13 BULLETS

A Vampire Tale

13 BULLETS

DAVID WELLINGTON

THREE RIVERS PRESS
NEW YORK

Published in the United States by Three Rivers Press,
an imprint of the Crown Publishing Group,
a division of Random House, Inc., New York.
www.crownpublishing.com

Three Rivers Press and the Tugboat design are registered
trademarks of Random House, Inc.

This work was previously serialized in slightly different form
on www.davidwellington.net.

Library of Congress Cataloging-in-Publication Data
Wellington, David.
     13 bullets / David Wellington.—1st ed.
          p.   cm.
     1. Policewomen—Fiction. 2. Pennsylvania—Fiction.
3. Vampires—Fiction. I. Title. II. Title: Thirteen bullets.
PS3623.E468A613   2007
813'.6—dc22   2006036175

ISBN 978-0-307-38143-9

Printed in the United States of America

DESIGN BY BARBARA STURMAN

10 9 8 7 6

First Edition

For my sister, Melissa,
who is less fragile than she thinks.
I should know, having leaned on her
shoulder often enough.

Though far and near the
bullets hiss,
I've 'scaped a bloodier
hour than this.

— George Gordon, Lord Byron, *The Giaour*

LARES

1.

Incident report filed by
Special Deputy Jameson Arkeley, 10/4/83
(recorded on reel-to-reel audiotape):

Through the rain there wasn't much to see. The all-night diner stood at the corner of two major streets. Its plate glass windows spilled a little light on the pavement. I handed the binoculars to Webster, my partner. "Do you see him?" I asked.

The subject in question, one Piter Byron Lares (probably an alias), sat at the diner's counter, hunched over in deep conversation with a middle-aged waitress. He would be a big man if he stood up, but leaning over like that, he didn't look so imposing. His face was very pale, and his black hair stood up in a wild shock of frizzy curls. An enormous red sweater hung off him—another attempt at camouflaging his size, I figured. He wore thick eyeglasses with tortoiseshell rims.

"I don't know what they teach you at Fed school, Arkeley, but I've never heard of one of them needing glasses," Webster said, handing me back the binoculars.

"Shut up." The week before I had found six dead girls in a cellar in Liverpool, West Virginia. They'd been having a slumber party. They were in so many pieces it took three lab technicians working night and day in a borrowed school gymnasium just to figure out how many bodies we had. I was not in a good mood. I had beaten one of the asshole's minions to dust with my bare hands just to find out his alias. I wasn't going to slow down now.

Lares stood up, his head still bowed, and took a leather wallet out of his pocket. He began to count out small bills. Then he seemed to think of something. He looked up, around the diner. He rose to his full height and looked out at the street.

"Did he just make us?" Webster demanded. "In this weather?"

"I'm not sure," I said. About a gallon of bright red blood erupted across the diner's front window. I couldn't see anything inside.

"Shit!" I screamed, and pushed my way out of the car, across the sidewalk, the rain soaking me instantly. I burst inside the diner, my star bright on my jacket, but he was already gone and there was nobody left alive inside to be impressed. The waitress lay on the floor, her head nearly torn off her body. You read about them and you expect vampire wounds to be dainty little things, maybe a pair of bad hickeys. Lares had chewed most of the woman's neck off. Her jugular vein stuck out like the neck of a deflated balloon.

Blood spilled off the counter and splattered the ceiling. I unholstered my service revolver and stepped around the body. There was a door in the back. I had to stop myself from racing to it. If he was in the back and I ran into him in the shadows by the men's room I wouldn't survive my curiosity. I headed back out into the rain where Webster already had the car running. He'd been busy rousing the locals. A helicopter swooped low over our heads with a racket that was sure to get complaints tomorrow morning. The chopper's spotlight blasted holes in the shadows all around the diner. Webster got us moving, pulled us around the alley behind the restaurant. I peered through the rain at the Dumpsters and the scattered garbage. Nothing happened. We had plenty of backup watching the front of the restaurant. We had heavy weapons guys coming in. The helicopter could stay up there all night if it needed to. I tried to relax.

"SWAT's moving," Webster told me. He replaced his radio handset.

The Dumpster in the alley shifted an inch. Like some homeless guy inside had rolled over in his sleep. Both of us froze for a second. Long enough to be sure we'd both seen it. I brought my weapon up and tested the action. I was loading JHPs for maximal tissue damage and I had sighted in the pistol myself. If I could have gotten my gun blessed by a priest I would have. There was no way this psychopath was walking away tonight.

"Special Deputy Arkeley, maybe we should back off and let SWAT negotiate with him," Webster told me. His using my official title meant he wanted to go on the record as doing everything possible to avoid a violent takedown. Covering his ass. We both knew there was no chance of Lares coming peacefully.

"Yeah, you're probably right," I said, my nerves all twisted up. "Yeah." I eased my grip on the pistol and kicked angrily at the floorboards.

The Dumpster came apart in pieces and a white blur launched itself out of the alley. It collided with our car hard enough to knock us up onto two wheels. My door caved in and pinned my arm to my side, trapping my weapon. Webster grabbed for his own handgun even as the car fell back to the road surface, throwing us both up against our seat belts, knocking the wind out of me.

Webster reached across me and discharged his weapon three times. I could feel my face and hands burning with spent powder. I could smell cordite and nothing else. I was deaf for a good thirty seconds. My window exploded outwards, but a few tiny cubes of glass danced and spun in my lap.

I turned my head sideways, feeling like I was trapped in molten glass—I could see everything normally but I could barely move. Framed perfectly in the shattered safety glass was Lares' grinning, torn-up face. Rain was washing the blood off his mouth but it didn't improve his looks. His glasses were ruined, twisted arms of tortoiseshell and cobwebbed lenses.

At least one of Webster's shots had gone in through Lares' right eye. The white jelly inside had burst outward and I could see red bone in the socket. The other two bullets had gone into the side of his nose and his right cheek. The wounds were horrible, bloody, and definitely fatal.

As I watched, they undid themselves. It was like when you run over one of those shatterproof trash cans and it slowly but surely undents itself, returning to its former shape in seconds. A puff of white smoke in Lares' vacant eye socket solidified, plumped out into a brand new eyeball. The wound in his nose shrank away to nothing and the one in his cheek might as well have been a trick of the light. Like a shadow it just disappeared.

When he was whole and clean again he slowly removed the broken glasses from his face and threw them over his shoulder. Then he opened his mouth and grinned. Every one of his teeth was sharpened to a point. It wasn't like in the movies at all. It looked more like the mouth of a shark, with row after row of tiny knives embedded in his gums. He gave us a good, long look at his mouth and then he jumped over our car. I could hear his feet beating on the roof, and he was all at once on the other side. He hit the ground running, running toward Liberty Avenue.

The SWAT team arrived at the corner before he did, sliding out of an armored van, four agents carrying MP5s. They wore full helmets and riot armor, but it wasn't standard issue. Their commanding officer had insisted I give them a chance to modify their kit. We all knew what we were getting into, he told me. We'd all seen plenty of movies before.

So the SWAT guys had crucifixes hot-glued all over them, everything they could get, from big carved-wood Roman Catholic models with gruesome Jesuses hanging from them to dime-store nickel-plated crosses like you would find on a kid's charm bracelet. I bet they felt pretty safe under all that junk.

Lares laughed out loud and tore off his red sweater. Underneath it his torso was one rippling mass of muscle. White skin, hairless, poreless, writhed over the submerged lumps of his vertebrae. He looked a lot less human with his shirt off. He looked more like some kind of albino bear. A wild animal. A man killer.

2.

Incident report filed by
Special Deputy Jameson Arkeley, 10/4/83
(continued):

"Don't fucking move!" one of the cross-covered SWATs shouted. The other three dropped to one knee and raised their MP5s to their shoulders.

Lares rolled forward from the waist, scooping his arms through the air like he could reach over and grab them from a distance. It was an aggressive movement. It was meant to be aggressive. The SWATs did what they'd been trained to do. They opened fire. Their weapons spat fire at the rain and bullets tore through the dark air, narrowly missing our unmarked car. Webster shoved his door open and stepped out into a big puddle. I was right behind him. If we could catch the bastard in a crossfire maybe we could damage him faster than he could heal.

"The heart!" I shouted. "You have to destroy his heart!"

The SWATs were professionals. They caught their target center mass more than they missed him. Lares' big body spun around in the rain. The helicopter came roaring overhead and lit him up with the spotlight so we could better see what we were shooting at. I fired three rounds into his back, one after the other. Webster emptied his clip.

Lares pitched forward like a tree falling down, right in the gutter. He put his hands down to try to stop his fall, but they slid out from under him. He lay there unmoving, not even breathing, his hands clutching at handfuls of the tiny yellow locust leaves that clogged up the sewer grate.

The SWATs traded hand signals. One of them moved in, weapon pointed at the back of Lares' neck, ready to take a brainstem shot, a traditional kill shot. He was aiming at the wrong place, but I didn't think it mattered at that point. There were no visible bullet holes in Lares—they must have healed instantly—but he wasn't moving. The SWAT stepped closer and kicked at one overly muscular leg.

Lares spun around on his side without any warning at all, far faster than a human being could move. He got one knee under him and grabbed at the SWAT's arm to pull himself up. He had no trouble whatsoever getting a grip on all those crosses. The SWAT started to react, bringing his MP5 up, ducking down in a firing crouch. Lares grabbed his helmet in two hands and twisted it right off. The policeman's head came with it.

For a second the decapitated SWAT stood there in a perfect firing crouch. Blood arced up from his gaping neck like a water fountain. Lares leaned forward and lapped at it, getting blood all over his face and chest. He was mocking us. He was goddamned making fun of us.

The SWAT leader started shouting, "Man down, man down!" into his radio, but Lares was already up and coming for him. He plowed through the rest of the SWATs in a single motion, his fingers tearing at their armor, his mouth fastening around the leader's neck. Those sharklike teeth bit right through the SWAT leader's padded collar. They bit right through a wooden cross and snapped it into pieces. I made a mental note: the cross thing was a myth.

The SWATs died one after the other and all I could do was watch. All I could do was stare. I brought up my weapon as Lares turned and jumped right at us. I would have fired, except

I was afraid I would hit Webster. Lares was that fast. He went low, diving to grasp Webster around the waist. My partner was still trying to reload his weapon.

Lares tore Webster's leg off at the thigh. He used his mouth. Blood was everywhere and Lares drank as much of it as he could get down his throat. Webster didn't start screaming for a long, horrible second or two. He had time to look at me, his face registering nothing but surprise.

When Lares had finished feeding, he rose to a standing posture and smiled at me. His half-naked body was caked with gore. His eyes were bloodshot and his cheeks were glowing pink and healthy. He leaned toward me. He was a good seven feet tall and he towered over me. He reached down and put his hands on my shoulders. His eyes stared into me, and I couldn't look away. The hand holding my weapon lost all strength and dangled at my side. He was weakening me, softening me up somehow. I could feel my brain itch—he was hypnotizing me, something, I didn't know. He could kill me anytime he wanted. Why was he wasting time with my brain?

Over our heads the helicopter chewed angrily at the air. The spotlight lit up Lares' back and made his hair glow. His eyes narrowed as if the light hurt him a little. He grabbed me around the waist and hauled me up to dangle over his shoulder. I could barely move. I tried to kick and hit and fight, but Lares just squeezed me harder until I felt my ribs popping like a string of fireworks. After that it was all I could do to breathe.

He didn't kill me. He had such strength in his arms that it would have been easy to kill me, to squeeze me so hard that my guts shot out of my mouth. He kept me alive, though, I assumed as a hostage.

He started to run. My body bounced and flopped on his shoulder. I could only see what was behind us. He was running toward the Strip District, toward the river. When I was planning this takedown I had convinced Pittsburgh Traffic to shut down a big patch of city, to keep the streets empty. I wanted a safe environment in which to pull off my showdown. Lares must have sensed the unusual quiet of the streets. He ran right out of my safe place, right into traffic, cars slaloming all around us, steam from the pouring rain rising from their hot lights like the breath of angry bulls. Horns shrieked all around us, and I panicked and called out for God—if one of those cars hit us it might not damage Lares at all, but I would surely be crushed, broken, impaled.

I could barely see for pain and wet eyes and the stabbing blare of headlights. I was barely cognizant of the fact that Lares had run out onto the Sixteenth Street Bridge. I could feel the helicopter above me, following me, its rotor blades pulsing in the dark. I felt Lares bend and flex his legs and then—freefall. The asshole had jumped right off the bridge.

We hit the freezing waters of the Allegheny River so hard and so fast that I must have broken half a dozen bones. The cold surged through me as if I were being stabbed with icicles all over my body. My heart lurched in my chest and I felt my entire circulatory system seizing up. Lares pulled me down, down into the darkness. I could barely see his white, white face framed by floating black hair like dead seaweed. Breath surged out of me and I started swallowing water.

We must have been under only a few seconds. I couldn't have survived any longer than that. Yet I remember him kicking, his legs snapping through the water. I remember the helicopter's searchlight slanting down through the murk, now this way, now that way, now too far away. Then I couldn't see anything. Air hit my face as if a mask of ice had been nailed onto my skull, but at least I could breathe. I sucked a great lungful of cold, cold air down inside of me until my body burned. Lares dragged me up over the fiberglass gunwale of a boat, a boat that bobbed and tilted alarmingly under our combined weight. He dragged me, only half alive, belowdecks.

3.

Incident report filed by
Special Deputy Jameson Arkeley, 10/4/83
(concluded):

Slowly, achingly, warmth returned to my fingertips, my toes. My brain spun inside my head for a while, and I couldn't make any sense of my surroundings. My ears rang. I felt like death had passed within inches of me.

Lares bent over me, his fingers probing in my ears and mouth. He tore my shirt away from my neck and shoulder and probed the veins, tapping at them to get the circulation going. Then he left me, unbound, all but forgotten. He hadn't said a single word to me. I wasn't supposed to be a hostage, I realized. I was going to be a midnight snack. I'd made enough heat for him that he felt he had to run home, to go to ground. That didn't mean he had to go hungry.

My eyes eventually adjusted to the near-absolute darkness of the boat's hold, and I began to make out some details. It was a cramped little space that smelled of diesel fuel and mildew. It was cold, not as cold as it had been in the river, but icy cold all the same. I guess if you're dead you don't need central heating. The usual boat stuff filled most corners of the room—life preservers like giant orange candies, a pair of aluminum oars, folded tarpaulins and sailcloth. Five coffins were leaned up against the shelves and bulwarks or lay flat on the floor. They were relatively plain, dark wood affairs in that elongated hexagonal shape that says "coffin" whenever you see it, even though I don't think anyone had built a coffin like that in fifty years. They had brass handles, and they were all propped open so I could see the overstuffed satin linings. One of them was empty. It was the biggest, and it looked about the right size for Lares. The other four were all occupied.

The bodies in the coffins were decayed beyond recognition. They were bones, mostly, tied together with scraps of flesh. Some showed old brown stains where blood had washed over them. One had nearly a full head of long white hair like uncombed cotton. One had a single eyeball still in its head, though it was shrunken and dried up like a white prune. None of the skulls were human. The jaws were thick, sturdy bone full of broken teeth. Just from the teeth I knew they were all vampires. Maybe they were Lares' family, in a perverse way. Maybe there was a whole lineage of them sleeping in that cramped little ship's hold.

There was something about them that made my skin crawl. It took me a long time to realize what it was: The bones in those coffins weren't dead. They were moving. Just barely, almost imperceptibly, but the bony hands were reaching out. The necks were craning forward. They wanted something. They were desperate for it, desperate enough to strain their dried-up sinews to get at it. As decayed and dilapidated as they might be, these corpses were still undead and still aware of their surroundings. Vampires were supposed to live forever, if they weren't killed. I guess maybe they didn't stay young forever, though. Maybe that was too much to ask.

Lares caught my attention as he started moving around the little space. He looked different. I focused my eyes and saw that the curly hair on top of his head had been a wig—it was gone now, and his head was as white and as round as the moon. Triangular ears poked out on either side. Those weren't human ears. I was finally seeing what a vampire really looked like. It wasn't pretty.

Lares knelt next to one of the coffins, his hands bracing him on the wooden lip. He lowered his head over the body and his back began to shake. One of his laughing eyes kept me pinned the whole time. With a horrible retching sound he vomited a half-pint of blood into the coffin, right over the corpse's face. He clutched at his sides and heaved again, and again, until the skull was bathed in clotted gore.

Steam rose from the hot blood in the cold room. Steam wreathed the skull, the rib cage of the corpse. Steam coalesced like watery light around the bones, wrapping the vampire's remains in illusory flesh and skin. The body plumped out and began to take on something like human form as the blood dripped into the corpse's mouth.

Lares moved to the next corpse. He started coughing and blood flecked his lips. Like a mother bird feeding her young, he coughed himself into a spasm until blood dangled in thick ropes from his mouth. Where it touched the corpse, steam rose up and a second transformation began. Skin like old mildewed paper rattled as it stretched around the second corpse's ruin. Dark skin, crisscrossed with scars. This one had a tattoo on his bicep. It read "SPQR" in jagged, sloppily done letters.

The pink hue I'd seen in Lares' cheeks before was gone. He was white as a sheet again. If he was going to feed all of his ancestors, he would need to find another blood donor, and soon.

I didn't like my chances.

He managed to vomit up blood all over a third corpse, just with what he had inside of him. He was throwing up death. The death of the waitress in the diner. The deaths of the SWATs we'd foolishly thought were safe under twenty pounds of crosses. He was throwing up bits of Webster, the good cop, throwing up part of Webster's body.

Lares turned to look at me directly. His whole body was shaking. Trembling, even shivering. Feeding his grandparents had taken everything he had. Before he'd fed on the waitress in the diner, had he been this shaky? He tried to meet my gaze, but I refused to let him hypnotize me again.

I looked down at my right hand. I was still carrying my sidearm. How I could have held onto it through being carried over Lares' shoulder, through the shock of hitting the river, through being dragged into the boat, was a mystery. The cold must have turned my hand into a solid claw around the weapon.

Lares lurched toward me. His speed was gone. His coordination was shot. However, he was still a bulletproof vampire.

I knew it was hopeless. The SWATs had hit him center left with full automatic machine-gun fire, but the bullets had never even pierced his skin. They hadn't even grazed his heart, his only vulnerable part. I had nothing better to do at that moment, though, than to shoot every last bullet I had.

I discharged my weapon into his chest. I shot him. Again and again until I was deaf with the noise and blind with the muzzle flash. I had three bullets left in my gun and I put all of them into his chest. The hollow-point rounds tore him open, splatted the boat's hold with bits and strips of his white, white skin. He tried to laugh, but his voice came out as a weak hiss, air escaping from a punctured tire.

I saw his rib cage torn open, exposed, flayed. I saw his lungs, slack and lifeless in his chest. He came closer. Closer. Closer. Close enough—I reached out with my left hand and grabbed at the twisted dark muscle that had once been his heart.

He howled in pain. So did I. His body was already repairing the damage I'd done, his cells knitting back together around the gunshot wounds. His ribs grew back like scissor blades crunching down on the more fragile bones of my wrist, trapping my hand inside of his body. His skin grew back over my arm and pulled at me, pulled me toward him.

I plucked his heart out like pulling a peach off a tree.

Lares' face turned dark with horror, his eyes wild, his mouth flapping open as if he couldn't control it, blood and spit flying from his chin. His nostrils flared and a stench like an open sewer bellowed up out of every one of his orifices. The heart leaped in my hand, trying to get back where it belonged, but I used the tiny shred of strength left in me to squeeze, to hold on. Lares slapped at me with his hands, but there was no real strength left in his muscles. He dropped to his knees and howled and howled and howled. It started to sound like mewling after a while. He was even losing the strength to scream.

Still he wouldn't just die. He was holding on to what strange kind of unlife he had ever possessed, clutching like a junkie at an empty syringe, trying through sheer willpower to not die.

His eyes met mine and he tried to suck me in. He tried to hypnotize me, to weaken me once more. It didn't work.

When he finally stopped moving it was nearly dawn. I held his heart in my clenched fist and it felt like an inert stone. The other vampires, the decayed ones, came slithering out of their coffins, reaching for him, reaching for me. They didn't understand what had happened. They were blind and deaf and dumb, and all they knew was the taste of blood. I kicked them away and, through the pain, through the shock, managed to get to my feet.

I found a can of gasoline in the engine room. I found a matchbook in the disused galley of the boat. I set them all on fire and stumbled up and out into the cold rain, pitched headlong onto a narrow wooden dock, and waited for the sun to come up, waited to see if the local police would find me first, or whether hypothermia and my injuries and shock would finish me off.

A fool there was and he
made his prayer
(Even as you and I)
To a rag and a bone and
a hank of hair
(We called her the woman
who did not care)
But the fool he called her
his lady fair.

— Rudyard Kipling, The Vampire

CONGREVE

4.

Pennsylvania State Trooper Laura Caxton pulled apart a road flare until red sparks shot across the leather elbow of her uniform jacket. She dropped the sputtering flare on the road and turned around. She'd felt something behind her, a presence, and on this particular night she had reason to be seriously creeped out.

The man behind her wore a tan trench coat over a black suit. His hair was the color of steel wool, cut short and close to his head. He looked to be in pretty good shape but had to be at least sixty. Maybe seventy. In the flickering light of four in the morning, the creases on his face could have been wrinkles or they could have been scars. His eyes were hooded by deep, pouchy lids, and his mouth was nothing more than a narrow slot in the bottom half of his face.

"Good evening," he said, his voice thick and a little hoarse. His face folded up like a gas station road map. He was smiling, the kind of smile you give a child you don't particularly like. The smile submerged his tiny eyes entirely. "You don't have a badge on your uniform," he went on, making it sound like she'd forgotten to wash behind her ears.

"We don't wear them," she told him. This guy was starting to piss her off. "The state policeman's good conduct is the only badge he needs," she said, more or less quoting what she'd been taught as a cadet. The black suit and the trench coat gave him away at once—he might as well have had FED written on his back in big white block letters—but she scanned his chest and found *his* badge, a five-pointed star in a circle. The badge of the

U.S. Marshals Service. "The Sergeant said he was going to call the FBI," she said.

"And they called me, just like they're supposed to. I only live a few hours away, and you could say that I've been waiting for this for a very long time. Please, don't make me wait any longer. When I arrived your sergeant told me to find you. He said you were the last one still here who saw what happened."

Caxton nodded. She unstrapped her wide-brimmed trooper's hat and scratched the top of her head. Fatigue and shock were fighting over which got to make her sit down first. So far she'd beaten both of them back. "I suppose that's right." She held out her hand. Maybe her dislike of this man merely stemmed from how much she disliked this night in general.

He didn't take her hand. He just stood there as if both of his arms were paralyzed. "My name is Special Deputy Arkeley, if that's what you wanted. Can we just get on with this and worry about the civilities later?"

Maybe he was just an asshole. She shrugged and pushed past him, assuming he would probably follow. When she got to the top of the rise she turned around and pointed at the roadblock just in front of the Turnpike on-ramp. The DUI enforcement trailer stood in the middle of the road, abandoned for the time being. Orange lights up on sawhorses stabbed at the dark, their light skittering around the dead tree branches that arched over the road. The strobing light made Caxton's eye sockets ache. "We're Troop T. We're highway patrol for the Turnpike, and that's all. We were not prepared for this." He didn't look like he cared. She went on. "Three fellow officers and I were working a standard sobriety check right here. Nothing special, we do this every Saturday night. It was about fifteen minutes past ten and we had three cars lined up for us. Another car, a late-model black luxury vehicle, stopped about fifty feet short of entering the line. The driver hesitated, then attempted to perform a U-turn. That's something we see a lot of. People realize they're going to fail the tests, so they try to evade us. We know how to handle it."

He stood there as quiet as a church mouse. He was just listening, his posture said. Absorbing whatever she was going to give him. She went on.

"Two units, troopers Wright and Leuski, had been at station in their patrol cars there and there." She pointed to where the cars had been waiting on the shoulders of the road. "They engaged the subject in a classic pincers maneuver and forced him to a stop. At that time he opened the door of his car and rolled out onto the road surface. Before Wright and Leuski could apprehend him, he ran to the west, toward that line of trees." She pointed again. "The subject evaded arrest, though not before he left some evidence behind."

Arkeley nodded. He started walking away from her, toward the subject's abandoned vehicle. It was a Cadillac, a CTS with a big blocky nose. A little pale mud flecked the running boards, and there was a bad scratch down the driver's-side door, but otherwise the car was in immaculate condition. It had been left just as it had been abandoned except that its trunk had been opened. Its flashers pulsed mournfully in imitation of the brighter lights up at the roadblock.

"What did your people do then?" Arkeley asked.

Caxton closed her eyes and tried to remember the exact series of events. "Leuski went after the subject and found the, well, the evidence. He came back and opened the subject vehicle's trunk, believing he had enough in the way of exigent circumstance to warrant an intrusive search. When we saw what was inside we realized this wasn't just some drunk running away so he didn't have to face the Intoxilyzer. Wright called it in, just like he was supposed to. We're highway patrol. We don't handle these kinds of criminal matters; we turn them over to the local police."

Arkeley frowned, which fit his face a lot better than his smile. "I don't see any of them here."

Caxton almost blushed. It was embarrassing. "This is a pretty rural area. The cops here work weekdays, mostly. Someone's always supposed to be on call, but this late at night the system tends to break down. We have a cellular number for the local guy, but he isn't answering."

Arkeley's face didn't show any surprise. That was alright. Caxton didn't have the energy left to make excuses for anybody else.

"We put in a call to the county authorities, but there was a multi-car pileup near Reading and the sheriff's office was tied up. They sent one guy to collect fibers, DNA, and prints, but he left three hours ago. They'll have more people here by morning, they said, which leaves us standing watch here all night. The Sergeant noticed this." She indicated the car's license plate. It was a Maryland tag. "There was clear evidence of an alleged criminal crossing state borders. And it was bad, pretty much bad enough that the Sergeant felt that bringing in the FBI made some sense. Now you're here."

Walking around behind the car, Arkeley ignored her as he studied the contents of the trunk. She expected him to gag or at least wince, but he didn't. Well, Caxton had met plenty of guys who tried to look tough when they saw carnage. She stepped around to the trunk to stand beside him. "We think there are three people in there. A man and two children, genders unknown. There's enough left of the man's left hand to get prints. We might get lucky there."

Arkeley kept staring down into the trunk. Maybe he was too shocked to speak. Caxton doubted it. She'd been working highway patrol for three years now and she'd seen plenty of wrecks. Despite the barbarous nature of the murders and despite the fact that the bodies had been shredded and heavily mutilated, she could honestly say she'd seen worse. For one thing, there was no blood in the trunk. Not so much as a drop. It also helped that the faces had been completely obliterated. It made it easier to not think of them as human beings.

After a while Arkeley looked away. "Alright. This is going to be my case," he said. Just like that.

"Now, wait a second—you were brought in as a consultant, that's all."

He ignored her. "Where's the evidence the subject left behind?"

"It's up by the tree line. But goddamn it, tell me what you meant by that. How is this your case?"

He did stop then. He stopped and gave her that nasty smile that made her feel about six years old. He explained it to her in a voice that made her feel about five. "This is my case because the thing that killed those people in that trunk, the thing that drank their blood, was a vampire. And I'm in charge of vampires."

"Come on, be serious. Nobody's seen a vampire since the eighties. I mean, there was that one they caught in Singapore two years ago, the one they burned at the stake. But that was a long way from here."

He might as well not have heard her. He walked up toward the trees then, and she had to rush to catch up. He was about four inches taller than she was and had a longer stride. They pushed a few branches aside and saw that the wild trees grew only a single stand deep, that beyond lay the long perfect rows of a peach orchard, its dormant trees silver and gnarled in the faint moonlight. A wicked-looking five-strand barbed-wire fence stretched across their path. They stopped together when they reached the fence. "There it is," she said. She didn't want to look at it. It was a lot worse than what was in the car's trunk.

5.

Arkeley squatted down next to the fence and took a small flashlight out of his pocket. Its beam was impressively bright in the gloom. It traveled the length of the evidence, a human hand and part of a forearm. The skin had been torn right off, leaving exposed bone and tendons and flayed blood vessels like fleshy creepers. At the stump end the blood vessels curled up on themselves while the remaining flesh looked crushed and raw, hacked at with a not-so-sharp knife. The arm was tangled inextricably into the barbed wire. There would be no way to remove it without cutting the fence.

Caxton had seen lots of bad things. She'd seen decapitations and eviscerations and people whose bodies were turned almost inside out. This was worse. Because it was still moving. The fingers clutched at nothing. The muscles in the forearm tensed and pulled and then fell back, exhausted. It had been doing that for nearly six hours since it was torn off the body of the subject.

"What does it mean?" Caxton asked. She was tired of fighting and thought Arkeley might actually know. "How does that happen?"

"When a vampire drinks your blood," he told her, his voice almost friendly, "his curse gets inside of you. It eats at you, at your corpse. He can make you rise and you do his bidding because he's all that's left in your heart and your brain. You live for him. You serve him. The curse burns inside of you and makes you an unclean thing. Your body starts to decay faster than it should. Your skin peels off like a cast-aside shroud. Your soul curdles. We call them half-deads. In Europe they used to be called the Faceless."

"This guy was a vampire's slave?" Caxton asked. "I've

heard about vampires having slaves, but I didn't know you could cut their arms off and they would keep moving. They don't talk about that in the movies."

"He was disposing of his master's victims. That's why he didn't want to be stopped. He was heading out to the woods to bury the bodies in shallow graves. Shallow enough, maybe, that when they came back to life they would be able to claw their way out and rise to serve their new master. We need to cremate the corpses."

"The families might not like that. Especially since we don't know who they are." Caxton shook her head. "Maybe we can post a guard down at the morgue or something."

"I'll take care of the paperwork." Arkeley took a Leatherman multitool out of his breast pocket and snipped at the barbed wire with a tiny bolt-cutter. Soon enough he had the flayed arm free. He clutched it to his chest, where the fingers tried to grasp at his buttons. They were too weak to get a good grip.

"I assume you're going to take that thing without even giving me a receipt," she said as he stood up, cradling the arm like a pet. "I could shoot you for interfering with an official investigation. You're supposed to be a consultant!"

He heard her. He didn't face her or do anything, really, but she could tell he'd heard her. His body stopped moving and sagged in place as if he'd been switched off. The words that came out of him next were like wind escaping from a dying set of bagpipes. "Nobody ever knows what it's like," he said. She had no idea what he meant. "They think they do. They've seen all those movies, all those idiotic movies. They think vampires are something you can reason with. Something you can explain away. They don't understand. They don't understand that we're fighting animals. Wild beasts."

"At least tell me what you plan on doing with the evidence." She couldn't bring herself to call it an arm.

He nodded and started up again. His power source replaced.

"There's a hospital near Arabella Furnace with the facilities I need. You can call there tomorrow and talk to them about getting it back, if you really want it. My advice is to burn it, but apparently we haven't reached the point yet where you're comfortable taking my advice."

"What's the number of this hospital?" she asked.

"I'll tell you tomorrow. I'm going to be in Harrisburg, at the state police headquarters. I want you to report there so you can repeat everything you told me to the Commissioner."

Caxton must have looked shocked. Honestly, she didn't know why the Commissioner would want to hear her report in person. But she knew better than to ignore a direct order from a Fed.

"Go home now. Get some sleep, and I'll see you tomorrow," he told her. Then he walked away, into the night.

The Sergeant grabbed her shoulder when she came back to the roadblock. She must have looked like she was going to pass out. "I'm okay, I'm okay," she told him, and he backed off. He didn't say a word when she announced she was going home.

The drive back to the house flickered in and out of her consciousness. She couldn't remember falling asleep at the wheel, but whole mile markers would go by without her noticing them. She stopped at the first diner she found and drank two big cups of coffee. It helped a little. She kept her speed down on the back-country roads she used for the last third of the journey, lightless, often unpaved stretches of track where the trees pressed in close on either side, their curving arms flashing at her in the headlights, the gray weeds that sprouted up out of the ground before her waving like seaweed.

She couldn't escape the feeling that the whole world had changed. That something horrible and new had come to life in the darkness outside, the chilly blackness that filled up the sky. Something big and dangerous and toothy, still made shapeless by her ignorance. It infected everything, it had gotten inside her head. Her teeth felt encrusted. She could sense the dirt under her fingernails. It was just exhaustion and low-grade fear, she knew, but it still made her itch inside her own skin. Everything had turned bad. The old familiar roads she'd driven a thousand times, ten thousand times, seemed more bendy, less friendly. Usually the car seemed to know the way to go, but tonight every turn and jog of the path took more strength out of her arms. She rode the brake down every hill and felt the car labor beneath her as she crested another rise.

Eventually, finally, she pulled her patrol car carefully into the wide driveway next to the Mazda and switched everything off. She sat there in the driver's seat for a moment, listening to the car ping, listening to the thinned-out rise and fall of the last of the year's cicadas. Then she popped open the door and slipped in through the garage. The ranch house she shared with her partner was perfectly quiet inside and mostly dark. She didn't want to disturb the stillness, didn't want to track any horror into her own home, so she left the lights off. She unstrapped her holster and hung it in the closet as she passed through the kitchen with its humming refrigerator, passed through the hall, unbuttoning her uniform shirt, pulling it down over her arms. She wadded it up inside her hat and put them both on the chair next to the bedroom door. Inside Deanna lay sleeping in their queen-sized bed, only a tuft of spiky red hair sticking up above the covers at the top, and, at the other end, three perfect little toes that had sneaked out from underneath. Caxton smiled. It was going to feel so good to climb into that bed, to feel Deanna's bony back, her sharp little shoulders. She would try as hard as she could not to wake her. Caxton unzipped her uniform pants and pulled off her boots one at a time. Suppressing the groan of pleasure it gave her to have her feet finally free, she stood there for a moment in just her bra and panties and stretched her arms above her head.

Behind her something tapped on the window. She pulled

the curtain aside and shrieked like an infant. Someone stood out there, a man, his face torn into strips of hanging skin. She screamed again. He slapped a white hand against the window, the fingers wide. His face beckoned at her. She screamed again. Then he broke away and ran. As Deanna stirred behind her and freed herself from the duvet, Caxton couldn't look away from the dark silhouette that loped across the garden behind the house. She watched until he slipped between the dog kennels and Deanna's shed and disappeared from view.

"Pumpkin, what is it, what is it?" Deanna shouted again and again, grabbing Caxton from behind.

"He only had one arm," the trooper gasped.

6.

The state police headquarters in Harrisburg was a brick box with big square windows, surmounted by a radio mast. It sat just north of the city in an underdeveloped patch full of road-salt domes and baseball diamonds. Trooper Caxton spent most of the day sitting around out back, waiting for Arkeley to show up. It was supposed to be her day off. She and Deanna were supposed to go up to the Rockvale Square Outlet stores and get some new winter clothes. Instead she sat around watching the civilian radio operators come out for their smoke breaks and then hurry back inside again. It was a chilly November day.

·The sun was up, though, which was a wonderful thing. Caxton hadn't been able to sleep after the half-dead tapped on her window. Deanna had somehow managed to curl back up under the warm sheets and doze off, but Caxton had sat up and waited for the local police to come and pick at the dead plants in her garden. She'd sat up and talked to them and watched them make a hundred mistakes, but it didn't matter. There was no evidence in the garden, no sign the half-dead had ever been there. She had expected as much.

Now, in the sun, in the fresh air, she could almost pretend it hadn't happened. That it was some kind of dream. She sat on a picnic table behind the headquarters lunch room with her hat in her hands and tried to will herself back into having a normal life.

There was the question, of course, that kept tugging and pulling at her. The question of why. Why the half-dead had come to her house. Her house specifically. If it had gone after Wright or Leuski, that might have made a certain amount of sense. Those two had chased the thing right into barbed wire. But why her? She'd been running the Intoxilyzer. She'd been in the trailer the whole time. It just didn't make sense.

If she concentrated very hard, she could not ask herself the question for whole long minutes at a time. She refused to let it rattle her. She was a state trooper, for fuck's sake. A soldier of the law—that's what they'd called her when she graduated from the academy. A soldier, and soldiers don't panic just because somebody tries to give them a little scare. She told herself that enough times to start believing it.

She read case reports and pursuit logs to fill the time, which was only slightly less boring than watching the smokers come in and out. Arkeley came for her at three o'clock. By that point she was ready to sign out and go home. "I've been waiting here all day," she told him when he stepped through the back door to collect her.

"I've spent all day getting search warrants and court orders. Which one of us had more fun, I wonder?"

"Stop talking to me like a child," she demanded.

His smile only deepened.

He led her up to the Commissioner's office, a corner office with two glass walls on the top floor. The other two walls were lined with deer antlers and the head of one very large twelve-point buck. A rack of antique fowling guns sat immediately behind the desk, as if the Commissioner wanted to be able to perforate anyone who brought him bad news.

Arkeley would have been a good candidate. After Caxton finished giving her report and Arkeley had made an introductory statement, the Commissioner gave him a look of pure hatred. "I don't like this, but you probably already guessed as much. The nastiest, ugliest multiple homicide in decades, and you just come in and take it away from us. A U.S. Marshal. You guys guard courthouses," he said, leaning way back in his chair. He was bald on top, but it hadn't reached his forehead yet. The bottom button of his uniform strained a little at keeping his gut in. He had a full colonel's birds on his shoulders, though, so Caxton stood at attention the whole time he was talking.

Arkeley sat in his chair as if his anatomy was constructed for some other kind of conveyance, as if his spine didn't bend properly. "We also capture the majority of federal fugitives," he told the Commissioner.

"Trooper," the Commissioner said, without looking at her. "What do you think of this piece of shit? Should I run him out of town?"

She was pretty sure it was a rhetorical question, but she answered anyway. "Sir," she said, "he's the only living American to have successfully hunted vampires, sir." She stayed at attention, staring up at the brim of her hat like she'd been taught.

The Commissioner sighed. "I could block this." He gestured at the paperwork spread across his desk. Most of it was signed by the lieutenant governor. "I could hold it all up, demand verification, demand copies in triplicate. I could stall your investigation long enough for my own boys to take care of the vampire."

"In which case, young man, more than a few people would die in a most horrible fashion." Arkeley wasn't smiling when he said it. "There's a cycle to these things. At first the vampires try to hide among us. They disguise themselves and bury their kills in privacy and seclusion. But over time the bloodlust grows. They need more and more blood every night to maintain their unlife. Soon they forget why they were trying to be discreet. And then they just start killing wholesale, with no moral compunction and no mercy. Until this vampire is brought down, the body count will continue to rise."

"Why have you got such a hard-on for this?" the Commissioner demanded. "You're willing to make enemies, just so you can horn in on this."

"If you're asking why I chose to take this case, I have my own reasons and I'm not going to share them with you." Arkeley stood up and picked his papers off the desk one at a time. "Now, if you're done pissing on my shoes, there are some things I need. I'd like to talk to your area response team. I need a vehicle, preferably a patrol car. And I need a liaison, someone who can coordinate operations between the various local police agencies. A partner, if you will."

"Yeah, alright." The Commissioner leaned forward and tapped a few keys on his computer. "I've got a couple of guys for you, real hotshots from the criminal investigations unit. Cowboy types, grew up in the mountains and learned how to shoot before they started playing with themselves. I've got six names to start—"

"No," Arkeley said. The temperature in the room dropped ten degrees. At least it felt that way to Caxton. "You misunderstood. I didn't ask to be assigned someone. I've already picked my liaison. I'm taking her."

Caxton was looking at her hat. She didn't see Arkeley point. It took her way too long to realize he meant he wanted her to ride with him.

"Beg your pardon, sir," she said, when the rushing in her

ears had passed, "but I'm a patrol unit. Highway patrol," she reiterated. "I don't feel I'd be appropriate for what you want."

For once at least it seemed he was willing to explain a decision. "You said I was the only living American to kill a vampire. You must have read something about me," he told her.

She'd read everything she could find while she waited for him to show up. It wasn't much. "I read your incident report on the Piter Lares case, yes, sir."

"Then you're the second-best-informed person in this building. Commissioner, I want you to release her from her current duties."

"For how long?" the Commissioner asked.

"Until I'm done with her. Now. You," he said, looking at Caxton, "follow me and stay close. I keep a certain steady pace, and I expect you to match me, or you'll forever be asking me to slow down."

She looked at the Commissioner but he just shrugged. "He's a Fed," his expression seemed to say. "What are you going to do?"

Arkeley led her down to the area response team's firing range out back. The ART was the antiterrorism squad, but they were also the ones who were called in to break up protests in the capital. They had the equipment and the tactics for mass arrests and crowd control, and they had a sizeable budget for less-lethal weapons (which Caxton knew used to be called nonlethal weapons, until somebody got accidentally killed). The ART guys were all gun nuts and gadget freaks and had an experimental weapons firing range behind the HQ where they could test out their toys before they actually had to deploy them. It also let them get in a little target shooting whenever they got the itch. Caxton kept her hands over her ears as they came up on the range officer, who was firing what looked like an antique musket. It was loud enough to make her think he must be using black powder.

Arkeley eventually yelled loud enough to get the range officer's attention. The RO took off his ear protectors and the two men had a brief discussion. Whatever Arkeley said made the RO snort in laughter, but he disappeared into an ammunition shed and came back out with a box of bullets.

Arkeley lined up thirteen of them on the firing stand and carefully, methodically loaded the magazine of his weapon. It was a Glock 23, Caxton saw. More firepower than most police handguns, but it was no hand cannon. "You only load thirteen?" she asked, looking over his shoulder.

"That's the capacity of the magazine," he said, his voice thick with condescension. It was going to take a lot to warm up to this guy.

"Most people would load an extra round in the chamber, so they're ready to shoot at a second's notice. I do," she said, patting the Beretta 92 on her belt.

"Tell me, do you not wear a seat belt while you're driving, so you can save half a second when you get in and out of your car?"

Caxton frowned and wanted to spit. She dug one of the bullets out of the box and studied it. The slugs were semijacketed lead, about what she had expected and not enough to make the range officer so excited. Two perpendicular cuts had been made in the nose of each round, forming a perfect cross. She thought maybe she'd caught him in a mistake. "I read your report—you said crosses had no effect on vampires."

"Luckily for me, they work wonders on bullets." Arkeley shouted to clear the range and sighted on a target thirty yards away, a paper target stapled to a plywood two-by-four. Caxton covered her ears. He fired one round and the target shredded. The two-by-four exploded in a cloud of wood chips. "The slug mushrooms and breaks apart inside the target," he explained to her. "Each piece of shrapnel has its own wound track and its own momentum. It's like every bullet is a little fragmentation grenade."

As much as she hated him, she had to let out a low whistle at that. So this was what you shot vampires with, she thought. She asked the RO to bring out another box in 9mm for herself.

"I can do that," he said, his voice low enough to count as a whisper, "but they won't be parabellum. Cross points are against the Hague Convention."

"I'll never tell," Arkeley said. "Load her up."

7.

"Down here, take the next right," Arkeley said, stabbing one finger at the windshield. He settled back in the passenger seat, looking more comfortable there than he had on the chair in the Commissioner's office. Maybe he spent more time in cars than offices, she thought. Yeah, that was probably right.

Caxton wheeled their unmarked patrol car around a stand of ailanthus saplings that bounced and shimmered over the hood. Twilight was about to be over: the night was just starting. According to the map they were right in the middle of the township of Arabella Furnace, named after a cold-blast pig-iron furnace that would once have employed the whole population of the town. There was nothing left of the furnace itself except a square foundation of ancient bricks, most of them crumbled down to dust. There was a visitor's center there, and Caxton had learned all about the history of cold-blast furnaces while Arkeley took a pit stop.

Other than barking out directions he had very little to say. She had tried talking to him about the skinless face in her window the night before. She had not presented it as something that had scared her, though it still did, especially as the daylight dwindled in her rearview mirror. She presented it as part of the case. He grunted affirmatively at her suggestion that he should know what had happened. But then he failed to add so much as a comment.

"What do you think it was about?" she asked. "Why was it there?"

"It sounds," he said, "as if the half-dead wanted to scare you. If it had wanted to hurt or kill you it probably could have." Any attempt on her part to get anything further out of him resulted in shrugs or, worse, complete apathy.

"Jesus!" she shouted, finally, and stopped the car short so they both hit their seat belts. "A freak with a torn-up face follows me home and all you can say is that it probably just wanted to scare me? Does this happen so often in your life that you can be so jaded about it?"

"It used to," he said.

"But not anymore? What did you do? How did you stop it?"

"I killed a bunch of vampires. Can we continue, please? We haven't got a lot of time before the bodies start showing up in heaps."

She studied him the whole length of the drive. She wanted to get the drop on him at least once, to prove that she wasn't a complete child. So far she'd failed. "You're from West Virginia," she suggested. It was the best she had. "There's a hint of a drawl in your voice." Plus she had read that his investigation of the Lares case had begun in Wheeling, but she left out that detail.

"North Carolina, originally," he replied. "Make a left."

Fuming a little, she crept forward onto the road he indicated. It looked more like a nature trail. In the headlights she could see it had been paved once with cobblestones, but time had turned them into jagged rocks that could pop a tire if she drove too quickly. The drive wound between two copses of whispering trees, mixed maple and ash. Leaves had fallen in great sweeps across the way, suggesting that this road led nowhere but the ancient past. Yet perhaps not—the way was never actually blocked. Someone might have tried to make the place look forbidding, but they had stopped short of actually cutting off access.

"There's no parking lot; there hasn't been for fifty years. You can just drive up onto the main lawn and stop somewhere unobtrusive," Arkeley told her.

Main lawn? All she could see was increasingly dense forest, the thick dark woods that had given Pennsylvania its name centuries earlier. The trees rose sixty feet high in places, in places even higher. She switched on her headlights—and then she saw the lawn.

It was not the manicured stretch of bluegrass she had expected. More like a fallow field aggressively reclaimed by weeds. Yet she could make out low stone walls and even, in the distance, a dry fountain streaked green and black by algae. She stopped the car and they got out. Darkness closed around them like a fog once the car's lights flicked off. Arkeley started at once toward the fountain and she followed him, and then she saw their destination looming up in the starlight. A great Victorian pile, a gabled brick mound with wings stretching away from its central mass. On one side stood a greenhouse with almost no glass left in it at all, just a skeletal iron frame festooned with vines. A wing on the far side had completely collapsed and partially burned, perhaps having been struck by lightning. A concrete bas relief above the main entrance named the place:

ARABELLA FURNACE
STATE HOSPITAL

"Let me guess," Caxton said. "You've brought me to an abandoned lunatic asylum."

"You couldn't be less correct," he told her. The smile on his face was different this time. It almost looked wistful, as if he wished it were an asylum. They approached the fountain and he laid a hand on the broken stone. Together they looked up at the statue of a woman pouring out a great urn that rested on her hip. The urn had gone dry years before. Caxton could see rust inside its mouth where the waterworks had been. The statue's free arm, maybe twice the size of a human appendage, stretched toward them in benediction or welcome. Her face, whatever expression it may once have offered to visitors, had been completely eroded. Acid rain, time, maybe vandalism had effaced it until the front of her head was just a rough mask of featureless stone.

"This wasn't an asylum, it was a sanatorium. They used to bring tuberculosis patients here for a rest cure," Arkeley explained.

"Did it work?" she asked.

He shook his head. "Three out of every four patients died in the first year. The rest just lingered on and on. Mostly the health authorities just wanted them out of the way so they wouldn't infect anyone else. The cure amounted to fresh air and simple manual labor to pay for their keep. Still, the patients received three meals a day and all the cigarettes they could smoke."

"You're kidding. Cigarettes for people with a respiratory disease?"

"The cigarette companies built this place, and all the other sanatoria like it all over the country. They probably suspected a link between smoking and tuberculosis—smoking made you cough, after all, and so did consumption. Who knows? Maybe they just felt sorry for the infected."

Caxton stared at him. "I wasn't expecting a history lesson tonight," she said. He didn't reply. "You said that I couldn't be more wrong. How else was I wrong?"

"Arabella Furnace was closed in the fifties, but it isn't abandoned. There are still patients here. Well, one patient."

She was left, as usual, without further information. She had to imagine what kind of hospital would be kept open for a single patient.

They entered through the front door, where a single watchman in a navy blue uniform waited, an M4 rifle slung over the back of his chair. He wore the patches of a Bureau of Prisons corrections officer. He looked bored. He appeared to recognize Arkeley, though he made no attempt at greeting the marshal.

"I've never heard of this place," she said.

"They don't advertise."

They passed through a main hall with narrow spiral staircases at each corner, leading both up and down. Large square vaulted chambers stood at every compass point. Arches here and there were sealed off with bricks, then pierced with narrow doorways with elaborate locks. Power lines and Ethernet cables hung in thick bundles against the walls or stretched away across open space, held up by metal hooks secured in the ceiling.

Caxton touched the dark stone of a wall and felt the massive coolness, the strength of it. Someone had scratched their initials in the wall right next to where her hand lay, a complicated acronym from a time of rigidly defined names: G.F.X.MCC., A.D. 1912.

Arkeley didn't allow her to absorb the atmosphere. He strode forward briskly, his squeaking footfalls rolling around the ceiling, echoes that followed her close behind as she rushed to keep up. They passed through a steel doorway and she saw where the paint had been rubbed away from the jamb by countless hands over time. They moved through a white corridor with plaster walls, studded by a dozen more doorways, all of them wreathed with cobwebs. At the far end a sheet of plastic hung down over an empty doorway. Arkeley lifted the plastic aside for her, a strangely comforting gesture, and Caxton stepped inside.

The ward beyond was bathed in a deep blue glow that came from a massive lighting fixture in the ceiling. The bulbs up there had been painted so that everything red in the room appeared to be black. The contents of the room were varied, and somewhat startling. There were rows and racks of obsolete medical equipment, enameled steel cabinets with Bakelite knobs that might have been part of the hospital's official equipment. There were laptop computers and what looked like a miniature MRI scanner. In the middle of the room was a tapered wooden coffin with brass handles and a deeply upholstered interior. Cameras, microphones, and other sensors Caxton couldn't identify hung down over the coffin on thick curled cables so the coffin's contents could be constantly and exhaustively monitored.

An electrical junction box with a single button mounted on its face stood next to the doorway. Arkeley pushed the button and a buzzer sounded deep inside the sanatorium. "You read my report. You know I set fire to all the vampires on that boat in Pittsburgh."

Caxton nodded. She could guess what came next.

"You'll also remember Lares only had enough blood to revivify three of his ancestors. There was a fourth one who went without nourishment. Strangely enough, the ones with skin and flesh burned just fine. The one without was merely charred. She survived the blaze."

"But vampires are extinct in America," she protested.

"Extinct in the wild," Arkeley corrected her.

A plastic barrier lifted at the far side of the room and a wheelchair was steered into the coffin chamber. The man who pushed it wore a white lab coat with the sleeves rolled up to his elbows. He was a little skinny—otherwise he had no distinguishing features at all. Then again, he was likely to appear nondescript in comparison to his charge. The woman in the wheelchair wore a tattered mauve dress, moth-eaten and sheer with use. She was little more than bones wrapped in translucent white skin as thin as tissue paper.

There was no hair on her head except for a few spindly eyelashes. The skin had broken and parted from the bones of her skull, in places having worn away altogether, leaving visible shiny patches of bone. She had one plump eyeball, the iris colorless in the blue light. Her ears were long, sharply triangular, and riddled with sores. Her mouth looked broken, somehow, or at least wrong. It was full of shards, translucent jagged bits of bone. Caxton slowly made out that these were teeth. The woman had hundreds of them, and they weren't broken. They were just sharp. This was what she had read about in Arkeley's report. This was one of the creatures he'd set on fire in the belly of the boat—a vampire, an old, blood-starved vampire. She'd never seen anything more horrible, not even the near-faceless halfdead who had peered in through her window the night before.

"Hello, Deputy. You're on schedule—it's just about feeding time at the zoo." It was the man in the lab coat who spoke. He pushed the wheelchair closer to them than Caxton would have liked. She felt nothing from the vampire, no sense of humanity, just coldness. It was like standing next to the freezer cabinet in a grocery store on a hot summer day. The chill was palpable, and real, and wholly unnatural.

"Special Deputy," Arkeley corrected.

"Feeding time?" Caxton asked, appalled.

The vampire's eye brightened noticeably.

8.

"This blue light we're standing in," Caxton said. "It must be some, I don't know, some wavelength vampires can't see, right? So she can't see us?"

"Actually, she can see you just fine. She would see you in perfect darkness. She's told me," the man in the lab coat said. "She can see your life glowing like a lamp. This light is less damaging to her skin than even soft white fluorescents." He held out a hand. "I'm Doctor Hazlitt. I don't think we've met."

Caxton tore her gaze away from the vampire's single, rolling eyeball to look at the man. She began to reach for his hand, to shake it. Then she stopped. His sleeve was rolled up to his bicep and she saw a plastic tube embedded in the soft flesh inside his elbow. A trickle of dried-up blood, perfectly black in the blue light, stained the end of the tube.

"It's a shunt," he told her. "It's easier than using a syringe every time."

Arkeley squatted down to look at the vampire eye to eye. Her fleshless hands moved compulsively in her lap as if she were trying to get away, as if he terrified her. Caxton supposed she had every right—the Fed had once set her on fire and left her for dead. "Hazlitt here feeds her his own blood, out of the goodness of his heart," Arkeley announced. "So to speak."

"I know it seems grisly," the doctor told her. "We tried a number of alternatives—fractionated plasma and platelets from a blood bank, animal blood, a chemical the Army is trying out as a blood surrogate. None of it worked. It has to be human, it has to be warm and it has to be fresh. I don't mind sharing a little." He stepped over to a workbench a few yards away from the wheelchair and took a Pyrex beaker out of a cabinet. A length of rubber tubing went into the shunt, its free end draped over the lip of the beaker. Caxton looked away.

"Why?" she asked Arkeley. "Why feed it at all?" Her first instinct as a cop—to ask questions until she understood exactly what was going on—demanded answers.

"She's not an 'it'! Her name," Hazlitt said, and he stopped for a moment to grunt in moderate-sounding pain, "is Malvern.

Justinia Malvern. And she was a human being once. That might have been three hundred years ago but please, show some respect."

Caxton shook her head in frustration. "I don't understand. You nearly got killed trying to destroy her. Now you're protecting her, here, and even giving her blood?"

"It wasn't my decision." Arkeley patted his coat pocket as if that should mean something to her. It didn't. He sighed deeply and kept staring at the vampire as he explained. "When we found her at the bottom of the Allegheny, still in her coffin, we didn't know what to do. I was still in the hospital and nobody much listened to me anyway. My bosses turned her body over to the Smithsonian. The Smithsonian said they would love to have her remains, but while she was still alive they couldn't take her. They asked us to euthanize her so they could put her on display. Then somebody made a mistake and asked a lawyer what to do. Since as far as we know she's never killed an American citizen—she's been moribund like this since before the American Revolution—the Justice Department decided we didn't have a right to execute her. Funny, huh? Lares was up and moving and showing signs of intelligence, but nobody filed any charges when I put him down. Malvern here was half rotted away in her coffin, but if I put a stake through her heart they were willing to call it murder. Well, that's how it goes. She had no family or friends, for obvious reasons, so they made her a ward of the court. Technically I'm responsible for her welfare. I have to clothe her, shelter her, and yes, feed her. Nobody knows whether cutting off her blood supply will kill her, but without a federal court order we're not allowed to stop."

"She's earned her keep a dozen times over," Hazlitt said. He was dismantling the siphon that had drawn blood out of his arm. "I've been studying her for seven years now and every single day and night of it has been rewarding."

"Yeah? What have you learned?" Caxton asked.

The vampire's face curled up. Her nose lifted in the air and rippled obscenely. She had smelled the blood.

"We've learned that blue light is best for her. We've learned how much blood she needs to maintain partial mobility. We've learned what level of humidity she likes and what extremes of temperature affect her."

Caxton shook her head. "All of which helps keep her alive. How does it benefit us?"

For the very first time Arkeley looked at her with a light of approval in his eyes.

"We're going to find a cure here." Hazlitt came around a bank of equipment, his face sharp. "Here, in this room. I'll cure her. And then we'll have a vaccine and that will benefit society."

"We don't need a vaccine if they're extinct," Arkeley said.

The two of them exchanged a hot stare for a moment of pure, easy hatred.

"Excuse me, I really do need to feed her." Hazlitt knelt before the wheelchair-bound vampire and held up the beaker to show her the ounce or two of black blood at the bottom.

"Jesus, how long have you been studying her?" Caxton asked. "You said you've been doing this for seven years. But she must have been here for two decades. Who worked here before you?"

"Dr. Gerald Armonk."

"The late Dr. Armonk," Arkeley said.

Hazlitt shrugged. "There was an unfortunate accident. Dr. Armonk and Justinia had a very special relationship. He used to feed her directly, cutting open the pad of his thumb and allowing her to suck out his blood. She had a bad spell of depression in the nineties, you see, and even attempted to hurt herself a few times. Perhaps it wasn't the wisest thing to do, to feed her that way, but it seemed to cheer her immensely."

"Armonk had a doctorate. From Harvard, if you can believe it," Arkeley said.

"For the first few days that I worked here, she was flush with life and really, actually, quite beautiful," Hazlitt said. "Then she began to fade like a wilting rose. What little blood I had for her just wasn't enough." He raised the beaker as if to press it to her bony lips. Arkeley grabbed it out of his hands, sloshing the thick liquid.

"Maybe not quite yet," he said.

The vampire lifted a shaking hand. Anger flared in her eye.

For a lingering moment no one said anything. Hazlitt opened his mouth only to shut it again quickly. Caxton realized he must be terrified of Arkeley. He had recognized the marshal when he arrived, had even spoken to him with a certain familiarity. How many times in the previous twenty years had Arkeley come to this little room, Caxton wondered? How many times had he grabbed the beaker?

But no. This was a familiar scene for everyone but herself. Yet she understood, from the relative postures of the two men, that Arkeley had never interrupted the ritual before this night.

It was Arkeley who broke the silence. Clutching the beaker in both hands, he looked right into the vampire's eye. "We've had reports of half-dead activity," he said, quietly. Softly, even. "Faceless. The woman over there saw one. I burned its arm this morning. There's only one way to make a half-dead, and it takes a young, active vampire. A new vampire. Have you been naughty, Miss Malvern? Have you done something foolish?"

The vampire's head rolled to the left and then the right on the thin column of her neck.

"I have a hard time believing you," Arkeley said. "Who else can make a vampire but you? Give me a name. Give me a last known address and I'll leave you alone. Better yet: Tell me how you do it. Tell me how you birthed the monstrosity."

The vampire didn't reply at all, except to let her one eye roll downward until it was focused on the blood in the beaker.

"Don't be a bastard," Hazlitt hissed. "At least not more than usual. You know how much she needs that blood. And look. It's already clotting."

"Alright." Arkeley lifted the beaker and pressed it into the vampire's outstretched hand. She clutched it in a shaky death grip that turned her knuckles even whiter. "Enjoy it while you still can."

"What is your problem?" Hazlitt nearly shrieked.

Arkeley straightened up and tapped his jacket pocket again. It made a tiny snare sound—there was a piece of paper in there. "I said we couldn't cut off her blood supply unless we had a court order. Well, this new vampire activity lit some fires under some very important posteriors." He drew out a long piece of paper embossed with a notary's seal. "You are hereby ordered to cease and desist feeding this vampire as of right now." He smiled quite broadly. "Sometimes it helps to be the guy who guards courthouses."

The vampire stopped with the beaker halfway to her mouth. Her eye swiveled upward to squint at Arkeley.

"If you were human you would try to make it last," the Fed told her. "You'd know it was your last taste, ever, and you'd try to savor it. But you're not human, and you can't resist, can you?"

The vampire's mouth drew back in a kind of sneer. Then a long gray tongue snaked out between all those teeth and started lapping hungrily at the blood in the beaker, licking long black streaks up the side. It was gone in mere seconds.

9.

"It will start with palsy. Uncontrollable shaking. Then she'll begin losing tissue mass. The skin will peel back from her hands and then the muscles will rot. They'll become lifeless claws. Her legs will atrophy even more quickly and become nothing but dead stumps. In time her eye will dry up and collapse."

Hazlitt sat on top of an antique electrocardiogram machine, its pens splayed outward, and puffed occasionally on a cigarette that mostly sat ignored between two fingers. "Maybe, eventually, she'll die. We don't know."

"If it keeps her from making more vampires I don't care," Arkeley said. "Is there a real reason why we're bothering with this?" he asked.

In the center of the room, near the coffin, Justinia Malvern sat in her wheelchair, the empty blood beaker clutched in one near-lifeless hand. Her other hand rested on the keyboard of a laptop computer perched on top of the coffin.

"You know she can't speak. Her larynx rotted away years ago. This is the only way she can express herself." Hazlitt rubbed the bridge of his nose with one thumb. He smiled at his charge as she worked up the strength to peck at one of the keys with a talonlike finger. "You should be more patient, Arkeley," the doctor said. "You might learn something from someone so old and wise." When she had finished, she folded her hands in her lap and looked up at them, her face quivering with emotion. Hazlitt turned the laptop around so they could see the screen. In thirty-six-point italic letters Malvern had spelled out:

my Brood shall Devour ye utterly

Arkeley chuckled. Then he stood up and started walking out of the room. "I'll be back to check on you both," he told Hazlitt. "Frequently." Caxton followed him out.

In the white light of the hallway Caxton blinked and rubbed at her eyes. She followed Arkeley's footsteps around to a desk in the hub of the building where a corrections officer with a sergeant's bars sat watching a portable television, a sitcom maybe. The reception was so bad that the laugh track was indistinguishable from static.

"What can I do you for, Mr. Marshal?" The CO slowly took his feet down from the desk and picked up the keyboard of his computer.

"Good evening, Tucker. I need some information on the staff here. More specifically I need to know the name and current address of everyone who worked here in, say, the last two years. I need to know if they still work here and if not, why they left. Can you get me that information?"

"Not a problem." Tucker fiddled with his mouse for a while and hit a key. Down the hall a laser printer rattled out three sheets of paper.

Arkeley smiled, an altogether warmer and more human smile than he'd ever given Caxton. "You have to love this modern world. It used to take days to get a report like that. Listen, Tucker, what's the turnover here?"

The guard shrugged. "Shit, it gets creepy at night. Some people can't take it. Others, like me, we've got balls enough to stick around. I'd say half of the faces I see come through here don't last a week. Maybe ten guys in the last year. Then there's cleaning, maintenance, construction crews, safety inspectors, whatever. They come through here so fast they never introduce themselves."

Arkeley nodded. "I was afraid of that." He turned to Caxton. "Any of those people could have had contact with Malvern."

"Which means any of them could be our vampire now," Caxton responded.

Arkeley nodded. She'd gotten something right. She felt embarrassed and vindicated at the same time. Arkeley grabbed the sheets of paper off the printer and jogged back to where she waited. "Hazlitt is supposed to keep her in isolation, but you saw him. He'll do whatever she asks." Arkeley shook his head in disgust. "Every doctor we bring in here falls in love with her."

"Does she hypnotize them?" Caxton remembered that part of the report.

"She has far more to offer them than just her piercing gaze," Arkeley replied, scanning the sheets.

"So why not drag him out of here right now, have him replaced?" Caxton demanded. "You have some funny ideas about police work."

Arkeley nodded, accepting what she said. "Listen," he told her, "if somebody wants to be your enemy, there's only one thing you can do. You give them exactly what they want. It confuses them and makes them wonder what you're up to. If I fired Hazlitt tonight he would start thinking about ways of breaking Malvern out of here. If I let him keep her company at least I know where to find them both." He shook his papers. "Alright. Now we go home and get some rest. In the morning we'll start running down these names. It's always better to hunt for vampires by daylight."

Caxton could understand the good sense in that. They headed back out to the parking lot, where dew had collected on the hood of the car and fogged up the windows. Caxton got the car started and drove back out toward the nearest highway, Route 322, which would take them most of the way back to Harrisburg.

She turned up the heater, trying to dispel the chill of the night air. It was hard to get warm after the things she'd seen and been exposed to in the previous two days. The cold seemed to have seeped into her flesh. It made her bones hurt. She wanted to turn on the radio but didn't dare—what if Arkeley disapproved of her taste in music? It wouldn't be worth the fight, or what it might do to her self-esteem. She got it, really: she was just a highway patrol trooper, he was some kind of big-time Fed. She was willing to bow to his experience, to treat him with respect. Yet whenever he chastised her she felt as if she were a complete failure. She needed to grow a thicker skin, at least when she was around Arkeley.

She was surprised, so deep in these thoughts as she was, when he was the one to break the silence. She was almost shocked when he commended her. "You asked some excellent questions back there," he said. "With some training you might make an adequate detective some day." She had imagined, in her private thoughts, that when he said such a thing (presumably after he found her standing over a heap of dead vampires) he would sound a little sheepish, as if he should have seen the potential in her all along but had been blinded by his own arrogance. Instead he sounded like he always had—like an elementary school teacher handing out report cards. But this one had a B-plus on it. She would take what she could get.

"I need to learn about these monsters," she said, "if I'm going to be any help to you. And I want to be a help to you."

"You will, one way or another. And I'll help you, too. No matter what happens, this is going to be a big case. When I went up against Lares it meant a big step up in my career," he told her. "You will no doubt be promoted if we can stop this thing from killing too many people."

She shook her head. She hadn't really thought about that. "I didn't become a trooper to get sergeant's bars. Don't get me wrong, I wouldn't mind a raise in pay grade. I'm in this car, though, because I believe in what I do. When we graduate from the academy, they make us say the honor call. They make us say it a lot, until we start believing it. 'I am a Pennsylvania state trooper. I am a soldier of the law. To me is entrusted the honor of the force.' They used to really mean that bit about being soldiers. Troopers weren't allowed to marry and they lived together in barracks, just like soldiers. They didn't let women join until the seventies."

Arkeley was quiet for a while. When he spoke again he

sounded almost pensive. "It must not have been easy for you to enter such a conservative organization. I imagine there would be some resistance to women being in your position, even now."

"Wow, you're preaching to the choir," she laughed.

"In fact you've probably faced some direct adversity yourself. A woman doing a man's job—there would have been talk. Idle talk, in the locker room, perhaps."

"Sure. A lot of the guys like to mouth off," she said.

"They would have made you a figure of fun. They would have names for you. Hurtful names, though perhaps accurate."

Caxton started to blush. She wasn't sure where he was going with that line of inquiry. "Yes, they call me names. They call everybody something, so—"

"They probably make a good deal out of your lesbianism."

Her lips pressed together and she heard a roaring in her ears. She watched the other cars passing them in the left lane. She was driving too fast and she made herself ease up on the gas.

"You are a lesbian, aren't you? I made the assumption based simply on your haircut," Arkeley told her. "I could be wrong."

She shifted in her seat and glared at him. "Yes, I'm gay!" she shouted. She couldn't seem to control her voice. "Which means what to you? I don't care if you know. I don't care who knows. I'm proud of who I am. But that doesn't give you a right to—to—it should mean nothing. It has nothing to do with this fucking case!"

"Quite true," he agreed, looking completely unruffled.

"Then why would you say something like that to somebody? Goddamn it, Arkeley!"

He cleared his throat. "I took the time to play this little game with you because I need to train you out of the habit of bullshitting me, Trooper. You may talk about being a soldier of the law all you like. You may say you want to help me. It's completely immaterial. You're in this car for only one reason."

A metallic blue Honda shot past them going at least ninety and stopped him from finishing his thought. The unmarked patrol car rocked on its shocks with the near collision and Caxton slapped her horn. The Honda slowed down just enough to pull right in front of them, dangerously close.

"What the hell?" she demanded, and hit the horn again. She took her foot off the gas completely and went for the brake.

Another car, a Chevrolet Cavalier that desperately needed a wash, came up on her left. It matched her speed. As she tried to slow down, the Chevy's driver copied her. In the rearview mirror she saw a third car coming up from behind. They were boxing her in. She glanced across at the driver of the Chevy just as he looked at her. His face was torn to ribbons.

10.

"They're following me—they were at my house and now they're following me," Caxton said. In the rearview she saw her half-dead pursuer drift ever closer toward the bumper of her patrol car.

"I doubt it," Arkeley told her. "Hold on." The car behind them—a Hummer H2—smashed into them and the patrol car shrieked as metal tore into metal. The half-dead back there wasn't trying to make them crash. Caxton had enough experience with police pursuits to understand. The driver behind her was showing her the limits of the box. She sped up a little, keeping just inches away from the car boxing them in from the front, and whirled around in her seat to keep all three assailants in sight.

"They're not here for me?" she asked.

"No, I don't think so." Arkeley took his weapon from its holster. "When I took down Lares he was feeding his ancestors.

He brought them blood. I did some more research and I found others who'd seen similar behavior. Vampires lust for blood, but they worship the creatures who gave them the curse. When I threatened Malvern back in the hospital I brought this on us. Roll down your window and lean back."

She did as he asked only a moment before he lurched across her body and fired two shots into the Chevy on her left. The half-dead driver threw his hands across his face, but they exploded in clouds of bone fragments and withered flesh. His head cracked and pulled apart, and the car spun off the road and smacked into a tree. Caxton watched in her rearview as the Chevy's headlights swiveled out crazily, pointing in different directions, a moment before they went dark.

From behind the Hummer H2 rammed them again. The half-deads were not pleased. Caxton grabbed the steering wheel so hard she felt it in her shoulders. "Okay, my turn," she said. She spun the wheel and stamped on the gas. The patrol car shot forward and smacked into the rear right wheel of the Honda in front of them. The tire slipped on the pavement and the car spun out to the left, letting Caxton surge forward and around the out-of-control vehicle. Like everyone in the highway patrol, she'd had three days' training in pursuit evasion tactics. As they sped into the darkness ahead, finally free of the box, she turned to grin at Arkeley, truly pleased with herself. "Do you know how to use the car radio?" she asked him, gesturing at the dashboard set with her chin. "Go ahead and call Troop H dispatch. We need every available unit."

Arkeley stared at her. "You little idiot," he breathed. She didn't look at him, just focused on keeping control of the car. She was doing better than ninety on a road rated for sixty at the most. "If we had let them, they would have taken us right to their master."

"To the vampire," she said.

"Yes."

"But you shot that guy!" she protested.

"I had to make it look like we weren't just playing along."

Caxton gritted her teeth and glanced in her mirrors. The Hummer H2 was still back there, laboring to keep pace with her. She eased off the gas a hair—not enough to make him think she was letting him catch up. The Honda was still trying to get turned around after its sudden stop. A green traffic sign flashed by. "The exit for New Holland is coming up. Do I take it or not?"

"We'll have to try to guess from their behavior which way they want us to go." Arkeley bit off the words and spat them out. He was holding on to the door handle with one hand while the other held his weapon up, barrel pointed up. If the bouncing, jostling car made him fire by accident the bullet would exit the car as quickly as possible through the roof. "If he starts to weave to the left—"

He didn't need to finish the sentence. Two motorcycles came screaming up the on-ramp behind them and rumbled quickly up behind the patrol car. The riders weren't wearing helmets, but then they didn't have faces, either. One of the half-dead riders pulled up on the right of Caxton, forcing her into the left lane, away from the New Holland exit. At least that answered her question. The other motorcyclist gunned his engine with a sustained explosive noise and pulled up next to her left front wheel.

The motorcycles weren't much of a threat on their own— she could ram them off the road with one swivel of her wheel. The rider on her right, though, had a big rusty hunk of metal in his hand, a cleaver, at least eighteen inches long. He brought it back with a straight arm and swung it right into the side of the car. There was more noise than damage to the car's body, but her right-side headlight flickered out in a shower of sparks and she was half blind, hurtling through the Stygian woods at eighty-five miles an hour. Reflexively, even as he was pulling his cleaver free, she swerved to the left to get away from him. The biker on that side swung out wide and narrowly missed getting clipped by her left front wheel. Glass and bits of metal smacked and skittered and danced across the windshield as the patrol car rocked up and down on its shock absorbers and the wheels slipped away from her.

Caxton struggled to regain control of the car. Her remaining headlight washed the road surface from left to right as the car sagged on its tires, but she was good at this. She'd had years of practice driving under hazardous conditions, and she didn't panic. She straightened out the car and poured on a little more speed. Maybe the Hummer would have trouble keeping up, but she figured the bikers knew where they were taking her.

"Are you sure they're not trying to kill us?" Caxton demanded.

"Ninety percent so," Arkeley replied. "Normally half-deads herd victims to the master. After all, if we die out here the vampire can't drink our blood. Then again, if they think I'm enough of a threat they may not want to take any chances."

"You're a known vampire killer," Caxton said. "If I were them I'd consider you a pretty serious threat. Can we just call for some damned backup?"

He nodded. He didn't waste time suggesting that maybe she was right for once and maybe he was wrong. He picked up the radio handset and called it in, just like he should have ten minutes earlier. Dispatch from Troop H started calling in cars.

Then an orange sign flashed by them so fast she could barely see it, its phosphorescent paint glowing eerily in the near-total darkness. She didn't have a chance to read it, but she knew what the color meant: road work ahead.

She took her foot off the gas. The Hummer behind her grew bigger in her rearview, but she tried not to sweat it. She had no idea what was coming—anything from a lane shift to a complete road closure. She could feel panic rising in her chest.

The biker on her left had a monkey wrench. He started to draw back his arm, clearly intending to smash in her remaining headlight. There were no streetlamps on this stretch of highway—this was a rural route where people were expected to bring their own lights. If he smashed her lamp she was going to be blind.

With a desperation she'd never felt before, she rolled the wheel over and slammed right into him. The bike twisted under the impact, its front wheel flying up. The biker, pinned against the side of the patrol car, shot out his hands and tried to grab onto her door, but his skinless fingers scrabbled uselessly on the slick metal and glass. He disappeared from view, there one second, far behind her in the dark the next. His motorcycle spun on the asphalt, kicking up sparks.

She stood on the brake and the Hummer swerved to avoid hitting her. The other biker passed her by, his broken face turning to watch her go. While he wasn't watching the road, his machine continued in a perfectly straight line, right into an orange traffic cone. The PVC cone was meant to survive even the worst collisions, but his bike wasn't. It flipped end over end and landed on top of its operator.

Caxton pumped the brakes. She could read the signs now. There was an emergency detour she couldn't quite make. There was a complete closure of the road in front of her. Behind her the Hummer stopped short, its brakes howling.

She rolled toward a stop, the car unwilling to slow as quickly as she wanted it to. Sheer willpower wasn't helping. The road surface was covered in a chalky dust, and in places it had been peeled away to reveal a much rougher layer below. The car jumped and bounced, and Arkeley shoved his handgun into its holster. Finally, at last, the car ground to a halt, sliding the last few feet. It rocked forward, then back, throwing the two of them around in their seat belts. Dust drooped from the air, settling again on the road, and silence fell with it.

Directly in front of them stood a roadblock of sawhorses and bright yellow collision barriers. Beyond, the road surface had been completely cut up and torn through, leaving a six-foot-deep pit in the earth. Mud-spattered construction vehicles, abandoned power tools, boxes of rags and supplies, and stacks of traffic cones littered the hole. Overhead an ancient and gnarled silver maple arched across the roadway, its twinned propeller-like seeds spinning down through the night air.

High up in the mostly denuded branches something huge and white caught a few rays of light from Caxton's headlamp. As she watched, about a quarter of the white thing broke off from the main mass and fell like a stone. It hit the hood of her patrol car hard enough to make her scream. When she'd recovered herself she looked through the windshield and saw a construction worker in an orange vest staring back at her with dead eyes. His throat had been completely torn out, as had part of his collarbone and shoulder. His skin was pale, and there was no blood on him at all.

Before the car had time to stop trembling from the impact, the vampire leaped down from the tree to land right next to her, separated from her fragile body by only the width of her door. His eyes met hers and she could not look away.

11.

The vampire stood at least six and a half feet tall. He was not as muscular as she had expected—perhaps she had thought every vampire would be as big as Piter Lares. This one had a thin, whiplike quality that made her think of a predatory cat—fast, vicious, overdesigned. He was completely naked and completely hairless. His ears stuck up on either side of his head and came to sharp points.

Caxton studied him. He didn't seem to be in any kind of hurry—it was as if he would kill them when he felt like it, when he got around to it. His eyes were reddish and bright. Seed pods from the maple tree had stuck to his skin here and there—a faint sheen of sweat covered him from head to toe. His skin, which had looked so white before, actually had a slight tinge of pink. He had just sucked the blood of the dead construction worker, after all. The poor dead man must have been the only one around the work site, perhaps a night watchman.

The vampire cleared his throat as if he wanted her to look at him some more. Was he vain? Did he want her to think him beautiful? Did she find him beautiful? Like Malvern in the hospital, he radiated no humanity at all. It was strange: she would never have said that Arkeley was particularly human-seeming. Yet the Fed gave off some kind of aura, a human warmth, or perhaps it was just a smell. The vampire had none of this. The only comparison she could make was that the vampire was like a marble statue of a person. Its lines and contours could be perfectly carved, immaculately replicated, but you would never mistake him for something alive. He was like Michelangelo's statue of David. Perfect but hard and cold. His penis drooped flaccidly against his thighs and she wondered if he had any use for it. Did he find humans attractive? Did vampires have sex with their own kind?

He padded closer to the car and placed one hand on the frame of the open window. He bent down to look inside, his lower jaw falling open to show his frightening number of teeth. From behind her Caxton was aware of an irritating buzz like the droning wings of a mosquito. As the vampire's face came closer to her the noise doubled in volume. It really was quite annoying. It was Arkeley, she realized. He was saying something, but she couldn't make out the words. Well, he'd never said anything she particularly wanted to hear before, so she saw no reason to pay attention to him now.

The vampire's hands came down around her, his powerful fingers clutching at her uniform shirt and her belt. She moved through space, dragged inexorably along by his power. In one slightly sickening, perfectly fluid motion she was outside of the car and dangling from his hands. She was floating, weightless, and she felt like a little girl again; she felt as she had when her father used to pick her up and carry her around. How wonderful it had been to surrender everything to that embrace. How much joy she had taken in being a doll in her father's arms.

She looked for the vampire's eyes again, but his face was turned away from her. She frowned, wanting very much for him to look at her once more. A hole appeared in his forehead, a gaping, fluttering black hole that spat dark fluids and fragments of bone. A second hole appeared in his cheek. She saw the back of his head burst open and suddenly, quite suddenly, she was falling.

Bang—she hit the ground. And pain flashed like lightning in her arm.

The ground drove the wind from her lungs. She gasped. She hadn't realized she had been holding her breath. She could hear again—she hadn't know she was deaf a moment earlier. She looked down at her hands, then up at the vampire. There was no marble statue up there. There was a beast, a thing of sharp teeth and bloody eyes, and it was going to kill her. In fact it—he—had been in the process of killing her when Arkeley shot him twice in the face.

"Jesus!" she shrieked. "Jesus!" The vampire had been shot twice in the head and all he did was drop her. He was hit—hit badly—but she knew it wouldn't be enough. She raced away from him, scuttling on hands and feet. Panic erupted in her throat and she nearly threw up.

The fucker had hypnotized her. She grabbed for her gun and turned to shoot him in the heart, as many times as possible.

Before she could do more than free her weapon from its holster the vampire's hand closed on her neck. As fast as she had moved away from him, he had come at her even faster. He picked her up and threw her away, even as two more gunshots made the night air jump and shiver. She was flying and this time she knew she was going to hit hard, knew it was going to hurt. She collided with an orange-and-white sawhorse. It caught her right below her navel, right at the top of her thighs, and she kept going, twisting over it, agony jarring through her femurs as they flexed and twisted and nearly shattered. She slumped forward and her momentum carried her right over the barrier and into the exposed pit beyond, the place where the road had been peeled away.

Caxton fell for six feet that felt like six miles, her hands clawing at naked air, her legs pinwheeling. She landed with a splash in a puddle of freezing cold mud that got in her eyes, her mouth, her nose, threatening to choke her, to drown her. She sputtered, clawed at her face, and sucked in one painful breath that made her ribs ache.

She was still alive.

Up above, beyond the pitch-dark wall of the trench, two more gunshots sounded. Then another one. She waited for a fourth shot, but it didn't come. Was Arkeley dead? If he was, she was all alone in the bottom of the hole. She sat up and looked around but couldn't see any way out—no ladder, no ramp, not even a rope she could climb. Given enough time, she could probably find a way up to the top. She doubted she would be given enough time.

Even as she thought it, the vampire appeared on top of the barricade. He looked down at her and his eyes were red mirrors that caught the starlight and reflected it down to her. With a wave of nausea she tore her gaze away from his.

"You." His voice was thick, and low, and it had a raspy, rumbling growl in the back of it. "Are you Arkeley?"

He didn't know? He'd laid such an elaborate trap to catch the Fed, but nobody had bothered to tell him if Arkeley was a man or a woman? Caxton didn't think before she answered. "Yeah, I'm Arkeley." He looked doubtful, so she tried to convince him. "I'm the famous vampire killer, bloodmunch. I tore your daddy's heart out, that's right."

He stared down at her and she looked at her feet. She could feel his gaze on her like the laser sights of two sniper rifles painting her back. Finally she heard him laugh. It sounded a little like a dog choking on a half-swallowed bone.

"Little liar," the vampire said, still chuckling. "Lares was no kin of mine. You're the other one, the partner. I'll be back for you," he sang. And then he disappeared from view.

"Damn," she said, not entirely sure why she'd wanted to pretend to be Arkeley. Surely if he'd believed her the vampire would have come down and snuffed out her life on the instant. Yet perhaps that would have given the real Arkeley a chance to get away, or at least to gather reinforcements. That idea was based on the presumption, with no basis in known fact, that the vampire hadn't already killed the Fed.

She pounded at the walls of the pit with her fists, scattering clods of dirt and pebbles and achieving nothing whatsoever else. "Fuck!" she shouted.

As if in echo, she heard another gunshot, this time from a different direction.

12.

"Freeze!" someone shouted, and she heard a whole volley of shots. "This is the state police!" came next. It was followed by horrible screams.

The pit was full of road grading equipment and supplies.

Caxton searched through boxes of tools, looking for anything she could use to help her get up top again. Her reinforcements had arrived—the backup Arkeley had called for, back when the half-deads were chasing them. The troopers had arrived and they were getting slaughtered.

Two beams of light shot over her head—someone had a car up above and had turned on the headlights. The vampire must have been right in the path of the beams. She heard him hiss in pain. He appeared at the top of the pit again, this time as a silhouette against the new light, his left forearm pressed tight against his eyes. A severed human head with part of its neck still attached dangled by its hair from the curled fingers of the vampire's left hand. Caxton prayed silently that it wasn't Arkeley's head.

Exit wounds appeared on the vampire's back, dozens of them spraying bloodless translucent tissue. The vampire staggered backwards until it was crouched on top of the barricade, howling in pain. Caxton drew her own weapon and sighted on his back.

He dropped the head. He lowered his forearm. Then he fell backwards like a tree falling in the woods. When his long body hit the ground at the bottom of the pit it cracked the loose pavement there.

Caxton remembered Arkeley's report, had all but memorized it. She knew that unless the vampire's heart was destroyed it would get up again. She had only a few seconds. Bullets were pretty much useless—even if she emptied her clip into his chest she knew she couldn't be assured of hitting the heart dead on. She looked to her side, to the boxes of tools, and found what she wanted. A pile of palings had been left in the pit, the kind of wooden poles surveyors use to mark out where a new highway will go. She lifted one, a square-cut, mud-stained length of unfinished wood maybe six feet long and an inch and a half thick.

It even had a Day-Glo orange ribbon tied to its flat end like a pennon on a lance. She took it up in both hands, lifted it over her head to stab directly downwards.

With all of her strength she brought it down, sharp end first, right into the vampire's rib cage, right into that white skin like carved marble. It might as well have been stone she attacked. The stake shivered all the way up its length, driving long splinters into the meat of her hand. Its point splayed out, twisted and broken.

She brushed away the debris and found a tiny pink point on the vampire's skin where she'd stabbed him.

"That skin is tougher than steel," Arkeley said. She looked up and saw his head and shoulders above the barricade. He had a bad scrape up one side of his face but otherwise looked unharmed. While she stood there, surprised, he lowered himself down into the pit to stand next to her. She didn't think to ask him to help her out of the pit until it was too late.

The vampire didn't move, didn't so much as breathe. He was a dead thing and he looked far more natural that way. Caxton lifted her hand to her mouth and tried to pull out a splinter with her teeth. "What do we do next?" she asked, as blood welled up out of the ball of her thumb. In the dark she could barely see it drip, a tiny fleck of it splattering on the vampire's foot.

The effect, however, was sudden and electric. The vampire sat up and his mouth opened wide. He swam toward her out of the sharp shadows at the bottom of the pit, some deep-sea fish that could swallow her whole. She started to scream, but she also started to jump out of the way. It wasn't going to matter— the vampire was faster than she was.

Luckily for her, Arkeley had been ready all along. He fired one of his cross points right into the vampire's mouth and broke off a dozen of his teeth. It didn't look as if it even hurt the monster, but it changed his course, slightly, enough that his leaping attack missed Caxton by a hairbreadth.

"Help me," Arkeley insisted. Caxton slowly got to her feet, badly shaken by the near miss. "I can't hold it for long," he shouted, and she shook herself into action. Arkeley fired two shots into the vampire's center mass. He must be running out of bullets, she realized.

He had slowed the vampire down, at least. The monster knelt in the mud, his balled fists punching at the ground, his head bowed. He started to get up and Arkeley shot him again. He'd had thirteen bullets to start with—how many did he have left?

Caxton looked at the tools around her, but she knew they wouldn't be enough. She ran to the far side of the pit and found what she wanted. It was a compact little vehicle with an exposed driver's seat and a simple three-speed transmission. It was designed to cut very narrow defiles through concrete or asphalt. To this purpose its entire front comprised a single three-foot-wide wheel rimmed with vicious shiny steel teeth. On its side the manufacturer's name was painted in black letters: DITCH WITCH. Caxton jumped up into the driver's seat and reached for the starter.

Nothing happened. She slapped the control panel in frustration when she saw there was no key in the ignition. The cutter had been immobilized for the night, presumably so teenagers wouldn't steal it and go for joyrides, cutting up the highway.

Arkeley fired again but the vampire was on his feet. He tottered back and forth, then took a step toward the Fed. It was impossible for someone to take so much damage, to incur so much trauma, and still walk, but the vampire was doing it. He was perhaps six feet from Arkeley. He would close that distance in seconds.

Caxton grabbed the gearshift of the Ditch Witch and threw it into neutral, then shot back the hand brake. She jumped off the back and shoved the machine forward. The pit's floor was slightly uneven and the whole compact mass of the construction machine rolled slowly, inexorably forward. Caxton drew her own weapon and fired at the vampire's head, one shot after another, blasting apart his eyes, his nose, his ears.

The vampire laughed at her, at the futility of her shots. His shattered eyes repaired themselves as she watched, filling in his broken eye sockets. Yet in the second or two it took him to heal he was blind. He couldn't see the Ditch Witch rolling right toward him until it was too late.

The toothed wheel dug deep into his thigh, his groin. He fell backwards as the mass of the machine rumbled on top of him and stopped, pinning him to the ground. He tried to get up, tried to shift the Ditch Witch's mass, but even he wasn't strong enough to lift a half-ton vehicle with almost no leverage.

"Hey," someone shouted. Caxton looked up and saw a state trooper on the rim of the pit, his wide-brimmed hat silhouetted against the low light. "Hey, are you alright down there?"

"Get the power on!" Arkeley shouted. "There should be a master switch up there. Get the power on!"

The trooper disappeared from view. A moment later they heard an electric generator sputter to life, then settle down to a throbbing growl. Caxton had no idea what Arkeley had in mind. A trooper brought a portable floodlight up to the barricade and blasted the pit with white light that made Caxton look away. The vampire, still trying to free himself, let out a yowl like an injured mountain lion. They didn't like light, she decided. Well, they were nocturnal after all. It made sense.

Arkeley limped over to the tool cases. He found what he wanted and plugged it into a junction box. Caxton could hardly believe it when he came to stand next to the vampire's side, an electric jackhammer in his hands.

He shoved the bit into the vampire's chest, just to the right of his left nipple. The same place Caxton had hit him with her wooden stake. Arkeley switched on the hammer and pressed down hard with all his weight. The vampire's skin resisted for a moment, but then it split wide open and watery fluids—no blood, of course—gouted from the wound. As the hammer's bit dug through the vampire's ribs the monster started to squirm and shake, but Arkeley didn't move an inch. Strips of skin and then bits of muscle tissue like cooked chicken—all white meat—sputtered out of the wound. The vampire screamed with a noise she could hear just fine over the stuttering racket of the power tool, and then . . . and then it was over. The vampire's head fell back and his mouth fell open and he was dead. Truly dead. Arkeley laid the jackhammer down and reached into the vampire's chest cavity with his bare hands, searching around inside to make sure the heart was truly destroyed. Eventually he pulled his hands free and sat down on the ground. The body just lay there, inert, a thing now, as if it had never been a person.

The troopers lifted them both out of the pit and Caxton saw what had happened up top while she was trapped. Two dozen state troopers had shown up to support her. Five of them were dead, their bodies torn to pieces and their blood completely drained. She knew them all by sight, though thankfully they were from a different troop than her, Troop H, while she was Troop T. She wouldn't have called them friends. She felt a lightness in her head, in her spirit as she passed by the bodies, as if she couldn't quite connect with what had happened.

Caxton was barely aware of her own body when they sat her down in the back of a patrol car and made sure she was okay. An EMT checked her for injuries and the surviving troopers asked endless questions about what had happened, about the car chase, about the naked vampire, about how many times she'd discharged her weapon. She would open her mouth and an answer would come out, surprising her every time. She was in shock, which felt pretty much like being hypnotized by a vampire, she realized.

Eventually they let her go home.

It is the nature of vampires to increase and multiply, but according to an ascertained and ghostly law.

—Joseph Sheridan Le Fanu, Carmilla

REYES

13.

In the morning, with sunlight coming in through the windows, Caxton got up without disturbing Deanna and pulled on some clothes, anything, really. It was freezing in the little house and there was frost on the garden. She turned on the coffeemaker and left it belching and hissing, then went and fed the dogs out in the kennel. Their breath plumed out of the cages. They sang for her when she came in, the ages-old greyhound song that is unlike a noise any other dog can make, a warbling, atonal screech. To Caxton it was a symphony. They were happy to see her. She let them out to run around for a while on the wet grass, none of them willing to test the limits of the Invisible Fence, content, for the moment, to stay in their safe little patch of lawn bordered by winter-quiet trees. She watched them play, snapping at one another, knocking each other over, the same game dogs had been playing for a hundred thousand years, and still nobody ever won. It made her smile. She felt surprisingly good, maybe a little stiff where she'd fallen on her arms and her ribs the night before, a few bruises here and there from when the vampire had yanked her out of the car. But mostly she felt good, and healthy, and like she'd achieved something.

So she was quite confused when she started crying. Not big noisy sobs, just a little leakage from the eyes, but it didn't seem to want to stop. She wiped it away, blew her nose, and felt her heart jump in her chest.

"Pumpkin?" Deanna asked, standing mostly naked in the back door, just a sleeveless T-shirt on that covered everything the law required. Deanna's red hair stood up in a bed-head shock of spikes, and she shivered visibly. She'd never looked more beautiful. "Pumpkin, what's wrong?" she asked.

Caxton wanted to go to her, to grab her around the waist, to ravage her. But she couldn't. She couldn't stop crying. "It's nothing. I mean, really, I have no idea why I'm crying. I'm not sad or . . . or anything, really." She wiped at her eyes with her fingers. It had to be a delayed stress reaction. They'd taught her about those in the academy, and told her she was no tougher than any civilian. Like everyone else in her class, she had thought, yeah, right, and fallen asleep during the seminar. She was plenty tough. She was a soldier of the law. But she couldn't stop crying.

Deanna rushed out on the grass, the dew squishing up between her toes, and grabbed Caxton up in a stiff kind of back-patting embrace. "There's some guy at the door who wants to see you. Do you want me to send him away?"

"Let me guess. Old guy, lots of wrinkles, with a silver star on his lapel." Caxton pushed Deanna away, not ungently. She grabbed the flesh of her own upper arm near her armpit through her shirt and gave it a good twist. The pain was sudden and real, and it stopped the crying instantly.

At the front door Arkeley stood waiting patiently, his mouth a meaningless slot again. When he saw Deanna, though, his face started to glow. She opened the door to let him into the kitchen and asked if he wanted a cup of coffee. Caxton stayed a little away from him, not wanting him to see her irritated eyes.

He smiled even more broadly but shook his head. "I can't drink the stuff. It gives me ulcers. Good morning, Trooper."

Caxton nodded at him. "I didn't expect to see you here," she said. "I thought we were done after last night."

He shrugged. "While we were busy having so much fun yesterday, some people were out there doing real police work. Fingerprints, dental records from the half-deads, what have you, have turned up no identification on the vampire yet, not even a name. But we do have this." He handed her a computer printout. She recognized it immediately as an entry from the national car license plate registry. It listed the license plate number from the Cadillac CTS that had started the vampire investigation, the car full of bodies that the one-armed half-dead had abandoned. The sheet listed the name and all known addresses of the car's owner.

"This is our vampire?" Caxton asked.

Arkeley shook his head. "Our best guess is that it's the victim. The one in the trunk. His fingerprints turned up nothing, but his son's did, and blood typing suggests everyone who was in that car was related."

"What kid has been fingerprinted?" Deanna asked, her nose wrinkling up. "I thought you only got printed if you got arrested." She poured some cereal in a bowl but didn't bother with milk. Breakfast tended to be an informal affair at their house.

"We've been printing kids as fast as we can for a couple years now," Caxton told her. "It helps identify them if they get kidnapped. At least that's what we tell their parents. It also means the next generation of criminals will almost all have their fingerprints on file when they start committing crimes."

Arkeley sat down unbidden in one of the cheap Ikea chairs around the kitchen table. He had that same uncomfortable posture she'd seen before whenever he sat in a chair. He must have seen the question in her face. "The Lares case nearly killed me," he explained. "I had to have three vertebrae fused together. This one last night was easy."

Caxton frowned and studied the printout. It indicated that the car's owner had been named Farrel Morton and that he owned a hunting camp near Caernarvon. Not too far from where she'd been working a standard Intoxilyzer sweep just two nights earlier. She put the pieces together. "Jesus. He took his kids hunting and the whole family got eaten alive. Then the living dead stole his car."

"There are human remains at his hunting camp. A lot of them," Arkeley told her.

Deanna stamped her bare foot on the floor. "No fucking shop talk in the kitchen!" she shouted. It was a habitual war cry and Caxton winced.

"Quite right. There'll be time enough for the gory details later." He and Deanna traded a look of complete understanding that made Caxton wince again. He would never have looked at her like that. Maybe she shouldn't have cared, but she did.

"You've got quite the partner here, Trooper," Arkeley said, rising painfully to his feet. "Have you two been together for very long?"

"Almost five years," Caxton said. "Should we get going? The crime scene is getting old by now." Not that it was likely to matter much with the perpetrator dead, but there were rules in police work.

"How did you meet?" he asked.

Caxton froze. She had to decide, at that moment, whether she was going to let him inside of her real life or not. The cop stuff, the vampire fighting, that was important, sure, but this was her home, her dogs, her Deanna. The side she didn't let anybody see, not even her fellow troopers. Of course she'd never had a work partner before. He was her partner at least for the duration of the investigation, and you were supposed to have your partner over for dinner and stuff like that. He would be going away soon, now that the vampire was dead. She decided the danger of letting him inside was minimal. "I rescue greyhounds," she said. "From the dog tracks. When one of the animals gets injured or just too old they put them down. I give them a more humane option—I save the dogs and raise them to be pets. It's an expensive hobby—most of the dogs you save are injured or sick and they need a lot of medical help. Deanna used to work as a veterinary technician. She used to sneak out heartworm pills and rabies sticks for me. She got fired for it, actually."

Deanna leaned across the kitchen cupboards, stretching, one leg up in the air. "It was a shit job anyway. We were putting down animals all the time because people didn't want to pay to fix them up."

"I can imagine that would get disheartening," Arkeley soothed. Deanna's face grew radiant under the warmth of his sympathy.

Jealousy spiked upwards through Caxton's guts. "Now she just does her art."

"Aha, I knew it," Arkeley said. "You've got an artist's hands."

Deanna waggled them for him and laughed. "Do you want to see the piece I'm working on?" she asked.

"Oh, honey, I don't know," Caxton tried. She looked at Arkeley. "It's contemporary. It's not for everybody. Listen, you can see my dogs instead. Everybody likes dogs, right?"

"When they're safely behind a fence, sure," Arkeley told her. "I can't stand the way they lick. But really, Trooper, I'd love to see your partner's work."

There was nothing for it but to head out to Deanna's shed. Deanna put on shoes and a padded winter coat and headed across the lawn to work the combination lock. Caxton and Arkeley followed along a little more slowly.

"What the fuck are you doing?" Caxton asked, once Deanna was out of earshot.

Arkeley didn't play coy. "You always make nice with your partner's wife. It gets you invited to dinner more often," he told her.

They entered the shed with roses on their cheeks—it was going to be a truly cold day, it seemed. Caxton moved to stand up against one wall of the shed, extremely embarrassed. Her cheeks burned, not just because of the cold.

Deanna was as unabashed as ever. She'd shown her work to every person she could find who was even slightly willing to look at it. Most of the time she got polite silence in response.

Some people would deem her work "interesting" or "engaging" and go on for a while about theories of body politics or post-feminism until they ran out of steam. The people who actually appreciated her work scared Caxton. They didn't seem all there—and worse, they made her wonder if maybe Deanna wasn't altogether normal herself.

Arkeley moved around the shed carefully, taking it all in. Three white sheets—queen-sized—hung from the shed's rafters with a few feet of empty air between them. They moved softly in the cold empty air of the shed, lit only by the early morning sun coming through the door. Each sheet was spotted with hundreds of nearly identical marks, roughly rectangular, all of them the same reddish brown. There was no smell on such a cold day, but even in the height of summer the marks gave off only the faintest tang of iron.

"Blood," Arkeley announced when he'd walked around all three sheets.

"Menstrual blood," Deanna corrected him.

Here it comes, Caxton thought, the moment when Arkeley gets skeeved out and calls Deanna a freak. It had happened before. A lot. But it didn't come. He nodded and kept studying the sheets, his head tilted back to take it all in. When he didn't say anything more for a full minute, Caxton started to feel nervous. Deanna looked confused.

"It's about taking something hidden," Caxton blurted out, and they both looked at her. "Something that is normally hidden away, disposed of in secrecy, and putting it up on display."

The pride in Deanna's face made Caxton want to melt on the spot. But she had to juggle her two partners. She couldn't let Arkeley see any sign of weakness, especially not here in this deepest sanctum.

Arkeley breathed deeply. "This is powerful," he said. He didn't bother trying to interpret it, which was good. He didn't try to explain it away.

Deanna bowed for him. "It's taken me years to get it this far and it's not nearly done. There's a guy in Arizona who is doing something similar—I saw him at Burning Man a while ago—but he's using any kind of blood and he lets anybody contribute. This is all me. Well, Laura has helped a few times."

Caxton's hands started shaking. "Okay, too much information," she let out. It just came out of her. They both looked at her, but she just shook her head.

"Perhaps we should get to the crime scene," Arkeley suggested. She had never been so glad to receive an order.

14.

"What about garlic?" Caxton asked. By day the dead trees that lined the highways looked a lot less threatening. She supposed it helped that the vampire was dead. There were some half-deads out there unaccounted for—the one driving the Hummer H2 that had rammed them and the one-armed one that had scared the hell out of her, at least—but by all accounts they would be easy to round up and subdue now that their master was gone. The vampire was dead—it made the whole world look better. She was finally giving in to her curiosity, which she had kept leashed before because she was terrified of the answers to her questions. Now they seemed harmless, academic. "Will garlic keep a vampire away?"

Arkeley snorted. "No. In ninety-three I did a little extemporaneous experimentation on Malvern. I brought a jar of minced garlic into her room and when Armonk wasn't looking I dumped it all over her. It made a pretty good mess and it pissed her off, but no, no lasting harm. It might have been mayonnaise for all she cared."

"How about mirrors? Do they show up in mirrors?"

"From what she's said she loved looking at her reflection

back in the good old days. She doesn't like the way she looks now, that much is certain." He shrugged. "I suppose that one has a grain of truth in it. The old ones will break any mirror they see. The young ones don't care."

"You already ruled out crosses. What about holy water, communion wafers, hell, I don't know. What about other religions? What about the star of David or statues of Buddha? Do they run away from a copy of the Koran?"

"None of that works. They don't worship Satan—and yes, I did ask—and they don't practice black magic. They're unnatural. If that makes them unholy, well, it doesn't seem to hurt them any."

"Silver," she tried. "Or is that werewolves?"

"It was vampires, originally. No one has actually reported a werewolf sighting in two hundred years, so I couldn't tell you about their vulnerabilities. As far as vampires go, silver has no effect." He shifted in the passenger seat. He looked a lot less flexible than he had the day before. Fighting vampires took it out of him, she guessed. "We tried all these things out on Malvern in the first couple of years, back before Armonk started worshipping her and moaning about her rights. Light, we found out, is obnoxious to her. It doesn't set her on fire, but it causes her pain. Pretty much every kind of light causes her pain. She has to sleep during the day; there's no way to keep her awake. Her body literally changes while the sun is up, repairing whatever damage she took during the previous night. You'll have to come see the metamorphosis some time. It's gruesome but fascinating."

"No thanks," Caxton said. "When this case is closed I'm done with monsters. You can keep your title as the only American vampire hunter. I think I'll stick with DUIs and fender-benders. So how did all these stories get started if nothing works?"

"Simple. Nobody likes a story with an unhappy ending. Until the last century—and the advent of reliable firearms—

vampires pretty much had their way with us. The poets and the writers changed the details so as not to depress their readers with how bad the world could really be."

"But if they had the reality to compare to—"

"That's just it—they didn't." Arkeley sighed. "Every time a vampire pops up people say the same thing: 'I thought they were extinct.' It's because there's never more than a handful of them anywhere in the world at a given time. And thank God for that. If they were any more common, if they were better organized, we'd all be dead."

Caxton frowned with the effort of trying not to think too hard about that. She drove the rest of the way to Caernarvon and the hunting camp without small talk. Arkeley was good at silence, a fact she was just beginning to appreciate. Some things weren't worth talking about.

Patrol cars from three different jurisdictions sat parked on rolling grass near the hunting camp when they arrived—state police, the county sheriff, and a sole vehicle for the local policeman, a middle-aged man in a dark blue uniform who stood outside looking like he wanted to throw up. Technically it was his crime scene, and he had to authorize Caxton and Arkeley before they could go in. They waited until he felt well enough to check their ID.

"Are you going to be able to handle this?" Arkeley asked her. It didn't sound like a dare, but that was how she intended to take it. "This won't be pretty."

"I've scraped prom queens off the asphalt, tough guy," she said. "I've dug teeth out of dashboards so we could match dental records."

Arkeley gave her a dry little chuckle for her bravado.

It didn't look so bad from fifty feet away. The camp itself was a more elaborate affair than Caxton had imagined. It stood next to a chirping stream, protected in the shadow of some tall willows. Most camps in Caxton's experience were drafty little log cabins with steeply peaked roofs so they didn't collapse under the weight of winter snows. Farrel Morton's place might more accurately have been deemed a hunting lodge. A big main structure with lots of windows branched off into a newer wing and what Caxton judged had to be a semidetached kitchen, taking a clue from all the chimneys and vents. A porch ran the full length of the building, well supplied with rocking chairs made of rough-hewn logs with the bark still on. Under the peak of the roof Morton had mounted a brightly painted hex sign, an old Pennsylvania Dutch ward against evil.

Apparently it hadn't worked too well. Cops with their uniform shirts unbuttoned and their hats set aside were digging holes in the kitchen yard and out around back. They didn't have to dig too deep.

"I thought the vampire's victims all came back as half-deads," Caxton said, looking down at a pile of bones and broken flesh that had come out of one of those holes. Maggots made the ribcage quiver. She had to look away. This was worse than traffic fatalities. Those were fresh and the colors were normal. These smelled bad. Really bad.

"Only if he bade them to rise," Arkeley explained. "He wouldn't need very many servants, especially if he was trying to stay under our radar. Half-deads can't disguise themselves as well as vampires can. His bloodlust would force him to keep taking more victims, but he wouldn't want thirty slaves wandering around, doing nothing but drawing attention to themselves."

"Closer on a hundred, if you count the ones inside." It was the local cop. He still looked green, but he had their identification in his hands. He returned it to them and let them head inside.

When she saw the kitchen, Caxton almost wished he'd refused them. The scene inside made no sense, and her brain refused to accept it. The smell kept screwing with her head. It was bad, extremely bad, but more than that, it was wrong. The reptilian part of her brain knew that smell meant death. It knew enough to want to get away. She could feel it squirming at the base of her skull, trying to crawl away down her spine.

She focused on the details, trying not to see the big picture. That was tough. There were cops everywhere in different uniforms, milling around, bagging evidence, doing their jobs. She could barely see them for the bones. It was like a crypt in there, not like a house at all. Bones were stacked like cordwood along the wall, on top of the white enamel stove, shoved into closets. Someone had sorted them into skulls, pelvises, ribs, limbs. "Obsessive compulsive disorder," Caxton breathed.

"Now, that may be something real," Arkeley told her. "In Eastern Europe they used to sprinkle mustard seeds around a vampire's coffin. They thought he would have to count them all before he could move on, and if they left enough he would still be counting when dawn came. We don't know much about what vampires and half-deads do when they're not actively hunting. We know they don't watch television—it confuses them. They don't understand our culture and it doesn't interest them. Maybe they have their own entertainment. Maybe they sit around sorting their bones."

Caxton moved into the main room, mostly just wanting to get away from all the bones. What she found in the living room was worse. She crossed her arms over her stomach and held on tight. A couch and three comfortable-looking chairs stood in a semi-circle around a big fireplace. Human bodies in various states of decomposition sat as if posed, some with their arms around others, some leaning forward on their elbows. Baling wire had been used to keep them upright and in comfortable-looking postures. "Jesus." It was too much. It made no sense. "I don't get it. The vampire ate all these people. He kept their bodies around. Then he killed Farrel Morton and his kids and he felt like he needed to hide their corpses. Why the sudden change? What was different about Morton?"

"Somebody might miss him." It was a photographer from the sheriff's office. She was an Asian woman with long bangs draped cross her forehead. Caxton had seen her before somewhere. Some crime scene or other. "As far as we can tell, the victims here are all Latino and Hispanic males, between fifteen and forty years of age."

Arkeley, strangely enough, squinted in confusion. "And what does that suggest?" he asked.

It was Caxton's turn to shine, finally. Her nausea was swept away by her need to impress Arkeley. "It suggests they were migrant workers. Mexicans, Guatemalans, Peruvians—they come up here every year to work in the mushroom sheds or pick fruit in the orchards. They move from town to town according to the growing season and they pay cash for whatever they buy, so they don't leave a paper trail."

"Illegal immigrants," Arkeley said, nodding. "That makes sense."

"It's smart," the photographer said. She looked angry, pissed off even. Caxton knew some cops turned their fear and disgust into rage. It helped them do their job. The photographer lifted her camera and snapped off three quick shots of a defleshed pelvis sitting on the coffee table. Someone had used it as an ashtray. "Real fucking smart. Nobody keeps track of migrants. Even if somebody back home misses them, what are they going to do? Come up here and ask the American police for help? Not a chance. They'd just get deported."

"So the vampire was living here for months, feeding on invisible people," Caxton said. "Then the owner showed up with his kids. Damn," she said, thinking it through. "The half-deads weren't taking the bodies off to make more half-deads out of them. They were going to dump them someplace else, to draw attention away from here."

"Yeah," the photographer spat. "Don't want to shit where

you eat." She snapped another picture, this time of an umbrella stand half full of umbrellas and half full of femurs.

"Alright, Clara." A burly sheriff's deputy grabbed the photographer's arm. "Alright, we have enough pictures." He looked up at Arkeley and Caxton. "Have you two seen the basement yet?"

Caxton's mind reeled. The basement. The camp had a basement. What kind of vault of horrors awaited them? They passed through a mudroom and down a flight of stairs, Caxton holding one hand against the smooth drywall, the other gripping the banister. They headed down past shelves of preserves, thick and cloying in their Mason jars. They climbed over stacks of scattered sports equipment and roofing supplies. At the far end of the narrow cellar a group of state troopers wearing latex gloves stood in a semicircle. What were they guarding? They stepped aside when they saw Arkeley and his star.

Caxton moved forward. She felt like she floated rather than walked. She felt like a ghost in the haunted camp. She pushed through the standing troopers. Beyond them in a shadowy alcove stood three identical coffins, all of them open, all of them empty.

Three coffins. "No," she blurted. "No." It wasn't over. There were more of them, more vampires out there.

Arkeley kicked one of the coffins shut with a hollow sound.

15.

Outside Caxton sat down on the grass and put her head between her knees. It wasn't over. She had thought they were safe again. She had looked at all the dead human bodies in the camp and she had thought that yes, they were horrible, but it was okay, okay in some sad way, because the vampire was dead. Because nobody else was going to get torn apart, nobody else's blood was going to be drained from a still-twitching carcass.

"She said 'brood.' She said her brood would devour me," Arkeley said. He stared out at a distant line of blue hills above the water. Mist rose from between the trees over there and it looked like ghosts to Caxton, like wandering ghosts coming out to plead, to beg for their life back.

Ghosts. Ghosts could scare you, but they couldn't hurt you, not really. They couldn't pull you to pieces and suck your life out. They didn't use your bones as furniture.

"I was fooled. I thought she was being poetic." Arkeley kicked at a spill of stones and they went clattering into the stream. "I thought Lares was pretty smart. He could pass as human, he was such a good actor. Malvern has real cunning, though. She knew I would be watching her. She knew that one vampire, just one, would be bad, would create all kinds of havoc. But it wouldn't be enough. What does it cost her to birth one of these monstrosities? And to do it while she's being monitored night and day. For twenty years I thought we were safe. Clearly she was just taking her time, gathering her strength."

Caxton's chest heaved. She wasn't sure if it was a sob or the precursor to vomiting. It was convulsive and spontaneous. It happened again, her ribs flexing as if something inside were pushing to get out.

"Let's go," Arkeley said. "We have to start chasing down our leads. All we have to go on is the list of people who worked at Arabella Furnace. Who knows. Who the fuck knows? We might get lucky."

"Hold on," she said. The thing in her midriff squirmed in annoyance. She wasn't supposed to talk. A cough exploded out of her lungs.

"We're wasting daylight," he told her. "Get up."

She shook her head. That was a bad idea. She hiccoughed

and a ribbon of bile shot out from between her lips. Her break-fast came up in one great rush, a brown spray she couldn't hold in. She rolled over on her side, her body shivering uncontrollably. "I don't expect you to care about my feelings," she whimpered. "But I can't do this anymore."

He squatted next to her. He jammed two fingers into her neck, feeling for her pulse. He took his hand away and she looked up at him, her cheek against the cool grass, her eye following his face. Then he slapped her.

The impact made her cry out, and her body shook. She rolled up to a sitting posture and then forced herself to stand, pushing her back against the side of the building, pushing herself up to a standing position. She stared at him, hot, pure hate coming out of her. He stood there and took it.

"There are dead people in that house," he told her. "There will be more dead people tonight. And every night. Until we bag the other two."

Five minutes later they were in the car. He drove this time. He kept his speed low, kept his eyes on the road. She sat in the passenger seat with the window rolled down. It was freezing, but the icy air on her face seemed to help. She spent most of the ride on her cell phone, coordinating with the area response team, trying to eliminate some of the seventy-nine suspects on Arkeley's list. It was tough even talking, much less trying to keep straight in her head the various units she was assigning to various missions. The Bureau of Forensic Services had to be connected with the records and identification unit so they could work up a profile of what a vampire killing looked like, which was then sent on to the Bureau of Investigation so they could detach units from the troop-level criminal investigations units. Meanwhile the media were yammering for details and interviews with the vampire killers. She was under orders from the Commissioner to send a prepared statement to his office for release to the press. She kept it as brief and nonsensational as possible. By the time she finished and signed off, they were nearing Centre County.

When she hung up the phone she felt as if her soul was going ninety miles an hour in a school zone. "I'm not cut out for this," she suggested.

"What, working the bureaucracy? I've seen worse."

"No," she said. "I'm not cut out for vampire hunting." She closed her eyes, but she just saw bones, human bones. "Last night the vampire hypnotized me."

"I remember," he told her. "I was there."

"No, I mean, there was nothing I could do. I couldn't fight it. What if the next one hypnotizes me, but you can't shoot it in time?"

"Then you'll die." His eyes stayed on the road.

"I'm not a weak person," she insisted.

"That has nothing to do with it. Susceptibility to hypnotism is like hair color or height. It's genetic and it means very little, most of the time."

"But I'm susceptible, that's what you're saying. I'm not strong enough, mentally, to fight vampires. Seriously. I'm not cut out for this. I can't do it." Fear ate her like a wolf swallowing a gobbet of flesh. She shivered and her teeth chattered and her skin stood up. Proud flesh, her mother used to call it. Her father called it goosebumps. Just sitting there, knowing she would have to face another vampire, was scaring the hell out of her.

"When I slapped you, you were ready to bring me up on charges. And you would have been in the right. But you didn't. Instead you came with me. That means you're in the right place," he told her.

She shook her head. She needed to stop talking and start doing something. It might help, anyway. "What's our next step?"

Arkeley surprised her by pulling off the road to get some lunch.

"You're hungry? I feel like I got kicked in the belly," she said.

He shrugged. "Try not throwing up next time." He rolled into the parking lot of Peachey's Diner, right next to a shiny black Amish buggy. The horse gave Caxton a look as she stepped out of the car. It swished its tail and she made clucking noises to calm it down. Arkeley headed inside without waiting to see if she would follow. Caxton looked up at the ridgeline opposite the restaurant and sighed. In the deep, dark heart of her state the earth was wrinkled into high limbs of rock that blocked cell phones and radio waves and left the fertile valleys secluded from most of human society. It was why the Amish thrived there. Caxton had never liked this stretch of Pennsylvania too much, though. It was a place where her kind weren't exactly welcome, a power center for the Ku Klux Klan and the neo-Nazis. Elsewhere in the state you saw billboards for Penn's Cave or the outlet malls clogging up every roadside, but here they disappeared. In their place you saw smaller, less colorful signs sponsored by the local churches with messages like: "WORSHIP Your LORD In Fear" and "How did you SIN today?" This was the zone of central Pennsylvania called "Pennsyltucky" by outsiders, and they didn't mean it as a compliment.

She stepped inside. The restaurant was familiar to her. It was neutral territory where all the valley's inhabitants could come together in peace. Peachey's catered to farmers who needed to fuel up for a day of hard manual labor and also to people who liked huge portions and weren't watching their cholesterol. Arkeley went through the buffet and heaped up a plate of fried chicken, German potato salad, and sweetened baked beans swimming with bits of gristly bacon. Caxton slid into an artificial wood-grain booth and ordered a small diet soda. She looked across the aisle at an Amish family: a gray-bearded patriarch with a mole on his cheek; his wife, whose face had the texture of a dried apple; and their two cherubic sons, who wore bright blue shirts and wide straw hats. Their eyes were closed, their hands folded. They were saying grace. The table between them was laden with plates of pork chops and bowls overflowing with mashed potatoes with brown bits of skin half-submerged under the starchy surface.

Arkeley folded himself painfully into the booth and dug into his food. The thought of all that oily, greasy chicken being shredded between Arkeley's teeth made Caxton look away. She studied a woman in an enormous sweatshirt with a howling wolf painted on the front. She was shoveling red Jell-O into her mouth. Caxton just closed her eyes and tried to breathe normally.

"They drink blood, just like we eat food," she said. Talking helped her ignore all the food being consumed. "You talked before about how they need more and more the older they get. Like those things in Lares' boat."

He nodded. "Malvern would need to bathe in blood to restore herself. It would take half a dozen kills to make her whole again, and she would need that much blood again the next night. And every night after that."

"Christ," Caxton said. The Amish man across the aisle shot her a nasty look for taking his Lord's name in vain. She resisted the urge to show him her middle finger. "They always need more? It has to level out after a while, right? Otherwise there wouldn't be enough blood in the world after a while."

"You've never seen evil before, have you?" Arkeley asked. He held up a spoon laden with ambrosia salad that vibrated with his breath. "Not true evil."

She thought about it for a while. The horrors of the hunting camp were still with her. She only had to close her eyes and she saw them again. Still. She had seen killers before, human killers, and they had failed to terrorize her like this. They had been sick, sad little people who lacked the imagination to solve their problems in any nonviolent way. That didn't make them evil—it made them damaged, but certainly not evil. "I'm not sure evil exists, not like you mean." She put both hands on the tabletop and pushed against the edge, stretching her arms. "I mean, there's a moral component to our lives, sure, and if you know you're doing something wrong—"

"Evil," Arkeley interrupted, "is never satisfied. Evil has no ending, no bottom." He swallowed noisily. "If it isn't stopped it will swallow the world. Vampires are unnatural. They are dead things that get up and enact a mockery of living and it costs them, badly, to do it. The universe abhors them even more than it abhors a vacuum."

She nodded, not really understanding. But she could feel how much of it he believed. How much he needed to destroy the remaining vampires. She could feel, also, the beginning of something inside of herself that matched his need. She wanted to close the remaining coffins. She wanted to destroy the vampires. She was standing on the edge of that desire and she wasn't sure that, if she stepped off, there would ever be a bottom to her wanting. Which, she realized, was exactly what had happened to him. He wanted to kill vampires the same way vampires wanted his blood.

"It's dangerous, isn't it, to learn too much about them?" she asked. "You start becoming something unnatural yourself." She looked around at the normal, healthy, happy people all just eating lunch. They weren't monstrous. They weren't disgusting. They weren't good or evil. They were natural. "Why did you bring me here?" she asked. "None of the suspects lived this far west."

"I want you to meet somebody," he said, and reached for the check.

16.

The road took them over a ridge and down the other side, then swerved to follow the course of a winding creek. The sun rode next to them, skipping along on top of the water. It kept getting in Caxton's eyes and eventually she put on a pair of sunglasses, which helped a little.

Arkeley turned again later to take them across a covered bridge. Though they rolled along at only ten miles an hour, the bridge rumbled and shook around them. Beyond, the valley turned golden and brown, the grassy pastureland changing to cornfields that stretched for miles. Ancient electric fencing stretched alongside the road, rusted and intermittent. They passed old shacks that had collapsed in the wind and the rain, their wooden planks silvered with decay. She saw an aluminum silo that had been struck by lightning years earlier, its domed top blasted open as if by a giant can opener.

The road narrowed down to a single unpaved lane, but Caxton wasn't worried about oncoming traffic. There was something old and quiescent about the valley they sped through. There were crows out in the corn, enormous black birds that took turns leaping into the air and scouting for danger. There were surely mice in those fields, and gophers and hares and snakes, but there were no people anywhere.

"You sure your friend is out this way?" she asked. "It looks pretty deserted."

"That's the way he likes it." The road forked and Arkeley took a left. Within minutes the road had disappeared almost completely, replaced by a pair of narrow ruts in a strip of grass between two cornfields. The car bounced and jumped and threw Caxton around but eventually, finally, Arkeley pulled to a stop in a cloud of dust. Caxton got out and looked around, hugging her arms against the chill in the air.

There were buildings around them—old, very old farm buildings. A two-story house, white with gingerbread trim. A barn with an open hayloft. A silo made of metal slats that looked as though it would leak pretty badly. Sunlight slanted through it and striped the side of the house.

A black-and-white hex sign hung above the house's front door, painted with geometric patterns more elaborate and more delicate than any she'd seen before, and Caxton had seen a lot of hex signs in her life. Typically they looked quaint and colorful. This one looked spiky and almost malevolent. It made her not want to go inside. Caxton saw a flash of yellow at one of the windows and saw a little blonde girl looking down at her. The girl twitched shut a curtain and was gone.

"Urie!" Arkeley shouted. Presumably he was calling his friend. "Urie Polder!"

"I'm here, I'm in here," someone said from behind the door of the barn. The voice was very soft, as if coming from far away, and thick with an accent she hadn't heard since she was a kid. They walked around the side of the door and into the barn and Caxton took off her sunglasses to let her eyes adjust to the barn's dimness.

She didn't know what she'd expected to find inside. Perhaps cows or goats or horses. Instead the barn was used as a drying shed for some kind of animal skins hanging in almost-perfect darkness. They were draped on equally spaced racks about as tall as her shoulder. They were not uniform in shape or size, but they shared a pallor so intense that they were almost luminous in the dark barn. Caxton reached out toward one, wanting to know its texture. Before she could touch it, however, a shadow passed across its surface, or rather five small, oval shadows like the tips of fingers pressing on it from behind. She gasped and yanked her hand back. Had she made contact, she knew, she would have felt a hand pressing back against hers, and yet there was no one behind the skin, no one anywhere near.

"What is this?" she demanded. Arkeley frowned.

"Teleplasm," he told her. She didn't know what that meant. "Go ahead, head in," he said.

She shook her head. "I've had about enough of weird shit." But his face didn't change. He would wait there all day until she walked farther into the barn.

Caxton walked between two racks and stepped into darkness. The shadow inside the barn was nearly complete—after a few steps she was inching forward in almost complete blackness, the only light coming from the luminescent skins on either side. The substance drew her eyes, since there was nothing else to look at. She couldn't see her own hands held out before her, fingers outstretched, reaching for the far wall of the barn, but she could make out every tear and fold and blemish on the skins. They seemed to shimmer, or perhaps they were simply fluttering in a draft. They had an illusory depth, as if they were windows into some moonlit place. She felt like she could look through their textured surfaces, where faces seemed to pass and vanish as fast as breath on a cold pane of glass. The only thing about them that stayed the same from one moment to the next was their color, though occasionally from the corner of her eye she would think she had caught a flash of pigment, a reddish tinge like a bloodstain fading from view.

She walked carefully so as not to trip in the darkness, but also so she wouldn't touch the skins. After her first encounter with the ghostly fingers she'd had enough.

She was nearly at the far end of the barn—or so she guessed, as the racks of skins suddenly stopped and beyond lay only darkness—when something seemed to brush her hair. She spun around and heard a faint voice whisper her name. Or had she imagined it? Before she'd even really heard the voice it was gone and the barn's silence was so complete, so certain that it seemed impossible she had heard anything.

"Arkeley," she cried out, "what are you doing to me now?"

There was no answer. She turned around and saw that the barn's doors had been shut behind her. She was shut inside with the skins, the teleplasm, whatever that was, and she wanted to scream for help, or just scream, scream for the sake of screaming—

"Laura," someone said, and this time it wasn't just in her head. But that voice—so familiar, so impossible. It was her father's voice.

He stood there. Behind her. One of the skins had lifted away from the rack, flapped away and folded itself into a mostly human shape. It had her father's voice, and his eyes. It was wrapped in chains that rattled as he glided toward her, chains that shook and dragged on the floor of the barn, holding him down, holding him back. She put out a hand, either to touch him or to push him away, she didn't know. He'd been dead for so long. She knew it wasn't really him. Was it? Was it some remnant of him, left over after his flesh had rotted away?

A smell of him, of shampoo and Old Spice, flooded the air around her. The temperature in the barn dropped twenty degrees in the space of a few seconds. He was close to her, so close she could feel the roughness of his hands. She could feel the hair on the backs of his arms, though they had yet to actually touch. She had missed him so much. She had thought of him every day, she had even thought of him when the vampire had held her up in the air the night before. Nothing had been as good since he'd died, nothing had been right, not even when she met Deanna, it hadn't healed that wound.

"Daddy," she breathed, stepping into his embrace. And then the lights switched on and there was just a skin, like an animal pelt, hanging on a wooden bar.

"Right you are," someone said. A very human, very live

voice. A man was standing behind the racks, a Caterpillar baseball cap on his head, his sideburns growing down to meet each other under his chin. His eyes were soft and deep. He was staring right at her. His voice was pure Pennsyltucky, down to the throat-clearing swallow he used like audible punctuation. "Right you are, Arkeley. They's drawn to her, ahum. She's ghost bait."

"It's not the ghosts I'm concerned with," Arkeley said. He was standing no more than ten feet away from her.

The other man—Urie Polder, she presumed—stepped around one of his racks and came up to her. He was tall enough to look down into her face and try to hold her eye. She broke his gaze, though, as she imagined most people did when they met him. He was missing his left arm. The sleeve of his T-shirt dangled over a wooden branch that he wore in the arm's place, a length of gray-barked tree limb that had a knotted elbow and even three twiglike fingers.

What really freaked her out about Urie Polder's arm wasn't that it was made of wood. It was the fact that it moved. Its thin fingers wove around his belt buckle and hitched up his pants. His wooden shoulder and his flesh shoulder shrugged at the same time. "We oughter take her into the house, ahum. Vesta'll do it there."

"Yes, alright," Arkeley said. He looked worried.

Caxton rubbed at her eyes with her hands. "My father—that was my father's ghost. You showed me my father's ghost just to—just to—" She stopped. "What the hell is teleplasm?"

"Most folks'd say 'ectoplasm,' which is all but the same, but then you might have guessed," Polder told her. "It's ghost skin, ahum."

"How do you skin a ghost?" she demanded.

"Well, now," he said, grinning sheepishly, "not in any way the ghost might like, ahum."

17.

It was cold in the barn. It was cold outside for an autumn day, but in the barn it was pure winter. The two men turned toward the open barn door to leave, but she stood rooted to the spot. Caxton felt rage bubble and spit in her stomach. "Hold on," she said, and surprisingly enough they both stopped. "That was my father. You have my father's ghost hanging on a rack." She had no idea how it had happened, no idea at all why her father's ghost in particular was in the barn, but she wasn't taking another step until she'd figured it out.

"Well, now, ghosts, them's tricky, ahum." Polder scratched his chin with his wooden hand. "It don't really come down to that."

She shook her head angrily. "I know his voice. I saw his eyes."

"Yes," Arkeley said. "It might even have been him. His spirit, anyway—or it could have been any kind of mischievous spook who wanted to toy with you. It might not even have been a human apparition. But whoever it was isn't trapped here in one of these pelts. The teleplasms aren't ghosts themselves. They're more like clothing that ghosts can pick up and put on. It's a substance that occupies this world and the other simultaneously, that's all."

She nodded at Arkeley. "I can guess what this was all about, though I'm pissed off at you all the same. If the teleplasm reacts strongly to me, that means I'm somehow open to psychic phenomena. I'm a 'sensitive.'"

"Young lady, based on what we just saw, I think you could moonlight as a medium," Polder said. "Please, we need to go inside the house. Your visit with your father made a lot of noise in the spirit world. Anyone who was listening would have heard it—and they might come looking for you."

As they pushed her toward the house she said, "So if I'm sensitive to ghosts I'm also sensitive to vampires. This explains how the vampire was able to hypnotize me so effortlessly last night."

Arkeley confirmed it. "I was surprised how little resistance you had. So I brought you here, where we can do something about it."

Polder stood before the hex sign over his front door and waved his arm at it, his real arm. He drew a complicated pattern on his forehead with his thumb, and something invisible relaxed. Caxton could feel the hex sign let go.

"Urie is a hexenmeister. I imagine you know the term?"

"Mostly where I grew up we called them pow-wow doctors, because they were supposed to have all kinds of secret Indian magic." Caxton had never taken the old stories that seriously, but then she'd never really believed in vampires either. After her adventures of the previous night and what she'd seen in the barn, she was willing to suspend a little skepticism.

They headed inside the house, where a woman waited for them. She wore a long black dress with a tight collar around her throat. Her blonde hair stood out from her head in enormous frizzy waves. Her long white fingers were covered in dozens of identical gold rings. "Vesta, it's been too long," Arkeley said, and he kissed her cheek. The woman's eyes never moved from Caxton's face.

"I've got water on for tea. Darjeeling, just as you like it," she said. "With sugar, not honey, and a touch of milk. Please, don't be surprised, Laura Beth Caxton. I know a large number of things about you already. I intend to learn many more."

Caxton didn't even open her mouth. She turned her head because she'd seen a flash of yellow out of the corner of her eye.

It was the girl she'd seen in the window, and she vanished as quickly as she had before.

"Now you, Special Deputy, you should be kinder to this one. She's risking much to help you in your vicious crusade."

Arkeley hung his head.

"Don't look so glum. I have a little something for your wife's foot, here," Vesta said, and handed the Fed a plastic bag full of a reddish, fibrous plant matter. "Make it into a poultice and have her wear it every night until she feels better."

"You have a wife?" Caxton demanded.

"I killed a vampire twenty years ago, and another one last night. I had to keep myself busy in the meantime," he told her. He thanked Vesta for her remedy, and then he and Urie Polder went deeper into the house. Caxton was not invited. Instead Vesta Polder led her into a sitting room, a dark but tidy space with a raging fire and a lot of heavy, dark wooden furniture. Six straight-backed chairs stood against the wall. A round table with a velvet cloth sat in the middle of the room, a horsehair-stuffed armchair crouching behind it. Vesta took this chair, lounging across it with one leg hooked over an arm. Caxton stood before the table for a long while before she thought to take one of the chairs from the wall and put it across the table from Vesta.

On the table were the teapot and a single teacup as well as a large, carved wooden box with a Chinese dragon on its lid and a slim deck of cards. "You've seen these before, in a movie," she said, tapping the cards against her wrist and then shuffling them with one hand. "But you don't know what they're called. They're Zener cards." She fanned a few of them as if she were demonstrating a poker hand. "They are used by parapsychologists to test extrasensory perception. They possess other virtues, as well." On one side each card showed a single symbol in thick black lines: a triangle, a star, a circle, three wavy lines, or a square.

"Now," she said, "your instinct is going to be to tell me what you see." She cut the cards and held one up so that Caxton could see it—a star.

"It's a star," she said.

"Yes, dear, I know it is." Vesta put the card down on the coffee table and opened the carved box. "I see all. Now, please. From here on don't say anything. Don't try to project, don't give me any clues. Just look at the cards."

Caxton never touched the tea. One by one Vesta lifted the cards so that only Caxton could see them. After a moment she would put them facedown on the table. Occasionally she paused to study Caxton's face as intently as if she were sketching it. Then she would reach into her Chinese box and take out a long brown cigarette and an equally long match. She would puff at the cigarette, filling the room with pungent, foul smoke until Caxton's eyes watered. Then she would draw another card. This went on until she ran out of cards: then Vesta would shuffle the cards and start again. With each shuffle there were new instructions. Caxton should try not to look at the card. She should speak the card's symbol in her mind, rather than visualizing it. She should try to clear her mind of thoughts altogether. Time seemed to slow down, or perhaps stop. Maybe there was something more in the cigarettes than tobacco.

Vesta gathered up the deck and shuffled it again. "Alright. This time, try to think of a symbol other than the one you see." Caxton nodded and got to it. After they'd gone through five or six cards, Vesta surprised her. "You're worried about Deanna."

It was hard to concentrate on the card in front of her, but Vesta rattled it between two fingers and Caxton looked away from the other woman's face. "She's been out of work for a long time."

"She's been having bad dreams. Violent dreams—you had

to wake her up last night because you were scared she would hurt herself. She's scared too, scared that you'll be killed."

That makes two of us, Caxton thought.

"Focus on the card in your head, even when you look at the card in my hand. She is afraid of the future, it sounds like to me. Afraid because she does not know if you will let her stay with you. Yet you have never even considered asking her to leave."

Caxton bit her lip. It was hard to even see the card in Vesta's hand when she thought of Deanna. "You can read her mind, too? But she's fifty miles from here."

Vesta sighed. She put down the cards and took another cigarette out of her box. It was her fifth so far. "I see the portion of her that exists within you." She scattered the cards on the table. "This is hopeless. Some people grasp the technique in a moment, while others need additional help. Given enough time, enough sessions, I might teach you some rudiments of psychic self-defense. For now, this must do." She opened her box again and took out a brass charm on a black cord. "Wear it always, and try not to make eye contact with anyone who might harm you."

Caxton took the pendant from Vesta and slipped it around her neck. The charm was a tightly wound spiral that she could pass off as jewelry. Caxton was glad for it—she had half expected a pentacle or a gruesome crucifix.

"Those wouldn't work for you. Their power requires faith which you do not possess."

Caxton touched the cool metal at her throat. Deanna. Now that she was thinking about Deanna she couldn't stop. "It's not just a question of not kicking her out. I don't want to lose her the way I lost my mother."

Vesta stared at her and said nothing. It was as if she expected Caxton to tell her all about the sad, sorry tale of her mother's insanity, the depression that had struck her after her husband's death, her eventual suicide.

"She hanged herself," Caxton said, finally, blushing. "In her bedroom. A neighbor found her and cut her down and tried to make her look presentable. My mother had always been very proud of her looks. When I got there she was laid out on the bed and her hair had been brushed and someone had even put some makeup on her. But they couldn't hide the rope burn all the way around her neck."

Vesta nodded and exhaled a plume of smoke. "You worry about losing Deanna. Well, that's just natural. But when the time comes you'll be ready to let her go. You'll have to be. I see it as strongly as I see the waves in your mind's eye."

That last bit confused Caxton—until she finally looked at the card in Vesta's hand. It showed three wavy lines.

"Now, come, let's collect the boys." They rose and headed into the kitchen, where Arkeley and Urie sat around an enormous table that had once been a door and now was mounted on plain wooden trestles. They had between them a pile of small objects, triangular in shape and almost pearlescent in color. Caxton picked one up and saw it was a vampire's tooth. After killing the vampire the night before, the Fed must have pulled out all his teeth with a pair of pliers.

Urie Polder swept the teeth into a satin bag and tied it closed with a thong. "Now that'll do just fine, in way of payment, ahum."

"What are you going to do with those?" Caxton asked.

"He'll find something they're useful for," Vesta told her, ushering her toward the front door. "Waste not, want not."

As they drove away the little blonde girl watched them from the window. Caxton had not gotten to meet her, and didn't even know her name.

18.

Caxton drove to State College, only a dozen or so miles away, just to get out of the suffocating atmosphere of Pennsyltucky. The tree-lined avenues of the university town were full of students in bright and colorful parkas and windbreakers. They walked in pairs or groups of four or more, laughing amongst themselves, shouldering backpacks, their faces red with the cold but their heads bare. They were alive; that was the main thing. Very much alive, and their concerns were for the simplest things—sex, grades, beer. None of them wanted to skin a ghost or drain the blood of a living victim. They were young, too, unwrinkled, innocent in their own fashion. It did her good to see them.

She was losing it, and she knew it. That she would drive so far just to see young people made her realize how dark her life had become in such a brief period of time. She pulled into a parking space on College Avenue before a big stone gate that let her look all the way up the quadrangle. She undid her seat belt but didn't get out of the car.

Arkeley looked up. He'd been studying his Blackberry since she'd started driving. "Good news," he told her. "The investigative unit has ruled out seventeen of the suspects. They decided to run down the medical personnel and corrections officers first—the ones who might have actually had physical contact with Malvern. They're about half done."

Caxton nodded. That was good news. "Malvern. It all comes back to Malvern. How did she get here?" she asked. "She was in Pittsburgh when you found her, but she wasn't born there, right?"

"No," he said. He put the Blackberry in his coat pocket. "Vampires move around a lot—it's how they stay one step ahead of people like us. It took me years to trace her route and I'm not done yet. I know she was born in Manchester, in England, around 1695. She terrorized that city for about sixty-five years before the bloodlust got too much and she couldn't rise any more from her coffin. She lived for a while under the care of another vampire, Thomas Easling, who was burned at the stake in Leeds in 1783. Malvern's body was found among Easling's property, and it was assumed at the time that she was dead, just a mummified corpse. A curio. She was purchased for thirty-five British pounds by a Virginian plantation owner, one Josiah Caryl Chess, who fancied himself a scholar of natural history. He had quite a collection of dinosaur and mammal fossils, so a moribund vampire must have been a prize find. He never bothered to remove her heart. She couldn't move, after all, and even though he must have known she was still alive in there in some fashion—he may have even fed her—he was certain she was beyond harming anyone. Most likely she had him under her spell, though his journals suggest just the opposite. He was physically intimate with her at least once."

"Shit, no," Caxton said, her stomach squeezing down like a rubber ball. Caxton remembered what Arkeley had said about Malvern and her current attendant, Doctor Hazlitt. *She had more to offer him*, Arkeley had said, *than her piercing gaze*. "But she would be all . . . look, I'm sorry if this is gross, but she'd be too dry."

"Personal lubricants have been widely available throughout history. I know the ancient Romans used olive oil. And if you let her, if you play along, she can make herself look however you want. Your ideal woman. The illusion lasts as long as she wants it to."

Something in Arkeley's voice worried her. "You've seen her do it?" Caxton asked. She really wanted to ask if she'd changed her appearance for him—and if he'd succumbed. She couldn't ask that, though, not in so many words.

He chuckled. "She's tried plenty of tricks on me. I've been visiting her every few weeks for two decades now—she's been trying to get me on her side this whole time. So far I've resisted." He made it sound as if he couldn't guarantee, even to himself, that he would always be successful. "Anyway. Chess died of blood loss, of course. No one ever officially put the blame on Malvern. She had never moved from her coffin, which was mounted in a front room as a kind of conversation piece. Looking back now, it's pretty obvious that she sucked Chess dry, but at the time they blamed a mutinous slave for his death. They locked Malvern up in the attic and forgot about her. The plantation was burned to the ground during the Civil War and she disappeared for a while. In fact the next time anyone has a record of her is when she showed up in the possession of Piter Byron Lares, and you know how that story goes."

"Lares had plenty of moribund vampires, not just Malvern."

Arkeley agreed. "They take care of their own. It's almost like ancestor worship, and it's one of the very few things that can make them act irrationally. I assumed originally that the four vampires in Lares' boat were all of one lineage, that one of them had made Lares while another had made the one who made Lares, and so on. I was wrong. By the time I discovered him Lares had been collecting old vampires for decades. Maybe he thought that by getting blood for them he was doing something good and nurturing. Maybe it helped assuage his conscience, assuming he had some kind of conscience. I don't know. I've been studying vampires for twenty years myself and I still don't know how they think. They're just too alien to us."

Caxton scratched under her armpit. She stared out through the windshield at the eighteen-year-olds walking by, their arms clutched around each other for warmth, their faces so clean. None of them knew what the future would hold, or what they would become. "You've been working the same case all this time."

"Lots of cops define their careers with one case. The

murderer who got away, the child who went missing and never showed up again." Arkeley shrugged. "Alright. You got me. I've never been able to get the Lares case out of my mind. I moved here, to Pennsylvania, to follow up on it. I've spent years getting to know people like the Polders who might have some information. And I've watched Malvern like a hawk."

"And now when someone calls the FBI to say they have a vampire killing, they call you." Caxton frowned. "That's a lot of weight to carry around."

"I do alright," Arkeley told her.

Whatever. She should be focusing on the case, not feeling sorry for Arkeley. "This is my first serious investigation," she told him. "I'm no detective. But I think I have an idea of what's been going on. Lares kept Malvern going until you killed him. Then, through various bureaucratic channels, she got installed at that hospital, at Arabella Furnace."

"Right."

"She tried to charm her way out, to talk her way out, she even ate one of the doctors, but it's been no good. You're sitting on her, just waiting for her to do something bad so you can punish her. She can't just give up, though. She's going to live forever, locked up in a withered corpse of a body forever, so the only option is to keep planning an escape, even if it takes twenty years to pull off. She's getting a little blood, but not enough to sustain her. She needs more muscle. So she creates three vampires."

"More likely she created one of them and he created the other two—it would involve less direct risk for her."

Caxton clucked her tongue. "Why three, though? Why do they even need to bring the blood to her? One vampire could just steal her, coffin and all, and hide her where we'd never find her. Then he could bring her back on his own timetable."

"Her body is too frail to be moved around like that. If she

broke in two pieces right now she might never have the strength to put herself back together. She needs to walk out of Arabella Furnace under her own power."

Caxton added that to her store of facts. "Okay. So the big plan is to bring blood to her, the way Lares used to. But a lot of blood this time, enough to completely heal her. To make that happen she creates a vampire. He goes out into the woods and takes over Farrel Morton's hunting camp, makes it his base of operations. He creates some half-deads to keep the place going and creates two more vampires. For months they stay on the down low, eating migrant workers, not showing themselves. Biding their time. But why? Why haven't they tried to free Malvern yet? Do vampires get stronger over time?"

"No—they're never stronger than the first night they rise to hunt."

Caxton nodded. "So the longer they wait the weaker they get, and the more risk they have to live with. Risk that somebody's going to wander by the hunting camp and notice that it's been turned into a mausoleum. Which is in fact pretty much what did happen. If that half-dead hadn't come up against my sobriety check we wouldn't know that any of this was going on. Farrel Morton shows up with his kids, looking for a weekend in the woods. He finds himself in a house of horrors instead. The vampires are so afraid of being discovered that they send a half-dead to dump the bodies somewhere else, to make it look like Morton never even went to the camp. Why go to such lengths? When it didn't work they had to leave home so fast they left their coffins behind. They've got to be desperate by now."

Arkeley nodded.

"Desperate enough to attack the hospital?"

"Malvern's plan isn't ready to be put into action—not yet. She can be an astonishingly patient creature, when it suits her. Still, she doesn't waste opportunities. She'll have a backup plan and she will put it into action as soon as possible. Still, I don't expect an attack right away. I believe I know why the three of them were biding their time."

"Yeah?"

"It's simple logistics. She needs a certain quantity of blood. Three vampires couldn't bring her enough blood to fully revivify her. Four of them could. They were going to make another one."

"Christ. But now—they're down to two, half of what they need. That's something, right? It's a good thing."

Arkeley scowled at her. "It buys us some time, that's all."

Caxton looked up. While they'd been sitting there talking the last of the afternoon had faded away. A streak of yellow marked the western horizon—the sun was going down. In perhaps fifteen minutes it would be dark. "People," she said, "are going to die tonight, one way or the other."

Arkeley didn't bother to confirm it. He was too busy reaching for the Blackberry that buzzed in his jacket pocket. When her cell phone began to ring as well, she knew something must have happened. Something bad.

19.

Caxton drove fast but safe, keeping her wheels on the road. The blue flasher on the dashboard played hell with her night vision, but she'd trained for this. When they reached Farrel Morton's hunting camp she switched off the flasher and her headlights and rolled up in the darkness. No need to make themselves a target.

An hour earlier, at dusk, the state troopers stationed at the camp had failed to report in on schedule. They were good men with many years of experience between them—they wouldn't just have forgotten to call headquarters. The local cop had called Troop J dispatch and told them he would drop by and see what had happened. He expected the troopers were having radio trouble. He'd reported back twenty minutes later with the news that the troopers were nowhere to be found. He was going to take a look around the surrounding woods and see what he could turn up. He had not called since and his cell phone rang for a while and then went to voicemail.

The sheriff was sending two units. Troop J out of Lancaster was sending every available car. Caxton and Arkeley hadn't waited to hear what came next. They were the closest to the camp, and Arkeley seemed to like it that way.

"You're almost smiling," she said, taking the key out of the ignition. "You hoping that somehow this is all a big misunderstanding, that everybody's okay?"

"No," he told her. "I'm hoping this is exactly what it looks like. I'm hoping we get a second vampire tonight. I doubt it, though. They aren't stupid."

Caxton popped the trunk of the unmarked patrol car. She lifted out a riot shotgun, a Remington 870, and slung it over her shoulder. The weapon had a shortened barrel and no buttstock so that it was easier to carry around, a black coating so it wouldn't glimmer in the low light. It would be worthless against vampires—the relatively small #1 buckshot was meant to stop a human being in his tracks, but it wouldn't even penetrate vampiric skin. Against half-deads it might be more effective.

"They weren't supposed to come back here," she said, closing the trunk as quietly as possible. "That was the idea, right? It was too dangerous for the vampires to come back. They would know we were watching the place. They left their coffins behind and they weren't coming back for them. That's what you told me."

"Are you going to blame me," he asked, "when we don't even know what happened yet?"

Caxton pumped the shotgun to put a round in the chamber. With her other hand she unlatched the holster of her pistol. "You want to lead?" she asked.

"With that kind of firepower behind me? Not a chance. You'd cut me in half at the first sign of any danger. You go first and I'll cover you."

The camp was dark, only a single light burning on the side of the building. It made the shadows deeper. She headed around the side of the kitchen wing, staying low, the shotgun pointing straight up. She came to an open window and decided to chance it. She flicked on the flashlight mounted to the top of the shotgun and checked to make sure he had her back. He did, of course. He might not like her very much, but he was a skilled cop. Caxton stood up and pointed her light inside the house. Nobody jumped out at her, so she took a quick look, panning the light from one side of the room to the other just as she'd been taught.

She saw what she'd expected. Stove. Refrigerator. Piles of bones. A half-dead could have hidden anywhere in the room, in the shadows, out of her light beam. She didn't see any movement, though. She circled the house with Arkeley following behind her.

When she got to the back of the house, near the stream, a harsh, cackling laugh wafted through the trees and ran cold down her spine. She froze, ducked down into a firing squat, and scanned the darkness all around. Her flashlight rippled across the trees on the far side of the stream and stopped when she found the source of the laugh. A half-dead was hanging in one of the trees. No, not hanging. It was secured to the tree with lengths of baling wire, its arms and legs bound securely.

She thought immediately of the dead people wired into sitting postures in the camp's living room. "Don't fucking move!" she shrieked.

The creep laughed again. The sound of it irritated her. It got on her skin and made her feel grimy, like her skin was crawling with dirt and cold sweat. "Oh, I promise," it said. Its voice wasn't human at all, nor was it anything like a vampire's voice. It was squeaky and infantile and nasty.

Arkeley came up on her left, his weapon pointed at the sky. He didn't look at her, just at the half-dead.

"I have a message for you, but I'll only tell if you're nice," the half-dead cackled. Before she could reply Arkeley shot it in the chest. Its ribs and the stringy flesh holding them together snapped open and shattered. Pieces of bone flew tumbling away from the tree. The half-dead screamed, a sound strangely similar to its laugh.

"Tell me now or I'll shoot off your feet," Arkeley said.

"My master awaits you, and you won't like him so much!" the half-dead crowed. "He says you're going to die!"

"Tell us the goddamned message," Caxton growled.

The half-dead shook and rattled, its bones straining against the wire. As if the simple effort cost it enormously, it lifted an arm and pointed one bony finger across the stream, deeper into the forest.

"Where is he?" Arkeley demanded. "Tell me where he is. Tell me."

The half-dead was still shaking, though, convulsing, tearing itself to pieces. Without warning, its head slumped forward and crashed to the ground. Clearly they wouldn't get any more answers out of it.

Its arm remained pointing toward the shadowy woods.

Caxton stared at the outstretched finger. "This is a trap," she said.

"Yes," Arkeley told her. Then he splashed across the creek and into the trees. She rushed forward to catch up with him and take the lead again. Her boots hit the stream with a splash and freezing water soaked her socks. On the far side she hurried into the dark, her flashlight bobbing through the trees, its light swinging across the trunks, leaping up among the branches, searching among the roots.

When it became clear they weren't going to die instantly, she figured she could afford to ask more questions. "What happened to being cautious?" she asked. "To wearing seat belts and not keeping a round in the chamber?"

He turned to look at her in the near dark. "This way we know we're in danger. If we headed back to the car they might spring on us without warning. When you know your enemy is trying to trap you the only course of action is to rush forward. Hopefully you can spring the trap before your enemy is fully prepared."

Half the time she thought he said things like that just so that he could be right and she could be wrong. She tramped after him into the gloom.

It didn't take long to find the two state troopers and the local cop. They were wired to the trees just as the half-dead had been. Their bodies were twisted and broken. They had died in terrible pain.

"The vampire," Caxton breathed.

"No." Arkeley grabbed the barrel of her shotgun and pushed it to move the flashlight around until it shone on the face of the dead policeman. Blood dripped from his lacerated nose, blood still steaming with residual body heat. "No vampire would leave a body like that. They wouldn't spill out blood on the ground, not if they had time to clean it up."

"Lares spilled blood all over the place. I read your report."

"Lares was desperate and in a hurry. This vampire can afford to take his time. We don't even know his name." He let go of her weapon. "We're wasting our time."

She turned to go.

Arkeley shook his head. "I didn't say we were done here."

Caxton spun around and saw it—a patch of dirt between two trees lifted and cracked open. A skeletal hand shot up and clutched at the air. She turned again and saw a half-dead coming at her between the trees, a butcher knife in either hand. She lifted the shotgun and fired.

The half-dead's body exploded in a fountain of ash and dust, bones splintering into fragments, soft tissues bursting open, tearing, bouncing off the trees. The knives flashed forward and clattered together on the ground.

"Jesus!" she shouted. The thing had just . . . blown up, its body literally shredded by the tungsten shot.

"They rot pretty quickly. After a week or ten days they can barely hold body and soul together," Arkeley explained. A half-dead appeared at his elbow and he pistol-whipped its jaw off, then fired one of his cross points right through its left eye.

Suddenly there were dozens of them, cackling in the darkness, running between the tree trunks, their weapons shining in the moonlight, glinting in Caxton's flashlight beam.

Reinforcements were on the way. The sheriff was sending two cars. She wanted to grab her cell phone and find out how soon they would arrive, but that would mean taking one hand off her shotgun. And there was no chance of that.

Something sharp dug into the flesh of her calf just above her boot. She screamed and kicked at a skinless hand that was reaching up to grab at her. Finger bones went flying as her boot connected, but the half-dead under her feet kept trying to climb up out of the dirt. She resisted the urge to shoot straight down, which would probably destroy her own foot in the process. Instead she waited for the half-dead's scalp to crown up out of the dark earth, then kicked it in with her boot. "Watch out," Caxton shouted, "they're coming up from the ground!"

Arkeley scowled at the darkness. "We don't have enough bullets."

Caxton pressed her back up against a tree and pumped the shotgun. Where the hell were the reinforcements?

20.

"**D**o any of them have guns?" she asked, petrified.

"Not likely," Arkeley told her. "They don't have the coordination to shoot straight. They'll be armed, though. I've never seen one those bastards who didn't have a thing for knives."

"I think we should head back to the house," Caxton said, doing her best to keep control of the obvious fear in her voice. She wanted to start screaming for help, but that wouldn't do anyone any good. "Let's at least get out of these trees." The half-deads were surrounding them. They were taking their time pressing the attack, and Caxton could imagine why. The assailants wanted to mob them: one on one they couldn't even get close, but if a crowd attacked all at the same time, Caxton and the Fed would be overrun, unable to shoot fast enough to keep all the knife-wielding monsters at bay.

Arkeley raised his weapon and fired. A half-dead she hadn't even seen disintegrated in midair. "We can't afford to lose them by going too far. But I agree, we're in unnecessary risk here." He turned to face the stream that ran between them and the house. A half-dead stepped out from behind a tree in front of him, and Arkeley punched it with his free hand hard enough to send it spinning to the leaf-littered ground. Caxton stomped it as she followed close behind.

"Follow my lead," he hissed at her. "If we don't scare them off, we might just learn something tonight."

They made it nearly all the way to the water without opposition. At the stream five of the half-deads waited for them, nearly invisible in the darkness. Caxton saw a hatchet come tumbling through the air toward her head, and she turned her body just in time for the weapon to tear through her jacket sleeve. If her reflexes hadn't taken over at just the right moment the hatchet would have embedded itself in her sternum. She put it out of her mind and lifted the shotgun. Her shot destroyed one of the half-deads completely and took the arm off another. Arkeley fired two shots, one after the other, and a pair of half-deads fell into the water, no more than heaps of old bones.

That left only one half-dead standing and unharmed. It charged them even as they were recovering from their shots, a shovel held above its head in both hands. It squealed in rage as it closed the distance, then brought the shovel down hard, blade first, right at Caxton's shoulder.

The shovel bit into her. She felt the impact, first, pain twanging up and down her arm and well into her chest. The blow didn't stop there, though—she felt the blade tear through layer after layer of cloth and finally lodge deep in her skin. Trickles of blood rolled down between her breasts and over the knobs of her spinal column. Her flesh stretched and tore, and her muscles screamed in panic as they were wedged open. It felt like she was going to die, like her body was being torn apart.

Arkeley took his time, lined up the perfect shot, and blew off what remained of the half-dead's face.

"Get up," he told her.

"I don't want to alarm you," she panted, pushing at a tree trunk, getting back to her feet, "but I think I'm hurt." She hadn't even realized she'd fallen down. The wound hurt, bad, and she was shivering as she finally stood up and pawed at the torn sleeve of her jacket. "I think . . . I think it's bad."

"You're fine," he told her, though he hadn't even looked at her wound. He stared up and back, at the way they had come. In the trees back there the half-deads were rallying. In a moment they would come running, rolling right over them. "Walk it off," he told her.

She thought she might die there, in that dark place, because he wouldn't take her seriously. She thought she might never see

Deanna again. She followed him, her feet like frozen chunks of beef, as he bounded across the stream. Her breath came fast but without rhythm, and she could hear her heart pounding in her chest, louder than the sound of her feet splashing in the water.

"I can't . . . I can't go any farther," she said. The pain was making her dizzy.

He turned and stared at her, his eyes very thin slits in his face. They didn't have time to stop like this, and she knew it. She was holding him back. He looked right into her and said, "In a second I'm going to ask you if you're okay. Your answer is extremely important. If you can keep fighting, or at least keep running, you have to say 'yes.' Otherwise we have to run away and let them win this one. Now. Are you okay?"

A thickness in her throat kept her from answering one way or another. She managed to shake her head. No, she wasn't okay. She was hurt, she'd been stabbed with a shovel. She was bleeding to death in the dark with enemies all around. She wasn't alright at all.

The look on his face changed to one of utter displeasure. Whether he was worried about her or about losing the fight she couldn't tell. "Then let's get the hell out of here," he said, and pushed her forward.

She dashed up the far bank and right up to the solid stability of the camp. She pressed her good shoulder against the wall and reached up to explore her wound.

"You do that later, when you're safe," Arkeley said, his voice very loud. He tore at her hands and pulled her away from the wall.

Arkeley pushed open the front door and shoved her inside. He locked the door and turned around to scan the grim tableau of the main room, with its corpses wired into lifelike postures. The barrel of his Glock 23 traversed from left to right before he even switched on the lights.

Outside the half-deads screamed for their blood. Where the

hell was the sheriff? Where were the cars from Troop J? Caxton began to sit down—she was feeling shaky, as if she might faint—but Arkeley scowled at her and she got back up. They both pivoted around when they heard a noise from the kitchen—something was trying to get in. "There's an open window in there," she said. The same window she'd looked through when they'd arrived.

He dashed into the kitchen wing and fired two shots. Then he slammed the window shut and bolted it. "This won't hold them for long," he called.

Out on the porch the half-deads started beating at the camp's walls, demanding to be let in. Their voices called out to her to let them in, to surrender. One of them called out her name and she whimpered, but she shoved her hands over her ears and slowly regained control. When Arkeley came back into the main room she pointed at the far wing, the bunk room. There was only one window in there, a square vent high up in the wall that let in a few stray beams of moonlight.

"If we go in there we stay in there," he said. "We can barricade the door and it will keep them out for a while. Maybe not long enough." He looked up and pointed to a skylight in the pitched ceiling, maybe ten feet up. A length of white rope dangled from its latch, presumably so that someone could open it to catch the breeze on a warm evening. Arkeley shoved a chair underneath the skylight and climbed up to grab the rope. He yanked downward and the skylight fell open. "Alright, come on," he said.

"I can't." Caxton held her injured shoulder and shook her head. "I can't climb up there, not like this."

Arkeley studied her face for a second. Then he grabbed the wrist of her hurt arm and pulled it around in a looping spiral that forced her into a pirouette.

Black spots burst inside her eyes. Her brain trembled with the pain.

He didn't seem to think it was so bad. "If anything was broken it would have made you pass out. Now get up there. I'll help as much as I can."

She didn't want to. She didn't want to do anything except climb into an ambulance and get pumped full of painkillers. She climbed up on the chair and reached up. She could almost touch the frame of the skylight, but not quite.

"Use the rope," he suggested.

"Will it hold my weight?" she asked.

"I only know one way to find out. Do it already!"

Sucking on her lower lip, she wrapped the end of the rope around her fist. Then she jumped up and grabbed onto the frame. The thin metal dug into her palm and opened up a fresh wound, but she managed to hold on. The rope dug into her other hand. She could feel it shredding under her weight, but it would hold for the moment. From below Arkeley shoved her, hard, and suddenly she was outside in the cold, dark air. A few stars shone down and illuminated the shingled roof. It looked too steep, as if she would fall if she didn't hold onto the skylight. She needed to help Arkeley up, though. Turning from the waist, her legs spread out for some minimal purchase, she reached down with her good arm and heaved him upward. He was a lot heavier than she'd expected.

On the way up he brought the rope with him. He pulled the skylight shut. Unless one of the half-deads was seven feet tall, there would be no way for them to follow Arkeley onto the roof. They were safe—more or less.

In the yard below, the half-deads gathered around the front of the camp. Their torn faces were white and vicious in the starlight. "Come down from there!" one shouted, its nasty voice unnerving Caxton. "Come down and we'll talk," it said. "We just want to get to know you a little better, Laura!"

She lifted the shotgun, then thought better. From ten yards away the shot would spread too wide to do much damage, even to a barely-intact half-dead. She reached with her bleeding hand into her jacket and drew her pistol.

"You're going to be one of us, Laura!" the half-dead crooned. "It's just a matter of time! Our master got inside of you, inside of your brains!"

She lined up her shot, but Arkeley stopped her. "Don't waste the bullet." He pried up one of the shingles from the roof and held it loosely in his hand. It was nearly a foot square, and when hurled it flew like a Frisbee. It bounced off the half-dead's chest, but it was enough to make the thing run away, howling in terror.

"They're cowards. You need to learn that. Now," he said, "we can look at your shoulder."

Caxton could barely balance on the pitched roof, but she managed to shrug off her jacket. The cold air chilled her instantly, and she started shivering again. "Am I in shock?" she asked, remembering a keyword from the first aid course she'd taken at the academy. You were supposed to repeat it every other year, but nobody ever checked if you did or not and she'd never gotten around to it.

He tore at the sleeve of her uniform shirt and exposed her skin to the night air. He touched the wound and his fingers came away bloody. She'd expected that, but then she'd expected them to come away caked in gore. His fingers were barely stained.

"For God's sake," he said, his voice scornful. She yanked away from his hands.

"What? What is it? Tell me!" she shouted. "Am I going to die?"

He stared at her in pure disgust. "That," he said, gesturing at the wound on her shoulder, "isn't deep enough to kill a house cat. Let me put it this way. Next time you get hurt this badly, don't even bother telling me. I can't believe we threw away a real opportunity because you got a little scratch."

"Jesus," she said, and turned away from him. "It felt like I was getting cut in half."

He only clucked his tongue at her in response. Down in the yard the half-deads laughed at her. She kicked at the shingles until several of them fell away and slid down toward the crowd below. That just made the half-deads laugh harder.

21.

Eventually the reinforcements came, their lights strobing through the trees, their sirens drowning out the cackling noises from below. Caxton sat up and nearly rolled off the roof. Arkeley grabbed her but wouldn't look at her as she scrabbled for handholds.

There was a lot of shooting, none of which she could see. She remembered being down in the pit when they took down the vampire. "Jesus, I thought I was going to die."

"When it's time for you to die I'll let you know." There was a sneer in Arkeley's voice. "Damn." He pointed and she saw a crowd of half-deads running into the trees. "They're going to get away. I wanted to capture at least one so we could torture some information out of it."

"I don't know if I could watch you torture something. Not even one of those freaks," she said.

"Then I'll just have to do it while you're not looking."

When the sheriff and the state troopers below had finished securing the hunting camp, they put a ladder up against the roof so Caxton and Arkeley could climb down. An ambulance waited for her, while the sheriff wanted to talk to the Fed.

"Take off your shirt and sit down here," an EMT in plastic gloves said. She did as she was told, sitting on the edge of the open back of the ambulance. It was freezing out and she didn't like sitting there in just her bra, but another EMT wrapped a silver antishock blanket around her and that helped. The first medic cleaned out her wound with antiseptic that turned her skin orange and made her cut look like spicy taco meat. "This isn't so bad," she said. "I've seen a lot worse."

So had Caxton, of course. She'd just never been injured herself before, not even so unseriously. "Do I need to go to the hospital?" she asked.

"You'll need a tetanus shot, and a doctor will need to change your bandage every three days. But you can go home tonight and sleep—that's the most important thing."

Sleep. It would be nice. Over the last few nights she'd gotten maybe six hours of sleep, total. She closed her eyes right there, but the ambulance's spinning lights pulsed blue on her eyelids and she came to again. The medic wrapped her shoulder with an Ace bandage and sent her on her way. Her shoulder ached, but she could move her arm just fine. She went looking for Arkeley and found him on the porch of the camp, studying a big state map. The sheriff stood rigidly next to him, holding a flashlight at just the right angle so the Fed could run his finger along the various routes and back roads. "Here, right?" Arkeley asked.

"Yeah, it's called Bitumen Hollow. Tiny little place."

Caxton bent down next to Arkeley. The Fed turned to stare at her as if she was in his light. She wasn't. "What?" she demanded.

He replied as if she'd asked what was happening. Which would have been her second question. "The vampires struck tonight. This," he said, waving his arm at the woods where they'd been ambushed by the half-deads, "wasn't a trap. It was a diversion from what was happening here." He poked at the map with his finger.

"You said the vampires struck tonight. Vampires, as in plural," she said.

Arkeley bared his teeth at her and stared down at the map as if he wanted to burn a hole right through it. "They worked together. The reports we have are pretty much useless in terms of piecing together a flow of events. We have a couple of panicked nine-one-one calls, a few cell phone recordings the sheriff was kind enough to share with me. No real details, but they all agreed on one fact: there were two of them, two males, and they were hungry. They took down an entire village. We're going there right now to see what kind of evidence they might have left behind."

She nodded and reached for her car keys. They were in her jacket, which happened to still be up on the camp's roof. Arkeley stalked away in disgust when she told him as much. The sheriff turned off his light and folded up his map. "Not the most friendly sumbitch, is he?" the man asked. He had a handlebar mustache and a scar across his forehead that cut his eyebrow in half.

"I've been thinking I might have more fun working for the vampires," she said, and he chuckled. She glanced at the map to memorize where they were headed. A sergeant from Troop J climbed up and fetched her jacket. He tossed it down to her and she snatched it as it fluttered through the air.

Back in the car Arkeley wouldn't even talk to her. She started up the cruiser and got it back on the highway. They were only half an hour from the village. About halfway there she realized she couldn't handle his silence for the duration of the trip. "Listen, I don't know what I did to piss you off, but I'm sorry."

For once he was in a mood to talk. "If I had known you weren't really hurt, I wouldn't have retreated so hastily," he said, as if he were writing out a report. "I was counting on capturing at least one of them. Why else did you think I walked right into that trap? Maybe this night wouldn't have been such a fiasco. Maybe we would have been in time to reach Bitumen Hollow while there was still a chance to help."

"Now you're blaming me before we even know what's happened." But of course she knew what they would find, just as he did. She didn't want to see the village, or what was left of it. She didn't want to do any of this. "If I'm not tough enough for you—"

"You will be. You're going to toughen up in a hurry," he told her.

"Or what?"

"There is no 'or what.' You're going to toughen up and that's it. I don't have time to find a new partner. I don't have time to teach anyone else just how dangerous this game can be. Don't let me down again."

It was all he had to say. She had learned one thing, at least—she had learned to tell when he was through talking and there was no point in asking more questions. She let him ride in brooding silence until they arrived.

Bitumen Hollow was just across the Turnpike, near French Creek State Park. It turned out to be a little depot town straddling the railroad line. A century earlier it might have served as a railhead for the local coal mines, judging by the giant rusting bins behind the town's single real street. Now it served merely as a place for the local farmers to buy feed and fertilizer. Or rather it had served that purpose until a few hours previous. There was a little coffee shop, a Christian bookstore, a discount shoe store, and a post office. Lights burned in all four places of business, but nobody was home.

A ribbon of yellow police tape stretched across the road at either end of the street. Inside that cordon there were no living people at all. There were plenty of human bodies.

Arkeley wasn't speaking to her. That was okay. She didn't need any more guilt. She ducked under the fluttering tape and walked the length of the street. She counted fourteen corpses. She kept meeting their eyes, which were open and wide. A teenaged girl hung over a bench, her midsection crushed by some unspeakable blow. The sleeve of her puffy coat had been torn open and the arm underneath was little more than torn meat. Caxton couldn't look away from the girl's face. Strands of thin blonde hair draped across her forehead, her nose. They stuck to the drying saliva at the corner of her mouth. In the darkness it was hard to tell what color her eyes were, but they were very pretty—or at least they had been.

In the Christian bookstore three bodies had been shoved behind the counter, all of their throats torn out. Whether they had run back there to hide or whether the vampires had stashed them back there for their own reasons, she didn't know. There was a man who looked a little like Deanna's big brother, Elvin. He was wearing a hunting cap with red plaid flaps.

At the end of the street a late-model car, a Prius, had collided with a lamp post. The driver was spread across the front seats. Caxton couldn't tell if it had been a man or a woman. The face was completely removed and the bloodless tissue underneath didn't look like a human head at all.

An explosion of light stunned Caxton. She blinked away the afterimage and looked up to see about twenty sheriff's deputies standing on the other side of the police tape. They waited respectfully, like people lined up to watch a parade. Clara, the photographer, had taken a picture—that had been the source of the flash. She'd been photographing the crashed car's license plate. "Hi," she said, and Caxton nodded back in greeting.

"Whenever you're ready, Trooper," the sheriff said. "Take your time." She realized they were waiting for her and Arkeley to finish their investigation. They had been given the right to the first look at the crime scene. The sheriff's department would take over as soon as they were done.

"Arkeley," she said, "are you finding anything useful?"

The Fed was bent over the teenaged girl. "Nothing I haven't seen before. Alright, let them in." He walked past her and lifted up the police tape. "Maybe they'll see something I've missed. I'm extremely tired, young lady, and I think I want to go home."

She blinked at him, then stepped aside to let the sheriff's deputies pass under the tape. "Alright," she said, more than a little surprised. "Let me bring the car around."

"Actually," he told her, "if you don't mind, I'd like to be by myself. I'm sure the sheriff can give you a ride home."

Very strange, she thought. Arkeley had to be up to something. He was going to do something he didn't want her to see. "Okay," she said. She was pretty sure she didn't want to see it, either. She handed over the keys to the patrol car. "Come pick me up tomorrow, whenever," she told him, but he was already walking away.

"What's eating him?" Clara asked her, but Caxton could only shake her head.

22.

Clara knelt down on the pavement to get a picture of the teenaged girl's hand. There was a bloodless laceration running down the side of her palm. "This looks like a defensive wound," she said, her uniform tie dangling between her knees. "Don't you think?"

"I'm not really trained for that sort of stuff," Caxton apologized. She wasn't entirely sure what she was still doing in Bitumen Hollow except waiting for a ride home. She checked her watch and was surprised to find it was only half past eight. The fight with the half-deads had felt like it took all night, but in fact little more than an hour had passed, even with all the time they spent waiting on the camp's roof.

She had been following Clara around because the photographer was a familiar face, the only member of the Lancaster

County sheriff's department whom she knew by name. Supposedly she was keeping control of the crime scene, which technically belonged to Arkeley and the U.S. Marshals Service. From time to time one of the sheriff's detectives would come up to her and get her to sign off on a form or a waiver. She didn't even bother reading them. It was pretty clear Arkeley wasn't interested in traditional police work. His modus operandi was to put himself (and everyone around him) in danger and then let violence work everything out.

Where he had gone—by himself, in a state police patrol car that she was responsible for—remained a mystery to her. She recalled him talking about torturing half-deads for information. She had said she couldn't sit by and watch that happen, and he had suggested he would just do it while she wasn't looking. Yet there were no half-deads in police custody. Where would he find one?

She might have been more diligent in trying to unravel his mystery if she hadn't been so tired. She sank down on a bench in front of the Christian bookstore and rubbed at her eyes. Clara came and stood next to her. "Do you need something?" she asked. "I've got a whole pharmacy in my purse. It's back in my car—I'll go get it."

"No, no," Caxton said, waving one hand at the photographer. "I'll be fine. I've just been running on fumes for a while. A good night's sleep and I'll be one hundred percent." She smiled at the sheriff's deputy, who just shrugged. Clara went over to the corpse of a farmer in a leather jacket who lay sprawled across the pavement not ten feet away. One of the farmer's arms had been torn off and thrown in a trash can. Much of his chest was missing altogether, as well as all of his throat. Clara hovered over him, not eighteen inches from the slack white skin of his face, and took a picture with her digital camera. "You're fearless," Caxton said, admiring the other woman. "I can't handle the gore."

Clara stood up and stared at her. "I thought you were in on that vampire kill last night on three twenty-two?"

"That's different. When you're fighting for your life the adrenaline keeps you going. But when it's dead bodies just lying there, I can't handle it. Too many traumatic memories, you know?"

Clara nodded and came over to the bench again. "It used to bother me too, and I mean a lot. Let me show you a trick, though." She handed Caxton the camera and mimed taking a picture. Caxton pointed the camera at the dead man in the road and studied the small LCD screen on the back of the camera. She wanted to turn away, but Clara stopped her. "No. Look. Is the picture too dark?"

"Well, yeah," Caxton said. "It's nighttime. You need the flash."

"Right." Clara indicated the flash button and Caxton turned it on. "Now try to frame the picture better. Get all the details in, but without too much background. Now, how's the color balance?"

Caxton got the point all at once. "Yeah. Okay. It's not a human being anymore. It's a picture of a human being. That's not so bad."

Clara nodded happily. "It's all just colors and shadows and composition. I worry more about getting the color of the blood right than how much blood there is. Now," she said, but she stopped and turned her head as if she'd heard something.

Caxton jumped up. "What? What is it?" But then she heard it as well. It wasn't difficult. Someone was screaming. A man, screaming, distant and muffled as if he were trapped underground. Caxton followed the sound until she saw a manhole cover in the middle of the street. Shouting for help, she and Clara got down on the road surface and tried to pry open the cover with their fingers. It was like trying to push a dead patrol car uphill. A sheriff's deputy with a crowbar rushed up and shifted the lid with a lot of grunting and straining. When the lid came off, the streetlights revealed a rusted metal ladder leading downward into pure black darkness. Caxton took the lead, her feet dancing down the groaning rungs until she reached the bottom. She felt sewage squishing under her feet, and the smell nearly overpowered her. She reached into her pocket and found her Maglite. Its narrow beam showed her weathered brick walls that curved up over her head, and she felt as if they would close in on her at any moment.

She shined the light farther down the passage and caught the shaking figure of a man clutching a large wooden cross in his arms, the wood maybe three feet long and two wide. His eyes flashed terror when the light hit him, and he screamed again. "No, no," he gibbered, "no, no, no. Keep away, keep away from me, behind me, get behind me, the Lord, the Lord, the Lord!"

Caxton moved toward him slowly, one hand outstretched to show him it was empty, the other holding the light. He was no vampire and no half-dead, but he clearly wasn't thinking straight, either.

"I didn't mean to scream," he whispered. "I didn't want to give away my position! Lord, oh Lord, oh Lord. They can't have me. They can't have my blood!"

"I'm with the state police, sir," she said, her voice low and soft and almost crooning. "Everything's okay now. The vampires are gone." She was close enough to touch him, almost. She reached out to touch his shoulder, the way she'd been trained. A nice, reassuring touch that wouldn't threaten anyone.

"The power of Christ compels you!" he shouted, and swung his crucifix at her like a baseball bat. It caught her in the stomach and knocked the wind right out of her. She dropped her Maglite in the muck and doubled over, the sudden darkness falling on her like a cave-in. "The power of Christ preserves me!" he screamed, and tried to hit her again. She heard the cross whistling through the dark air and shot out her hand to stop it.

Twisting from the waist, she pulled it away from him. The effort made her see stars. She dropped the cross and grabbed him around the waist, catching both of his arms. She hoped he didn't try to bite her. She brought her knee up into his groin, hard enough to do serious damage.

Someone came up behind her with a more powerful light, and she saw the man's pupils constrict wildly. His face was inches from her own, his mouth open wide, his teeth glinting with saliva. But they were human teeth. He was gasping for breath—she had squeezed him so hard he couldn't breathe.

Dumb, she thought. Fighting with vampires had made her forget everything she knew about subduing human beings. She could have really hurt the guy, whose only real crime was being scared. She released him, and sheriff's deputies pushed past her to cuff him and check him for weapons. "He's not a perp," she said, one hand over her face, deeply ashamed. "He's a survivor."

Up top, up on the street level again, she examined her own injuries. Just a bruise on her stomach, but it was tender and would be yellow and purple come morning. Well, she thought, she could just add it to the cut on her hand and the shovel wound on her shoulder and call it a night's work.

"Listen, somebody else can take the pictures," Clara said. "I'll take you home now."

Caxton nodded, but she wasn't quite finished with Bitumen Hollow. "Who is he?" she asked.

"The assistant manager of the bookstore," Clara told her. "He calmed down once we got him out of the sewer. As far as we can tell he's the only one in the entire town who made it." She frowned in anger. "He says he doesn't remember how he got down in that sewer. The deputies are with him right now, working the virtual Identikit on the sheriff's laptop."

There had been no ID on the vampire they'd killed. What if they got a facial recognition match on one of the others? It could be a good break, just the kind they needed. "I need what-ever they find sent right to my PDA, okay?" she said.

"Yeah, sure," Clara told her. "I'll send you the full report and all my pictures if you have the bandwidth."

Caxton nodded. The state police were testing out new handhelds that had more memory and better wireless Internet connections than the laptops in the patrol cars. "I can handle it. Now," she said, scratching her nose, "let's get me out of here."

"I'll just sign out with the sheriff." Clara dashed off and left Caxton there to nurse her new bruise. When she returned she'd taken off her tie and undone the top button of her uniform shirt. "Come on," she said. "You can sleep in the car."

23.

She couldn't sleep in the car. Clara's car was a rebuilt Crown Victoria like almost every other police car in the world. It was a lot like Caxton's own patrol car. It was de-signed to provide a cop with all the information she needed to do her job. The dashboard was studded with instrumentation: the readout for a radar gun, the ubiquitous mounted laptop for checking license plates, the video recorder that monitored everything that happened both inside the car and from the per-spective of its front bumper. The various radios squawked and muttered at random intervals. The seat couldn't recline because of the bulletproof partition immediately behind Caxton's head to protect the driver and front-seat passenger from anyone in the rear compartment. The car was a workplace, not a bed-room. After trying to relax for fifteen minutes, she grabbed handfuls of her hair and pulled, too frustrated to even speak.

Clara glanced over at her. "I know what you need," she said, and took the next exit. She pulled into the lot of a one-story building with white Christmas lights strung up under its eaves. A little tavern, bright, cheery light leaking from all its windows, along with the muffled sound of a jukebox playing some bad country song. They went inside and grabbed a couple of bar stools and Clara ordered them Coronas with extra lime. "There's no way you're going to sleep now. You're wound up as tight as a spring."

Caxton knew it was true. She didn't particularly want the beer, though she didn't refuse it. She wasn't much of a drinker— she was a morning person, really, and had never managed to close out a bar in her life. Yet with the cold wet bottle in her hand and the taste of the lime on her lips, she realized she'd been missing for a long time the easy good humor that comes from sitting in a bar with friendly people around you. She probably hadn't been in a place like this since she'd met Deanna.

A fifty-inch plasma screen at the far end of the bar showed a football game. Caxton didn't watch much television, either, and the bright light and constant motion kept drawing her eye. She didn't care whatsoever about football, but the bland normalcy of it was kind of nice.

Slowly her shoulders slid down away from her neck. Slowly her posture let up a little and she slumped forward on the bar stool. "This," she said, "is not so bad."

"Hey, look," Clara said, pointing at the television. The local station had cut away to a news report. It was just ten o'clock. They were leading with video shot out in the woods, with lots of strobing lights and a reporter who kept looking back at the camera with wide eyes and a tightly pursed mouth. Caxton had no idea what was going on until she saw her own face, looking pale and ghostly as it swam up out of the darkness to be flooded with video camera lights. "Turn on the sound, will you?" Clara asked the bartender.

"I don't remember any cameras," Caxton said, realizing

that she was looking at the scene of the vampire kill. The after-math, anyway.

"Still haven't been allowed to see the body, I have to say," the reporter droned, "there's a real sense of secrecy here, as if the Marshals Service is covering something up. We have no information on the alleged vampire yet, even twenty-four hours later. Authorities haven't even released his name."

Twenty-four hours? Had it really been only one day? Caxton put a hand over her mouth. On the television screen her emotionless face kept turning away from the light. She had a vague memory of being annoyed by a light, but she hadn't realized at all that the media were there while she was being debriefed. The fight with the vampire had shocked her so much that she must have been in a daze.

"A source in the Pennsylvania State Police gave us an interview this afternoon under condition that we didn't reveal his identity. He says the alleged vampire was not given any kind of warning or any chance to surrender to authorities. Diane, there's sure to be a lot more to this story in the coming days."

"Thanks, Arturo," the anchorwoman said. She looked calm and unfazed. "Stay tuned for more coverage of—"

"That what you wanted to hear?" the bartender asked. When Clara nodded, he muted the sound again and switched over to a reality show about lingerie models working in a butcher's shop.

"Wow, you're going to be a celebrity, you know that?" Clara asked. "Every news station in the country is going to want an interview."

"Assuming I survive long enough," Caxton said, under her breath.

"What?" Clara asked. When Caxton didn't reiterate, she shook her head. "Wow. So what was the vampire like?"

"Pale. Big. Toothy," the trooper answered.

"I was so obsessed with vampires when I was in high school. My friends and I would put on capes and fake fangs and make little movies of us hypnotizing each other with our best sexy looks. Man, I looked pretty good as a vampire."

"I doubt it," Caxton said. Clara's eyebrows went up in what could have turned into real offense. "Don't get me wrong. I bet you looked great. But not if you looked like a vampire. They're bald as cue balls, for one thing. And those pointy little fangs? Believe me, you don't want to see the reality."

Clara slapped the bar. "Vampires are, too, sexy," she announced, her tone jaunty. "Stop trying to ruin my schoolgirl fantasy! I don't mind if they're bald. I say, as long as we're here in this bar, everything about vampires is sexy. Very, very sexy."

Caxton smiled in spite of herself. "Oh yeah?" she asked.

"Hells yeah!" She reached over and grabbed Caxton by the bicep. "And big tough vampire hunters are even sexier!" They both laughed. That felt good, that comfortable, friendly laugh. "Don't you think she's sexy?" she demanded from the bartender. Her hand lingered on Caxton's arm, doing nothing objectionable. Clara didn't even look at her, just sucked at her beer bottle, but she didn't take her hand away.

"I'd do her," the bartender said, watching the lingerie models make sausage with an industrial meat grinder.

"I'll be right back," Caxton said, pulling away as she slid off her stool. Clara's hand moved to the bar. Caxton ran back to the ladies' room, where she threw some water on her face. Wow, she thought. Wow. The hand on her arm hadn't just been warm. It had been hot, physically hot. She knew it was just an illusion, but wow. She hadn't felt like that in a very long time. She missed feeling like that. She missed it.

When she stepped out of the bathroom, Clara was standing next to the pay phone. She was smiling from ear to ear and her eyes showed nothing. She was trying to play it cool and be aggressive at the same time. Caxton remembered that dance, she even remembered pulling off the same moves. When Clara lowered her eyes and stepped to the left, just as Caxton was stepping to the right, she knew exactly how it felt: the little, trembling fears that multiplied the longer you held back, the big hope you shoved down so it wouldn't overwhelm you, but that kept busting out.

There was even a good song on the jukebox. She couldn't remember the name of the artist or the title, but it was a good song.

She missed that feeling: the butterflies in the stomach, the cold prickles on the back of her neck. She missed it so much that as Clara raised her hands she stepped right into them, closed her eyes as the hands touched her face, those hot little fingers tracing the smooth line of her jaw. Caxton just had time to exhale before Clara's soft lips touched hers, moist, soft, exactly the right temperature. She had missed that most of all, those first, exploring kisses. The very first taste of a woman's lips. Clara's mouth started to move and Caxton raised her own hands, not to touch Clara's face but to gently, ever so gently, break contact.

Clara's eyes were moist, her mouth a pursed question. "Aren't you . . . ?" she asked, a whisper.

"I'm in a relationship," Caxton said. She was sweating under the bandage on her shoulder. "I need to go home. To her."

Clara nodded and stepped to the right, to let Caxton past. Except Caxton chose the same moment to step left. They nearly collided with each other, and it was enough to break the tension. They both sighed out a little shared laugh. Caxton covered the bar tab and they climbed back into the sheriff's department car. They said very little on the ride to Caxton's house, but a tiny smile played on Clara's lips the whole time. When she stopped the car out front, they sat there for a moment listening to the dogs singing in their kennels. Normally her greyhounds were quiet, but Caxton wasn't too concerned. They were reacting to the presence of a stranger. "I love dogs," Clara said. "What kind?"

"Rescue greyhounds," Caxton said, as if she were admitting to a crime.

Clara's eyes lit up. "Maybe sometime you'll introduce me to them?"

"Sure—sometime, maybe," Caxton said. She was blushing. Only when she popped open the door and felt the cold air on her cheeks did she realize she'd been blushing all the way home. No wonder Clara had kept smiling at her. "Thanks for the ride, anyway," she said. "I'll, uh, see you."

"Don't worry," Clara told her. "I can wait a while to get my cute little fangs in that neck of yours." She was laughing as she drove off.

Caxton fed the dogs—Deanna had forgotten again, even their water bowls were dry—and headed inside. She stripped in the kitchen and then dashed into the bed, burrowing under the covers before she could get cold. Deanna's body under the duvet was sharp and angular, but Caxton snaked a hand around her lover's stomach and up to cup one of her breasts. Deanna stirred in her sleep, and Caxton started kissing her ear.

"Oh, Pumpkin, not tonight," Deanna hissed. "You smell all bloody."

With the wounds on her hand and her shoulder, Caxton supposed that was fair enough.

She sat in the shower for a long time, playing with the spiral pendant Vesta Polder had given her, watching the steam roll and roil around her until she finally, blessedly, began to nod off. It took the last of her energy to dry off and climb into bed, and she was asleep before she knew it.

24.

In the morning she played with the dogs for a while. It was cold outside and the kennels were well heated, so she stayed with them and let them dance around her, snapping their teeth at her hair and her face, the way greyhounds showed affection. They were beautiful, the lines of their bodies so sleek and perfect. Wilbur, who had only three legs but a truly beautiful blue fawn coat, kept curling up in her lap, twisting around and around as if trying to tie himself in a knot before plopping down on her folded legs. She rubbed him behind his ears and told him he was a good dog. Lola, an Italian greyhound who already had a good home lined up in upstate New York, kept pressing her long nose against the door, but whenever Caxton would push it open she would dance backwards from the frosty gust that burst in, snapping at the air with her teeth and rearing up on her hind legs to fight off the wind.

When Deanna found her there, covered in greyhounds, Caxton felt almost human again. Deanna just smirked at her as if she'd caught her with her hand in the cookie jar. She handed Caxton her PDA and disappeared again without a word.

She had a new email from "Hsu_C@lcsd.pa.us," which she figured had to be Clara. Her hand trembled as she opened it—what if Deanna had seen it? What if Clara had called instead of emailing, and Deanna had picked up? But she was just being paranoid. For one thing, she'd done nothing wrong. She had stopped Clara before anything real could happen. For another, Clara's email wasn't embarrassing at all. It was one of the most professional correspondences she'd ever read, and it contained nothing except the sheriff's department report from Bitumen Hollow. There wasn't so much as a cordial salutation.

She actually felt a little let down. Clara coming on to her was a problem, really, but still . . . it had been so nice. She put the thought out of her mind and studied the report. It was cold and clinical and she tried to keep it that way, refusing to feel the horror of the people who had died in the sleepy village the night before. Most of the report was based on the eyewitness testimony of the assistant manager of the Christian bookstore, the one who had hit her with the big cross. Once he'd calmed down he had turned out to be a pretty good observer. He'd seen the vampires enter the main street of the town, both of them dressed in black overcoats with the collars turned up to hide their mouths. If they'd been trying to pass as human they needn't have bothered. Everyone in Bitumen Hollow knew everyone else—the two giant vampires (both well over six feet tall) stuck out like torn-off thumbs. The first to die had been the teenaged girl, Victim #1, Helena Saunders. One of them picked her bodily up off the ground while the other tore open the sleeve of her coat and bit into her arm, in the words of the survivor, "Like you would gnaw on a ear of corn." From there things just got nasty.

There had been no attempt to defend the town. No one had even fought back, though a loaded hunting rifle was found under the counter of the coffee shop and the woman who ran the post office (Victim #4) had a licensed handgun in her car. No police presence reached the town until it was far too late. It didn't surprise Caxton much. A town that small wouldn't have a police department of its own, instead relying on the local sheriff.

Caxton skimmed through much of the report. There were fourteen victims in total and she really didn't need to know how they all had died.

Fourteen. The two vampires that had attacked Bitumen Hollow were pretty fresh. Their need for blood should have been easily quenched—at most they might have required a single victim each. Yet they had completely depopulated the village. Why? She thought about Piter Lares, who had intentionally overfed and stuffed himself full of blood so he could feed his elders, including Justinia Malvern. The new assailants (the report listed them as Actor #1 and Actor #2, police-speak for the person who "acted" upon the victims) could have been gorging themselves to feed Malvern, but no, they needed four vampires to restore her. Anyway, she was still safely behind stone walls at Arabella Furnace.

As far as she knew.

A cold finger ran down her spine at the thought that the vampires might have attacked the abandoned sanatorium, that even now Malvern might be free, but no, surely Arkeley would have called her to tell her as much.

Unless they had attacked, and Arkeley had been killed.

She quickly fed and watered the dogs and headed back into the house. She didn't want to jump the gun on a paranoid whim, but she had to know. There was no listing for Arabella Furnace State Hospital in the phone book, and the state police databases she had access to via the Internet didn't even list it. While she dressed she called the Bureau of Prisons to ask for the number, but they said any such inquiries had to go through official channels. The man on the other end of the line wouldn't even admit that such a place existed, of course.

"Look, the people there could be in danger. I know all about the place. I've been there. It's a hospital for just one patient, and she's a vampire. Justinia Malvern."

"Calm down, lady," he said. "Look, we don't do hospitals. We do prisons."

She somehow managed not to yell at him. He said he would pass on her message. Hanging up the phone, Caxton stormed into the bedroom. "Dee?" she yelled. "Dee? I need to borrow your car."

Deanna was in the living room, lying on the couch and

watching television. The remote was clutched in one hand, which spilled down onto the floor and lay half-buried in the shag carpet. "I had one of my dreams about you last night," she said. Caxton came storming in. "You were tied to a post and Roman soldiers were whipping your naked back. Blood was trickling down your hips in long, red tracks that looked kind of like chocolate syrup. I don't think you should go anywhere today."

Caxton made a fist and shoved it into her pocket. She didn't have time for this. "I really, really need to borrow your car."

"Why?" she asked. "Maybe I have things to do today."

"Do you?" Caxton asked. It wasn't the day Deanna did the shopping. Most days her car sat unused in the driveway. "Look, this is super important. Seriously, or I wouldn't even ask."

Deanna shrugged and looked at the TV. "Alright, if you want me to be a prisoner in my own home."

Caxton was holding her breath, she realized. She blew it out slowly and then inhaled, just as slowly. Deanna's keys were hanging on a hook in the kitchen, right next to the closet where Caxton kept her pistol. She fetched them both. Outside the air was a little more than crisp. She pulled her uniform jacket around her chest and jumped into Deanna's little red Mazda. She took off her hat and went to put it on the passenger seat, but the remains of a takeout lunch from McDonald's, including half a hamburger, were spread across the already stained fabric. The narrow backseat was full of cans of paint and unopened packages of brushes and rollers, even though Deanna hadn't painted anything in six months. She'd been restricting herself to the untitled project in the shed.

Caxton balanced her hat on top of an open can of paint that had dried to the consistency of hard plastic and hoped for the best. Backing out of the driveway, she adjusted the mirrors and in minutes was on the highway, headed for Arabella Furnace. On the way she played with the car's radio, looking for a news report. There was another IED explosion in Iraq and some kind of golf scandal—Caxton didn't really follow sports and didn't understand what they were saying. There were no reports of vampire attacks on abandoned tuberculosis rest homes, no bugles playing "Taps" for a Fed who had died in the course of his duty, but the lack of news failed to reassure her.

By the time she arrived it was well past noon and sprinkling rain. The sun was blinking on the wet leaves that dotted the road, and the narrow track that led to the hospital had gone to mud. The little Mazda nearly got stuck, but Caxton had years of training in getting cars through bad patches of road. She pulled up on the lawn below the faceless statue of Health or Hygiene or whatever it was and felt a little relieved, but just a little, to see her own patrol car parked on the same stretch of grass. Arkeley had come to Arabella Furnace the night before. When he'd indicated he wanted to be alone, he must have gone to see Malvern.

It occurred to her that he might have taken one look at Bitumen Hollow and known the vampires were gorging themselves and would attack that night. But then why would he have gone alone and left her behind?

Because he didn't trust her, of course. Because she'd acted like a wimp when she got stabbed with a shovel. Because she couldn't watch him torture a half-dead. He'd decided she was a liability.

The corrections officer at the front desk recognized her but still made her sign in. When she saw him she knew her worst fears hadn't come true. Malvern was still behind locked doors.

"What happened here last night?" she asked, placing the pen back down on his sign-in sheet.

"Something happened, something big," he said, his eyes wide.

"Something? What kind of something?"

He shrugged. "I just work days. This place, at night? You'd have to nail my feet to the floor to keep me from running away."

She wanted to ask him a million more questions but figured there might be better informants. From memory she tried to find Malvern's ward, only to get lost and have to circle back. Finally she retraced her steps, took a left instead of a right, and saw the plastic curtain that sealed off the ward. The hospital was immense and most of it was dark. She could easily have gotten lost for hours if she hadn't been shown the way before.

She pushed through the plastic and into the blue light and there, of course, was Arkeley, sitting patiently in a chair. He looked healthy enough, though he appeared not to have showered since she'd seen him last.

Malvern was nowhere to be seen, but the lid of her coffin was closed. Caxton went straight to Arkeley. "Are you alright?" she asked.

"Of course I am, Trooper. I've been having a lovely chat with my old friend." He knocked on the coffin. There was no answer, but Caxton assumed Malvern was safely inside. "Why don't you sit down?"

Caxton nodded. She looked around but didn't see Hazlitt. Maybe he slept during the day. "I thought—I know it sounds crazy, but I had this idea. The vampires that slaughtered everyone in Bitumen Hollow last night were gorging on blood. I thought they might attack this place, that they were gathering blood for her. I guess I jumped to a dumb conclusion."

"Hardly," he said. "They did exactly as you thought. Or at least they tried."

25.

The previous night, when Caxton was being kissed by a pretty girl in a bar, Arkeley had been fighting for his life. He laid out the story for her quite calmly and without a lot of recrimination. He never once said he wished she'd been there to help.

Arkeley had taken one look at the corpses in Bitumen Hollow and knew trouble was brewing. He had seen the number of bodies, and he knew how many vampires were responsible. He did the math in his head. Remembering the way Lares had fed his ancestors—"Not that I'd ever forgotten it," he said, with a shudder of distaste—he had realized the vampires were through waiting. The two of them couldn't hold enough blood to fully revivify her, but they could at least get her up and walking under her own power. They would strike that very night—he was certain of it. So he had taken the patrol car and proceeded immediately to Arabella Furnace.

"Without me," she said, in a partial huff.

"Shall I finish my story, or should we argue?" he asked.

He arrived at the hospital at nine o'clock. He warned the corrections officers about what was coming and then he went into Malvern's private ward. He found her significantly decayed from when he'd last seen her, when he'd cut off her blood supply. She was unable to sit up and was reclining in her coffin. Most of the skin on her skull had worn away and her single eye was dry and irritated. One arm was crossed over her chest. The other hung limply out of the coffin, its talonlike fingers draped across the keyboard of a laptop computer. Arkeley had thought she had simply flung it out in despair, but her index finger trembled and stabbed at the "E" key, then fell back as if that slight effort had completely exhausted her.

Hazlitt appeared, his manner suggesting he was unhappy about something. He explained that Malvern was averaging four keystrokes a minute. The doctor allowed Arkeley to view what she had written so far:

a drop lad it is ye sole remedie
a drop a drop one onlie

"You're killing her, Arkeley," the doctor told the Fed. "I don't care if she's already dead. I don't care if this can go on forever. To me it's death, or worse."

"If she wants to live so badly she should conserve her energy," Arkeley said. "Maybe you should take that computer away from her."

Hazlitt looked as if he'd been struck. "It's the only connection she has to the outside world," he insisted.

Arkeley dismissed the argument with a shrug. He sent the doctor home at ten P.M., although Hazlitt had indicated he wished to stay with his patient. Arkeley assured him that he would keep her safe through the night.

Alone with her, the only distraction the sporadic click of her withered nail on the keyboard, Arkeley drew his weapon and placed it on a heart monitor outside of Malvern's reach. He did not, in fact, get a chance to use it.

The vampires, the remaining two members of Malvern's brood, came to him around two in the morning. Their cheeks were pink and their bodies radiated palpable heat. They appeared without a sound, one from the main entry to the ward, the other rising up out of the blue-edged shadows of the room. Arkeley had not seen them come in, though he'd been expecting them.

One of them tried to hypnotize the special deputy. The other moved fast as lightning across the room, his hands out to grab Arkeley's shoulders, his mouth wide to bite off his head.

Both of them stopped in midattack when they saw what Arkeley held in his hand.

Before they arrived he had taken certain precautions using surgical instruments that were readily available in the ward. With a bonesaw and a pair of pliers he had removed part of Malvern's rib cage. A young healthy vampire could repair that kind of damage almost instantly, but Malvern was starved of blood and far too old to even feel what he was doing. His amateur surgery had revealed Malvern's heart, a cold lump of black muscle that felt like a charcoal briquette in his hand.

When the two male vampires came at him, he gave her heart a little squeeze. It started to crumble under the slightest pressure. As weak as she was, she found the energy to crane her head back, her toothy mouth yawning open in a voiceless scream.

The vampires froze in place. They looked at each other as if communing silently about what to do next.

"I'm going to present you with a few options," Arkeley told them. He refused to make eye contact with either one—though he believed himself able to resist their wills, he didn't want to find out the hard way. "You can kill me. Either of you could do it in a heartbeat. Unfortunately, my last spasm of life would travel down my arm and I would crush this heart into oblivion. You can stand there all night waiting for my arm to get tired, but you only have four hours before the sun comes up. How far are you from your coffins?"

They didn't answer. They stood there, their red eyes watching him, and waited to hear a third option.

"You can just leave now," he said, trying to sound reasonable. "That way everybody survives."

"Why should we trust you?" one of them asked. His voice was rough and thick with the blood that surged in his throat.

"You slaughtered our brother," the other said, biting his words into the air. "You could destroy her the moment we step away."

"If I kill her I'll have to face trial as a murderer. I know, it doesn't make any sense to me, either." Arkeley started to shrug, but the gesture would have moved his hand and pulled Malvern's heart right out of her chest. The moment that happened, there would be no reason for the vampires to let him live. "If I'm going to die tonight, I'm going to take her with me."

The vampires disappeared without another word, leaving as quickly as they had come.

When he was sure they were gone, Arkeley made the rounds of the guards in the hospital. They had done as he had told them. The vampires had no need for blood—they were replete with it—and when the corrections officers gave them no resistance they walked right past. Nobody in the abandoned hospital had been harmed in the slightest.

When Arkeley returned to the private ward he found that Malvern had typed a new line on her computer:

boys my boys take him

Luckily for Arkeley, her brood hadn't received the command until it was too late.

"You," Caxton said, when he'd finished his story, "haven't got any blood in your whole body. Just ice water."

"I'm glad you think so. While they were standing there I was sure my hand was going to cramp up." He smiled, not his condescending smile, not the smile he showed his partner's girlfriend. Just a normal human smile. It looked out of place on him but not entirely repellent. "Eventually the sun came up. She pulled in her arm and I put the lid on her coffin. And now here we are."

"You should have brought me along. We could have fought them together," Caxton insisted.

"Not like that. They were so full of blood a bazooka couldn't have made a dent in them. There's a reason they always feed before they fight. There's an upside to this, however. They were bringing that blood for her, to regurgitate it all over her just like Lares did that night on the boat. Now they'll have to digest it on their own. It'll make them strong, but it'll slow them down, too. Tonight, and maybe tomorrow night as well, they won't want to feed at all."

"So you didn't invite me along because you thought I would be a liability. You thought I would screw up your plan."

"I thought," he told her, "that you would get hurt. Do we have to do this now? I haven't slept all night."

Caxton seethed but knew better than to argue with him at that moment. "Fine. You're done with me, that's fine. I'll go home to my dogs, then."

He shook his head. "No. We're changing your duties, but you're still on the team. You can coordinate the detective work, find me some names and street addresses for Malvern's boys. There will always be something for you to do."

"Gee, thanks," she spat.

"Don't be like that. Few people have what it takes to fight vampires, Trooper. You gave it your best. Just because that wasn't enough is no reason to feel bad about yourself. Hey." He looked down at the coffin, then back at her and raised his eyebrows. "Want a peek?"

26.

"I don't—" she said, but she wasn't sure. She wasn't even sure what she was rejecting. Did she even want to stay on the case? Did she want to know another single thing about vampires, about evil and how nasty the world could really be?

"It's like seeing a caterpillar turning into a moth. It's foul, but fascinating if you have the stomach for it."

She was ready to say no. She was going to say no, and turn away.

"Every morning she goes through this, transforming like a larva in a chrysalis. Her body has to change so it can repair all the damage she took the night before." He lifted up the lid. A weird animal smell came out, hot and musky but unnatural. It made her think of the way the dog kennels smelled when the dogs were sick. "This is what immortality means."

No. She just had to say no and he would put the lid back down. She was done with this case, with vampires. If he wanted her working a desk, that was fine.

She stepped closer to the coffin. He threw the lid back and she looked down.

Malvern's bones lay askew on the upholstery. Her enormous lower jaw had fallen away from the upper part of the skull. Her heart, which looked like a rotten plum, lay inside her rib cage, unattached to anything else. All the rest of her flesh had been reduced to a mucilaginous soup that stained the silk lining of the coffin, a gloppy mass that covered her pelvis and part of her spine. Pools of it lingered in the corners of the coffin and filled one of her eye sockets. Flecks of what looked like charred skin hung submerged in the fluid, while tiny curved things like fingernail clippings clustered at the center of the mess. The smell was very, very strong, almost overpowering. Caxton leaned forward a little and studied the fingernail clippings. She could just make out little hooks protruding from one end, and the rings that segmented their tiny bodies.

"Maggots," she gasped. Her face was inches from a maggot mass. Rearing up, she nearly screamed. Now that she could see them for what they were, it was impossible to pretend they were something else. Her skin crawled, writhed away from the coffin. Her lips retracted in a grimace of horror.

"One of evolution's greatest wonders," he told her. He looked completely serious. "If you can see past your own prejudices, anyway. They eat the dead and pass the living by. Their mouths are designed so that they can only survive on food of a certain viscosity. They are so adept at working together to break down necrotic tissue that they literally share a common digestive system. Isn't that astounding?"

"Jesus Christ, Arkeley," she said, bile touching the back of her tongue. "You've made your point. Cover her up, please."

"But there's so much you haven't seen yet. Don't you want to watch her come back to life when the sun goes down? Don't you want to see her tissues recompose, her eyeball inflate, her heart reattach?"

"Just close it," she breathed. She hugged her stomach, but that just made it worse. She tried to breathe calmly. "That smell."

"It's wrong, isn't it? That's not how natural things smell." She heard the coffin lid scrape closed behind her back. It helped, a little. "The maggots don't seem to mind, but dogs will howl if they smell her and cows will stop giving milk if she passes them by. People notice eventually. Something feels wrong about her, something's just not right. Of course, by then she'll already have ripped one of the big veins out of your arm so she can gulp down all the blood in your body."

"You're enjoying this, aren't you?" she demanded. "It makes you feel good to put the little girl in her place." Caxton stalked to the far corner of the room, as far as she could get from the coffin. "It must make you feel tough."

He let out a long, elaborate sigh. She turned around. There was no joy in his face. No desire to hurt her, she could tell. Just weariness.

"You were grooming me to be your replacement," she said. "Someone to keep fighting vampires after you're gone."

He shook his head. "No, Trooper, no. I never even considered you a candidate. I won't bullshit you. I owe you at least that much, since you've been honest with me."

She nodded heavily. There was no way she could win the argument. It was like when she used to fight with her father. He was a good man, too, but the rule was that in his house he was always right. It had been harder to remember that when she was a teenager.

Jesus, she thought, why was she thinking about her dad so much lately? Ever since the vampire, the now-dead vampire, had hypnotized her, she'd been thinking about him a lot. And she'd told Vesta Polder about her mom. It had taken her months to talk to Deanna about her dead parents. Arkeley had dredged all that up to the surface in record time.

Enough. It was over. She'd thought that when she'd seen the first vampire die. But now it was actually true. "I've got something you should see, too," she said, and he looked at her expectantly. The argument hadn't bothered him at all, because he knew that it was his investigation and that made him right. Fine, whatever, okay, she thought, knowing she would blow up later when he wasn't around. She took out her PDA and scrolled to Clara's email. She opened up two of the picture attachments and displayed them side by side. "A survivor in Bitumen Hollow gave us these," she said.

He bent close to look at the pictures on the small screen. She'd studied them already and she knew what he would see. The pictures had been assembled from a virtual Identikit, mix-and-match software that let the sheriff's department create full-color composite sketches of Actors #1 and #2. Like all such images, they weren't exact and they looked blocky and strange, more like pictures of Frankenstein's monster than vampires. The skin tone was all wrong, because the Identikit didn't have an option for deathly pale, nor did it have red eyes (a kind of rich, warm brown was the best it could do) and it certainly had nothing like a vampire's jawline and teeth.

Yet the images struck a chord with Arkeley right away. "Yes. This is them," he said, looking up at her. "This is good. It's useful."

Caxton nodded. "I thought so too. And look, we even have an identifying mark for one of them." The Identikit artist had sketched in the long triangular ears of Actor #2. The survivor had insisted, however, that Actor #1 had normal human ears that were discolored on top, almost black. "His ears are different."

"Because he tears them off daily," Arkeley agreed.

"He what?"

The Fed picked up the PDA and brought it very close to his face. "The ears are a dead giveaway. Some vampires, young vampires, will try to hide them, to make themselves look more human. Lares did it for camouflage. I've read of others who did it out of self-loathing. They wanted to look human again. They'll wear wigs and blue contact lenses and even put rouge on their cheeks and noses to look more like us."

"But every day . . . this guy tears his own ears off every day?"

Arkeley shrugged. "Every night. At dusk, when he wakes, he'll find they've grown back."

That just made Caxton think about the maggot mass in the coffin. "Some of them must hate themselves. They must hate themselves and what they have to do."

"No one knows. The movies suggest they have deep and brooding inner lives, but I don't buy it. I think they sit around all night thinking about blood. About how good it tastes and how bad they feel when they don't get it. About how to get more without being found and executed. And about how long it will be before they stop caring about being found."

Caxton suddenly felt cold. She held herself close. "Like junkies," she said. Before she'd dropped out of college, she'd known some girls there who did heroin. They were individual people with thoughts and feelings before they started using the drug. Afterwards they were interchangeable, their personalities completely submerged beneath their need. "Like junkies who can't quit their habit."

"There's a difference," he told her. "Junkies eventually die."

27.

"**S**omething happened here last night, didn't it? Something that could have been bad," Sergeant Tucker said, staring across his desk at them. The last time Caxton had seen him he'd had his feet up on the desk and he'd been watching television. Now he was leaning forward, his eyes scanning the hallways that led off in four directions from his station. "We had twenty-three COs on duty last night, but I can't get a straight answer out of anyone. One guy saw shadows moving around like his room was full of candles and they were flickering and shit. Another guy definitely saw a vampire walking across the lawn, pale skin, lots of teeth, bald as an egg, but he had orders not to even tell the asshole to halt."

"That was my order," Arkeley confirmed.

Tucker nodded. "And then at two-fourteen in the A.M., the temperature in the hospital wing dropped by seven degrees. I got a recording right here on my computer. It was sixty-two, then it was fifty-five. By half past two it was back up to sixty. I've got video footage of something pale and blurry running across the pool room so fast I can't even get image enhancement to work." Tucker's eyes narrowed. "If you hadn't been here, if it had just been my men—"

"I was here. The situation was under control the whole time."

Tucker studied Arkeley's face for a long time, then looked away and scratched at his close-cropped hair. "Yeah, alright. What can I do for you now?"

Caxton handed over her PDA and Tucker stared at the pictures on the screen. "These are the vampires who were here last night," Arkeley explained. "I need to know if they resemble any of the people on my list."

Tucker tapped at his keyboard. "Right, the list of all the

people who worked here in the last two years. I can't say I recognize either of them but let's look." He swiveled his monitor around so they could see. The names from the list came up on the screen and he clicked each one to show them a picture.

"This is a pretty sophisticated database," Caxton marveled.

Tucker pursed his lips and clicked through the names, one by one. "It has to be. I don't know what this place looks like to you, but to me, it's a corrections facility. I run it like I would any prison—which means I keep very close tabs on who goes in and out."

"There," Arkeley said, pointing at the screen. "Stop and go back a few."

Tucker did so and soon they were all staring at a picture of one Efrain Zacapa Reyes, an electrician with the Bureau of Prisons who had come through Arabella Furnace the previous year. "I remember this guy, a little. He came in to replace some fluorescents and to set up the blue lights Hazlitt wanted in the hospital wing."

A chill ran down Caxton's spine.

Arkeley frowned. "So he would have been close enough to communicate with her. Close enough for her to pass on the curse."

Caxton started to ask a question, but then she remembered something. She wasn't really on the case anymore. She could help Arkeley out in whatever capacity he chose for her, but her thoughts and opinions were no longer welcome. She felt a weird pang of loss, weird because it was very similar to how she'd felt when Clara had kissed her. Like she could see a whole new and exciting aspect of life, only to know she would never be allowed to explore it.

"I'll admit there's a similarity, but this ain't your guy," Tucker said, startling her back to attention.

"And why is that?" Arkeley asked.

"Well, he was only on the hospital wing maybe like an hour. All he did was screw in some lightbulbs, and I had three COs in there with him while he was doing it. If he'd tried anything they would have beaten him down on the spot—we do not fuck around at Arabella Furnace. Nobody mentioned anybody swapping blood or spit or anything wet."

Arkeley nodded, but he clearly hadn't written off Reyes as a suspect. Caxton stared at the two pictures, the one on her PDA, the one on the screen. There was a distinct resemblance in the forehead and nose between one of the vampires and the electrician. There was one major difference, though.

"He's Latin," Caxton said. The picture on the computer screen showed Reyes as having skin the color of ripe walnut shells. The vampire, of course, was snowy white.

"Others," Arkeley intoned, "have made that mistake. Others who are now dead. When vampires rise from the grave their skin loses all of its pigment. It doesn't matter if they were black, Japanese, or Eskimo beforehand, they end up white. You saw for yourself," he said to Caxton, "that vampires aren't just Caucasian. They're albino. This," he said, tapping the computer screen, "is one of our men."

Tucker wasted no time printing off Reyes's vital statistics. Caxton ran to the printer to gather up the printouts.

"Tell me his LKA," Arkeley said, referring to his last known address. "We flushed them out of the hunting camp. They'll need a new hiding place, and most likely they'll turn to a place where they feel comfortable."

She found the information easily enough but shook her head. "It's an apartment building in Villanova. They won't want that, will they? Too much activity, too much chance of being noticed when they go in and out."

Arkeley nodded. "They prefer ruins and farms."

"Then there's nothing here. Reyes lived in the same building for years, at least since 2001. Listen, let me try a cold call and see if I turn something up." Maybe—maybe if she could turn up some useful information, then Arkeley wouldn't consider her such a failure. She cursed herself for using his opinion to define her self-esteem. What stupider thing could she possibly do? Still. She took her cell phone out of her pocket and dialed the emergency contact number, which was also the number of the manager for the apartment building. When she'd established she was a police officer the manager was more than willing to talk to her. She got what details she could and hung up.

"So?" Arkeley asked.

"Efrain Reyes was a nice guy, kept pretty much to himself, no wife or girlfriend, no family, or at least no family that ever visited. The building manager thought maybe he was an illegal immigrant but had no proof of that."

"He would at least need a green card to get in here," Tucker clarified.

Caxton nodded. "The man I spoke to liked Reyes a lot, because Reyes fixed a problem with the building's circuit breakers a couple of years ago for no charge. He was informed by the local police that Efrain Reyes died seven months ago in an accident at his workplace. He says he wanted to attend the funeral but was told that because no one had claimed the body it had been given a quick burial at the state's expense in the potter's field in Philadelphia. He's holding Reyes's few personal effects in a box—he says there's nothing unusual among them, just some clothes and toiletries. The apartment was furnished and Reyes doesn't seem to have added anything to it."

"He sounds like a ghost, not a vampire," Tucker suggested.

Caxton shrugged. "From what I heard he sounded like a severe depressive. Apparently the only thing he ever complained about was being tired, but the building manager suggested he missed more than a few days of work, especially in the winter.

Judging by the mail he got, he read a lot of men's magazines—*Playboy, FHM, Maxim*—but never went on a date or anything more social than a movie."

Arkeley nodded as if it was all starting to make sense. "A virtual nonentity who no one really missed when he was gone. Tell me how he died."

"Industrial accident. He touched a live wire or something and died of cardiac arrest before the ambulance could even arrive. That's what the building manager told me." She studied the printout in her hand. "It happened at an electrical substation outside of Kennett Square." She checked the printout again. "Let me make another call."

Arkeley stood stock still while she called the substation's offices. Tucker started a game of computer solitaire, then had to close it out when she hung up her phone after less than a minute. "You're going to love this," she said.

Arkeley's eyebrows inched up toward his hairline.

"He wasn't working at the substation. He was helping to dismantle it. The substation was a hundred years old and they were closing it down. Most of the buildings onsite are still standing but have been permasealed. Which means all the windows are going to be covered with plywood and the doors padlocked."

"A vampire could tear a padlock off with his bare hands," Arkeley said. His face started to crease into a very wide smile.

"You said they liked ruins. Should we get on the road? We don't have too much daylight left, but we could at least scope the place out, and maybe get an order of exhumation for Reyes's grave."

The smile on Arkeley's face stopped short. "We?" he asked.

Caxton was about to reply when her phone rang again. She expected it was the building manager with a detail he'd just remembered, but it wasn't—the call was coming from state police headquarters, from the Commissioner's office. "Trooper Laura Caxton," she answered, placing the phone to her ear. When the Commissioner's assistant had finished relaying his message, she hung up once more. "We've been instructed to come to Harrisburg immediately."

"We?" Arkeley asked again.

"We, you and me. The Commissioner wants us, and he says it's urgent."

28.

The Commissioner stood in his doorway when they arrived—never a good sign. It meant he was looking forward to having them at his mercy. They filed into his office and sat down across from his desk. The air in the room felt hot and becalmed, and Caxton wished she could undo the top button of her uniform shirt, loosen her tie; but she knew it wouldn't be allowed. There was a dress code to maintain. Arkeley just sat down in his awkward fashion, his fused vertebrae making it impossible for him to sit comfortably. He did his best to appear as if this were just a routine meeting, perhaps a chance to prepare a new strategy. While Caxton stewed in uncomfortable silence the Commissioner busied himself at the front of the desk for a while, saying nothing, working with paper and tape.

When he was done five letter-sized color laser prints hung down from the edge of the desk. Portraits of state troopers, probably taken the day they graduated from the academy. They wore their hats with the chinstraps actually under their chins (by the next day, Caxton knew, they would learn to wear the straps across the backs of their heads) and looked out of the paper and over her shoulder as if toward some bright tomorrow.

"Would you like to know their names?" the Commissioner

asked when they'd had time to look at the portraits. "There's Eric Strauss. And Shane Herkimer. And Philip Toynbee. And—"

"I resent your implication," Arkeley said. As evenly and dispassionately as he said anything. His left hand gripped the desk, and he leaned forward to stare right into the Commissioner's eyes.

"I haven't even begun to imply," the Commissioner fired back. He leaned forward in his chair and grasped either branch of a pair of antlers that had been turned into a pen and pencil set. "These five men died two nights ago. They were Troop H, and they responded to a call for backup. Their deaths are inexcusable—five men lost to bring down one bad guy? These were well-trained troopers. They would have known how to handle themselves in a hazardous situation. That is, if they had known what to expect. They were not given sufficient information, and they died because no one told them they were facing off against a vampire."

Caxton was confused. She knew it wasn't her place to speak out—the two men expected her to remain silent throughout this interview—but she couldn't help it. "We didn't know either, when we called for them," Caxton tried, but Arkeley held up one hand to quiet her. He looked at the other man as if he was ready to hear what came next.

The Commissioner made a low sound in his throat. "And let us not forget the two troopers and the local policeman who died watching the hunting camp. They died because they were sitting on a porch."

Caxton shook her head. She wouldn't speak, not after Arkeley warned her off, but she had to make some gesture of her incomprehension.

"I sent my two best trackers down to that camp," the Commissioner said, looking at her as if he wanted to see her reaction. "They were Bureau of Investigation hotshots, top marks at the academy, lifelong hunters, mountain boys—these two have bow-hunted for bear and come out on top. They set up shop in a handmade blind a hundred yards from the camp and they waited to see if anybody was coming back to the scene of the crime. At least, that was the plan until your man Arkeley here called them and told them they were perfectly safe and they could sit on the porch, out in the open, where anyone could see them. Now they're dead."

She glanced across at Arkeley. He only nodded. He must have made the phone call while she was sitting with Vesta Polder. But why? What had made him think the porch was a safe place for the troopers? He must have at least suspected that the half-deads were coming back.

"I have their pictures here, too," the Commissioner said, shuffling some papers on his desk. "Want to see?"

Arkeley stirred in his chair and cleared his throat before speaking. "I'm not entirely sure what you're getting at, but I do know what you're missing. The thing you don't understand, Colonel, is that we are not fighting gangbangers, or terrorists, or drug dealers. We are fighting vampires."

The Commissioner sputtered, "I think I know—"

Arkeley cut him off. "In the dark ages a vampire could live for decades unopposed, feeding nightly on people whose only defense was to bar their windows and lock their doors and always, always, be home before sundown. When it became necessary to slay a vampire there was only one way it could be done. There were no guns and certainly no jackhammers at the time. The vampire slayers would gather up every able-bodied male in the community. The mob of them would go against the vampire with torches and spears and sticks if they had to. Very many of them would die in the first onslaught, but eventually enough of them would pile on top to hold the vampire down." He paused and raised one finger in the air. "Let me be clear about this, they quite literally climbed on top of the vampire to keep him from running away, pressing their own bodies against his, exposing themselves to his teeth by necessity. Those who made it this far would usually die as the vampire struggled to get free. Often enough the vampire *would* get free and the process would start over. Eventually our forefathers would prevail, but only through sheer dint of numbers. The men—and the boys—in those mobs did not shirk from their duty. They understood their terrible, grievous losses were the only way to protect their villages and their families."

Fuming, the Commissioner stood up from his desk and came around to the front, so close to Caxton that she had to move her knees to let him pass. "I'll use that story when I speak at the combined funeral next week. The families will be comforted, I'm sure. It will help them understand why their children had to be cremated before they were even allowed to say good-bye. It will help them understand why you felt it necessary to throw their babies to the wolves."

Arkeley rose as if he would leave.

"We'll finish this right now, right here," the Commissioner told him.

Arkeley was taller. It let him look down his nose when he said, "You have no authority over me whatsoever." He actually turned to go.

"Stop, Marshal," the Commissioner said.

Arkeley did as he was told, though he didn't turn to face the other man. The line of his back moved gently as he breathed. He didn't look like a man with fused vertebrae. He looked like somebody who ought to be holding a broadsword in one hand and a flag in the other. In the hot, close space of the office his body seemed enormous and powerful. He looked like a man who could fight vampires. Caxton wondered if she, herself, would ever come close to that kind of presence, that kind of confidence.

"I have authority over her," the Commissioner said. Arkeley

turned back around. "I'm taking trooper Caxton off this case right now. You want to try to fight me? I'll suspend her for using unauthorized ammunition in her weapon. Ha. I think I got you right there."

Arkeley stood in total silence, looking down at the other man. Caxton did not understand what was happening. She was a nothing, a nobody, somebody barely fit to make phone calls for the Fed. The two men were acting as if she were a bargaining chip. What did the Commissioner know? What did he suspect about Arkeley's motivations that was still such a mystery to her?

"You want her pretty bad, don't you? I saw it the last time you and I met, when you snatched her right up. I offered you ex-marines and special investigations boys, but you wanted one little slip of a girl from highway patrol." The Commissioner's smile was a gouge in the middle of his bright red face. "She's special. She's special for some reason and you need her."

Arkeley waited for him to finish. Then he cleared his throat, glanced at Caxton (the look was inscrutable), and sat back down. "What are you asking me for, really?" he said, finally. "Please, just spit it out. I'm a busy man."

"I want to protect my troopers," the Commissioner said. His attitude changed immeasurably—he had won, and he knew it. He sat down on the corner of his desk. He and Arkeley might have been two old friends working out who was going to pay for lunch. "That's all. I want you to let me do my job. There will be certain safeguards for anyone involved in this investigation, alright? There are two more vampire kills to be completed, but we are not going to lose any more personnel. This will be done by the book, by our best practices. My best practices. I will not let you use my boys as live bait anymore."

Caxton's mouth fell open.

"The survivors told me all about you, Arkeley. I've already

called your supervisors over in Washington. They were very interested in hearing about how you just let my boys die, one after the other, biding your time, hiding in the shadows. My troopers had no idea what they were up against, and you didn't seem to care. In twenty-some years of law enforcement work I have never heard of such—"

"Done," Arkeley said.

"I—you—wait. What do you mean?" the Commissioner stumbled.

"I mean that I agree to your conditions. The rest of it, all this nonsense about using state troopers as bait, the threat of calling my superiors, is immaterial. I really don't care what you think happened the last two nights. I was there and you weren't. However, if you're going to hold trooper Caxton hostage, then I am acceding to your demands."

Caxton's brain reeled in the heat of the office. "This is about me?" she asked.

Apparently it was.

29.

Arkeley rose again, and this time he was going to leave. Caxton could just feel it. "Any questions?" he asked.

The Commissioner nodded. "Oh yeah. I want to know what you're doing every step of the way. I've got so many questions you're going to feel like directory assistance from now on."

Arkeley smiled, his most gruesome, face-folding smile. The one he used when he wanted someone to feel small. "Well, sir, I intend to raid a vampire lair tomorrow morning at dawn. That's my next step. I'll need some support on the ground, and your troopers are my best resource for that. Take whatever safety measures you think are appropriate—gas masks, Kevlar vests, whatever, but have them ready and mustered at the station nearest Kennett Square by four-thirty tomorrow morning. Trooper Caxton need not be among them." He turned to look at her and gave her a new kind of smile. This one looked a little melancholy. "You, young lady, can sleep in. You've been enough help locating Reyes's hiding place."

She had the presence of mind to nod and shake his hand. He left without saying good-bye or anything else—well, she had expected that. But there was still one thing she needed from him, something she had to know.

The Commissioner gave her the rest of the day off. She started by racing down to the motor pool to catch Arkeley before he could leave. She needed to know the answer to a question she couldn't have asked in the overheated office. In the parking lot Arkeley was signing for an unmarked patrol car of his own so he wouldn't have to rely on her vehicle. He looked mildly peeved to see her, but at least he didn't drive off while she just stood there.

"I have a right to know," she told him. "In the Commissioner's office you gave up as soon as he tried to take me off the case. You're a tough guy, but you caved over me." She tried to push a little self-esteem into what she said next, but it still came out sounding as if she doubted her own worth as a human being. "What is it about me that's so important? Why can't you afford to lose me?" Originally she'd been convinced by his story that because she had actually read his report she was the best prepared to fight vampires. Later she'd thought he might be grooming her as a replacement. When he took her to the Polders, she honestly believed he wanted to keep her alive, that he was actually worried about her safety—but then after her failure at the hunting camp he'd been willing to write her off. She didn't understand any of it. She didn't understand why he valued her or why he disregarded her so easily. Why he tried to physically protect her or why he didn't seem to care if she got hurt.

"The night I took over this case," he said, his face neutral. "The night we met, a half-dead followed you home."

She didn't understand what that had meant, either. "I remember," she said.

"You were on this case before I was. You're part of it. The vampires know you and they want something from you. I'd be a fool to let you out of my sight."

She remembered what he'd said about Hazlitt. If someone was determined to be your enemy you gave them exactly what they wanted. The vampires wanted her. They were out to consume her, one way or another. So he would dangle her before their toothy mouths just so he could get close enough to jump down their throats.

"That's . . . it?" she asked. Her heart sank in her chest. All the time she'd spent trying to prove herself, to impress him, was wasted.

"That's it," he said. He opened the car door and climbed inside. She let him go.

She was vampire bait. That was all that she was.

She watched him drive away. She had no idea where he was headed. Perhaps he wanted to check out the substation near Kennett Square by himself, or maybe he wanted to exhume Efrain Reyes. Maybe he just didn't want to be around her. Maybe he was afraid she would be angry.

She was, of course. And confused. And sad. And afraid. And just a little bit relieved.

Relieved because she had finally found how she fit into the vampire investigation. Because now she knew exactly where she stood with Arkeley.

She collected her own car and drove in the general direction of home, her overworked brain a little assuaged by the sound of her wheels hissing on the asphalt and the rising and falling roar of the engine. She rubbed at her eyes and blinked a lot, as if she was going to cry, but she didn't. She didn't even know why she expected to. Of all the emotions struggling inside of her, none stood out so strongly as to require such an overreaction.

She felt hungry, and knew it had to be bad if it could compete with all of her other concerns. She pulled over at a place in Reading where they made good cheesesteaks and ordered one "wit wiz," which meant she wanted onions and Cheese Whiz, the traditional condiments. She sat down in a little booth with her steak and a diet Coke and chewed on the sandwich. It was good, but her mind kept wandering, her tongue stopped tasting anything. She was half done with her meal before she stopped to think about the real issue, the thing that should have consumed her with panic and really made her cry.

The vampires wanted her for something. Something specific, something specific to her life. The half-dead who followed her home the first night had been sent on a mission. But what mission? Just to scare her? In that case it had been successful. But she couldn't imagine the vampires would waste time just to give her a shock.

She thought backwards, a little desperately, searching for anything that might explain the vampiric interest. She thought of previous cases she'd worked on, but nothing stood out. She worked highway patrol—how could that mean anything to Malvern and her brood? She tried to remember the car wrecks she'd seen, tried to draw some kind of connection, but nothing came to her. She'd sent some people to prison for driving under the influence, for possession of drugs. She had caught them, arrested them, testified against them in court. The perpetrators had been sad, broken people, people who needed to drink or inject methamphetamines more than they needed to stay out of jail. None of them had put up much of a fight, and they could never look her in the eye when they went to trial. How could a few drunk businessmen and stoned teenagers possibly matter to Justinia Malvern?

It had to be something personal, then. But what? She wasn't the kind of person who made a lot of enemies. She didn't have a lot of friends, either—and that made her think of Efrain Reyes. A nonentity, Arkeley had called him. Someone with no real life. Someone no one would miss when he died. Caxton had a life, of sorts, but there were holes in it. Her parents were dead and she had no siblings. She had a few friends in the troop, but they rarely hung out. The beer she'd shared with Clara Hsu was the first time she'd been in a bar in months. Clara—Clara would wonder what had happened to her if she disappeared, but not for long. Deanna would be devastated, mentally destroyed, but the only real change in Deanna's life post-Caxton would be that she would have to go back to living with her alcoholic mother. If the one person who defined your life had no life herself, what did that say about you? She had the dogs, who would miss her very much, but Caxton didn't suppose dogs counted.

Malvern had been looking for a fourth candidate, someone she could add to her brood. Every cell in Caxton's body squirmed at the same time. She stared down at the mess of grease and gristle on her plate and felt bile frothing in her throat. Would Malvern—could Malvern—turn her into a vampire?

She got back in her car and rushed home. She needed to get inside and be safe for a while. She would definitely sleep in the next morning, she decided, and let other, more qualified people raid the substation.

She knew the road back to her house like the lines on her palm. She could drive the route half-asleep, and often did. Yet as she approached her own driveway she felt suddenly as if she'd never seen the place before. As if she were no longer welcome in her own house.

Unnatural, Arkeley kept saying. Vampires were abominations against nature. Was this how that felt? To be around life and warmth and comfort and feel like you were visiting some alien world?

She started to pull into the driveway and stopped short because she'd heard something. A crash, a bright melody of glass breaking, as if a window had been knocked in. She unholstered her weapon and slowly, taking every possible precaution, stepped down onto the grass of her lawn. She couldn't see anything from the front of the house, so she edged around the side, toward the kennels and Deanna's shed.

Shards of broken windowpane littered the side yard, long triangular pieces leaning up against the side of the house. Someone wearing a hooded sweatshirt, maybe a teenaged boy, was standing next to the shattered window, his hands resting on the empty frame. He looked as if he were talking to someone inside the house.

"Freeze," she barked.

The boy turned to look at her. Flesh hung in tatters on his face. He was a half-dead. She discharged her weapon without thinking, and the half-dead's fragile body split into pieces. The chunks slumped to the ground. The stink coming off of him made her eyes water. She stepped closer anyway, intending to search his pockets, when she finally had a chance to look in through the window.

Deanna stood there, naked from the waist up, her outstretched hands, her lower face, her bare chest all covered in bright red blood.

30.

"Jesus, Dee, Jesus, what did he do to you?" Caxton sobbed. She wiped at Deanna's face with a wet washcloth and found a three-inch-long wound along the edge of her chin. It was going to need stitches, even if she could get Deanna to a hospital before she bled to death. Caxton picked the larger slivers of glass out of the cut, but that just made it bleed more. She pulled open the drawer where they kept their scissors and their twine and found a roll of thick masking tape. Lacking any better idea, she stretched a length of it across the cut and pressed down.

Deanna howled with pain. Her eyes were clenched tightly shut and her knees were up against her chest where she lay on the kitchen floor. Her hands were wrapped up in an old T-shirt that was already soaked through with blood. She had wounds all over the front of her body as well, tiny cuts and big lacerations. Caxton had called 911 and they were sending an ambulance, but the blood kept flowing and flowing.

"What did he do to you?" Caxton asked again, smearing blood on her own face as she tried to wipe away her tears. If the ambulance didn't come soon she would lose Deanna, just like she'd lost her mother. It was more than she could bear. "What did he do?"

"Who?" Deanna wailed. She had been hypnotized, or perhaps was just in shock, when Caxton found her, but now she was recovering herself and the pain was coming. Caxton shushed her and stroked her red hair, but the bleeding just wouldn't stop. She didn't know what to do, how to save Deanna. She didn't know what to do. She wanted to scream herself. "Who?" Deanna asked again.

"The half-dead, the thing in the window," Caxton gasped.

"There was nobody—" Deanna paused to howl with pain. "Nobody here. Nobody but me and I—I couldn't seem to wake up, I was having a dream and I couldn't, I couldn't—" She screamed again and Caxton picked her up and held her close. Caxton was crying so hard that she couldn't see where the blood was and what was clean. "I dreamed you were being crushed under this, this, this heavy stone and your insides were squirting out, all of your blood. I woke up but only halfway, I kept seeing your body torn apart, in pieces, I kept seeing it when I closed my eyes."

"Shhh," Caxton said, and held Deanna closer. Then she worried that if she put pressure on Deanna's wounds they might reopen. She loosened her grip.

"I came in here," Deanna whined, "into the kitchen because I heard something cracking, some glass, some glass was cracking. I went to the window and there was a crack running from the top to the side and there was a drop of blood rolling down from the crack. I couldn't stand to see that, so I tried to mop up the blood with my hand, but then more blood came and when I pressed, when I pressed on the crack it just split open and there was glass everywhere." She buried her face in Caxton's shirt. "There was blood everywhere."

In the bedroom something crashed to the floor. Caxton looked up, alert again with a suddenness that surprised her. A soft voice swore in Spanish, a voice that wasn't human.

There was another half-dead, inside the house.

"Dee, I have to let go for a second," she whispered. "I have to do something, but you'll be okay."

"No," Deanna begged.

"You'll be okay. The ambulance will be here any minute. Just do whatever the paramedics say, and I'll be right back."

"No, please, please don't leave me," Deanna mewled. But there was nothing for it. Caxton gently lowered her back onto the kitchen floor. She checked the tape on Deanna's cheek and saw that it was starting to peel away. She pushed it back down and it stayed, mostly. She drew her weapon again and glided down the hallway, toward the bedroom.

"Pumpkin, come back!" Deanna shrieked. "It really hurts!"

Caxton knew what had to be done, though. She stepped into the bedroom. A half-dead wearing a baseball cap and a football jersey stood next to the closet door. He had knocked over her nightstand, and her clock radio lay in pieces on the hardwood floor.

"*Hostia puta,*" he squeaked. He looked from side to side, his flayed arms spread against the wall. It was pretty clear what he planned to do next. He was all the way across the room from the open window. If he could run faster than she, he could easily get away.

Before he'd taken three steps Caxton knocked his legs out from under him, smashing his upper body down to the floor. He called out, but she sat down hard on his pelvis and lower spine and he could do no more than move his arms and legs along the floor as if he were trying to swim away.

"What did you do to her?" she asked, as coldly as she could manage. If she lost control now she would just crack his skull and that would be the end of it. Not that she would mind, but she needed information more than she desired revenge. "Tell me and I'll let you go."

"*La concha de tu hermana!*" the half-dead shouted, wriggling underneath her, trying to break free. She was stronger and it must have known that. It wasn't going to get away without tearing itself to pieces.

"You came here looking for me, didn't you? You wanted me, but you tried to kill Deanna. Why? Why?" She bounced up and down on top of the half-dead until it screamed.

"I don't know who you are, lady," it cried out in English. "I got no idea!"

"You came here for me. Tell me why."

The half-dead shook violently. "If I say something he'll rip me up."

"He who? The vampire, Reyes?" she demanded.

"I ain't talking about President Bush, lady!" The half-dead grunted and groaned and rose a fraction of an inch off the floor, lifting her weight at the same time in a supernal act of will. With a gasp of frustration he collapsed again. "*Me cago en Jesus y la*

Virgen, you might as well kill me now and get it over with, huh?"

Caxton thought about Arkeley and what the Fed would do to get the information. She knew he would torture the half-dead. He would do exactly what the half-dead feared to receive at the hands of the vampire. The half-dead was less afraid of oblivion than of pain. She had said at the time that she would not be able to stand by while Arkeley did that. She couldn't countenance torture, she'd told him.

Of course at that point no one had tried to kill Deanna.

She reached down and grabbed the index finger of the half-dead's left hand. It felt wrong in her grip, not at all like a human finger. There was no skin on it and very little flesh—it was more like holding an uncooked sparerib. She twisted it with all her strength and it came right off the half-dead's hand.

"Coño!" the half-dead screamed, a pure, horrible noise, a sound of perfect pain.

The disembodied finger wriggled in her hand like a centipede. She threw it away from her. Then she reached down and grabbed the middle finger of the same hand. She gave the half-dead a second to think about what was going to happen, and then, without a word, she tore the middle finger off, too.

His left hand had nothing but a thumb when he finally spoke. "He told us to come here and pick up whoever we found, that's all, lady, please, stop now!"

"Who told you? Efrain Reyes?"

"Yeah, that's who! He said to come get you, your *tortillera* girlfriend, your dogs, anybody who was here. He even told us how, with the *hechizo.*" She grabbed the thumb and asked what a *hechizo* was. "It's a spell, a magic spell, kind of! Hey, lady, I'm telling you what you want to know, be nice, okay?"

"You hypnotized her? You hypnotized Deanna, is that it?"

The half-dead struggled again, but he was growing weaker

by the minute. He had no blood to spill, but the pain seemed to take the fight out of him. "Yeah, but it only works when she's asleep and dreaming."

"Why us? Why were you sent to this house?"

"He doesn't tell us that. He doesn't fill us in on his big plans, he just says, *vamos,* and I go. Please, lady, please, I told you all I know."

A siren wailed through the walls of the house. Caxton heard doors slamming and people running up to the door. "Alright," she said. Then she grabbed her pistol and smashed in the back of the half-dead's skull. He stopped wriggling instantly. Slowly, stiffly, her clothes sticking together where the blood had dried in the folds, she rose from the floor and holstered her weapon. Then she walked into the kitchen and opened the door for the paramedics. On the floor Deanna was curled up in a tight ball, weeping piteously. Her blood was everywhere.

31.

A stretcher rolled past Caxton's face, barely three inches away. It was being pushed at high speed up the main ramp to the emergency room entrance, but to her it seemed to float, unattended, through boundless space, taking its time. The body on the stretcher was just a pile of bloodstained rags. She couldn't even see a face. But then the body reached out a hand to her. The skin was scorched and falling away in places. Thick clotted blood was smeared across the fingers. She couldn't even tell if it was a male or female hand.

Still. She reached out, touched it. The fingers curled around hers, but then the hand was ripped away from her, the stretcher flying up the ramp. Somebody shouted for plasma and she squinted and tried to clear her head.

She'd been sitting in the hallway for hours and hours with no stimulation except the constant parade of mutilated bodies that flew by. She shouldn't have been in the hallway at all—there was a waiting room for people like her, complete with six TV sets and a couple hundred pounds of straight women's magazines—but being a cop had its privileges. Most of the EMTs and nurses who passed by didn't even give her a second glance; they assumed she was just guarding the entrance. In fact it just let her be a couple hundred feet closer to Deanna. They wouldn't let her into the operating room or the recovery room. The hallway was as close as she was going to get.

That hand. It had been like something out of a dream, but she knew it was real. It had touched her. She looked down and saw real blood on her fingers. Her hand smelled like gasoline and shit, a smell she knew all too well. The smell of a really bad car accident. The hand had been real and warm and alive.

Unlike the half-dead she had tortured and executed on her bedroom floor. Unlike the vampires who were coming to destroy her life.

Caxton sighed and crossed her arms and waited. She had tried reading a magazine, but she was too distracted. Images and words jumped into her head unbidden. Not even things related to the investigation, not even memories of Deanna, just weird little scraps of thought. She kept wondering if the milk sitting out on the kitchen counter was going to go bad. The kitchen had to be as cold as the outside air, since the window was completely gone. Pretty much anybody could climb in through the hole where the window had been—should she call someone, have them check the house, have them put cardboard, at least, over the window? If she did that, should she ask them to go inside and put the milk back in the fridge?

She couldn't shut her mind down. It didn't work that way. Only sleep could turn off the brain, and she was a long way from sleep. The banal thoughts, the endless, cycling inanities had their purpose, as excruciating as they were. They kept her from thinking the big thoughts, the real thoughts. The things that scared her.

Thoughts like the fact that vampires wanted her dead. So badly they would send their minions to kill everyone in her house. Everyone. The half-deads would have killed her dogs, probably, just to be thorough about it.

Thoughts like, Arkeley had turned his back on her. She couldn't even count on him to defend her against the dark things that wanted her life. He wasn't done with her, he had some purpose for her, but she wasn't going to be an active part of his investigation.

Thoughts like: Is there really any difference between someone being hypnotized into breaking a window and impaling themselves on broken glass . . . and someone whose brain chemistry stops working one day, and they hang themselves in their bedroom? Her mother had had a good job and plenty of money. She had a perfectly good daughter to live for, a nice house, partners for bridge, church socials, potluck dinners. Holidays. Family. Vacations. Retirement. Her suicide had been a complete mystery to everyone who knew her. It had been a mistake, really, it had to have been.

Deanna had nothing to keep her living. No job, family who loathed her for what she was. A partner who cared and who tried but who just didn't have the time to be there for her. No future. Art that nobody understood.

Was it still suicide, if you had an excuse? If you were driven to it?

"Officer," someone said, nearby. It was like the ghost that had called her in Urie Polder's barn, a directionless, bodiless voice. "Officer," the voice said again. Caxton frowned and turned her head. A nurse stood there in bloodstained scrubs, a middle-aged woman with white hair up in a bun on top of her head. She wore heavy gloves, the kind you wear when you wash dishes. "Officer, she's awake," the nurse said.

Caxton followed her through halls, around corners, up stairs. She could not have found her way back if she was called upon to do so. They came to a room, a semiprivate room with two beds. One held a morbidly obese woman whose entire lower body and thighs were wrapped up in plaster. A surgical gown had been draped over her breasts. The other bed held something that had been stitched together out of spare parts.

Jesus, Caxton realized, it was Deanna. "You look like Frankenstein's monster," Caxton said.

Deanna tried to smile, but the stitches in her jawline kept her from moving her mouth too much. "Pumpkin . . . you left me," she mumbled. Caxton took off her hat and leaned down to kiss Deanna's puffy lips. The obese woman in the other bed let out a half-gasp, half-cluck of disdain, but Caxton had learned to ignore that sound a long time before. She stood back up and took a better look at Deanna. The view didn't improve the second time around. Glinting staples held the side of Deanna's face together. The sharp ends of stitches, black and coarse like horsehair, stuck up out of the flesh of her chest and shoulders, while bandages wrapped her hands so that she looked like she was wearing bloody mittens. "You left me all alone," Deanna said.

"Don't talk, Dee. Just rest." Caxton reached down and gently brushed the staples in Deanna's face. They were real, solid, and the flesh underneath was red and inflamed.

A doctor came into the room. Caxton didn't even look at him. She held Deanna's eyes with her own and refused to let go.

"I'd like to bring in someone to talk with her. I know you probably don't want to hear that, but I'm not sure you have the right to stop me, either—do you have a civil union?"

They didn't. They'd never bothered, since it wouldn't be legally recognized anyway. It didn't matter. "I don't object," Caxton said. She started to reach for Deanna's hands, but they were so badly damaged that she didn't want to touch them. She held onto the railing on the side of the bed instead.

Deanna started to protest, but Caxton just moved her chin back and forth a little and said, "Shh, it's just to talk."

"She's pretty lucky, all things considered. She could easily have died. She lost a lot of blood, and some of the fragments of glass went pretty deep. We'll wait and see if there's any nerve damage to her hands. The cut in her face is going to require reconstructive surgery, and even then there will be scarring."

Caxton held onto the railing as if she would be swept away on a dark sea if she lost her grip. It didn't matter, she told herself. Deanna was going to live. At least, she would live until the next time someone tried to kill her. Maybe the next time Reyes would come for her himself. "I'm going to call in for a guard to stand watch outside this room, Doctor. This was an attempted murder." The words sounded ridiculous coming out of her mouth, like something she'd made up. It was real, though, she needed to convince herself it was real. "I'll stay with her until the first shift arrives."

"Very well." The doctor moved to check on the obese woman in the next bed. "It's almost two o'clock now, but I'll call down to the desk and have them set something up."

"Two o'clock?" Caxton asked, surprised. She glanced down at her watch and saw he was correct. "Shit. Dee, honey," she said, "I have to go."

"Whuh?" Deanna asked.

"There's someplace I have to be." It was something she'd figured out in those long hours in the hallway. It was her next move.

32.

Caxton couldn't figure out how to strap the vest around her stomach. One of the guys from the area response team had to pull it tight behind her back and buckle it there. He also helped her with the knee, shin, and shoulder guards. She figured out the helmet for herself. "Larry Reynolds," he told her, and stuck out a gloved hand. She shook it and introduced herself.

"I'm sorry I'm so unfamiliar with this stuff. This is my first time in riot gear." She squirmed for a moment, embarrassed, then admitted, "Normally I'm highway patrol."

"You were in on that vampire kill a couple of nights ago, right? That's what they told us when we got assigned to this detail." Reynolds had black paint under his eyes and it made it hard to read his expression. She couldn't tell if he was annoyed to be saddled with such an untrained whelp as herself and was hiding it well, or if he was honestly trying to be friendly. "Stick with us, keep your head down, and you'll be alright."

Another ART detective came up and slapped Reynolds on the top of his helmet. "Keeping his head down is about ninety percent of Larry's job." Reynolds faked punching the new guy in the kidney and they broke away, laughing, dancing around each other like Caxton's greyhounds. "I'm DeForrest, and I'll be your stewardess this morning," the new guy told her. He had Reynolds in a headlock. "We hope you enjoy your trip with Granola Roller airlines."

Caxton had no idea what he was talking about, but she smiled anyway. It had taken a lot of pleading to get assigned to this detail and she didn't want the ART guys to resent her presence. When a woman in riot gear came and offered her coffee from a thermos she took it as graciously as she could.

Truth be told, she needed the caffeine as much as she needed to be accepted. She hadn't slept, even for a moment, not since she'd woken up the day before and realized why the vampires had decimated Bitumen Hollow. Her hands were shaking, and if she looked at anything too closely or for too long its outlines grew fuzzy and indistinct.

"They're infantile, I know, but they're good men," the woman with the coffee said. "DeForrest was a firefighter before he took this job. He was bored, he said. I assumed the first time I met him that he just wanted to play with guns, like a lot of people who sign up for the ART. He's never discharged his weapon, not once, since he came to work with us, even when bad guys have fired on him. Reynolds dislocated his shoulder last year getting a five-year-old out of a trailer knocked over in a tornado."

"Wow," Caxton said.

"I'm Suzie Jesuroga. Captain Suzie," the woman said, and shook Caxton's hand.

"Laura Caxton. Trooper."

Captain Suzie smiled. "I know exactly who you are. We've all been briefed about that vampire kill you pulled off over on Route three twenty-two. The Commissioner made us go over all the details. Today's trip should be a little less hairy, considering we've got good daylight conditions and the extra precautions we're taking, but I'm still glad to have you along. You want to get started?"

The four of them finished suiting up and ran through an equipment and weapons check. They'd been issued M4 carbines, military-grade assault rifles with underslung shotgun attachments. Caxton also carried her Beretta, loaded up with cross points. The others had their own personal weapons—combat knives, revolvers, tear gas and smoke grenades. The ART had a little latitude, it seemed, in how they kitted out for an operation. Together they headed out of the locker room of the Harrisburg

HQ and down to a parking lot secluded by a row of trees. Darkness tinged the deep, rich blue of an impending dawn, lain over the lot like a comforter. Arkeley waited for them there, wearing no protective gear at all, just his overcoat. It hung open and she could tell he wasn't carrying anything other than his Glock 23 with its thirteen bullets.

"Captain," he said, when they greeted him, "I'll express one more time my desire to leave this vehicle behind." He nodded his chin at a giant white truck that took up two spaces in the parking lot. It was based on the chassis of a Humvee, Caxton thought, but it had been uparmored as if it were meant to roll through Tikrit instead of Scranton. Heavy metal plates had been welded to its doors, its hood, its roof, and all of the windows had been almost completely obscured except for small slits. Even the truck's tires had been reinforced with heavy chains. What looked like a homemade air cannon had been mounted on the roof.

"It's pretty noisy when it gets up to speed, I'll admit," Captain Suzie told Arkeley. "Are you afraid we'll wake the vampires?"

Arkeley's upper lip twitched in distaste. "No. Vampires don't sleep during the day. They literally die anew every morning. It's the half-deads I'm worried about."

Captain Suzie just shrugged. "The Commissioner gave me my orders himself. You can talk to him if you want to change the plan, but he doesn't even come in to the office until nine. I'd just as soon get on the road now."

Arkeley narrowed his eyes, but he nodded and stalked off toward his own car, an unmarked patrol car that looked puny by comparison.

One by one the ART climbed inside the armored vehicle. The interior was packed with so much gear, and the team members were so bulky in their riot armor, that there was barely room for the four of them. Reynolds drove and DeForrest took shotgun—almost literally, since he rode with his weapon in his hands. Captain Suzie rode beside Caxton in the backseat.

A man came out of the main building, his uniform shirt unbuttoned and his face unshaven. Caxton recognized the range officer from the less-lethal weapons test area, the one who had supplied her with her cross points. He popped open the hood of the armored vehicle and played around with the engine for a minute.

"It's the old man's baby, and he never lets it out without a personal inspection," DeForrest told Caxton, craning around in his seat to look at her, his helmet catching on the headrest of his seat and tilting over one eye. "He built the Granola Roller nearly from scratch."

"I'm guessing I'm sitting in the very same Granola Roller," Caxton said.

Reynolds snorted. "Yeah. It was never really meant for hunting vampires. The old man designed it for crowd control, you know, at demonstrations and protests and riots and such. Sometimes we call it 'Extra Chunky,' too."

Caxton tried to figure it out, but her fatigued brain couldn't make sense of the name. "Why's that?" she finally asked.

"Because," DeForrest said, barely able to contain his mirth, "when you run over a hippie with this thing, extra chunky is about all that's left."

"Don't be gross," Captain Suzie said as DeForrest and Reynolds laughed in each other's faces. She turned to Caxton. "I'm sure that I'll have to do this about a hundred times today, but now, for the first time, I officially apologize for my men. Reynolds, have you forgotten how to drive a stick shift, or are we waiting for the vampire to die of old age? Let's get moving!"

"Yes, Ma'am," Reynolds said, and he started up the armored vehicle with a noise like boulders falling down a mountainside. The range officer waved them off and started buttoning his shirt.

They followed Arkeley's car onto the highway and settled in for the long ride to Kennett Square, which was all the way down by the Delaware border. The armored vehicle's groaning and grunting engine noise made it impossible to speak and be heard inside the cabin, but Caxton didn't mind so much. She could barely form a coherent sentence in her head, much less make one come out of her mouth.

She had to hunch over against the door to look out the view-slit in her window, which meant exposing her bones to a constant jouncing vibration as the heavy truck ground over every minor imperfection in the roadway. Somehow she survived, though. She watched suburban lawns speed by, silver with frost and dark with fallen leaves. As they rolled out into more rural zones she let her eyes linger on the geometric regularity of farmers' fields or the shaking, surging rattle of dark tree branches that leaned close over the road.

Every time she closed her eyes she saw a death's head, and felt wriggling finger bones rattling in her hands. She saw Deanna covered in blood. She remembered what it was like to be hypnotized by a vampire, to feel as if she were drowning in death, as if the air had turned to glass and she were suspended inside of it. She reached up and touched Vesta Polder's amulet through the thick nylon and Kevlar layers of her ballistic vest.

As the sun began to climb up from behind the ridges, a lemon-colored sliver on the horizon, she began to feel a little better. She was taking action, taking up arms against the thing that was trying to kill her, which had nearly killed Deanna. Arkeley, when he heard she had requested to come along on this raid, had said absolutely not. He had thought, he told her, that he had made himself quite clear. He didn't want her endangered. He didn't think she could handle it.

She had told him about torturing a half-dead, how she had

pulled the bastard's fingers off, and slowly, almost imperceptibly, he had come around. He'd never actually said it was alright, but he had stopped insisting quite so strongly that she stay behind. It was as good as she was going to get, she knew.

33.

They had to stop for gas outside of Lancaster. When the jumping, swaying truck finally came to a stop, the ensuing quiet and calm shocked Caxton. She climbed out of the Granola Roller to stretch her legs and then leaned against the side of the vehicle with Captain Suzie while DeForrest pumped the gas. He had to unbolt a layer of armor from the truck's side to get at the gas tank. Inside the gas station the attendant watched them with dull eyes, as if he saw state troopers in full combat gear every morning. Eventually Caxton realized he was asleep, sleeping sitting up in his chair. They were probably the first customers of his shift.

DeForrest froze, suddenly, even as Caxton was thinking about waking up the attendant to get some snacks. The ART guy let go of the nozzle and stepped away from the pump. He looked at Captain Suzie and without a word pointed up at a line of trees across the highway. "Over there," he said.

"Can you confirm his sighting, Caxton?" Captain Suzie asked.

Fear stuck icy needles into her heart. "Confirm . . . what?" she asked. She scanned the dead trees for the broken faces of half-deads, the shocking white skin of vampires, even just for movement of any kind. Then she noticed flecks of darkness, like pieces of shadow, swooping and darting among the trees.

A smile lifted her face a little and she turned around, shaking her head. The ART members behind her had dropped to shooting crouches, their weapons up and at their shoulders. They were deadly serious. They were terrified, and they were all looking at her.

"Those are just bats," she said. "They're nocturnal, and the sun's coming up. They're flying home." She shrugged her shoulders. "Bats."

Captain Suzie frowned and put her weapon up but didn't move from her defensive crouch. "So there's no danger?"

"No," Caxton said. "There's no connection. That's just a myth." She realized with a start that the ART members didn't resent her presence. As they climbed back inside the vehicle to resume their journey, she understood that they were glad to have her along. She was their trained vampire killer.

She just hoped the mission's success didn't depend on her expertise.

They pulled into Kennett Square just as dawn made the white lines on the road glow and seem to float above the dark asphalt. Maybe it was just Caxton's lack of sleep. With the sun creeping up over the trees they moved through the quaint little town, which the map showed as being quite literally square.

"What's that smell?" Reynolds asked. Caxton had noticed it too, a thick, earthy smell that occasionally sharpened into something pretty nasty.

"This is the mushroom capital of the world," Captain Suzie told him. "Didn't you know that? That smell is the stuff they grow mushrooms in."

DeForrest sniffed the air. "Shit?" he asked.

Captain Suzie shrugged. "Manure, anyway. They have to cook it in these long sheds, night and day, to sterilize it. This whole part of the state smells like that, pretty much all the time. I used to live around here. You get used to it."

"You get used to the smell of cooking shit," Reynolds said, as if he were trying on the idea for size.

"So you hardly even notice it anymore," Captain Suzie assured him. "After a couple of days you can get used to anything."

What about torture, Caxton wondered? Could you get used to torturing your enemies for information? She was afraid she knew the answer.

They passed over a set of train tracks that made the Granola Roller rumble ominously, and then they were there—the substation. The hideout of Efrain Reyes, if they were lucky. Or maybe if they weren't.

Caxton checked her weapons, working the actions, chambering and unchambering rounds. The ART followed her example. Arkeley pulled up outside the substation's fence and got out of his car. "What is he doing?" Captain Suzie asked.

The Fed answered for himself, slipping a hands-free phone attachment over his ear. He touched the tiny mouthpiece bud and the armored vehicle's radio squawked. DeForrest punched some buttons. "Say again, over," he announced.

"I was saying that I'm going from here on foot," Arkeley told them. "You can follow however you choose, but this place was never meant for a military parade."

"He's making fun of your truck," Caxton told Captain Suzie.

The other woman scowled. "He can make fun of my big nose, but I'm still not getting out and walking," she said, but she wasn't smiling.

The substation took up about two acres of ground, all of it surrounded by brick wall or chain-link fence. The ART had secured the plans of the place. It had been decommissioned by the local utility provider a year earlier (a bigger, better, and safer substation having already been built and hooked into the grid), and work crews were still taking it apart. There was more to it than simple demolition—there were all kinds of nasty chemicals and compounds inside the giant transformers that made up the bulk of the substation's equipment, from sulfur hexafluoride gas to liquid PCBs. The transformers had to be taken apart piece by piece by trained professionals. Electrical engineers, to be specific—men like Efrain Reyes before he died.

Arkeley had gotten permission from the substation's owners to search the place. They'd given him a key to the padlock on the gate. There had been some concern that Reyes might have changed the lock, but the key worked just fine. Arkeley pushed open the heavy gate and went inside.

Reynolds put the Granola Roller into gear and crept forward, staying twenty-five feet behind Arkeley at all times. The Fed moved forward briskly, as if he knew what he was looking for. They passed down a narrow aisle flanked by two rows of tall switches adorned with stacks of round insulators that made them look like the spires of futuristic churches. Beyond lay the transformers themselves, thick, sturdy metal blocks standing in perfect rows.

"I thought we were after vampires, not Frankenstein's monster," DeForrest joked. Everyone ignored him. "What's all this stuff for?"

"It steps down the voltage of electricity coming from the power plants," Caxton explained, "until it's safe to send to your house." She pressed her face against the gunport in her window and tried to see what Arkeley must be seeing.

Nothing stirred in the substation except a few fallen yellow leaves that skittered around in the breeze, chasing one another back and forth.

Up ahead at the end of the row stood an old switch house. It was where the original circuit breakers for the substation would have been housed—maybe even fuses, if the place was old enough. It was a one-story building made of dark brown brick with mullioned windows that didn't let much light in or out.

It had to be the place. Beyond lay the chain-link fence. Yellow cornstalks stood eight feet high outside the fence, fields of the dead vegetation running off in every other direction. If Reyes was hiding inside the substation, he was in the switch house.

Arkeley went to the door and pushed it open. Whatever might have been inside, the sun hadn't yet touched it. He unholstered his weapon and took a flashlight from the pocket of his overcoat. "I'm going in, if anyone cares to join me," Arkeley said over the radio.

"That's not how we planned this," Captain Suzie said into her own radio. "That's not what the Commissioner wanted. It could be dangerous."

"The sun's up. We're safe. Right? We're safe," Reynolds said. "The sun's up. Vampires can't come out in the daytime."

"That's right," Caxton told him.

"I don't care. We stay in the vehicle," Captain Suzie said. She stared forward at Arkeley as if she could meet his gaze from the backseat of the armored vehicle.

The Fed stepped into the darkness. None of the ART members moved.

"Deputy," Captain Suzie called. "Deputy? Come in, Deputy. Give me a status report, give me something. Anything."

"Special Deputy," Arkeley's voice corrected her. He remained out of sight. "I don't have a lot to report just now. I've found a large quantity of cobwebs and rusty equipment. Hold on. I just found a trapdoor. It looks like there's a lower level. I'm headed down."

Caxton pushed open her door and jumped down to the ground before she knew she was really going to do it. Captain Suzie grabbed for her, but Caxton slipped through her hands. She moved toward the switch house as the radio on her collar started yelling orders at her.

She was almost at the switch house's open door when something moved in the corner of her eye. She turned, her rifle in firing position, and saw it again. Outside of the fence something was definitely moving around. She looked left and right and saw that someone had cut a hole through the fence, big enough for a grown man to duck through. She ran over and twined her fingers through the chain link. "Arkeley," she called, "I've found a back exit to the substation. There's somebody out there."

"Caxton," he said. "Get back in that fucking truck. I've told you already—"

She stopped listening to him. Something was definitely moving, creeping through the cornfield. It wasn't an animal, either. It was a person, or maybe even several persons or . . . or several half-deads. She ducked under the fence and immediately heard rustling, a layered slithering sound as numerous bodies pushed through the dead stalks. She spun around, one eye down near the scope of her rifle, and then she saw them, six or maybe seven half-deads wearing hooded sweatshirts. They were dragging something through the corn, something big made of dark wood with brass hardware.

It was a coffin.

34.

She lifted her rifle to her shoulder and fired a quick burst of three shots, but she didn't hit anything, nor did she expect to. The half-deads were moving and obscured behind dozens of rows of cornstalks. With the power of the weapon in her hands she could mow down half of the cornfield, but she'd been trained better than that. A rifle bullet could travel half a mile before gravity brought it down. Unless she could guarantee there were no innocent bystanders within a half-mile radius, she couldn't fire blind like that.

She could only watch, then, as the half-deads dragged their coffin through the corn. "Arkeley," she said into her radio. "Arkeley, please come in. I have sighted a group of half-deads carrying a coffin. Please advise. Arkeley, what do I do?"

". . . bones, human bodies in . . . no sign of recent . . . a lot of dust," he said. She figured he must be talking about the basement of the switch house and what he had found there. He must not have been able to hear her—she could barely make out a fraction of what he was saying. Presumably the signal was being partially blocked by the layer of dirt between them. That was immaterial, though. The half-deads were getting away. She looked back through the fence and saw the armored vehicle just sitting there. One member of the ART leaned out of an open door, staring at her, open-mouthed.

"Captain Suzie," Caxton said, "I need backup over here. They're getting away!"

"My orders are to stay with the vehicle, no matter what. Our safety is more important than catching your vampire. Those are your orders, too, Trooper."

"Reyes will escape if we don't get him now," Caxton said. "If we get him now, by daylight, we can destroy his heart."

"You said there were maybe seven of those creatures. There's only three of us. You come back here right now, Caxton. If you won't take an order from the Commissioner, maybe you'll take one from me. Come back right now."

Caxton looked from the armored vehicle back to the cornfield. She could still hear the stalks rustling, but the sound was growing faint. She didn't know what to do. She knew what Arkeley would do, however, in her situation. She knew exactly what he would do.

She pushed through the papery stalks and ran after the half-deads, her boots sliding in dark mud.

The fibrous leaves of the stalks slithered across her helmet and lashed at her exposed wrists. The thick stems of the stalks resisted her, and she was certain that if she didn't catch the half-deads soon she would trip and twist an ankle, maybe even break it. How stupid would that be, she thought, to cripple herself because she was so intent on revenge? After the third fall, catching herself on her hands in the clinging dirt, she forced herself to slow down. The half-deads couldn't be moving as fast as she did, could they? Weighted down by the coffin, their frail bodies just couldn't make that much speed. She pushed through a line of stalks with her rifle and it snagged, just for a moment, but enough to make her sway.

Her radio squawked. "This is the ART, calling headquarters. We need immediate clarification of a standing order," it warbled. It sounded distant and thin. She knew Captain Suzie wasn't coming to help, and the knowledge bothered her but couldn't stop her. She couldn't let it stop her.

Weariness rose in her, seeping into her bones. She had to accept the fact that she was working on no sleep, that she couldn't trust her body. Gasping for breath, she tore her rifle off the cornstalk and slung it over her shoulder. It was a liability in that close space.

Standing still, she looked around herself, trying to get her wind back, trying to get her bearings. She was well on her way to getting lost in the tall corn. Already she wondered if she could find her way back—there were no landmarks, no way to tell one patch of plants from another.

That kind of thinking didn't help her, though. She was so close. Shaking her head, she sucked breath into her body and refused to give up.

She raced down one row of cornstalks and quickly found what she was looking for, a swath of vegetation that had been crushed by the passing coffin. She moved alongside the track, keeping to a crouch, sure she was getting closer. Soon she could hear the coffin dragging on the papery corn trash that littered the ground. A moment later she heard the half-deads whispering, not more than twenty feet from where she stood. She couldn't quite make out what they were saying. When the sound of the moving coffin suddenly stopped, she stopped, too.

"Do you see her, is there sign of her?" one of the half-deads hissed. There was no reply.

Slowly, careful not to make a sound, she brought her rifle around to a firing position. She grasped the shotgun attachment slung under the barrel with one gloved hand and moved forward slowly, steadily, her boots making very little noise in the soft mud. Ahead, through the close-planted stalks, she could make out shadowy figures. She took a step closer and parted the corn with the barrel of her weapon.

Through the narrow gap she could see open space, an aisle cut through the field as a firebreak. The clearing was full of half-deads. They were standing around the coffin, their heads low. One of them stood atop the casket, probably trying to get a better view of where she was.

She pointed the shotgun attachment and yanked the trigger. The half-dead on the coffin flew apart in filthy rags and shards of broken bone. The others started howling and running around in terror. One ran right past her, close enough to reach out and grab. She let it get away—she had more important business at hand. She stepped into the firebreak and spun slowly around, looking to see if any of the half-deads had been brave enough to stick around. She didn't see any. She forced herself to ignore the coffin until she was sure she was alone. Then she bent to take a closer look.

It was a casket, as opposed to a coffin—unlike the hexagonal pine boxes the other vampires used, Reyes had switched up to a deluxe model, rectangular and appointed with turned moldings. It had been, once, a handsome assemblage of polished cherrywood. The brass handles had probably been bright and metallic before the casket had been dragged through acre after acre of soggy dirt. Now the wood was splattered with dark earth, so thick on one end it looked as if it had been dipped in mud.

She stepped closer and put a hand on top of the wooden lid,

half expecting to feel some evil presence beneath, but there was nothing. She remembered the cold feeling she'd gotten near Malvern, the absence of humanity. This could be the same. She licked her lips and tried to open the lid. Something held it shut. Well, she supposed that made sense. The half-deads wouldn't want it flapping open as they moved it around. She felt around the edges and found three nails holding down the lid.

She tried her radio but got no response. Had she run so far that she was out of range? It seemed impossible. She felt as if she'd run no more than a quarter mile. She looked around. She couldn't really remember which direction she'd come from. She didn't think she'd be able to find her way back—and even if she did, that would mean leaving the casket behind. The safe thing, the smart thing to do, was to accept that, to just head back, try to make contact with the ART, and hopefully bring the others to the casket. But it sounded like such an impossible errand. If she left the casket even for a few minutes, surely the half-deads would come back for it. Wouldn't they?

Her vision blurred for a moment and took its time sharpening up again. She was really going to need to sleep soon. As soon as Reyes was dead, she decided. As soon as she'd killed him. She took the clip out of her rifle and emptied out the bullets. The empty container had a sharp metal edge she could use to break the nails. She would probably ruin the clip in the process, effectively destroying the rifle. She still had her Beretta, which she placed on top of the casket where she could grab it at a moment's notice.

She slid the edge of the clip between the lid and the body of the casket and tried to saw at the first nail. The clip moved back and forth a few times before it slipped right out of the gap and across the back of her wrist, gouging her skin. Tiny flecks of blood spattered the casket and her breath caught in her chest. She expected to hear Reyes stir inside, that the blood would call him somehow. But the casket remained motionless, as if it were completely empty.

She didn't relish the prospect of looking inside and seeing the maggots, the bones, the deliquescent remains like those she had seen in Malvern's coffin. Still. Reyes's heart would be in there, dried and shrunken until she could crush it in her hands. She took up the clip and wedged it under the coffin lid again. She put her back into it and the nail broke, the wood shrieking as it came loose. The second nail parted almost instantly when she put some pressure on it. Sweat was collecting under her helmet and running down the backs of her ears. Her back ached, and she knew that when she stood up it would scream with pain. Just one nail left. She got the clip under the lid one more time, but before she started to saw at the final nail she closed her eyes and thought of Deanna, bloody and helpless on the kitchen floor. It gave her back some strength, to think of just how badly she wanted to destroy Reyes. The third nail came out in pieces, so that she had to hack at the wood to get it free. The lid was open; she could just throw it back and look inside.

Some basic fear possessed her and she stopped for a moment, goosebumps breaking out all over her arms. She stood up, and the stiffness in her back made her groan. She picked up her Beretta from the top of the casket and looked around for any ruined faces peering out of the corn. She didn't see anything.

The heart. She had to destroy the heart. With her boot she pried open the lid, kicked it wide. She raised her weapon and pointed it down into the red silk-lined interior of the casket.

Nothing. It was empty. In her fatigued state she could hear the vampire laughing at her, cackling in cold delight.

Then something cut her across the back of her legs, slicing right through her uniform pants and making her body sing with pain. She collapsed, falling forward, right into the casket. It all happened in the time it took her to switch off the safety on her pistol. The lid of the casket came down across her back and knocked her onto the upholstery. It had all been a trick.

35.

Light dripped into the casket from a crack where she'd damaged the lid. Otherwise she would have been trapped in total darkness. She tried to heave, to buck open the casket, but the half-deads were sitting on it, laughing at her. She heard them drive nails through the lid, sealing it shut again. She couldn't get any leverage to push against them—she could barely roll over. Her legs burned with a narrow edge of pain where she'd been cut. They would bury her alive.

She screamed to think of it, to imagine being buried under six feet of dirt. Already she could smell nothing but her own sweat and her own fear, the air in the coffin growing stale as it circulated in and out of her lungs. Every time it went out of her it had a little less oxygen in it. How long would it take to use up all the oxygen?

She screamed again, but it was no use. The only ones who could hear her would take delight in her distress. It didn't matter—she screamed a third time, and slapped at the padded lid of the casket, desperate to get free.

Her body slid around inside the casket and she realized the half-deads were dragging her away from the firebreak. She bounced painfully as the casket grated over ridges and furrows, broken cornstalks, stones half-buried in the ground. Caxton's heart raced and her breath came faster and faster. She couldn't stop it.

She could feel her Beretta flopping around at the bottom of the coffin. She must have dropped it inside when they'd cut her legs. She tried to reach for it but couldn't bend down far enough. The constriction drove home just how small her prison was, and she screamed again at the knowledge that she couldn't sit up, couldn't bring her knees up. Every muscle in her body twitched as it felt the constraint.

The casket jumped as it was dragged over some particularly large obstruction, and the pistol smacked her ankle with a smarting pain that turned the darkness around her green for a moment, an optical illusion born of exhaustion, panic, and physical pain. She tried to remember if the weapon's safety was still on, if she had chambered a round. If she had—if the gun was ready to fire—it could go off with the next bump. A cross point round could come out of its barrel faster than the speed of sound. It could shoot off in any direction, but a lot of those directions intersected her body.

Just one more thing to scream about.

She worked her hand down as far as she could. Her fingertips glanced off the hard edge of the gun's barrel, and she could feel the slickness of the metal. Her shoulder dug through the casket's upholstery, came up hard against the wood beneath. She lunged, and shoved, and tried to brace herself with her legs.

Another bump, a jostling bump that smashed the bones of her shoulder together and made her grunt in shock, but the Beretta slid half an inch closer. She grabbed it with her fingertips and drew it, millimeter by millimeter, closer to her palm. It kept trying to bounce away again, but she refused to let it go. Finally she had it in her hand. The weight and power of the weapon helped to calm her, made her breathe just a little easier.

"Yes!" she shouted, as she worked her finger through the trigger guard.

The casket stopped moving with a sudden lurch that wrenched her back. One of the half-deads knocked on the lid. Its voice, though muffled, was as irritating as ever as it asked, "Everything okay in there?"

She tried to figure out where the voice was coming from using just her ears. It was difficult—the acoustics in the casket were terrible, echoes rolling back and forth in the narrow space. She pressed the barrel of the pistol against the casket lid.

The half-dead giggled at her. "I'd get comfortable if I were you. It's a long—"

She squeezed the trigger, and light and heat and noise filled the casket in a wave of overpressure that made blood drip from her ears. She was blind and deaf, her hands were burning, and she realized what a terrible mistake she'd made. What if the shock wave from the explosion had ruptured her eardrums?

Her vision came back slowly. A slanting ray of weak sunlight poured through a nearly perfect circular hole in the lid of the coffin. She could see sky through the hole, the yellow of the dead cornstalks. Whether or not she'd hit the half-dead who had been taunting her, she didn't know.

The stench of cordite filled her nostrils and she wanted to retch, to stop breathing the fumes altogether, but her body knew better than her brain. It sucked deeply from the fresh oxygen coming in through the bullet hole.

For a long time nothing happened. The casket didn't move. She could hear her heart beating, but it sounded strange, deeper and slower than she'd expected. Then she heard a sound at last, a faint, twittering sound, a bird calling somewhere out in the corn. Her eardrums were intact.

The casket started moving again, bouncing and jumping over the rough ground, faster if anything than before. She held on as best she could, shoving her weapon into its holster and grabbing at handfuls of upholstery to keep from being thrown around. The slick silk kept slipping through her hands, and soon they ached from the constant exertion of just holding on.

Minutes passed, long minutes she could measure only by counting slowly to herself. Onnnnne, twooooo, threeee . . . she was certainly counting too quickly or too slowly, but she had no other way to mark time. Her legs continued to twitch, either from the wounds on the backs of her calves or from being compressed in such a tiny space. She did not know which.

The half-deads picked up the casket and carried her after a while. They moved more slowly than they had while dragging the casket through the cornfield, but Caxton didn't mind. The ride was a lot less bumpy.

Darkness closed over the bullet hole in the lid. They might have covered the opening with a cloth. She stuck her pinky finger through the hole, careful not to extend it too far, to not give the half-deads an excuse to grab it and do something horrible with it. She felt nothing out there but cool air. She tried again and again felt nothing.

The casket suddenly tilted forward at a very steep angle, and she slid up into the top half, her head jammed painfully to one side. She struggled to push her arms up past her shoulders, to push against the top of the casket with her hands and take the pressure off of her neck.

The coffin lifted and fell. Again it lifted and fell. Again, a moment's respite and then it lifted—to fall again. She realized what was happening. The bullet hole had gone dark because they were inside of a building. The lifts and falls came from the motion of the casket as the half-deads carried it down a flight of stairs.

She tried to count the risers but lost track every time the casket lurched. It was a long way down and she had lost track of how much time had passed. She felt as if she were floating unbound in space and then grasped tightly by enormous fingers, her body shaken violently by a giant spectral hand with each step down.

She didn't notice at first when the downward motion stopped. The half-deads set her down without any fanfare, the casket creaking on a stone or concrete floor. Then she heard their footfalls, and the echoes of their footfalls, getting softer as they walked away from her.

Then there was no sound at all.

She slapped the lid of the coffin again and again, but got no reply.

"Hello?" she said, willing to hear their squeaking voices if that was the reply she got. "Hello?" she shouted, wanting someone, anyone, to speak to her. Sure, she had shot at them, but wouldn't that make them want to taunt her even more? "Hey you fuckers!" she screamed. "Hey, calling all faceless geeks out there, somebody say something!"

She heard her own echoes but nothing more.

"You can't just leave me here!" she screamed hysterically. She knew they could do, and had done, just that.

36.

Caxton slept.

Somehow her body had given out, whole hours of panic had ebbed away, all force spent, and little bits of sleep had rushed in, dark breakers on the shores of a planet with no sun. Inside the casket her breathing had become more shallow, her eyes had rolled back in her head. She had slept.

If there were dreams in that dark slumber, she could remember little of them afterward. She had a sense of rolling over in blackness, of tumbling, of falling free through infinite lightless space. There was no fear in the dream, though when it ended she screamed, her body thundering around her, her pulse beating very hard. Her eyes fluttered open and she was awake, awake and lying silently on the upholstery of the casket. She cleared her throat and blinked her eyes and tried to reconcile where she was with waking life. It wasn't easy.

A tiny finger of light slipped in through the bullet hole in the casket lid. It was so pale and faint that she thought it might be a hallucination, but it grew stronger as she watched it. It danced and shifted from side to side and soon a sound came to join it, a repetitive slapping sound, a rasping two-part sound, slip slap, slip slap.

Bare feet walking on stone. And the light—it possessed the guttering motion and the warm yellow color of a candle flame.

"Hello," she breathed, but her throat was dry, painfully dry, so it felt like it was stuck shut. She tried to clear her esophagus, but nothing would come loose. She coughed and coughed and the footfalls stopped and she held her breath, wanting them to come back, terrified they would leave her alone inside the casket, even though she knew that whatever made that sound, whatever horror was approaching her, would not be a friend, or a rescuer, but a monstrosity.

The feet came closer and the light brightened. It moved to one side and then stayed put, as if the owner of the feet had set the candle down beside the casket. Caxton tried to breathe as calmly as she could.

The casket rocked back and forth as the unseen monster tore at the lid. It made no sound, no grunt or gasp. The nails in the wood shrieked and tore. The wooden lid came away altogether, air rushing into the casket, her eyes narrowing in even the minuscule light of the candle. She saw the ceiling above her, perhaps fifteen feet away, a vaulted mass of bricks held up by stout square columns. On either side she saw the walls of the cellar room lined with shelves, the shelves heavy with jars and cardboard boxes and rolled-up blankets. She had no idea where she was.

A pale face slid into view. She'd been hoping for a half-dead, but her hopes were dashed. She saw the round, hairless head, the triangular ears, the face of Efrain Reyes looking down at her. His eyes were dark slits, vaguely reddish in the flickering light. His mouth was heavy with all those teeth. She sensed that he had just woken himself, that he was still half asleep, as she was. Had night just fallen? Had she been in the casket for an entire day, alone with her dreams?

Reyes wore nothing but a pair of drawstring pants. His skin was a snowy white but with just a tinge of pink that made him look feverish instead of healthy. He leaned down closer until his face was eighteen inches from hers. She felt the same absence of humanity or warmth she remembered from when she'd stood next to Justinia Malvern. It didn't surprise her this time.

He stared into her eyes. She tried to look away, but he grabbed her chin and held her, as sure and steady as if her face were bolted to his hand. She would never have the strength to break that grip.

His eyes went wider and she saw red tears wash across his pupils, as if blood had replaced every fluid in his body. She saw his pupils grow larger and larger until they filled up half her vision. She had been hypnotized by a vampire before, but this was nothing like the paralysis she had felt then. That had been a general deadening, an anesthetic effect. This time she was quite conscious, to an almost painful degree, of what was being done to her. Something passed between them, from his mind into hers. It moved silently, invisibly, but it was something very real. It was all in her mind, certainly, but it carried with it a physical sensation, a very real, very unpleasant feeling of being invaded.

Caxton had never been raped. There had been a boy in high school who hadn't understood what she'd meant when she'd said she wanted to wait, to save it. She hadn't understood herself, really, and hadn't known how to stop him when he would shove his hands inside her clothing and grab her, grab handfuls of her flesh in a painful grip. One day after school when they'd gone back to her house, he had taken out his penis and rubbed it up and down on the back of her hand, begging her to turn her hand over, to grasp him the way he was always grasping her. The boy's need, his absolute desperation, had sickened her and she had pulled away. He had stood up next to the bed and loomed over her then, and she had been very much aware of the fact that they were alone together, that her father wouldn't get home until after six. "Suck it," he had said, his appendage dangling in front of her. "Suck it." His voice had been something broken, and sharp, and potentially dangerous.

She had resorted to tears, big sobbing tears of panic, and the boy had been so ashamed that he went away and never spoke to her again. It was the last time she'd tried to date a boy—six months later she'd met her first female crush and finally understood who she was. Whenever she thought of the boy now, she cringed.

What Reyes was doing, though, was violating her worse than any teenaged fumbling ever could. He was forcing himself on her innermost thoughts, her secrets, the deepest, darkest parts of her. He read her like a book, picking at her memories. He found the memory of the boy and the tears and she could feel he was amused. She could feel him just as if he lay on top of her, the cold waxiness of his skin, the faint heat of blood, the smell of blood all over him. She was under his control, completely. She lacked the will to fight him, or even to struggle, to try to get away.

After a while the vampire closed his eyes. The violation stopped instantly, but she could still feel him, some remnant of his intrusion inside of her skull. It made her brain itch. Vesta Polder's amulet hadn't done a damned thing to help her. The vampire reached down into the casket, presumably to lift her up.

She wasn't going to get a better chance. She lifted the Beretta to the level of his heart and fired and fired and fired again, the noise splitting the silence wide open, the muzzle flashes so much brighter than the candle that it was as if the sun had entered the room. Spent gas wreathed around Caxton's face like smoke, and the stink was oppressive. Her already battered ears rang, and the vampire snarled like a wild animal.

When she stopped firing he grabbed the smoking hot barrel of the gun in one of his hands and threw it into a corner of the room. Her shots hadn't hurt him. She remembered what Arkeley had said: with so much blood in him, a bazooka probably couldn't scratch his skin. She had succeeded in one thing, though. The part of him inside her head lit up with rage. She knew she'd pissed him off, she could feel his anger burning inside of her. He reached down with both hands, picked her up, and threw her against the wall.

Her back collided with wooden shelves, dry and dusty, which broke under her momentum. Glass jars bounced over her shoulders and head and shattered on the floor. The pain woke her up and bent her double at the same time, made her want to pass out even as it brought her fully to consciousness.

He was going to kill her, she thought. He would tear off her head and drink from the stump. Or maybe he would just punch her face in. There were so many ways he could destroy her. Tears squirted from her eyes and she could do nothing but be afraid. She couldn't even call out Deanna's name. She didn't have time to worry what Arkeley would think about the mess she'd made. She had no energy to spend on anything but fear.

He strode toward her on his muscular legs, his eyes wide with hatred. Then he stopped, right in the middle of the cellar room, and stared at her. She had no idea what he was doing, but she could sense he was in pain. His body shook for a moment, a single, awful heave, and then his mouth opened and a thick scurf of clotted blood slid out and dripped down his jaw.

Reyes dropped to his knees, the impact with the stone floor sounding like a thunderclap in the vaulted chamber. He coughed and choked and spat old blood onto the flagstones. He clutched at his chest and tore at the skin there with his vicious fingernails, leaving long pink trails across his pectoral muscles. He shook violently, then collapsed totally on the floor and lay there in his own sick.

Caxton could do no more than take a few breaths while she watched him curl around himself in pain. In her head the relic of him howled and she clapped her hands over her ears, but the sound was inside of her. There was no shutting it out.

Eventually he recovered from his fit. She hadn't moved an inch. He got to his feet, grabbed her around the waist, threw her over his shoulder, and started climbing up the stairs.

37.

Reyes wasn't going to kill her—at least not right away. He was still too full of undigested blood from the devastation of Bitumen Hollow. Whenever he thought of drinking her blood, his reaction was pure nausea.

She could feel these things in her own head. He had violated her brain and left something of himself behind when he withdrew, a relic, an image of himself. Now she could feel his thoughts. No words came across that channel, nor even images. She could feel his unnatural heart pounding, though, pounding hard to move all that sluggish blood around, and she knew how sick he was. She got little bits of him, little inklings and fragments of thoughts. It was a link, and it was enough for her to know his moods and some of his motivations.

He wasn't going to kill her, because that would be a waste of blood. She remembered that when Hazlitt had fed Malvern he had said the blood had to be warm and fresh. If Reyes killed her now her blood would go to waste. He couldn't drink it and he couldn't store it.

There was more to it, though. He wasn't going to kill her, because he wanted something from her. That scared her, but she was getting used to being scared. Caxton's fear reaction was becoming so familiar to her that she felt strange when she wasn't scared. She felt, when she was unafraid, that she must be missing something.

Reyes carried her up the stairs. On the way down, in the dark of the casket, those stairs had seemed to descend forever. They emerged at the top of the staircase into a vast open space surrounded on every side by thick walls. The concrete floor was cracked everywhere and green weeds sprang up from below. The scale and the emptiness of the place made her think of an abandoned factory, but then her eyes adjusted to the moonlight slanting in through the long windows and she began to make out details. Chains hung from the ceiling in great profusion. Molds and casting equipment littered the floor like the playthings of a giant who had outgrown the need for toys. The tall windows were broken in places, panes of frosted glass having been replaced by plywood or filled in with ventilating fans. In the distance, at the far end of the concrete floor, stood an enormous coke-powered blast furnace that must have gone cold decades earlier. A thirty-foot-wide ladle, an enormous reinforced cup that had once held hundreds of tons of molten steel at a time, hung before the furnace on one thick chain, the other having given way. The ladle's lip dragged on the floor, mired in a vast wash of hardened slag. Reyes's hideout was a defunct steel mill. There were a lot of them in Pennsylvania, mostly around Pittsburgh, but she didn't think she'd been carried that far. She could be miles from the cornfield where they'd caught her, or only hundreds of yards away. In the sensory failure of the casket ride she'd had no way to accurately measure distances. Her mind spun wildly, trying to figure out how far they'd taken her, to no avail.

At least she was somewhere, somewhere with light and sound so that her mind wasn't adrift in darkness. She studied her surroundings as best she could while being bounced around on the vampire's back. Reyes and his half-deads were using only one small corner of the vast cracked floor. The faceless minions had a good campfire going and had set up some furniture, old chairs and couches with springs sticking up through rotting cushions. Fifteen or so of them were gathered around the fire, watching the flames leap and dance, giggling amongst themselves at some unspeakable joke. They fell quite silent as Reyes approached. He tossed Caxton onto a mildew-stained easy chair and then squatted next to the fire. He made no attempt to tie her up or otherwise constrain her.

"If you're not—" Caxton started, but she stopped instantly as they all turned to look at her at once. All those mutilated faces unnerved her and made her think of her own mortality. "If you're not going to kill me, then I need to go to the bathroom," she said.

She was expecting the half-deads to mock her, and they did. Their whining, high-pitched taunts made her cheeks red, but she really did need to urinate.

"Pee in your fucking pants, bitch," one of the half-deads screamed. His skinned jaw flapped open in amusement. "Yeah, come on, do it, I want to see this. Pee in your pants!" He started chanting it over and over and some of the others joined in.

Reyes stood up and grasped the half-dead's head in one long-fingered hand, his shoulder in the other. The vampire twisted his hands and the half-dead came apart in two pieces. Reyes threw them both into the fire. The flames leapt high as the broken body was consumed and a stink of unwashed horror rolled over them all.

There was no more chanting after that. Reyes searched about in a pile of junk for a moment and came up with a rusted tin bucket. He tossed it to her and she caught it.

"Gee, thanks," she said, and walked away from the fire. The vampire didn't even look at her as she walked far out onto the mill's floor, well away from the half-deads. He didn't need to. She could feel him inside her head and she knew she would never get away from him again. He was with her even as she squatted over the bucket. She closed her eyes and tried to block him out, but it was impossible.

She left the bucket there and walked back toward the fire. It was brutally cold in the unheated mill, and she figured that it was better to get over her squeamishness toward her captor than it was to die of hypothermia.

A half-dead waited for her, a bag of fast food in his bony hand. She took it and realized just how hungry she was. She hadn't eaten in well over a day, and while adrenaline had confused her body into ignoring food for a while, it couldn't last forever. She opened the bag and found a cold hamburger and a flat, watery soft drink inside. The hamburger already had a bite taken out of it. She wasn't sure whether the half-deads had gotten the food out of a Dumpster or if one of them had taken the bite. It didn't matter. She devoured the burger and washed it down with the syrupy soda. Her lips were chapped, she'd been so thirsty.

With her essential needs met she climbed back onto the easy chair and wrapped her arms around herself. She wasn't sure what she was supposed to do next.

Fatigue sapped her energy for a moment and she had to blink rapidly to clear her head. She wasn't tired, not really—she'd slept all day. The feeling came back, a wash of listlessness that made her arms so heavy she had to let them fall at her sides. Her neck ached with the weight of holding up her head.

It was Reyes, she realized. The vampire was playing tricks with her mind. Maybe he was just showing off the power he had over her—or maybe he really wanted her to sleep for some reason.

She thought of the half-dead she had tortured and killed on her bedroom floor. He had told her of the *hechizo* they used to make Deanna break the window. It only worked in dreams, he had said. Dreams. You had to be asleep to dream. Whatever he wanted her for, he would use magic to get it, and his magic only worked if she wasn't conscious enough to fight it off. She scowled at the vampire. "I don't feel the least bit sleepy. I feel like staying up till dawn," she told him, "so I can watch you melt into a puddle of goo."

His reaction made her feel as if the force of gravity had been doubled. Her limbs dragged her down into the cushions of the chair, her body curling over on itself, her eyelids squeezing shut. She fought it and had just enough willpower to push it back, to stay conscious. It took everything she had. She knew that the next time he tried to pull that trick she wouldn't have the strength to resist.

He still hadn't said a word to her. Piter Lares hadn't spoken to Arkeley, either, when he dragged him back to his lair. Caxton wished she knew what that meant. She wished she knew what the hell was going on.

Reyes didn't look at her. Instead he knelt on the floor and pushed one of his hands deep into the fire. Immediate pain rushed through him and Caxton's body curled up in response. She felt only a fraction of what he must, but it was enough to make her gasp in agony.

When he pulled his hand out of the blaze it was dark with soot. Some flesh had burned off of his fingers, revealing narrow bones beneath. The flesh grew back over the space of a few seconds, but the soot remained. Reyes came stomping over to her and dragged his fingers across her cheeks and forehead. She tried to turn her face away, but his strength was beyond her measure. He could hold her perfectly still, so still she couldn't even wriggle like a worm.

His hands smelled like woodsmoke and burned meat. She sensed his impatience as he drew complex symbols on her face with the soot under his fingernails. He was writing a word on her face, she realized, a single word:

SUEÑO

It should not take so much work to make her accept the curse. A glance had sufficed in his own case, a chance meeting of the eyes. She was fighting too hard and it was taking too long.

"What curse?" she asked.

Reyes's eyes went wide. Apparently she wasn't supposed to have heard so much of his thoughts. He frowned and grasped her head in both of his hands. She tried to close her eyes, but he pried them open with his thumbs.

His red eyes bored down into hers like drills biting into soft wood. He tore her consciousness away from her as if he were ripping off her clothes. She couldn't fight. She could barely utter a meek protest, a hissing "No . . ." under her breath.

In a moment she was asleep.

38.

Darkness claimed her, darkness far more complete than what she'd experienced inside the casket. There was no ground below her, nothing on either side of her, nothing above her. She lay motionless, unaware, inert.

Then something changed.

Where before there had been no light, there was suddenly a light. A dim orange spark glowing all alone, stranded in the dark with her. It pulsed and flared yellow for a moment as if she'd breathed on an ember, but then it sank back into dull orange. She reached for it, tried to keep it alive because she knew if she didn't, if she didn't do anything, it would blink out of existence and she would be all alone again.

The spark grew as she poured her will into it. It grew and smoldered and she smelled smoke and she was glad. It became an ember, and then a pool of burning radiance, and suddenly it gave off enough light for her to see where she was.

She was standing in the mill, right where she'd been when

she fell asleep. The spark she'd thought she was nurturing was thirty yards away in the bottom of the half-collapsed ladle. It was more than just a little ember, she saw. It had just looked like that because it was so far away. It was a pool of molten incandescent metal, and it swelled as she watched. It swelled and deepened and soon it spilled out over the ladle's thick lip.

The liquid metal ran down channels carved in the floor. It filled up molds and etched lines of fire through the cracks in the cement. It gathered in great glowing heaps of slag, cooling and turning black only to be melted again by new waves of superheated metal as more and more spilled out from the ladle.

Red light glared on every metal surface in the mill. Black smoke filled her lungs and she coughed wildly. The surging metal threatened to engulf her, and she had to climb up on top of a huge mold before her feet burned off.

Clouds of red sparks filled the air around the ladle. Torrents of dark smoke obscured the ceiling just as the metal covered the floor, a lake of fire. The heat was intense—it made her eyebrows curl up and it singed her nasal passages. She could barely breathe.

"No," she managed to shout before the fumes filled her throat and choked her. She coughed and coughed until she couldn't speak anymore. "This isn't real. This is just a dream!" Though it was like no dream she'd ever had before. She revised her statement: "It's all in my head!"

It was true, and she knew it. But it didn't matter. If she fell into the molten iron she would still burn. Her skin would crisp and pull away from her muscles, her hair would catch flame. The pain would still be excruciating.

The liquid metal kept rising. Caxton grabbed at a chain hanging from the ceiling. The metal links were hot enough to scorch her palms, but she knew she would climb up the chain if she had to.

The air roared around her, a hydrocarbon wind of burning

iron. Her lungs grew dry and shredded inside her chest as she sucked in the air, trying to get one clean breath. Then her legs wobbled underneath her. Caxton tottered on the mold as it started to melt under her feet. The smoke in her throat made it hard to keep her balance as she kept coughing, a reedy, dry cough that hurt her lungs. She grabbed at the chain again and the metal burned her hand so badly that she pulled it away, pure reflex. Her arm swung out and pulled her off balance as her feet shuffled on the mold, trying to find purchase as the metal edged up to touch her boots—

—and she opened her eyes.

She was awake.

She was lying facedown on the floor of the mill, her cheek pressed against the cold cement. The ladle stood empty and cold at the far end of the open space. Behind her the half-deads were gathered around their fire, giggling away. How she had gotten so far away from them while she slept was a mystery. She heard a sound like running water and looked up.

Reyes stood a dozen feet away. The drawstring pants were down below his buttocks and he was relieving himself on a pile of old, rusted metal, pissing out not urine but blood. When he was done he pulled up his pants and strode over to where she lay.

She didn't have the strength to get up. She didn't have the strength to lift her face from the icy floor. She couldn't see any of him but his pale white feet. The toenails were thick and ragged. They looked as though they could cut through flesh like steak knives.

"You don't scare me," she managed to croak. She expected her throat to be scorched—she could still taste smoke in the back of her mouth. But of course that had all been a dream. "You were human, once. You were a sad little man who stayed home and jacked off to the bra advertisements in magazines—"

One of his feet moved backward, lifting off the floor. It

swung away from her, and then it came back. He kicked her right in the stomach and she wasn't ready for it. She felt as if her guts liquefied inside of her body and came swimming up her throat, pressing down against her rectum. She clenched down hard and somehow kept everything together.

"You had nothing. You were nobody," she cried. "Now you're even less. You're unnatural. The light of the sun melts you, you—"

He drew his foot back for another blow. She called out and he stopped, his feet spread on the cement, ready to kick her if she didn't say what he wanted to hear. She would gladly have said anything, anything at all, but she had no idea what the right words would be. "What time is it?" she asked, just trying to stall.

The foot went back and hit her once more. It was like being struck by a moving car. She felt bones give way in her chest. The pain surged upward, to her brain, and without warning she—

—opened her eyes and saw black smoke drifting along the ceiling. She looked down and saw the red glow of the burning metal once more. She was back in the dream.

In the few moments while she'd been awake her dream-self had been busy. Ignoring the searing pain in her hands, Caxton had clambered up a thick chain and hung suspended perhaps ten feet above the surface of the molten metal. With her legs wrapped around the chain and her arms holding her in place she was, for the moment, safe, but she didn't see many options for what to do next. Nothing of the floor remained visible—the liquid iron had flooded the mill until the molds and tools and all but the uppermost lip of the ladle were submerged in burning, smoking metal. The mold she had stood on before had melted and was no more than a black stain on the reddish-orange surface of the bubbling sea below. The lake of fire was still rising, too—she could see it climbing up the windows, a thick meniscus of darkly glimmering slag spreading across the brick walls as still more molten steel poured from the ladle.

There was no way to go but up, and little enough above her worth climbing toward. She tried to wake up. She tried pinching herself, grabbing a thick fold of skin at her waist and twisting it, hard. The pain screamed through her belly, but nothing happened. She pulled off one of her gloves and dropped it into the heaving liquid below. It struck the surface with a hiss and a gout of flame, then disappeared forever. She got her teeth into the sensitive webbing between her thumb and forefinger and bit down, hard. Harder. Hard enough to draw blood.

The pain didn't wake her up. In desperation she closed her eyes and tried to imagine it all away, tried to find her way back to the waking world through sheer willpower. Again, she failed.

She thought of the cold mill, the long-defunct mill of reality where the half-deads waited to taunt her, where Reyes kept beating the shit out of her. Did she really want to go back there, she wondered? Was it so much better than the burning mill of her dream?

Desperate, alone, barely able to see or breathe for the smoke, she clutched to the hot chain and sobbed. She couldn't handle it anymore. The dream world was a hell of fire. Reality was pain and torture. There was a third option, she knew.

She could just let go.

She tried to shove the thought away, to ignore it, but it kept coming back. It haunted her. She could just let go. Let go, and fall, and fall forever.

39.

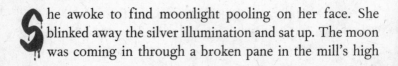

She awoke to find moonlight pooling on her face. She blinked away the silver illumination and sat up. The moon was coming in through a broken pane in the mill's high windows, painting a broad rectangular patch of floor with its light.

Caxton tried to stand up. It wasn't easy. Her midsection screamed with pain every time she moved, a tearing pain as if she were being pulled to pieces. Her legs ached where the half-deads had cut her the day before. Her head was full of ugly things and she kept having to snort and clear her throat and spit out bloody mucus. Some of the things in her lungs wouldn't come out no matter how much she blew her nose.

Slowly, mindful of her aching rib cage, she rose to her feet and looked around. Reyes was nowhere in sight. The half-deads and their fire were halfway across the mill. She had moved, or been moved, in her sleep until she was well out of earshot of her captors. Nobody was watching her. Nothing prevented her from running away.

She felt as if cold water was pouring down her back. It was impossible. She had been given a reprieve—somehow the vampire and his minions had just decided to ignore her. Did they think she was still unconscious, perhaps sleepwalking around the mill? Did they think that she was too weak to get away?

It was too good to be true—she knew that. It had to be some kind of trap, but she also knew she had to capitalize on whatever small freedom she'd been allowed. Keeping an eye on the half-deads around the fire, she hurried toward the wall of the mill. A pile of broken carts had been left there, miniature rail cars that had once moved ingots from one side of the mill to the other. The jagged wood and rusted wheels made a lot of noise as she clambered up to the top of the heap, but there was no way to silence them. The pile shifted under her feet and hands, but it was stable enough to let her get up to the bottom ledge of the tall windows.

She found a broken pane, an open space as wide as her hand filled with chicken wire. Shards of frosted glass still hung from the wire. She carefully brushed them away and looked out.

The moon lit up a rural landscape for her, a tableau of black trees swaying and bending in the cold wind. A vacant lot stood directly behind the mill, perhaps a parking lot once or a railyard that had been so overgrown by weeds it no long served any purpose at all. A few rows of fifty-gallon oil drums stood forgotten and skeletonized by rust directly below her.

There was no way out. She was perhaps twenty feet up in the air. Even if she could break the glass and somehow get through the wire, she would have to drop to an unknown surface and hope she didn't break her legs in the process.

Something moved behind her and she panicked and nearly fell off the heap of broken carts. She looked back and saw a group of half-deads in the center of the mill floor. They held torches and were muttering amongst themselves. They weren't looking at her, but they had to see her—didn't they? Maybe their vision wasn't as good as hers. Maybe she was overestimating them.

Caxton turned her face once more to the broken window. It was good, it was helpful, just to get a whiff of fresh air. In a moment she knew she would be discovered and put back to sleep. Just a glimpse of moonlight on trees was worth the effort.

She breathed in deeply—and nearly choked. The air outside was foul with the smell of baking manure. She turned away from the window and tried not to cough.

The half-deads were pulling on a chain hanging from the ceiling. The chain rattled through their skeletal hands and suddenly took on a life of its own. A counterweight descended quickly from the rafters as another chain shot toward the ceiling. A bundle wrapped in canvas was tied to the counterweight. Caxton was not surprised when the half-deads cut it loose and she saw it was a human corpse, a heavyset woman in the brown uniform of a UPS driver. She looked very pale, which meant she must have been drained of blood. One of Reyes's victims.

The half-deads laid her out carefully on the floor and unbuttoned her clothing but didn't remove any of it. It looked like they were trying to make her comfortable, strangely enough.

The vampire came out of the shadows then. He had been lying on a flow of hardened slag, a pale spot in the shadows. He had been no more than twenty feet away from her the whole time. Hope slipped away from Caxton like water down a drain. The whole time she'd been climbing the broken carts and sniffing the foul air outside, he must have been watching her. Well, of course he had. He wasn't stupid enough to let her wander around unsupervised.

He didn't so much as glance at her, though. He walked over to the corpse and touched the dead woman's chest with one of his hands. His hand pressed against where her heart would be. He stared deeply into her glassy, sightless eyes, and muttered something in his low, growling voice.

The woman's body started to twitch, muscles jumping here and there under her clothes. "Come back," Reyes said. He was calling her—literally calling her back from death. "Come back and serve me. Come back and serve me!" The twitches graduated into full-blown convulsions, her heels kicking against the floor, her head flopping back and forth like a fish cast up on a dry wooden wharf. Her body stiffened with the spasm and a sour reek split the air, similar to the manure smell from outside but much sharper and more pungent. The dead woman's hands curled into wicked claws as she reached for her face. Slowly, she sat up, while clawing again and again at the skin around her eyes.

She started to scream when strips of skin peeled off of her face, but she didn't stop gouging with her nails at her cheeks and forehead—if anything, her clawing grew more urgent. She was going to tear off her own face, piece by piece. Caxton was watching the birth of a new half-dead, a replacement for the one Reyes had thrown into the fire.

Reyes felt her disgust. The vampire turned to look at Caxton and for a long bad moment they just stared into each other's eyes. Caxton felt him squirming around inside of her head, almost as if he were rifling through the filing cabinets of her mind, looking for something and not finding it. The vampire was upset, angry, nervous—though as soon as she sensed those emotions in him he clamped down hard on the psychic connection they shared. Her body writhed as if she were touching a live wire. He looked away and Caxton's body collapsed backward onto the carts, her breath heaving in and out of her lungs. Her eyes fluttered closed and—

—she was back in the burning mill, still clinging to the chain.

She could hardly believe she hadn't let go yet. She wanted it, suddenly, wanted it very badly. She could visualize the whole process. Her body would fall for a few seconds through empty space. She would collide with the surface of the molten metal below. Her skin would burn off instantly. Her muscles and her flesh would take a moment longer. There would be pain. She was sure it would hurt beyond anything she had ever experienced. But only for a second. And then . . . what? Oblivion? Nothingness?

How tempting it was—how tempting to put everything behind her. She thought of her life even before she was imprisoned in the casket and how much of it had been utter misery. Working so hard for the approval of her superiors, the approval of Arkeley, the approval of her dead father. None of them had ever taken her seriously. Then there was Deanna, Deanna whom she loved so much, Deanna who was fading away while she watched. Deanna who had been vibrant and lively and sexy before, and now half the time couldn't get off the couch. Caxton would come home and find her there, wrapped up in a quilt, watching some celebrity gossip show on television. Or rather watching empty space, her eyes not even focused on the TV.

Caxton had vowed to save Deanna, to bring her back to life. But she was failing, she knew. If anything, Deanna was dragging *her* down.

The dogs—the greyhounds, her beautiful animals. They would miss her. They would howl for her. But somebody else would come along and feed them, and pet them, and soon enough they would forget. The whole world would forget Laura Caxton after a short season of formulaic grief. If she just ceased to exist, nothing, really, would change. Or rather, one thing would change. In the great balance sheet a certain amount of pain would be subtracted from the world. Wasn't that a good thing? If she had the opportunity to reduce the world's pain, by ending her own, wasn't that the *right* thing to do?

All she had to do was let go.

She took one hand off the chain, and somewhere, somewhere outside of the dream, she felt Reyes the vampire start to smile. She looked at her hand. He wanted her to let go. Reyes wanted her to end the dream.

It didn't matter. It didn't matter who wanted what. In a second she would be gone, erased from the world, and after that, who cared? Who cared if the vampires ate half of Pennsylvania? Who cared? She wouldn't be around to feel guilty.

She removed her other hand from the chain. The muscles in her thighs quivered as they were forced to support her entire weight. She started to lean back. So easy. So easy, and it would solve every problem she'd ever had.

Strong fingers clutched at her left wrist. She screamed, expecting pain, but the fingers just held her, they didn't dig into her flesh. They wouldn't let her fall. She tried to turn her head and see who was holding her, but it didn't work—her neck didn't bend that way. She couldn't see the fingers as they shifted their grip, closing like a pair of handcuffs around her wrist.

"You're not done yet," the owner of the fingers said. The

voice was quite soft and almost vanished in the furnace roar of the burning mill. She could tell, though, that the voice belonged to Arkeley.

40.

"Enough!" Reyes shouted, from somewhere, from nowhere. Everything stopped—time stopped, motion stopped. Caxton was all alone. The molten metal receded, draining away to reveal the mill floor once again. The steel still filled runnels in the floor, which provided some light, and the blast furnace still smoked and spat out great gusts of red sparks. But the heat became, if not bearable, at least survivable, and the air thinned out until Caxton could breathe without pain. The metal pouring from the giant ladle slowed to a trickle, and she climbed down her chain to stand on the mill's floor without being burned.

In one corner of the mill a trapdoor creaked open on rusty hinges. She walked toward the portal timidly, unsure of what was happening. She could see stairs leading downwards into darkness but nothing more.

On unsteady, tired feet, she stepped down onto the first riser. The stone step was cold against her bare foot, cold enough to make her toes curl. After spending so long in the conflagratory heat of the burning mill she'd forgotten what cold could really feel like. She took another step down and braced herself against the metal edge of the trapdoor. She was relatively certain that as soon as she descended far enough it would close after her with a tooth-loosening clang, or perhaps it would even snap shut when she was only a few steps down the stairs, closing like a mousetrap on her already-battered body. She wouldn't put anything past this nightmare.

"Laura, please, join me," someone said from down in the darkness. There was a lot of Central America in the voice, an accent she wasn't expecting. She took another step, and another. The trap didn't clang shut. Eventually she made out some light filtering up from below, yellow light that guttered like a flame in a mild breeze.

She walked down farther—and found that she knew this other room very well. A narrow vaulted space, the walls lined with shelves holding jars and boxes and rolled-up blankets. It was the same cellar storage area where she had first entered the mill. The place the half-deads had brought her in the casket. The offending piece of furniture was still there, its lid closed now. A candle in an antique holder stood at one end of the casket. Sitting on the other end was a man of average build and height. He wore a hooded sweatshirt (with the hood down) over an Oxford cloth white buttoned-down shirt. His skin was the color of walnut shells and he had a black roll of hair that looked carefully combed. He smiled at her and showed her a mouth of small, round teeth, very human teeth, but she knew this was Efrain Reyes. It was Reyes as he had appeared in life. Before he had died and become a vampire.

"When the mill was in use they would store borax and lime down here. That's what you smell," he told her. He patted the casket lid next to him, offering her a place to sit.

She hadn't smelled anything. The smoke from the burning mill had scalded her nasal passages and left her unable to smell at all. She didn't correct him, just sat down next to him. There wasn't enough room on the casket to sit apart, so she ended up touching him, hip to hip, arm to arm.

"I wanted to talk with you directly," he told her, once she was comfortable. "She advises against it." Caxton knew somehow he meant Malvern, that Justinia Malvern had made up the rules of this conversation. The information must have come through the part of Reyes inside Caxton's head. "This is all supposed to be done in silence. She even calls it the Silent Rite."

"You're in contact with her . . . right now?" Caxton asked.

Yes, she heard inside her mind, but he only shook his head. "I can't answer that." It was as if he wasn't aware of what she'd heard. As if he didn't know that their connection ran both ways. "I can't tell you anything until you've accepted the curse."

"Then what do we have to talk about? Because I refuse to . . . to do what you ask," she told him. She could no more do that than she could say the word out loud. "You'll have to kill me yourself."

"I'm not asking for anything. It has to be your own choice. You have to accept this thing to be one of us."

"I can't . . . I've seen Malvern, in her coffin . . ."

There was a rustle of silk behind her and Caxton tried to turn around, but she moved so slowly. Someone stood behind her, but no, there was nothing human back there. Finally she managed to turn enough to see that a woman had joined them. A female vampire, pressed up against the shelves as if she were holding on for dear life. She wore a long purple silk dress cut shockingly low in front, but fluffed out below with an honest-to-God hoop skirt. A powdered gray wig perched high on her bald head, concealing her pointed ears. She had a black satin eye-patch over one eye and clotted blood smeared around her lips.

It was Malvern. Justinia Malvern, as she must have looked when she was an active, well-fed vampire. An icon of strength and power. She didn't move, or smile, or speak. Her single eye studied Caxton without blinking. In that eye Caxton saw the truth that the strong appearance hid so well. Malvern was desperate. She was asking for help, and at the same time she was studying Caxton, trying to decide if she was worthy.

"She needs us, Laura. You can't imagine her suffering. We have to help her and to do that you need to become one of us. Your life is kind of pathetic, okay? I don't mean to be cruel." His voice changed as he spoke, the Central American accent coarsening, turning into a growl. Malvern vanished without warning, leaving nothing behind but a smell of blood that lingered in the air and slowly changed, almost fluidly, into the smell of baking manure.

Caxton didn't understand at first—then she slowly turned her head back to face him. The dream was over, and reality had returned. Nothing had changed. She was still sitting on the casket with him, and the only light still came from the flickering candle. He wanted her to think she was still in the dream—otherwise, why the subtle transition? But where he had been human before and fully dressed, now he wore only his sweatpants and his skin was whiter than soap flakes. She looked up and saw his bald head, his pointed ears. His mouth full of wicked teeth.

He had looked like an individual before, like a human being unique among all the others in the world. Now he looked just like the vampire she'd helped kill, the one Arkeley had destroyed with the jackhammer.

Congreve, she heard in her head. It was the name of the dead vampire. Reyes would never have volunteered as much, surely? Unless perhaps he didn't care anymore. If he was certain she was about to die, maybe.

"It's all up to you," he said, handing her something heavy and strangely shaped. She looked down, slowly, and saw that it was a handgun. Her own Beretta, in fact. "She thought maybe you would understand. That maybe you'd be willing to help? But this part's up to you. You lift that, and you put the barrel in your mouth."

Caxton frowned in confusion. Her hand lifted the weapon without any effort at all. Her muscles contracted to bring the pistol closer to her face. It would be harder, she knew, to put the gun down than to do as he said. She tried to call up the sense of oblivion she'd had in the dream. She tried to focus on how this one step would solve everything.

She wanted to please him. It startled her a little to realize it.

She'd tried to please and impress every authority figure in her life—her father, her superiors in the highway patrol, Arkeley. Why not the vampire who had taken such control of her?

"Come on, Laura. I've got other things to do, okay?" He didn't touch her or the weapon. "Most people figure this out pretty quick. When I saw her in her coffin, I got it right away. I knew what she was offering, and I knew I wanted it. It's immortality, Laura, and it's contagious! What a wonderful thing! Why are you holding back?"

Caxton hadn't thought she was. She thought she was being good. The gun kept coming closer, inching through the air toward her lips. Her teeth opened up. Her tongue pushed her dry lips open.

Her will and Reyes's will were fused together. She could feel him inside her like a worm burrowing between the hemispheres of her brain. Justinia Malvern had done this to Reyes, she realized, with just one look, by catching his eye for just a moment. The old vampire had raped the electrician from across a room in the time it took him to install a lightbulb. Now he was doing the same thing to her, using that same power. He had made Congreve and the other, the vampire who cut off his pointed ears daily. Reyes was an expert at this. How could she possibly hope to resist?

The handgun touched her lips. She felt the cold metal on her sensitive skin like an electric shock. Her eyes crossed as she looked down at the barrel. Just a few more inches. The weapon had only a few more inches to traverse and then she knew her finger would tighten on the trigger.

"Your mother did it. Your father smoked three packs a day, he understood," Reyes breathed. He was so close to her. He wasn't looking at her. "Your lover's well on her way. I did it without hesitation. It's not this hard."

Caxton's finger moved on the trigger. A tremor, a twitch.

Arkeley came down the stairs then, his feet making no sound on the risers. He came up behind her and put a hand on her shoulder. She couldn't see him, but she knew it was him. Just like in the burning mill. "You're not as fragile as you think," he told her. It was the nicest thing anyone had ever said to her. A nice, final thought to cap off her life.

You're not really here, she thought. But then she didn't understand—how could he be there, if she was wide awake? He'd appeared in her dream, but this, his presence in real life, was quite impossible.

As soon as she thought it he disappeared. His hand left nothing but a little warmth on her shoulder. Her own hand suddenly felt very, very heavy, and the gun fell away from her lips. It was still pointing at her flesh, but the barrel rested on her chest, just to the left of her sternum. If she fired, she would blow out her own heart.

"No," Reyes said, a huge noise in the little room. He moved fast, too fast for her to follow. The gun flew away from her, into a corner of the room, and her hand ached as if it had been slapped. "No. No, no, no. *Joder*," he moaned, "how are you so stupid? I don't have time for this." He looked at her then and his bloody eyes were filled with rage and hatred. His arm swung out and she flew off the casket and landed in a heap in the corner.

41.

Reyes got up and grabbed her hair in one enormous hand. He pulled her up, looking into her eyes, until she was standing.

"I thought the whole silence thing was *mierda* but I guess not. I want you to forget everything I said to you, okay? You forget everything and you sit right here and you don't move a muscle till I come for you again."

She nodded. She possessed no more willpower whatsoever. If he told her to stand on one foot and cluck like a chicken she would.

"Alright. Fine, damn it! You have to be so stubborn, well I can outstubborn you, *perra*. We'll start all over again tonight." He rubbed at his eyes and mouth in frustration and turned away from her. She expected that he would take the candle and leave her in the dark, that he would climb the stairs and leave her all alone. His destination, however, was a lot closer at hand. He opened up the casket on the floor and climbed in, leaving her to watch by the flickering light of the candle.

Day must be dawning outside, she realized. The night must be over.

The first night, anyway. How many more times would she be subjected to the dreams of the burning mill? How many nights would it take before she did shoot herself, before she did, finally, accept his curse?

A burbling, liquid noise came from the casket. He was so certain that she was safe, that she couldn't harm him, that he left her right there next to his deliquescing body. And he was right. She couldn't so much as twitch a thumb. To prove it, she looked down at her hands, at her right thumb. She prepared to will it to move, to pour all of her remaining psychic energy into making it jump just a little bit. A futile task, but one she felt she needed to perform before she just gave up. If she could prove to herself that even this, just twitching her thumb, was out of the question, then why should she fight even a moment longer? She would just do what Reyes asked of her. She started willing her thumb to move, but before she could really begin a voice out of nowhere startled her.

"What if it works?" Arkeley asked her. He was standing on the stairs, just out of sight. It was his voice, though.

What? she asked, unable to open her mouth. She could still think it.

"What if the thumb moves?" he asked. "What are you going to do then? Are you going to keep fighting?"

It was an absurd question. *You're not real,* she said, as she had said to him before. And just as before, it worked. He vanished. She felt a little bit pleased with her ability to at least control her own phantasms.

When he was gone she tried to return to the matter at hand, but it took her a long time to remember what she'd been doing. She couldn't seem to . . . to think right. Every time she would try to hold something in her head it would just fly away from her again. She was going to do something, she remembered. Something important. Some vital, last step. Yes. She was going to move her thumb.

She looked down at the thumb and thought, *Okay, if you can twitch, then twitch.*

The thumb moved. Just a little jerky spasm, a trembling almost. But it moved.

She looked up at the stairwell to see if Arkeley was there, ready to jeer, to ask her what happened next. He wasn't there, of course, because he'd never been there. He had not been real. But that didn't get her off the hook. What next? What did she do next?

Moving her whole hand seemed like a good idea. She tried to make a fist. Slowly, very slowly because she was so tired, the hand folded up into a weak fist.

She felt a very weird kind of anger. She'd really wanted her hand to disobey her, frankly. She was far more comfortable sitting there, doing nothing, waiting for Reyes to climb out of the coffin. But if she could make a fist, then she could probably stand up. And that meant she had to stand up.

"You'll need to do more than that," Arkeley told her. He was back, hidden somewhere, somewhere very close by, but not where she could see him. He was a presence in the room, but she couldn't have said where he might be. "You're going to need to open the casket."

She rose to her feet, taking her time about it. Not in any kind of hurry at all. If Arkeley had insisted she move more quickly, she would have banished him from her presence once again, maybe permanently. He didn't, though. He offered no encouragement nor any kind of derision. He was silent. But he was still there.

She shuffled over to the casket until she was standing right over it. She looked down at the scorched hole in the lid where she'd shot through the wood. A curling white maggot clung to the edge of the hole.

Caxton bent at the knees and got her hands under the lid of the casket. With one quick motion she threw it open. She was expecting what she found inside, but not so much of it. She saw Reyes's bones, just as she'd seen Malvern's skeleton, but where Malvern's flesh had been reduced to a quart or two of pasty glop, Reyes's casket was half full of the viscous soup. Well, he had a lot more flesh to liquefy than Malvern did. Some of the long bones floated near the top, with whole colonies of maggots clinging to their knobby protrusions. The skull was at the bottom, fully submerged, staring up at her with its lower jaw hinged wide.

"You have to take the heart," Arkeley told her.

She turned around, looking for the Fed. He was so close she could feel his body heat. Just like she felt the cold absence of Reyes's humanity. She couldn't see Arkeley, though. He was just in her head. She was careful not to say as much, though. Saying anything like that seemed to make him disappear, and she knew she could use his advice.

"Take the heart," he told her again.

She looked for the heart but couldn't see it. It wasn't floating near Reyes's spine, nor had it bobbed up out of the bottom of the rib cage. There was something shadowy at the bottom, resting on the silk upholstery of the casket. Something dark that wasn't a bone. She started to reach for it, then stopped. She didn't know if she could reach through the liquefied flesh.

"You twitched your thumb," Arkeley told her. "You promised yourself that if you did that, you would keep fighting. This is the only way."

She closed her eyes and plunged her arm into the casket. The liquid clung to her, sticking to the hairs on her wrist and forearm. She felt a bone bump against her skin, rough and terrifying. Maggots crawled on her skin, inching their way up her arm. She wanted to scream but was still too foggy to make a sound. If she hadn't been half-hypnotized, she knew, she would not have been able to take the heart.

In her semilucid state, though, she felt her fingers close around the shadowy organ and lift it free. The organic broth that was Reyes's daytime body dripped from the heart. It splattered her shoes. The heart itself was writhing with maggots. She tried to shake them off, but it didn't work—they clung tightly to it. The muscle in her hand pulsed gently against her palm, an almost imperceptible ticking rhythm. It told her she wasn't finished.

She looked around at the shelves. Reyes had said the vaulted cellar had once been used to store lime and borax, and now that she was half-awake she could, in fact, smell them, a sort of alkaline bite in the air. At some point the cellar had been converted into a general storehouse, however, and the shelves were full of all manner of things. There were jars full of nails, bolts, and other hardware. There were camping supplies and spare candles and box after box of materials data safety sheets, government-required forms that explained what chemicals were present in the mill and how toxic they all were.

She took the biggest jar she could find and emptied it into the mess in the casket. She crumpled a dozen or so sheets of paper and pushed them into the jar, careful to leave room for air to circulate. She'd been a Brownie once and she'd been camping enough times to know how to make a fire.

The candle Reyes had used to illuminate the cellar was guttering low when she was ready, but it only took a moment to light her makeshift fire starter. Bright orange flames dripped down the sides of the jar. The paper blackened and crumpled quickly, but she had plenty to work with and kept stuffing more and more inside. Then she dropped the heart into the jar.

She'd expected to have to feed the fire for hours as the wet heart dried out. Muscle tissue, especially the heart, was notorious for being hard to burn. This was not true of a vampire's heart. It might as well have been made of paraffin—it burst into flames instantly, blue flames so hot they shattered the glass jar and spat flaming refuse all over the cellar.

In the casket Reyes's skull floated to the surface, the jaw wide in a scream Caxton heard just fine, a drawn-out, horrified scream. The scream of a creature being burned alive but unable to roll or run or get away from the flames.

And that was it. She had expected—or hoped for—something more dramatic. After a few moments, though, the skull sank back down into the goo and was still once more. The scream in her head faded but remained, a distant sort of musical tone. It never quite disappeared, but it was swallowed up in the background noise of her own head.

"Don't feel bad for him," Arkeley told her.

She coughed to find her voice. "I don't. This son of a bitch raped me. Even now he's inside of me. I'm glad he can feel this."

She knelt down next to the burning heart and watched it shrivel and fall to pieces. When it was nothing but orange embers, when the screaming had stopped, she picked up a smoldering piece of the heart with a rolled-up piece of paper and tossed it into the casket. The liquefied flesh inside went up like a fireball and cheerful little lines of fire ran across the wooden molding on the casket's lip.

"What are you going to do next?" Arkeley asked her.

"I'm going upstairs," she told him, because it was just that simple. But first she paused to find her Beretta. It felt very good, and very important, in her hand.

42.

A pair of half-deads were standing near the trapdoor. They were carrying a coffin between them, a plain wooden box that might once have held tools but that was just about human-sized. The coffin was meant for Caxton, for her vampiric rebirth.

One of them wore a chrome Kaiser helmet. He had been a biker four days earlier, a massively built tough guy with a penchant for leather and grease. Reyes had taken him while he had stopped at a pay phone. Nobody remembered who he was going to call. "It can't be much longer now," the half-dead said, his voice high and shrill. He rubbed his skeletal hands together until bits of dried-up flesh flaked off. "The sun is almost up."

The other half-dead shook her fleshless head. "The sun. I didn't think I'd ever see the sun again. I would have paid cash money to see it and now . . . Jesus. What am I? What did he make me into?" she asked. She sounded confused and more than a little scared. Reyes had found her jogging just before dawn, out on a lonely rural road still carpeted with the night's haze. She had tried to run, but Reyes had been faster. "This is . . . this is hell. I'm in hell, I must be."

"Don't be so quick to write this off," the biker told her. "It's got its good points."

The female half-dead turned to look at her companion.

"Good points? Spending the rest of time as an undead freak with no face has an upside, is that what you're telling me? I can't eat, I can't sleep. My body is falling to pieces while I watch, literally corroded by contact with the air. Where the hell is the silver lining in this?"

"Well," he told her, "it only lasts about a week."

Caxton stepped out of the shadows then, a five-foot-long bar of solid iron in her hands. She brought it around in a sweeping blow that knocked the faceless head right off of the former biker's neck. His stringy body slowly collapsed to the floor.

She turned to face the other one, the female. The half-dead backed away from her, arms outstretched, begging. In a moment she was out of range and the heavy bar was an unwieldy weapon at best. Caxton threw it at her and winced as it clanged and rattled and banged on the concrete floor, well short of its target.

The half-dead turned and ran on wobbly legs. Caxton ran after her and caught her easily. She grabbed the female's hand and tore it free, threw it into the dark corner of the mill. She grabbed the left arm and it came off with barely any pulling at all.

The half-dead screamed and screamed. Finally she collapsed to the floor. Caxton stamped on her head with both feet until the screaming stopped.

She took a moment to breathe, just breathe. She stood alone in the darkness of the mill. The vampire was dead.

"You still need to get out of here alive," Arkeley told her. She'd stopped looking for him. He was nearby, that was what mattered. "All that noise will bring the others."

She nodded, accepting that he was right. She checked her Beretta. She had three bullets. There were at least thirteen half-deads still active in the mill. She couldn't take them all on at once. She couldn't take more than one or two at a time—she'd only prevailed against the biker and the jogger through the element of surprise. Her arms were shaky with stress and horror. She'd barely been able to lift the iron bar.

Okay, she thought, so if you can't fight, then run. The trouble was, she didn't know what direction to head in. The fire from the night before had burned out and the mill was filled with darkness, great clotted heaps of it. There had to be an exit from the mill, a doorway leading out into the day, but she had no idea where to find it.

"If you can't decide, head for the nearest landmark. That'll at least help you get your bearings," Arkeley told her. She turned and headed into the depths of the mill, toward the ladle and the cold-blast furnace. The sun had smeared a little white light on the tall windows and she could make out a few details here and there. She could see enough that she didn't trip over the piles of junk or the ankle-high molds that littered the floor.

She saw torn faces floating in the gloom, bodies swimming toward her out of the dark. She felt skeletal hands reaching for her. One touched her side, the wasted muscles of a half-dead hand closing on the fabric of her shirt. She swung her elbow backward, hard, and the hand fell away with a high-pitched squeak.

Ahead of her a red ruin of a face floated out of the gloom, and she raised the Beretta and fired as the half-dead's arms came up to grab her. The half-dead cracked apart and exploded, but that left her with only two more rounds. She ducked under the attack of another half-dead and ran around the side of the ladle. Ahead she saw a pair of double swinging doors. A thin line of bluish light sneaked in beneath them. She ran at the doors and threw her arms out to hit the pressure bars. The doors screamed open and she burst out into a courtyard enclosed by high brick walls on every side. Yellow grass burst from the ground all around her. She saw workbenches and old tool racks but there was no way out.

She was trapped.

At least there was blue sky over her head. At least she was outside. She smelled the baking manure smell of Kennett Square and knew she couldn't be far from help. The southeastern region of Pennsylvania was pretty heavily developed. If she could just get out of the courtyard she would be free.

There was no exit, however. No way out. She'd run right into a dead end. The walls on every side were solid, unbroken. They were too high to climb.

The double doors rattled and a half-dead poked its skeletal head out into the open air. She raised her pistol and it ducked back inside. "Arkeley," she said, "what do I do?"

He didn't answer. Maybe he had no better ideas than she did. She had two bullets and maybe ten or twelve half-deads chasing her. She had no time.

Caxton grabbed the rough edge of a wooden table—really just a big sheet of plywood nailed to some sawhorses—and dragged it toward the far wall. She jumped up on top of it, but she was still about seven feet too short to grab the top of the wall.

The double doors started moving again. One inched open, scraping on the uneven ground. She stared at it, almost as if she were hypnotized again, unable to move. If all the half-deads came out, if they were armed even with just knives or clubs, she was dead. She couldn't fight them all off.

"They're cowards," Arkeley told her. His voice was very soft.

"What?" she asked, but she understood. "I only have two bullets," she pleaded with him, but she knew perfectly well by that point that he was just inside her head. That he was her own survival instinct, compartmentalized, made abstract.

She waited a moment to let the half-deads get clustered, and then she fired both shots right into the crack between the two doors. She heard one high-pitched scream and a lot of excited shouts. Good enough. She shoved the empty gun into her holster. Then she jumped down and grabbed another work table, then a pile of two-by-fours. Soon she had a rickety heap of wood that looked like it might collapse under its own weight, much less hers. She stared up at the tottering pile and thought there was no way she could climb it, no way she could then jump from the top of the assemblage and grab the lip of the wall.

She knew what Arkeley would say. You only have to do it once, and if you fall and break your neck, it won't matter for very long.

With hands that shook badly, she hauled herself up the makeshift scaffolding. She got her feet on the top level, an over-turned wheelbarrow. She put one foot on a wheel and it spun away from her. Carefully, her body trembling like grass in the wind, she got to the top and launched herself up the side of the wall. The heap collapsed beneath her, leaving her ten feet up in the air with no support.

One of her hands found the top of the wall and clamped on, hard. Her other hand swung free, but she fought her momentum and made it grab the wall as well. Then she heaved, pulling her own weight up onto the top of the wall. From up there she could see that the courtyard was surrounded by mill buildings on three sides. The fourth side fronted a country lane. A road—which had to lead somewhere. It had to lead to safety. There was a fifteen-foot drop on that side. She didn't let herself think about it, just lowered herself down as far as she could with her arms and let go.

The ground came up very hard and very fast. It crushed the wind right out of her, making her broken ribs sing a high plaintive howl of agony, but the rest of her seemed okay. No broken limbs, anyway. She rolled to her feet and started running down the road, intending to flag down the first car she saw.

She was free.

His thoughts were red thoughts and his teeth were white.

—Saki, Sredni Vashtar

SCAPEGRACE

43.

They had a shower in the back of the local cop shop, with fresh towels and good soap and everything. It wasn't too surprising—the local chief of police was a woman. Caxton was a little disappointed not to find a bathtub, though she supposed that wouldn't be too professional. She spent a lot longer getting clean than she probably needed to.

While disrobing she found Vesta Polder's charm still hanging around her neck, grimy with her sweat and dirt. She cleaned it off, held it up to the light, and didn't see anything different than she had before. It was just a spiral of metal, cool to the touch. Whether it had helped her or failed her she had no idea. Maybe that was how such things worked. Maybe it was entirely psychosomatic, or maybe it had been the only thing that saved her from Reyes's domination. She imagined she would never know.

By the time she'd finished cleaning up, the paramedics had already arrived to take a look at her. They told her she'd been very lucky, that her ribs were merely sprained, not broken, and would heal nicely in a week or two. She had a lot of minor lacerations and contusions, which they painted with antiseptic and dressed with bandages before going away.

Caxton put on the street clothes the chief had offered her, which were only a little too big, and sat down in the break room with a yellow legal pad. She started to write down her story. Caxton had never been very good at long reports. They always made her think of writing papers in her abortive attempt at college. Still, she told the story as plainly as she could, with as much detail as she could remember. She stopped only when Clara arrived.

Clara. Caxton had asked specifically for the sheriff's photographer to come and drive her home. She had called Deanna, but mostly just to make sure she was okay. Deanna was still in the hospital and couldn't come for her. Caxton told herself that Clara had been her second choice. When Clara came into the break room, though, Caxton knew better, just by the way she felt seeing Clara again. She held out one bandaged hand and Clara took it, then came closer and stood there for a moment before awkwardly leaning down and kissing Caxton on the top of her head.

Warmth—stemming from both embarrassment and other causes—spread through Caxton's face and down her neck.

"We thought you were dead," Clara said, her voice a little shaky. "We looked all night. Somebody called me yesterday morning because . . . because they thought I would want to know you were missing, and I came right away and joined the search party. We looked everywhere. We even checked out that steel mill, but it was all locked up. Oh, my God, I looked that place over myself and I didn't see anything."

"Don't be too hard on yourself," Caxton heard Arkeley say. "They're masters of concealing their hiding places. They have charms to confuse the mind, especially by moonlight."

"He insisted on coming along," Clara said.

Caxton frowned. She wanted to ask what Clara meant, whether Clara had heard Arkeley's voice as well, but then the Fed walked into the break room and sat down on the edge of the table. Caxton slowly realized he wasn't just in her head anymore. It was the real Jameson Arkeley, vampire killer.

It was truly weird to see him again. She had internalized him, made his personality part of herself, and it was the only way she had survived being Reyes's captive. He had come to represent something vital and necessary to her. The flesh-and-blood Arkeley, by comparison, was someone she didn't necessarily want to see.

She sighed. She had so much to tell him, though. So much he had to hear.

"Special Deputy," she said, "I need to make a report to you."

His face contorted, the wrinkles all running in one direction, then another, as if he couldn't decide whether to smile or frown. He finally settled on a pained-looking grimace. "I've already got the Cliff's Notes version. You killed Reyes."

"I waited until dawn and then I burned his heart," she said.

"Unnecessary understatement is almost as bad as pointless embellishment."

She stared up at him, her face devoid of any emotion. What she had to say was going to be important to him. "He tried to make me one of them."

Nobody moved or spoke after that. Nobody dared break the silence until Arkeley reached up and rubbed the back of his neck with one hand. "Okay," he said. "Tell me while we drive."

She expressed her thanks to the local chief and they headed out back to where Clara's personal vehicle waited. It was a bright yellow Volkswagen, a New Beetle with a flower vase built into the dashboard. It was a lot like Clara herself—tiny, cute, and from a whole different world than the one Caxton inhabited. A world she could visit for a while but would never be allowed to stay in. The vampires would make sure of it.

Caxton crawled into the back while Arkeley took the front passenger seat. His fused vertebrae trumped her sprained ribs, he announced. She leaned forward between the front seats and told him about her ordeal. Clara drove not west, toward Harrisburg, but southeast, back toward Kennett Square. Nobody bothered to tell Caxton why, and she was too busy talking to ask.

"He used the Silent Rite on me, or at least that's what Malvern calls it. Just one of a long list of what she calls *orisons*. Reyes called it a *hechizo*." She didn't mention how she'd learned that word, how she'd tortured a half-dead by pulling his fingers off. She didn't want Clara to ever know about that. "It's a spell, or maybe some kind of psychic power. Either way, it's a violation of the brain. He shoved part of himself in through my eye sockets and took total control of my dreams. He could make me fall asleep against my will, and he kept me in and out of the dream state. He showed me a vision of hell, I guess, and waited for me to commit suicide."

"Hmph," Arkeley said.

"Something you want to add?" she asked.

He glared back at her with eyes wide, as if she'd forgotten her place. She supposed she'd never used that tone with him before. It made her want to say "Hmph" herself.

"I've studied every vampire I've killed," he told her. "It's central to the curse. In Europe every suicide was questionable. They used to have to bury suicides at crossroads, the thinking being that the vampires would be lost when they rose and wouldn't know the way home. In other times, in other places, they buried suicides with their heads cut off and turned upside down or fired a bullet through the heart."

"A silver bullet?" Clara asked.

"That's a myth," Arkeley and Caxton said at once. Another opportunity to glare at each other.

"The curse drives you to take your own life. Once it's in you the thought starts gnawing at you. You start thinking that all your problems would just go away if you were dead. That's the last step in the change, and it's necessary. He was very clear on that."

"Reyes went through this same process, most likely," Arkeley asked, voice neutral, just looking for data. "And Lares, and Malvern before him."

Caxton shook her head. "No. Reyes didn't require any of the dream magic bullshit. He already wanted to die. Malvern looked into his soul and he said yes, just like that. Congreve— that's the vampire we killed together—took about three hours to convince. Reyes did him and the other one, the one with docked ears. Congreve was a construction worker. That's why he picked that site for his ambush. He had a master's degree in Renaissance music but couldn't find a job with his degree, so he ended up working construction on a highway project. He hated it, hated everything about his life. Reyes capitalized on that and convinced Congreve to blow his own brains out. It was too hard for Malvern to make happy, healthy people into vampires, so she went looking for real losers. People with nothing to hold them to life."

"Jesus," Clara sighed. "I feel that way half the time."

Arkeley ignored her. "The other one. With the mangled ears. Do you have a name?" he asked.

Caxton thought about it for a second. She bit her lip. It suddenly occurred to her for no reason at all that Clara trusted her and probably wouldn't even try to stop her if she just reached forward and grabbed the steering wheel and gave it a quick yank to the right. They were driving along the wooded bank of a dry streambed that ran maybe thirty feet down. The New Beetle would crumple like a soda can when it hit the rocks down there.

She sat back in her seat and pressed her knuckles against the sides of her head and pushed the thought away. It wasn't her thought, though it had felt like any of the million other things in her head. It was Reyes, the part of Reyes that had colonized her brain. His curse was still trying to destroy her.

"Scapegrace," she said, coughing out the name. She had to fight to make Reyes let it go, but once she had the name she had the whole story. "Kevin Scapegrace. He was sixteen years old. Tall but skinny, too scared of his high school to get decent grades. The kids at school picked on him. One of them, an older boy, raped Kevin in the showers during gym class. Kevin was pretty sure that made him gay, and he couldn't live with himself anymore." Caxton's mouth hardened into a tight snarl. "He'd swallowed a bottle of aspirin when Reyes found him. Reyes sat with him while the half-deads raided a drugstore. They brought back a bottle of Valium, and Kevin took that, too. Kevin didn't really understand what he was being offered. He accused Reyes of raping him, too, and now he hates what he's become."

She looked up and saw Arkeley staring at her. Clara kept glancing back over her shoulder, and her eyes were tougher to meet. They were full of confusion and worry and a little fear.

"Reyes told you all that, before you killed him?" Arkeley asked, softly, as if he knew the answer already.

"No," Caxton replied. She suddenly wished Clara wasn't there. She licked her lips. "No. After."

Arkeley nodded patiently. Damn him. He was going to make her say it out loud. He was going to make her say it in front of Clara. "And how is that possible, Trooper?"

Caxton closed her eyes. "Because he's still inside my head."

44.

Clara drove them into the electrical substation, the same place they had originally thought Reyes was using as a lair. It might have been a completely different place the second time. For one thing, she arrived in a car about half as big as the Granola Roller, with no armor and very few weapons. For another thing, she knew the place was empty. Empty of everything except ghosts, anyway.

Clara stayed in the car while Arkeley led Caxton into the depths of the substation. The day was starting to cloud up and the air had a bitter chill to it. It might snow soon, she thought. As they walked between the switch towers Arkeley gave her a moment to pull her coat tighter, then started in with the questions.

"You can feel him in there? Even though he's dead?"

She shrugged, pulling her collar close around her neck.

"It's difficult to describe. There's a chunk of him in my head. I get thoughts that I know belong to him, not to me. I can access his memories as if they were my own."

"Does he tell you to do things? Do you hear his voice?"

She almost tripped over her own shadow. No, she didn't hear Reyes's voice. But she had heard Arkeley's, even when he wasn't there. She wasn't sure if that made her crazy. "He's . . . passive. It's like he's gone to sleep in there. Unless I want something from him he keeps to himself. If I do want something, like when you asked me about Kevin Scapegrace, then he wakes up and we fight. I'm winning, so far."

Arkeley looked like he could have spat. He didn't, he was far too cultured for that, she knew. "When Scapegrace and Malvern are dead we'll take you back to the Polders. They'll know how to get him out of there."

"Seriously?" she asked. The offer was almost kind, something she didn't expect from Arkeley.

"When Malvern is dead, yes."

She frowned. "I thought you had a court ruling saying you couldn't just kill her. She can't be executed."

"Not unless she breaks the law. It's hard to murder anyone when you can't climb out of your own coffin. If I can get some evidence that she conspired with Reyes and Congreve and Scapegrace, though—if I can pin Bitumen Hollow on her, do you think any judge in this state will refuse me that pleasure?"

Caxton frowned. She felt a lot of clues fall into place, as if jigsaw puzzle pieces had fallen out of the box and landed perfectly aligned with one another, their tabs already interlocked. She had something. "That's what this has all been about," she said.

"Don't oversimplify things."

"Oh, I think that's your job, and I wouldn't dare to step on your toes. For twenty years you've kept this case perfectly black and white. No matter what it takes, no matter who says not to, you've always wanted to kill Malvern. To finish the job you started in Pittsburgh." He didn't stop her. She went on. "You can't stand the fact that she survived. That you had a chance to destroy her but through simple chemistry she just didn't burn as fast as the others. You can't stand the fact that you failed. When the court ruled on her, when they said you couldn't kill her—that ate you alive, didn't it? You have a wife. Vesta Polder said you had a wife. Do you have kids?"

"Two. My son's in college, up at Syracuse. My daughter's an exchange student. She's in France." His face fell. He wasn't even looking at her—his eyes were turned up as if he were reading a note scribbled on the inside of his skull. "No," he said, "Belgium."

"You really had to work for that." She was being cruel, but she figured Arkeley could take it. "This case is all you have. It's your life's work. That's why you're such a hardass about it. Why you don't let anybody help you, because you won't share the eventual glory."

"I work mostly alone, that's true. It keeps other people from being killed. If you had slept in yesterday the way you were supposed to—"

She stopped him. "What's your son's major? At Syracuse."

He didn't try to answer. He didn't turn to upbraid her. He just trudged onward, toward the switch house.

"You'll do just about anything to get the goods on Malvern, won't you?"

"Yes," he said. "Anything." He pulled open the door of the switch house as if he wished he could tear it off its hinges. He turned on a flashlight and handed it to her. He had one of his own. They stepped inside, into almost perfect darkness. Only a diffuse yellow glow came in through the mullioned windows, a dull radiance that illuminated nothing. Caxton played her flashlight beam over massive constructions of coiled copper wire and varnished wooden switches as long and thick as her arm. They were as ornate as bedposts. They had to be the original circuit breakers from when the substation was opened a century earlier.

"What are we doing in here?" she asked. She shone her light on the floor and saw a trapdoor set in the cement. Just like the one at the steel mill. She didn't want to go down through it. She really didn't want to. "What's down there?"

He pointed his flashlight at her face. "You tell me," he said, his voice totally blank.

Maybe he was just being cruel to get back at her for questioning his private life. Maybe he really wanted to know.

"We were right, weren't we?" she asked. "Reyes did use this place as a lair. Before he moved to the mill." That much was guesswork. For anything more she needed to ask the vampire in her head. She sighed and closed her eyes. Arkeley moved his light away and she was in total darkness. She reached down into the darkest corner of her brain—and felt a pale hand grab for her. It was just a metaphor, though, and she easily slipped out of the ghost's grasp. "He spent a lot of lonely nights down there. Thinking. Planning. This is where he decided to trap one of us. Malvern didn't like the idea, but he thought it would be funny. He also knew that you and I were responsible for Congreve's death." She opened her eyes, but all she saw were colorful spills of light, phosphor afterimages. The things the eye sees when there is no other input. "He told Malvern he wanted to catch one of us and take us apart. It would be funny, and it would make them safe again. I imagine he probably would have preferred to get you, since you were the one who did the actual killing."

"Imagine again," Arkeley said. His clothing rustled as he moved in the dark. He lifted the trapdoor and she heard echoes roll up from below.

She pointed her light down the stairs and forced herself to

proceed. At the bottom she stood in a wide space full of damp air that smelled of mildew and decaying leaves and something fouler but fainter. She swung her beam around and saw bodies.

Dead bodies—lots of them. It was worse than the hunting camp. These bodies hung from the ceiling by their feet, their arms dangling down, water running across their fingers to the floor. They were fixed to the walls, held in place with giant iron staples that had rusted over time. They crouched in the corners as if hiding from the light, as if they would raise their rotting arms to protect themselves if she approached. They were wired in place, held in position.

In the center of the room a pair of bodies took pride of place. They were clearly meant as the masterpiece of the collection. They were both female and their skin was pale white, mottled with dark spots where fluids had gathered after they died. One was missing an arm, but otherwise they were still intact. Their hair had been yanked out of their scalps. They were locked in an intimate embrace, kissing.

No, no they weren't. Caxton moved closer for a better look. They weren't just kissing. Their lower faces had been fused together, the lips and teeth cut away so they were like Siamese twins joined at the mouth.

"Tell me if I'm wrong. But I think he wanted to capture you, specifically," Arkeley said. "I think you turned him on."

The sight failed to make her sick. She wanted to throw up, but her body wasn't in the mood. Her emotions weren't altogether her own. She wanted to have a visceral reaction to that much death. Reyes wouldn't let her. He was proud of what he'd achieved. And whatever he felt, she felt too. Seeing the bodies brought him back to life, a little. He curled inside her, excited to see his old home again. "I need to get out of here," she told Arkeley. Not because she wanted to flee in revulsion. Because she kind of liked what she was seeing.

"What was Reyes planning? What was his next step?" Arkeley asked her. He wanted the vampire to wake up, to surge inside of Caxton. This identification between herself and Reyes was just another tool for him. He thought it would make it easier for her to remember Reyes's plans. And it did, though the plans she recalled were from an earlier time, when he'd first learned of Laura Caxton's existence.

He had targeted her. She didn't have to fight at all for that piece of information. Reyes wanted her to play back that particular memory, as if it were a favorite record. Reyes had specifically gone after her, Pennsylvania State Trooper Laura Caxton, regardless of what he might have told Malvern. He hadn't really cared about removing the vampire killers. He'd wanted her, her body. When he had learned she was a lesbian, when his half-deads had gone to her house and seen her sleeping with Deanna (oh God, what had they seen? How many nights had they stood outside the windows and watched the two of them sleep?), he had become sexually aroused.

Vampires, she now knew, weren't supposed to think of living humans as sexual beings. It was like a human wanting to fuck a cow. But Reyes had become obsessed with her. He had remembered all those men's magazines he used to read when he was alive. He had always liked the girl-on-girl portfolios. They always got him hot. He would imagine them sucking each other off, desperate for a real man to come along and show them what they were missing. If he made her a vampire, then perhaps he could fuck her. Perhaps she would want to fuck him.

That memory, finally, was enough to make her sick. "Let me out of here," she screamed. She spun around and the bodies looked back at her, their dead eyes all focused on her face. How they had worshipped Reyes. Or feared him, yes, they all feared him, it was the last thing to pass through their faces, that fear. Reyes had loved that.

"What was his next move?" Arkeley asked. He stood in front of the stairs. "Was he going to make more vampires? Was he going to wait until he had four, to bring blood to Malvern? Where is Scapegrace right now?"

She shook her head. "Let me out," Caxton said. The bones. The bones of the dead—death itself. Death called to her, her own death, suicide, the death of others, murder. Reyes stretched inside her brain like a predatory cat, languid, pleased with what he had created. No, there was no creation in that cellar. Pleased with what he had destroyed. "Let me out! Get away from me," Caxton howled, unsure who she was talking to—the Fed or the vampire. "Leave me alone!"

45.

Up above ground, leaning against the side of Clara's Volkswagen, Caxton rubbed at her face over and over, trying to make sense of things. She wanted to throw up but kept thinking she would vomit up clotted blood, just as Reyes had. She wanted to sit down, but she knew if she did she wouldn't ever want to stand up again.

"The only reason I'm alive," she said, muttering to Arkeley, "is because I happened to fit into some vampire's kink. Not just any vampire. A depraved vampire." She tried to stop breathing. Her body freaked out, panicked, made her hyperventilate.

Vampires didn't breathe, of course. They were dead things and they didn't need to breathe. Living things, like state troopers, needed to breathe a lot.

"His curse is alive," she sighed. "His curse is alive in me."

Clara pushed a paper bag into her hands. Caxton realized that Clara must have been talking to her, but she couldn't hear her. She couldn't hear anything. She breathed into the bag and slowly, slowly, she calmed down. She felt things slow down all around her. She felt the air on her skin and smelled fruit, maybe strawberries.

She took the bag away from her face. "Strawberries?" she asked.

Clara's forehead wrinkled. "Strawberries and kiwi fruit, and a cup of unsweetened yogurt. How . . . how did you know what I had for breakfast?" The look on her face verged on fear.

Caxton waved it away. "I'm not psychic." She crinkled the bag in her fingers. "I just have a good nose." They laughed together. That helped. It helped an awful lot, actually.

"When you've stopped panicking, let me know," Arkeley said. "So we can go back down there."

With her eyes closed Caxton could pretend that Arkeley wasn't really there. That he was just in her head again. Then he had to talk again and ruin it.

"I can wait until tomorrow. I'm pretty sure that Scapegrace will still be too full to hunt tonight. I'd say, eighty percent sure. Which means that there's only a twenty percent chance he'll tear someone's throat out because you were too scared to help me."

She opened her eyes and saw Clara standing not two feet from the Fed.

"Hey, asshole," she said. She was a good foot and maybe three inches shorter than Arkeley. He outweighed her by nearly a hundred pounds. "Yeah, you, asshole," she said. "I'm not going to let you do this to her, not twice. I don't care what the stakes are."

"Laura, call off your dog, will you? She's yipping obnoxiously."

Clara's entire body tightened. Her muscles curled, and she looked ready to punch Arkeley right in the gut.

"Are you going to strike me, Sheriff's Deputy Hsu? Is that your intent? Because I have to say, the way you're telegraphing your punch, you'd be lucky to touch my coattails before I had you on the ground with two broken arms."

Clara rolled her shoulders and tilted her head side-to-side. "You're not worth the paperwork," she said, and suddenly she was standing down. She hadn't moved an inch, but her posture and the slump of her shoulders spoke volumes.

"If you're not going to hit me," Arkeley said, "then please leave us alone. The trooper and I have things to discuss."

Clara nodded and walked over to where Caxton leaned against her car. "You don't have to do anything you don't want to do," she said.

"I wish it were that simple," Caxton breathed.

Clara reached across the space between them and cradled Caxton's chin in her hand. She gave it a gentle squeeze, then made herself scarce behind a tower of switching gears. She could probably still hear them, but Arkeley didn't seem to mind.

"I want to help you," she told him. "I do."

He walked toward her as if he hadn't heard her at all. As if she hadn't said anything. She immediately felt guilty. She felt the way she had felt as a child when her father would give her the silent treatment. She tried to push that feeling out of her gut, but it was no use. She braced herself, almost expecting him to slap her.

"I will do anything you ask. Except I won't go back down in that hole."

He nodded and came even closer. Close enough to touch her, but he didn't.

"When I was down there he came swimming up to the surface, like he wanted to poke his nose out. Like he wanted to see his creation one last time. It was horrible. I felt the way he felt. I don't think my body can tell the difference between my emotions and his. I—I'm so sorry, but I can't help you like that."

"Alright," he said, a sigh coming out of him.

"No, no, it's not alright," she said, and felt herself on the verge of breaking down. "Reyes spoke to me down there. He spoke right into my head. Maybe not with words, but . . . but he was aware. Still alive in me, somehow."

He nodded. "Okay. I kind of expected that his ghost would plague you."

"You expected—you knew—how can you know? How can you know anything about what I'm going through?"

"I know," Arkeley told her.

"How?" Caxton said, squinting at him. "How do you know that?"

He picked up a stone and threw it hard at a transformer fifteen feet away. The metal box clanged. It made Caxton jump.

"Piter Byron Lares dragged me down into his hiding place and stuck me there through hypnosis. He didn't hurt me. He didn't take my weapon away. And he never spoke a word to me."

Caxton thought back to when she'd read his report. She'd read about how violent and uncaring Lares had been, tearing apart an entire SWAT team, and she'd been more than a little surprised when the vampire had taken the Fed down through the river and onto his boat still in one piece. But there had been an explanation. "He was saving you as a midnight snack," she said.

"No, he wasn't." Arkeley leaned on the car next to her and folded his arms.

"You can't be saying—"

"He had only started the process with me when I killed him. He didn't get anywhere near as far as Reyes got with you. I didn't even know I was being raped by that pale son of a bitch. But a part of him broke off in my head, just like a part of Reyes got stuck in yours. Not so much that I could feel him in there, no. Just enough that every once in a while, maybe twice a year, I dream of blood."

"You don't need to—"

Arkeley turned to stare at her. "It tastes like copper pennies on your tongue. It's hot, hotter than you expect, and very wet at first, but it clots even as it fills your mouth. It sticks in your throat, but you swallow it down, you can feel it stringy and dark in the back of your throat, but you force it down so you can have some more, another mouthful, and another. I know it so well now. The dryness of it, the clots in your teeth. The need."

She had to look away. Because it didn't sound as disgusting as he made it out to be. It sounded almost . . . tempting. She couldn't stand for him to see the naked desire she knew was lighting up her face.

"He remembers the taste. He's been dead so long there's nothing else left of him, just the longing for that taste. And it's never going to go away. If I killed myself today I don't know if I would come back as a vampire or not."

"But you know I would," she said. "You know that I'm already one of them, whether I like it or not. And there's no way back."

"That I don't know at all. I'm truly hoping the Polders know a way to exorcize this curse from you, Laura. The first step, though, has to be that we kill Scapegrace and Malvern. So nobody else has to share our dreams. So I want you to go back down that hole and look at those bodies again and tell me what his next step was going to be."

He adjusted his weight with a grunt and was standing in front of her. He held out his hand to her but she wouldn't take it.

"No," she told him.

"I beg your pardon?" he asked.

"No. I won't go back down there. I don't know how to get rid of this curse, but I know if I go down there it'll just make things worse. You find something else for me to do, some way to help you, and I will play along. But not if it means going down into that chamber of horrors again. Ever."

46.

"**C**hrist, it's not even Thanksgiving yet and look at this," Caxton exclaimed, gesturing up at the air above their heads. It was winter outside the car. Big white flakes of snow were coming down, swirling in the car's wake, gathering on the sills of the windows. The sky had turned a watery gray shot through with vaporous reefs of cloud. The road surface darkened and glistened with frost and Clara had to slow down to keep her little car on the road. In the backseat Caxton couldn't seem to get warm. Clara turned up the heat for her, but it wasn't enough. She clutched herself, her arms close so they wouldn't touch the cold glass of the window, and shivered. She was one of them. She was some kind of vampire in training. She thought of the cold feeling she'd gotten from the vampires—especially from Malvern, when she'd stood next to the dried-up monster in her wheelchair.

She needed to get away from death and horror for a while. She needed to go home and be with the dogs and not think about anything for a long time. She had a couple of stops to make before that, however.

They dropped Arkeley off at the police station. Caxton had to climb out of the back to take his seat, so she could sit up front with Clara and nearer to the heater. Her arms folded across her chest, she tried to make eye contact with the Fed, but he didn't look back, just swaggered over to his car and clambered inside.

Caxton threw herself back into the Volkswagen and yanked her door closed. The cold was sending her into convulsions, her body trembling violently, her teeth snapping at each other, chattering so loudly that she could hardly hear Clara ask if she was okay.

"I know it's a stupid question," Clara said when Caxton

didn't answer. The smaller woman looked straight ahead through the windshield. The wiper blades swung back and forth, a pendulum marking the time.

"Listen," Clara finally said. "Why don't you come home with me tonight?"

Caxton shook her head. Her whole body shook, so she reiterated in words, "You know I can't do that."

"No, not like that, we wouldn't sleep together. I mean, you could sleep in my bed. With me, because I don't have a guest room or even a real couch. But we would keep our clothes on. I just don't think it's a good idea for you to be alone tonight."

"You have no idea how alone I am right now," Caxton said. It sounded bitter, and she wanted to apologize. She opened her mouth to do just that, but the look on Clara's face stopped her in her tracks. The hurt there was too guarded—if Caxton acknowledged what had just happened, it would only hurt Clara more.

Clara started up the car and got them on the highway headed west, toward Harrisburg. Caxton needed to see Deanna before she did anything else. She needed to hold Dee's hand and figure out what her next step was.

They turned on the radio and drove in silence. Caxton watched the snow get thicker the farther they went and wished they could just magically be there. She was sure it would be warmer in the hospital. When they arrived, however, outside of Seidle Hospital, there was no parking available and they had to circle for blocks before they found a spot.

"You don't have to come in," Caxton said. She had meant it as a kindness, but it made Clara wince as if she'd been struck. "I mean, it would really help me if you did, but you don't have to."

"I've come this far," Clara said, almost aggressively, but there was a little smile on her face.

Caxton would have done anything for things to be comfortable between the two of them. But she guessed her life was just going to be complicated for a while. Together they made their way back to the hospital, a big modern monolith of a building that looked across the river at the ruins of the Walnut Street Bridge. Caxton had never gone in through the main entrance—they had brought Deanna in through the emergency room—so it took her a while to get her bearings. Eventually she took Clara up an elevator and down a long hallway full of equipment carts and bad, but colorful, paintings. "Listen. It's a semiprivate room, and her roommate doesn't approve of women like us," she told Clara. "Just so you know."

"I'll try not to stick my tongue down your throat while we're standing over the hospital bed of your horribly injured domestic partner," Clara told her, deadpan.

A laugh bubbled up inside Caxton's chest and she snorted out all her frustration, leaning hard against the wall and closing her eyes for a moment. God, she had needed that release. "Thanks," she said, and Clara just shrugged. Caxton knocked and pushed open the door, which sighed a little. The two of them passed silently by the bathroom and into the main room, which was lit only by the flickering glow of the television set. The obese woman in the other bed was asleep, her face turned to the wall, and Caxton tried to be quiet so as not to wake her. Clara waited by the door.

Caxton stepped over to Deanna's bed and gasped. It was empty.

She clapped a hand over her mouth and ran back out into the hall. Clara grabbed her arm and stroked her bicep. "They just moved her. Really," she said. "It's okay. They just moved her."

Caxton headed down to the nurse's station and scowled at the woman there, who was filling out a form on her computer. "Deanna Purfleet!" she shouted, when the nurse wouldn't look up. "Deanna Purfleet!"

The nurse turned slowly and nodded. "I'll call the doctor. It'll just be a second."

"Just tell me where they moved her to. I'm Laura Caxton. I'm her partner."

The nurse nodded again. "I know who you are." She put on a pair of reading glasses and looked down at a phone directory. "Please sit down and wait for the doctor. You'll want to talk to him."

Caxton didn't sit down. She paced back and forth around the nurse's station, studied the awards and plaques on the walls, took a cup of water when Clara brought it to her, but she couldn't sit down, not if she ever wanted to get up again. The doctor came out of an elevator down the hall and she ran to him. It wasn't the doctor she'd seen before. "Deanna Purfleet," she said.

"You're Ms. Caxton, I think?" he asked. He was a small Indian man with perfectly combed hair and very soulful eyes. He looked like he'd never smiled in his entire life. "I'm Dr. Prabinder. If you'd like to sit down—"

"Jesus, just tell me where she is! Won't anyone tell me where she is?"

"There was a complication," the doctor said, and everything turned rubbery and soft. The floor started to rise toward her face.

47.

Caxton sat in the morgue. Deanna's body lay on a gurney. Dr. Prabinder and Clara were nowhere to be seen. She was all alone in the semidarkened room, surrounded on every side by rolling partitions. How she'd gotten there she couldn't say. It was as if she had blacked out, except she hadn't, at all. The trip from the fourth floor down to the basement was all there in her memory. It was just so immaterial that she hadn't bothered to review the information.

There had been a complication, she remembered. She got up and walked around the gurney. She touched Deanna here and there. Twitched back the sheet that covered her. Deanna's face was calm, at least. Her eyes closed, her red hair clean. Her lips were pale, but otherwise she didn't look so bad. Caxton moved the sheet back a little more, and wished she hadn't. Deanna's breasts pointed in the wrong directions. Her chest was open like a ravenous mouth, her ribs like teeth reaching for a piece of meat. Her lungs and her heart lay collapsed at the bottom of that wound like a lolling tongue.

There had been a complication. Deanna had lost so much blood when she broke the kitchen window that she had required five new units of plasma. They had also given her some whole blood because she had started to show the signs of acute anemia—coldness in the extremities even while her trunk was warm, a lasting and dangerous shortness of breath.

There had been a complication. A blood clot had formed, perhaps from one of her wounds, possibly from a bad reaction to the transfused blood. Dr. Prabinder had refused to speculate. The clot had entered Deanna's bloodstream and probably roamed around her body several times before it reached her left lung.

There had been a complication. A pulmonary embolus, Dr. Prabinder had called it. When it was detected they had rushed her immediately into surgery, of course. They had tried to cut it out. And that was one complication too many.

"I really must insist, Ms. Caxton," the doctor said, pulling back one of the partitions. Clara stood next to him. "You're not supposed to be here at all, and truly, it's not appropriate for the morgue technicians to let you see her in this condition—"

"That's Trooper Caxton," Clara announced. She held up her badge.

"Oh, I . . . I didn't know," Doctor Prabinder said.

"This is a homicide investigation, Doctor." Clara put her badge away. What she was doing was highly illegal. She was well outside of her jurisdiction. So was Caxton. Lying about a criminal investigation could get them both fired.

Caxton wouldn't tell, if Clara didn't. She pulled the sheet back up over Deanna's chest. Blood soaked through it almost instantly.

"When?" Caxton asked. She couldn't get any more of the sentence out.

"What was the official time of death?" Clara asked.

The doctor checked his PDA. "Last night, about four-fifteen."

"Before dawn," Caxton said. While she had been fighting vampires in abandoned steel mills, Deanna had been slowly dying and nobody had known. There would have been nobody with her. Perhaps if there had been it could have been avoided. Perhaps if Caxton had been there, listening to Deanna's ragged breathing, she might have noticed some change. She could have summoned the doctor. They could have gotten Deanna into surgery that much quicker.

At the very least she could have held her hand. "I wasn't here," she said.

"No, no, come on," Clara said.

"Ah, ladies, I know it is not my place to ask, but is it acceptable for this woman to investigate the death of someone so close? Is there not a conflict of interest?"

"She was alone," Caxton said, ignoring him.

"Was there anyone in her room last night? Any visitors at all?" Clara asked.

The doctor shook his head in incomprehension. "No, of course not. We don't let visitors in after seven, and anyway she had posted a guard on the room." He pointed at Caxton with his PDA. "Did you not know about the guard?"

Clara glanced at her, then back at the doctor. "I was just brought in on this case. I'm still catching up."

"I . . . see." Doctor Prabinder straightened up and squared his shoulders. "Now let's get one thing clear. I wish to assist the police in any manner possible, of course. But this is my hospital, and—"

"Doctor," Caxton said, turning to face him for the first time. She gave him her best fisheye look. Caxton wasn't wearing her uniform, she didn't have a badge, and her weapon was still in the trunk of Clara's Volkswagen. It didn't matter. The look was what made you a cop. That perfectly uncaring, potentially violent look that could freeze most people in their tracks. "I need to know if anything unusual happened here last night. I need to know if anybody saw or heard anything weird or out of place. Anything at all."

"Of course, of course," he said. He looked down at his shoes. "But this is a hospital with a trauma ward in a major urban center. You must clarify for me, I have seen so many weird things . . ." His words trailed off.

"I'm not talking about freak accidents. I'm talking about people with no faces being seen in the hallways. I'm talking about vampire activity."

"Vampires, here?" He muttered something in Hindi that sounded like a brief prayer. "I saw on the news that—I hear some things, yes, and the bodies that came in—but oh, my, no, nothing like that last night! I swear it."

"Good." Caxton reached down and took Deanna's hand. It was freezing cold, but so was her own. "Now I need someone to sew this woman up so I can bury her. Can you arrange that?"

Dr. Prabinder nodded and took out his cell phone. "There will be papers to sign, of course, if that is not too much."

"Of course," Caxton said. She took out her own phone. Deanna's brother Elvin was in her stored phonebook. Hopefully he would know his—and Dee's—mother's number. There were suddenly a lot of things she needed to do.

"I'm so, so sorry," Clara said, and reached for her, but Caxton shrugged her away.

"I can't feel anything right now," Caxton tried to explain. She didn't know if the grief was just too big and she was defending herself from it, or if Reyes was in control of her emotions. To him Deanna's death was regrettable only in that all that blood was going to waste.

It helped that there were a lot of phone calls to make and a lot of questions to answer. Somebody had to be calm and in charge.

Elvin wasn't home. She left a message for him to call her back. Someone came and asked her about organ donation. She told them to take what they could. Deanna was wrapped up, taken away. They brought her back—her tissues weren't good candidates for donation. She'd been dead too long for the major organs to be useful, and her skin and eyes weren't the right type. Caxton called Elvin again. Someone from the transplant center came down and demanded to know who she thought she was, offering up Deanna's body parts for donation, when she wasn't even a relative. That conversation took far too long. For perhaps the first time she actually wished she'd bothered to get a civil union. It wouldn't have given her any more rights, but it might have forestalled a few of the less comfortable questions. She finally got hold of Elvin and he said he would come right away. He would bring Deanna's mother. Caxton flipped shut her phone and put it away. She turned around and there was Clara.

"How long have I been making phone calls?" she asked. She had a feeling a lot more time had passed than she was aware of. She was in a lounge, for one thing. Hadn't she just been in the morgue? Somehow she'd been moved to a well-heated lounge with a big window and comfortable chairs and lots of tattered magazines. Maybe Clara had brought her there.

"Well, I already had lunch. I got you a sandwich."

Caxton took the offered bag and opened it up. Tuna salad, white flesh in white mayonnaise on white bread. It didn't appeal to her at all. She wanted roast beef and felt almost childishly peevish about it—why couldn't Clara have gotten her roast beef? Why couldn't she go right now and get a big rare steak, all full of juice, of, of—of blood?

She clamped down on that thought immediately and started eating the tuna sandwich. She was not going to let the vampire live vicariously through her.

"Listen, there's something I haven't heard anyone mention, but I think it's important," Clara said. She frowned and pursed her lips and finally spat it out. "Do we need," she said, pronouncing each word separately, "to consider, well, cremation."

Caxton blinked rapidly. "You mean for Deanna?" she asked. "Of course you do. I mean, nobody else is dead right now. Yeah. Right. Cremation." She didn't so much think it through as let it come bubbling up in her head. "No."

"No," Clara repeated, tentatively.

"No. You saw all that blood. No vampire would leave so much blood on a body. It was just an accident, Clara. Just a stupid fucked-up accident, the kind that still happens, you know? Not everybody gets killed by monsters."

Clara nodded supportively, then opened her mouth to speak again. She stopped when the door behind her burst open. An enormous man with thin, straight red hair that fell past his shoulders came storming in. He wore a sheepskin coat and a look of absolute befuddlement. Behind him followed a woman with hair dyed to match his, though it showed gray at the roots. Her face was a mess of red blotches, as if she'd been crying, or drinking. Most likely both.

"Who's this, your new girlfriend?" Deanna's mother asked.

"Hello, Roxie," Caxton tried. She glanced up at the big red-headed man. "Oh, Elvin, I'm so sorry."

He nodded his massive head. "Yeah. Thanks. Thanks a lot," he said. He looked around as if unsure of where he was.

"I'm going to go now," Clara said.

"Jesus, don't leave on my account." Roxie Purfleet sneered at Caxton. "You work fast, huh? One of them's not even cold and you're on to the next."

Clara slipped past her without further comment. Caxton sat the Purfleets down and started to explain what had happened.

48.

Deanna was dead. It wasn't hard to accept on a factual basis. Caxton could hold the knowledge in her head, she could walk around it, see it from all angles. She could see the repercussions, the paperwork she would need to file. She would have to cancel all of Deanna's magazine subscriptions, for instance. She would have to change their insurance coverage, a precariously balanced set of documents that allowed Caxton to pay for Deanna's medical bills with her own state employee insurance.

That didn't begin to explain how she felt, however. The nitty gritty details of Deanna's life didn't add up to what had just happened. Deanna was dead. It was like the color blue had stopped existing. Something Caxton had always counted on, something she had built an entire life around, wasn't there anymore.

It wasn't fear of loneliness or loss of companionship that bothered her most. It was this existential hole in her worldview. Deanna was gone—forever—and it had happened just like that, in the time it took to say out loud: Deanna was dead.

She found herself driving home, much, much later, an hour or two after sunset. Roxie Purfleet had taken over her duties at the hospital, convinced she knew best what her daughter wanted done with her mortal remains. She'd refused to let Caxton even help plan the memorial service. Deanna's body would go back to Boalsburg, where she'd been born. Caxton had listened a million times to Deanna moan and bitch about the place, about how she'd longed to get away from it as early as elementary school. But that's where she would be forever, now.

Driving—Caxton was driving, she needed to focus on that. She watched the yellow lines on the road but soon found herself fixated on them, unable to look away. She forced herself to check her mirrors and her blind spot.

Deanna was dead. She wanted to call Deanna up and talk to her about what had just happened. She wanted to sit on the couch with the TV turned off for a second and just talk about what it all meant. Who else could she trust with such monumental news? Who else could she go to first?

Driving. Right. Caxton squinted as a semi roared past in the other direction, its headlights smearing brilliant light across her face. She blinked away the afterimages and focused on the car, on the speedometer, on the gas gauge. Anything to keep her in the here and now.

Elvin, who was perhaps the only person in the world with less of a grip on what had happened than herself, had been kind enough to drive her back to Troop H headquarters, where she'd left her car. It hadn't been moved since she'd suited up to get onboard the Granola Roller. She'd gone up and touched the patrol car's metal skin as if it were a special machine that could take her back in time, to before Deanna died, to before she became half of a vampire. Then she'd turned around because she felt Elvin behind her, just standing there. His body sort of hovered halfway between leaving and coming closer, a mass being turned this way and that by some sort of emotional physics. *Looming* was the word that came to mind. He loomed over her and frowned, deep and long, and finally spoke.

"She really loved you," he said. "She swore it. When I first found out she was a fag I was going to cream her, but then she said she really loved you, and I figured that made it okay. I mean, you don't pick who you love. Nobody does."

"I suppose not," Caxton had replied, unsure what he wanted. A hug? A reminiscence of his sister? "Thanks for the ride," she'd said, and he had nodded, and that was that.

She blinked back a half-formed, inexplicable tear. Oh, God, driving—she had to watch where she was driving. She'd just missed the turn-off. She stopped the car and looked behind her. There was no one on the road back there. Slowly, with a noise of rumbling gravel, she backed up and maneuvered until she was headed back the right way. Then she drove up to the house without losing track of time even once. She switched off the car. The headlights disappeared and everything was dark. She sat in the cooling car and stared at the dark house. Deanna had always left a light on for her before.

It was only the whining of the dogs that spurred her to action. She had forgotten them—how could she forget them? But she had. She had forgotten her dogs, and they hadn't eaten in over a day. They were watered automatically with a gravity bottle, but they hadn't eaten. They would be starving. She didn't even go into the house, just ran back to the kennels and grabbed a twenty-pound bag of kibble. She switched on the lights inside the kennel and gasped.

The dogs looked okay—but something had tried to tear their cages open. The greyhounds lay curled up behind warped and bent bars, crying and whining and yawning in fearful confusion. Blood and what looked like a strip of cloth hung on the bars near her. Caxton stepped closer and touched the damaged cage. It wasn't cloth. It was corroded flesh, torn off in a hurry. A half-dead had been there, and not very long before. Clearly it had meant to kill the dogs, only to get its arm torn open instead.

She let the dogs out and hugged them and poured them bowls of food. Hunger won out over their bewilderment, and they ate greedily. She squeezed vitamins from a plastic bottle into the kibble and left them at it. Then she went back to her car and retrieved her Beretta and the box of cross points. With fumbling, half-frozen hands she loaded the pistol, then went to the front door of the house.

Why had they come? She had expected they would leave the house alone, if nobody was inside. She couldn't figure it out. She touched the knob of the door and knew instantly that it was unlocked. Careful, wary of anyone who might be waiting just inside, she slipped on her flashlight and stepped through the door.

Cold silence blew past her, cold air rushing through the house. It leaked in around the cardboard over the kitchen window, the window that had killed Deanna. It swept down the hallway toward their bedroom. She reached for the light switch, but it did nothing when she flicked it. She looked up and saw that the light fixtures in the hall had been smashed, all the bulbs broken.

Even in the darkness she could see the house had been ransacked. Sheets lay twisted and strewn across the hall as if they'd been dragged off the bed. Plates and pots and the iron skillet had been jumbled all together and thrown in a corner. Some were broken, but there had been no method to it. Whoever had done this had been in a hurry, or perhaps a frenzy. The pictures were torn off the walls and thrown on the floor. Her flashlight beam struck one of them and dazzled her with the reflection off the glass. She looked closer. It was a picture of Deanna and Caxton at a canine agility tournament, the two of them bent low, beckoning Wilbur across a balance beam. God, what an amazing day that had been. The glass was cracked and the frame broken. She fished the photo out and put it in her pocket, trying to save something.

The bedroom was a mess. Sharp claws or maybe knives had torn up the mattress and bits and pieces of foam rubber were scattered everywhere. Caxton's closet had been rifled through, most of her clothes just dumped in a heap. It was going to take so long to clean this all up. She turned around and gasped again when she saw that the intruder had left her a message. It covered half the bedroom wall and looked like it had been painted in blood:

NO LIFE = NO SLEEP BE WITH ME

She didn't need a signature to know who had sent the message. Scapegrace, the last of Justinia Malvern's brood. He wanted her to finish the transformation that Reyes had started. He was waiting for her to commit suicide and come be his partner in reviving Malvern. He must have somehow convinced himself that destroying her home would be an incentive toward that end. Maybe he thought it would depress her.

The piece of Reyes still curled around her brain pulsed, rejecting the idea, and she understood, a little—or rather she knew how little Scapegrace understood. Vampirism had been a dark gift as far as the teenager was concerned. How could anyone not want that power and strength? He was telling her that she no longer needed to sleep, that she could break out of the prison of her frail human flesh and emotions and become so much more.

"Then why does he cut off his own ears every sundown?" she asked, but Reyes fell silent on that matter. Thinking of the dead boy made her more sad than angry. Petty destruction of other people's property was the only outlet left for his rage, now that he had destroyed himself.

She checked the rest of the house, but there was no one there. Scapegrace and his minions were long gone. She took another look at the bed and realized she would never be able to spend the night there. She decided to call Clara and see if her invitation still held. To get a better signal she headed out back, toward Deanna's shed. The door stood unlocked and ajar, of course. Scapegrace had tried to hurt her dogs. He hated everything about the living. He would have destroyed Deanna's art as well.

She stepped inside and closed her phone before she'd even found Clara's number. She switched on the lights and they actually worked, the bare hundred-watt bulbs in the ceiling flaring to life. The shed looked completely untouched. The three sheets hung slack from the ceiling, the light filtering yellow and red through the cloth. Perhaps Scapegrace had seen something in Deanna's art. Maybe he approved of using blood as a medium— though surely he wouldn't have known what kind of blood it was. She turned to head back outside, then stopped. She heard a footfall, but it wasn't hers.

"Laura," someone said, and for a moment she thought it was her father's ghost inhabiting the sheets, just as he had inhabited the teleplasm in Urie Polder's barn.

It was Arkeley who stepped out from behind the artwork, however.

"Special Deputy," she said, her heart racing at first. It slowed down as she watched him come closer. "I didn't expect to see you here."

His face was creased with sorrow. "Laura," he said again, "I'm so sorry. I didn't want to bring you this far into this."

Was he actually apologizing for getting Deanna killed? Grief was like some kind of thicker skin she'd put on. Whatever he was saying just didn't get through to her. "It's alright," she said. It wasn't, but the words came out of her like a yawn, completely unavoidable.

"I needed bait, you see. I needed you because they needed you. The only way to escape a trap is to spring it before they're ready, remember?"

"You've taught me so much." It was her body talking, not her heart. Her body wanted to go to bed. Clara. She had to call Clara. Clara had to come pick her up. It would be at least an hour before she could sleep. She started texting Clara because it was easier somehow than talking to her on the phone. She was done talking for the night.

"You don't understand—" Arkeley insisted, but she shook her head. "Laura, you need to focus right now." He stormed toward her and she was sure he was going to hit her again. She stopped breathing and her eyes went wide.

"What is so important?" she asked, finally finding her own voice. "What is so fucking important that I have to listen to you, tonight of all nights?"

Arkeley drew his weapon. A little gasp came out of her— she had no idea what he was doing.

"They're outside," he told her. "Waiting for us to walk out of here. Dozens of half-deads and at least two vampires."

49.

"What do you mean, two vampires?" Caxton demanded. "We killed them all except for Scapegrace. You don't mean Malvern—you can't mean that."

"No, I don't," Arkeley said. He checked the action on his Glock 23. He gestured at the Beretta that lay inert in her hand. She checked to see there was a round in the chamber, then raised the weapon to shoulder height, the barrel pointed at the ceiling. "Malvern is still at Arabella Furnace. I had Tucker check on her fifteen minutes ago and there was no change in her condition. So we have to assume that we made at least one mistake."

"We saw three coffins at the hunting camp," she insisted. She didn't want to hear what he said next, even though it was already echoing in the dark cloister of her own skull.

"That doesn't mean there couldn't have been another one somewhere else." Arkeley moved toward the light switch, careful to stay out of the shed's wide doorway. "Let's go over what I do know. I came here tonight to officially relieve you of duty. I was going to send you back to the highway patrol. Then I saw that something was wrong. There were maybe ten cars and trucks parked out on the road. I looked around, but none of your neighbors were having a party. I abandoned my own vehicle and came in here on foot, through the woods. By then they were already setting up their ambush. There are six half-deads hiding out by the driveway, there are five of them stationed in the yard next door, and three more of them on the roof of the kennels. There will be more—those are just the ones I found. I saw one vampire giving them orders. His ears were docked, so we have to assume that was Scapegrace. Then another vampire climbed out of your bedroom window."

"You're absolutely sure it was a vampire you saw coming through the window? How good a look did you get?"

He shook his head. "I can't be certain of anything. But I saw something with pale white skin and long ears. Its hands were stained red."

Caxton moved up to the other side of the doorway, just as she'd been trained. When they left the shed they would go together, facing in slightly different directions so they could cover each other's back.

She texted Clara and told her to summon reinforcements. She called in to headquarters to report an officer under fire. She knew nobody could get there in time—the closest barracks was miles away. They were going to have to fight their way out on their own, just the two of them. She looked up at Arkeley. "Do we have a plan?" she asked.

"Yes," he told her. "Shoot everything that moves."

Together they stepped through the doorway. Arkeley raised his weapon and fired even before her eyes had adjusted to the darkness. She saw a shadow coming toward her, a shadow with a broken face, and she shot its center mass. It crumpled and fell without a sound.

Suddenly they were everywhere.

Shadows detached from the trees, pale shapes darted around them like wolves circling to the attack. No warnings were given this time, no cryptic messages to draw them out. A half-dead whirled out of the dark, a six-inch knife in his hand, and Caxton smashed him across the face with her weapon. He went down, but not before three more sprang out at her. "There are too many!" she shouted. "We need to get out of here!"

"Go!" the Fed yelled back, though he was only three feet away. "Go now!"

Caxton broke away from Arkeley and dashed to the side of the kennels, intent on at least getting something behind her. Otherwise they might sneak up on her. She expected Arkeley to run for cover as well, to protect himself.

He didn't.

The Fed dropped into a firing crouch and moved out into the open space between the kennels and the house. His gun arm stood straight out from his body and swung back and forth like a weathervane as he tracked some assailant she couldn't see. He squeezed the trigger, and bright fire leaped from his barrel. To her side, just inches from her left shoulder, a half-dead slipped downward to writhe in agony on the ground.

Arkeley spun and fired again—and a third time. Shadows howled and flopped in the darkness, but more of them appeared as if emerging from out of the night, as if they'd dropped from the moon-colored clouds. One leaped onto his back and bit at his neck with sharp teeth. He smashed its nose with his free fist and knocked it away. Another rolled into his legs, dropping him to one knee. He shot her in the chest and she jerked backward.

A half-dead grabbed Arkeley's gun arm and twisted. He yelped in pain—Arkeley, of all people, cried out in pain. The half-dead must have caught him completely off his guard.

But Caxton had her own concerns. The half-deads were coming for her, too, though with far less force and in fewer numbers. Clearly they didn't consider her to be a threat on Arkeley's level. She found herself almost disappointed.

She fired at a dark shape that lunged down across the roof of the kennels, and it fell to the ground with a hiss of exhausted breath. She kicked it in the legs and felt its flesh yield. Another half-dead reached down to grab her shoulders. She lifted her gun and fired without even looking.

"Go!" Arkeley shouted again. She looked over in his direction but could barely see him. He was surrounded on every side by Scapegrace's servants. She discharged her weapon over and over, trying to thin out the crowd, even as she dashed out, away from the kennels. Arkeley was about to be overrun and she knew it, but there was very little she could do. She couldn't save him—she didn't have enough bullets. Her only hope was to get away herself and find some backup.

The problem was that she wasn't sure where to go next. The driveway led straight out to the road and the possibility of help. Any police response would come from that direction, assuming she lived long enough for anyone to arrive. Arkeley had said there were half-deads stationed out there, however. They would almost certainly be laying in wait.

Instead she turned to the back of the drive, to where a ten-foot privacy fence cut through the trees. She got a foot in between two of the boards and lunged up and grabbed at the branches that protruded over the top. Adrenaline carried her up and over and she slid down the trees on the other side, branches whipping at her face and digging up long scrapes on her hands and arms. She rolled down a steep embankment and into the parking lot of the elementary school next door. In the moonlight the black asphalt sparkled.

She heard gunfire from the other side of the fence. One shot—two more. Then nothing. She tried to breathe normally, tried to control her urge to panic. Arkeley was probably dead, but it didn't change her situation.

The trees by the fence shivered and their dry leaves whispered as they rubbed together. Two half-deads were climbing up after her. Chasing her. They would be on her in a second.

She checked her weapon. She had only one round left. She was better off saving it, she decided. She climbed to her feet and ran.

The school building was low and rectangular, a black edge in the night that guided her. She didn't know if half-deads could see in total darkness or not. Vampires could see your blood glowing in the gloom, but what about their servants? It was one of the many things she should have asked Arkeley back when she'd had the chance.

Back when he was still alive.

Guilt dripped down her spine as she dashed around a corner and up a short stairway. She could feel guilt and run at the same time. Ahead of her lay a backstop and a chain-link fence, the pale dirt of a baseball diamond. She dashed through a narrow gap in the fence and slid in a patch of mud. There were trees ahead of her. Not such a big surprise. There were trees everywhere in Pennsylvania. They might give her a little cover, she decided. They might shield her from half-dead eyes. She slipped between them and realized her mistake almost instantly. You can't run at night in a forest, or at least, you can't run very far. No matter how dark a night might look, it's ten times darker under a forest canopy. Unable to see, she could run right into a hardwood trunk or trip over exposed roots. She had a flashlight in her pocket, but turning it on would give away her position instantly.

Without light she could break her neck, or worse, break a leg. She could end up immobilized but still conscious, unable to walk and forced to wait for the half-deads to find her. She needed to get out of the woods—but going back was out of the question.

Ahead of her she saw a patch of wan radiance and headed toward it, her hands outstretched, feeling her way forward. Her boots shuffled forward spasmodically, just waiting to be trapped by thick underbrush or sucked down into a puddle of mud.

The light revealed a clearing maybe fifty yards on a side and strangely regular in shape. A few thin saplings grew there, but mostly it was covered with overgrown grass, yellow and thin with the season. She stepped out of the woods and into the relatively bright space, relief flooding through her body, and then she tripped over a rock. The hard, half-frozen ground connected with her chin and her teeth smashed together with a horrible clinking sound.

She struggled onto her side, then sat up and looked behind her. The stone she'd tripped over was pale, almost ghostly white in the moonlight. It was rough on top but straight on the sides, worn down by wind and rain over the course of centuries, but once, long ago, it must have been straight and smooth. A slab of rock planted upright in the soil. Like a gravestone.

She had stumbled right into an abandoned cemetery.

50.

When she knew what to look for it was obvious. The low stones were badly eroded, ground down by time's wheel until they were just tall enough to trip over. She could see where they made neat rows, however, and at the far end of the clearing she could see twisted bars of metal, the remains of a pair of wrought iron gates.

There were little graveyards like this all over the Pennsylvania countryside, Caxton knew. Developers hated them because they were legally required to move the bodies if they wanted to tear up the land. More often than not they just left them in place. It was no great shock to find one in the woods behind her house. There must have been a church nearby in some past decade or century, but it had been burned or pulled down since. There was nothing to fear from the graves, she told herself—vampires slept in coffins, yes, but they didn't bury themselves in ancient churchyards just for the ambience.

Something snapped maybe ten yards from her head. A fallen branch or maybe a crust of frost on the ground. It could have just been a cat or a deer—or it could have just been a branch finally giving way.

Caxton froze anyway. Her entire body craned toward her ears, her whole brain tuned up in anticipation of the next sound.

It came in a series of tiny pops, like a string of firecrackers going off but much, much softer. Perhaps something had trod on a carpet of pine needles. Caxton lowered herself inch by inch until she was lying flat on the ground, trying to make herself small, trying to make herself invisible.

"Did you see that?" someone warbled. It was the squeaky voice of a half-dead. After a moment she half-heard a muttered reply.

She cursed herself for lying down, for moving at all. In the darkness, if she'd been perfectly still, maybe they would have walked right past her.

She had one bullet left in her Beretta. The flesh of half-deads was rotten and soft and she could probably beat another one to pieces. If there were three of them, however, or if they were faster than she expected, it would all be over.

She tensed her body, ready to strike upward if anyone came close. She would try her best to destroy them, if there were two of them. If there were three, or more, she would shoot herself in the heart. It would prevent her from being raised as a vampire.

"There, what's that?" a half-dead asked.

There were two of them. There had to be two. She prayed there were two.

Then she heard a third voice.

"You two, leave us alone," someone else said, someone who had to be standing right behind her. She rolled over and looked up into a pale silhouette with a round head. It wore a pair of tight jeans and a black T-shirt. Its ears were dark and ragged-looking.

Scapegrace.

Caxton brought her pistol up and fired her last round point blank into the vampire's chest. The bullet tore through his shirt, then pranged off into the trees. It didn't even scratch his white body. She hadn't really expected to kill him—even in the dark she could see the pinkish glow of fresh blood moving beneath his skin—but at the least she'd expected to make him turn and snarl. He didn't even laugh at her. He just crouched down next to her and touched the grave marker she'd tripped over. He didn't look at her or touch her.

She tried to ask a question but her throat kept closing up. "What . . . what are you going to . . ."

"Don't talk to me," he said. "Don't say anything unless I speak to you first. I can kill you," he added. "I can kill you instantly. If you try to run away I can catch you. I'm much faster than I used to be. But I want to bring you in alive. I mean, those are my orders. I think you know what She wants. I've also been told that if I hurt you a little, that's okay. That it might even help."

He faced her, then, and she had a bad shock when she

saw how young he looked. Scapegrace had been a child when he killed himself. A teenager, maybe fifteen or sixteen at the most. His body was still painfully skinny and hunched. Death hadn't made him a grownup overnight. He still looked like a little boy.

"Please don't look at me like that," he said to her. "I hate it."

Caxton turned her face away hurriedly. She knew her own features had to be wracked by fear. Snot was running across her upper lip and cold sweat was breaking out on her forehead.

"I can see some things in the dark, but I can't read this," he told her, running his fingers across the headstone. The lettering there had mostly worn away, but here and there an angle or a fragment of a curved inscription could still be seen. "Maybe you can read it better. Read it to me."

Her throat shuddered and she thought she might throw up. She fought her body until it was back under her control. She couldn't quite read the letters, but maybe it would help to feel them, she thought, to trace them with her fingertips. Trembling fear lanced up her forearm as she ran one finger across the face of the stone. She could make out a little:

ST PH N DELANC
JU 854 – JULY 1854

She told him what she had discovered. "I think—I think it says Stephen Delancy, died July 1854. The date of birth is h-h-harder to m-m-make out," she chattered.

Caxton felt as if someone were pouring cold water over her back. It had to be at least partially the weird feeling she always got around vampires, the cold sensation that she got standing next to Malvern's coffin or whenever Reyes had touched her. But most of that skin-crawling horror had to come from the fact that at any moment he could kill her. Tear her to pieces before she could even raise her arms to ward him off.

"Do you think he was born in June or July? Did he live for a full month or only a few days?" Scapegrace knelt down beside her and ran a hand across the gravestone as if he were caressing the face of the infant buried below. "I guess there's one way to find out."

"No!" she screamed, as he dug his pale fingers into the soil and started tearing out clods of earth. She threw herself at his back and beat on his neck with her empty pistol. Finally she got a reaction out of him.

Turning from his kneeling posture, he grabbed her around the waist and slung her away from him. The empty Beretta flew out of her hand and into the darkness. She couldn't see where it went because she was too busy reeling across the graveyard. She tumbled backwards, her feet kicking at the ground point-lessly. She came down hard across another gravestone, this one nothing more than a stub of rock sticking out of the ground like a decayed tooth. Her elbow collided with the stone and wild pain leaped up and down her arm. She didn't think she'd broken anything—just hit her funny bone.

Scapegrace had made a hole three feet deep by the time she could stand again. The bones and cartilage of her hand still thrummed with agony, but she was going to be okay. She found herself crying, though, as he lifted a wooden box out of the ground. She couldn't stand it—between the fear and the horror of what he was doing, she thought she was going to start scream-ing, that she would run away even though she consciously knew he would just chase her down.

The box was of some light-colored wood, maybe pine, riddled with worm casts. It was decayed so badly that she couldn't tell if it had originally been ornate or plainly made. The baby-sized coffin broke apart in Scapegrace's hands, though he was clearly trying to be gentle with it. He brushed away the fragments of pulpy wood and the dirt and sediment that had collected around the body inside.

"My family had a big funeral for me," he told her. "I could kind of see what was happening, like I was a ghost floating around the ceiling of the church. Everybody from my school was there and they walked past and looked down at my face and some of them cried, and some of them said things. Sometimes it was people I didn't even know. Girls who would never have talked to me in the hall, not even if they needed a pen and I had a spare one. Some of them were really upset, like they finally understood what it was like, what they had done to me. That was kind of awesome. Nobody would touch me, though." Gently, with his thumb, he brushed debris away from the tiny body.

"Please," Caxton said, the word strained and stretched as it came out of her. "Please. Please." He didn't strike her but he didn't stop what he was doing, either. He shook the coffin a little and debris and dirt and other matter fell away. Vomit surged up her throat and she turned to the side, ashamed to show such disrespect but unable to stop herself from throwing up right then and there.

"When you're on the other side of it, death just isn't scary anymore. Actually, it becomes kind of fascinating. A lot of being a vampire is like that. It totally changes your perspective." He held something round in his left hand, something about the size of an apple. With a half twist he removed it from the coffin. The rest of the infant's remains went back in the hole and he kicked dirt over them. Then he turned around and showed her what he'd found.

It was the skull. Stephen Delancy's skull, which had been buried for a hundred and fifty years. "Look," he told her. "He was only a few days old when he died." He showed her the skull. It was packed full of dirt and smeared with dried fluids. It was horrible to behold, sickening. "Maybe he was never really born." He considered the baby-sized cranium at length. "This will work," he said. He rubbed at the skull with his thumbs and then stared deeply into its eye sockets as he chanted softly. She didn't understand the words—she wasn't even sure they were words he was speaking.

When he finished he closed his eyes and then held out one hand, the skull balanced on his white palm. After a moment the skull began to vibrate. She could see it blur with motion. A sound leaked out of it, a kind of wailing moan it couldn't possibly make on its own—it didn't even have a lower jaw. The scream grew louder and louder until she wanted to clamp her hands over her ears. Instead Scapegrace pressed it against her hands. "Take it," he said, and she could hear him just fine over the shrieking. "Go on—my ears are more sensitive than yours. Take it!"

She took it in her hands and the screaming stopped instantly.

"I'm going to take you with me, back to Her lair. I need you to behave, though. So we're going to play a little game. You're going to hold Stephen in both of your hands, because that's the only way to keep him quiet. Nod for me so I know you understand."

She shuddered. It made her head bob on her neck as if it weren't fully attached. She wrapped both hands around the skull. Something moved and chittered inside, some insect hidden in the dirt that filled the baby's sinus cavity. She moaned a little, but she didn't drop the skull.

"Now you take good care of that. If you take your hands away from it or if you drop it or if you crush it because you're holding it too hard, I'll hear it scream. Then I'll have to hurt you. Really, really badly." He squinted his red eyes and stared shrewdly into her face. "I'll break your back. You know I can do that, right?"

She nodded again. Her whole body trembled.

"Okay, Laura," he said. "Now move."

51.

Scapegrace led her out of the woods and back to the parking lot of the elementary school. She scanned the surrounding area with her eyes, desperately hoping someone would see them and call the police. No luck, though. She and Deanna had picked the place because it was out in the middle of the woods. Plenty of space for the shed and the kennels. Nobody around to complain about the sometimes bizarre noises greyhounds made. At night there was nobody around at all.

A car, a late-model white sedan, waited for them in the lot, its engine idling, its lights on. Doctor Hazlitt sat in the driver's seat, looking nervous.

"She promised Hazlitt he could be one of us," Scapegrace told her. He was standing behind her, so close she could feel his cold breath on her neck. "She promised him lots of things." The vampire held open the passenger door for her. She could hardly open it herself while she held the baby's cursed skull in her hands. She climbed in and realized she couldn't fasten her seat belt, either. She guessed that didn't matter.

"Hello, Officer," Hazlitt said. She didn't look at him. He sighed and tried again. "I know you have no reason to like me just now," he went on. "In a few hours, though, we will be allies. That's how this is going to work out. Can't we be civil to each other now?" When she didn't answer, he started up the car and turned onto the highway headed southeast. Toward the tuberculosis sanatorium where Justinia Malvern waited so patiently.

They were going to make her kill herself. She'd understood that before, but she hadn't considered how it might happen. Reyes had wanted it to be her own choice, and he had nearly succeeded in talking her into shooting herself. He'd wasted time trying to convince her—and before he could finish with her the sun had come up. Scapegrace wasn't going to make the same mistake. He would force her hand. Judging by the methods of persuasion he'd used so far, she imagined he would torture her until she begged for death. Then he would give her the means to do herself in.

Arkeley couldn't stop them this time. Arkeley was dead. *Tonight I'm going to die,* she thought, *and then tomorrow night I will rise as a vampire.*

She wanted to fight them. She wanted it so badly—her body was wracked with the urge to attack, the need to kill the vampire and the doctor. Whitecaps of adrenaline surged through her bloodstream, beckoning her on. But how? She had no weapons. She didn't know any martial arts.

On the verge of panic, she started breathing fast and shallow. Hyperventilating. She knew it was happening, but she didn't know how to make it stop. Hazlitt glanced over at her, concern wrinkling his face.

In the backseat Scapegrace seemed bigger than he actually was. He was like some enormous growth, white and flabby like a cancer, filling half the car. "She's just afraid. Her pulse is elevated. She might pass out."

"Yes, thank you," Hazlitt shot back. "I know the symptoms of an anxiety attack. Do you think we should sedate her? She could hurt herself or someone else."

"She might hurt you," Scapegrace said, laughing a little. "Don't worry. I'll grab her if she has a seizure or something."

Tiny sparks of light flashed inside Caxton's eyes. They swam across her vision and were gone as quickly as they'd come. Her throat felt dry and thick and very cold, with the air howling in and out of her body. She could hear her own heartbeat pulling in her chest. Then bars of darkness appeared at the top and bottom of her vision, like when they played old movies on television. The bars thickened and a high-pitched whining filled her head. Everything went soft and fuzzy and out of focus.

She could hear Hazlitt and Scapegrace talking, but only as if they were shouting through thick layers of wool. They were drowned out by the ringing in her ears. She could feel her body around her, but it was completely numb, rubbery, and dead. She could move if she really wanted to, but just then she didn't really want to.

The fear was gone altogether.

That was the best part. She knew things were still bad and that they wouldn't end well, but her fear was gone and she could think clearly again. She didn't want to sit up—that might break the spell—but she looked forward, through the windshield, and tried to see where they were going. There was something out there, but it wasn't the highway. It was pale and big and it had long triangular ears. It was a vampire, maybe Malvern. The vampire raised its hands to her and they were full of red blood. It was offering that redness to her, like a gift.

Scapegrace slapped her across the back of the head and her eyes whirled around in her head. She was back, the ringing gone from her ears.

"I said, are you okay?" Hazlitt yelled. He had one hand on her neck, maybe feeling for her pulse.

She wanted to bat him away, but she looked down and saw she was still holding the baby skull. Whatever had happened, she'd managed not to let it fall out of her hands. She remembered she wasn't allowed to let go of it. She pulled away from Hazlitt as best she could with her shoulders. "I'm fine," she managed to say. Her voice sounded weaker than she felt. "What happened?"

"You swooned," the doctor told her, his voice thick with gloating.

She scowled. She wasn't the kind of woman who swooned. She thought about it, though. Once, when she and Ashley (Deanna's predecessor) had been in Hershey on vacation, she had drunk chocolate martinis until she had literally passed out.

She had woken up on the floor of the ladies' room with a crowd of scared-looking cocktail waitresses peering down at her. It had felt a lot like what had just happened—but even that hadn't made her feel so much shame.

Wow, she thought. If Arkeley could have seen her just then, he would have had concrete proof of all the horrible things he'd ever said about her. Thank God he wasn't in the car. Because he was dead.

She worked her face muscles, stretching out her jaw, puffing out her cheeks, trying to revive herself. By the time they reached the hospital she felt pretty much recovered. Hazlitt drove up onto the main lawn next to the statue of Hygiene and they piled out of the car, Caxton very careful not to drop the skull even though her palms were clammy with sweat.

Twelve or thirteen other cars were already parked haphazardly on the grass. They were all empty. A bonfire burned close to the front doors of the hospital. Caxton was pretty sure that the corrections officers who ran the place weren't just having a weenie roast. She was right. As they walked up toward the entrance she saw the COs lined up on the ground near the fire, their hands tied behind their backs, their faces down in the grass.

She thought they must be dead. It was almost a relief to think that. When one of them moved, her body sagged with brand-new horror.

Tucker, the guard who had helped Arkeley find out Reyes's personal information, strained his neck trying to look up and see who had arrived. Caxton did everything she could to look away, to not be seen, but it didn't work. His eyes met hers for a moment and it was as if they had a conversation, as if they had some of the magic of the vampires and they could communicate with just the firelight that shook in their eyes.

I'm so sorry, she tried to say with her eyes. *But there's nothing I can do.*

His eyes were easy to read, even from twenty feet away. *Help me*, they said. *Please. Please help me*.

That was her job, of course. Helping people. At the moment she was indisposed, however. Tucker was going to die because she hadn't been strong enough. Just like everybody else. There was blood on her hands—the metaphorical kind, anyway.

"That guy means something to you?" Scapegrace asked. He didn't give her a chance to deny it. He stormed over to where Tucker lay on the grass and scooped up the big CO in one arm. Tucker outweighed the vampire by probably a hundred pounds, but it didn't seem to matter. Scapegrace fastened his big toothy mouth around Tucker's neck and bit down, almost gently. Like he was biting into an apple and didn't want to spurt any of the juice. Then he began to suck.

Caxton had no recourse but to scream for him to stop. She might as well have yelled at an avalanche—if anything, she just spurred him on. The CO's face went gray, then white. It never got as white as the vampire's skin. His eyes rolled around in his head and his body quivered, but he never screamed. Maybe Scapegrace had crushed his larynx. When it was over the vampire just threw the body down on the ground. It was useless. Blood ringed his mouth, bright red blood. "They're all going to die," he told her. Some of the other COs whimpered. One began praying in a sobbing, warbling voice. Scapegrace took him next.

After the third or fourth victim had been drained, Hazlitt cleared his throat. "Leave the rest for now," he said. "Justinia wants to talk to our guest."

Scapegrace jumped up and ran his forearm across his wet mouth. He moved across the grass so quickly that he left trails in the air. Suddenly he had his hands around Hazlitt's neck. He forced the doctor down to the ground until he was kneeling on the wet grass, looking up into the vampire's eyes, sheer terror beading waxy sweat on his forehead.

"You're not one of us yet," Scapegrace said. "You think you can remember that?"

The doctor nodded emphatically. The vampire let him up and they all went inside.

52.

The tiny skull in Caxton's hands quivered and she nearly dropped it. She did let out a little squealing noise. Scapegrace and Hazlitt stopped to look back at her. The vampire grinned cockily at her predicament.

A millipede with long, hairy feelers had crawled out of the skull's left eye socket and was working its way across the back of her hand. Its body looked wet and slimy. Its legs made her skin itch. It was all she could do not to jerk her hand away. If she did, though, she knew that Scapegrace would cripple her instantly. The teenaged vampire would probably put the millipede in her hair, afterwards, just to torture her.

She bent her knees and gritted her teeth and tried not to care. It was just a bug, she told herself. It was extremely unlikely that it was poisonous.

Carefully she raised the skull to the level of her mouth. She took a deep breath and blew on the millipede, trying to knock it off her hand. Its head waved in the jet of air, but then its back legs anchored between two of her knuckles. She blew harder, and harder, until she thought she might pass out again.

Scapegrace snorted out a mocking laugh. She sucked in air and then spat it at the millipede until it finally flew off of her hand. The vampire shook his head in amusement and then gestured for her to follow. "This way," he said, "if you're okay, now."

Hazlitt ran ahead into the darkness and switched on a light in the corridor ahead. All but one of the fluorescent tubes in the corridor had been smashed. They hung above her like jagged glass teeth, sparking now and again. What little light remained was barely enough for her to find her way to the far end of the passage. They were headed directly for Malvern's private ward—she recognized the route they took from her previous visits.

Scapegrace glanced at Hazlitt, then lifted aside the plastic curtain and went inside. Caxton started to follow, but the doctor touched her arm and shook his head. Together they waited for long minutes, listening to Scapegrace retch up his cargo of stolen blood. Tucker's blood, Caxton thought. Maybe Arkeley's blood. He was feeding Malvern, of course, just as Lares had the night that Arkeley killed him. When Scapegrace was finished and the noises had stopped, Hazlitt nodded at her. She pushed through the plastic curtain and stepped into the blue-lit room. Her eyes went out of focus for a moment, adjusting to the new light, and her head grew light. She thought she heard someone calling her name and she swam back to lucidity. She was so scared she thought she must be going crazy. "*Laura,*" she heard, again, a woman's voice. Was it Malvern? No, that was impossible. Malvern's vocal cords had dried up a hundred years ago. "Laura." It was as clear and as loud as if someone stood behind her, calling her. She turned, but she knew nobody would be there. It was as if a ghost were talking, like the ghost in Urie Polder's barn.

"Officer?" Hazlitt said, looking concerned.

"Nothing," she said. Her eyes were slowly adjusting to the blue light. She saw that the room had been changed around some. The medical equipment had all been shoved back into the corners, and the microphones and probes that had once hung down from the ceiling to constantly measure Malvern's status had all been cleared away. The laptop remained, sitting alone on a metal stool. Caxton glanced down at the coffin, which was propped up on its sawhorses. Blood filled the coffin almost to the rim. She was sure Malvern was in there, submerged under the dark fluid, but she couldn't even see a shadow beneath the still surface. Then, as if in response to her stare, a ripple ran across the blood and five tiny peaks appeared in the surface. They pressed upward out of the coffin and she saw they were fingernails.

Malvern's hand lifted from out of the blood, clotted fluid dripping and falling away from the fingers. There was more flesh on the bones than before—clearly, being soaked in human blood was having the desired effect on Malvern. She was rejuvenating, revivifying. Her hand reached for the laptop keyboard and she began to type. Character by character, she spelled out a message for her new guest:

well come, laura

When the vampire was done typing, her hand slithered back inside her coffin. It was all so quiet and stately and polite that Caxton felt an absurd urge to curtsy and thank her hostess for her kind hospitality. Scapegrace tapped Caxton's shoulder, then, and she turned back around, losing her breath at the sight before her. A noose hung from the ceiling, hovering over a simple wooden chair. "That's—for me," she stammered. "So I can—so I can—finish myself off and complete the rite."

"Yes," Hazlitt told her. "I want you to know I opted for a lethal injection. I have one made up for myself. They wouldn't hear of it."

"It's how your mother did it, right?" Scapegrace asked. He sounded almost solicitous, as if he really wanted to make sure he'd gotten it right. "She hanged herself? The symmetry of it appealed to us."

"Yes, that's right." She nodded, trying to fight back by being more nonchalant than he was. Her stomach boiled with acid, but she refused to let it show. Symmetry. The kind of thing that would appeal to a vampire's spiky, twisted, obsessive-compulsive mind. "She hanged herself. When I was very young. Is it time, now?" she asked, a lump in her throat. "Is it time for me to . . ." She couldn't finish the sentence. "You know."

"We're not quite finished," Scapegrace said.

A half-dead entered the room and climbed up a stepladder to hang a pair of thick iron chains from the ceiling. When he was done he took his ladder away and made room for two more half-deads, who dragged a big canvas sack into the room. There were ugly stains on one end of the sack. They grunted and cursed as they struggled with their burden, but they didn't complain openly. From time to time they looked up at Scapegrace as if they expected him to pounce at them and tear them apart just for fun.

Finally they got their bag open. Inside was a human body, a big one, dressed in a dark suit. There was so much blood on the hands and face that Caxton couldn't determine the race or even the sex of the cadaver.

No—wait, she thought. It wasn't dead. It moved, though surely only by reflex, a twitch here or there, a last shudder before the body could finally succumb to mortal wounds. The half-deads attached the dangling chains to the body's ankles and started hauling it up into the air. Scapegrace moved forward to help them lift it up, over the coffin, until the body dangled over Malvern's submerged form with its outstretched fingertips nearly brushing the surface of the pooled blood.

The body swung from side to side, first left, then right. Scapegrace and Hazlitt both kept looking at her face as if they expected her to have some kind of reaction. She'd seen worse, she wanted to tell them. She'd scraped prom queens off the asphalt. Then she realized why they wanted her to see this particular body.

It had a small silver badge on its lapel, a star in a circle. The badge of a special deputy of the U.S. Marshals Service.

53.

"**A**rkeley," she said. "Oh God, it's Arkeley. You've killed him." She had already known that he was dead, had already accepted it, but this—this was proof. Tears shot out of her eyes and splashed on her shirt.

"Oh, there's plenty of life left in him yet," Scapegrace announced. "There had better be." The half-deads shrank away from the coffin and she understood intuitively. When they attacked her house they had been under Scapegrace's orders to take both cops alive. Caxton so she could be turned into a vampire, and Arkeley so Scapegrace could torture him to death for what he'd done to Reyes and Congreve and Lares and Malvern and every vampire he could get his hands on.

Hazlitt touched the Fed's throat. "He still has a pulse. It's thready, but it's strong. And he's definitely breathing. Unconscious, though."

Scapegrace smiled. "So let's wake him up." He stepped over to the dangling body and took Arkeley's left hand in his own. He stroked the bloodstained skin for a moment, then lifted the hand to his mouth and with one quick motion bit off all four fingers down to the palm.

Fresh blood poured out of the wounds and mingled with the blood in the coffin. Arkeley's eyes flicked open and a mewling, catlike sound surged from his chest. He sucked in a horrible breath that caught on something broken inside of him, then he moved his lips as if trying to speak.

Scapegrace spat the severed fingers into Malvern's coffin. They sank into the blood without a trace. "What's that, Deputy? Speak up."

"Spuh," Arkeley rasped. It sounded like two pieces of paper being rubbed against each other. "Spesh."

"Special Deputy," Caxton said for him. A kind of gruesome smile, but yes, an actual smile appeared on the Fed's upside-down face.

"Cax," Arkeley sputtered. "Caxt—you. You knee." He took another grating breath. "Need to . . ." He couldn't seem to finish his thought.

Scapegrace didn't like it at all. He reached for Arkeley's other hand. "Do you have something more to say?" he asked. "Some last kind word for your young friend here? You've failed her, old man. She's going to die, you're going to die. Everyone is going to die. You've failed everybody. Maybe you'd like to say you're sorry. Go ahead. Whisper in her ear. We'll all wait here patiently for you to think up your dying words."

Caxton leaned close against the edge of the coffin. Her shirt trailed in the blood. "Jameson," she whispered. She'd never used his first name before and it felt strange in her mouth. "Please don't apologize."

"Kneel," the Fed told her. It wasn't what she was expecting. "Kneel before her."

She recoiled from the words, from the very idea. She sought his eyes, wanting to let him know how angry she was that he would just surrender like that, that he would want her to embrace her doom so wholeheartedly. The light in his eyes was wrong, though. There was a distinct streak of defiance in the wrinkles around his eyes.

He'd never been wrong before. She dropped to her knees and lowered her head as if she were praying in church. She knew very well that it would take more than a simple prayer to save herself, though.

Down on her knees, she saw something—a shadow tucked away in the near-perfect darkness under the coffin. She saw the triangular shapes of the sawhorses and between them something else, something flat and angular. She squinted and saw that something had been secured to the bottom of the coffin with a silver X of duct tape. She squinted again and finally understood. It was a handgun. A Glock 23.

He must have put it there earlier. Perhaps back on the night when Scapegrace and Reyes had come for Malvern and he had threatened to tear out her heart. He must have planned for this, just as he planned for every possible contingency. That was how you fought vampires—you never let them get the drop on you.

She glanced up at Arkeley's face. He wasn't giving anything away. She looked back at the pistol. She knew it held thirteen bullets—there would be nothing in the chamber. She looked up and around the room. "Scapegrace," she said.

The vampire stepped closer. He was no more than five feet away. "Hmm?"

"Catch," she said, and tossed the skull into the air. Instantly its high unearthly shriek split the air. Scapegrace grabbed at it, his white hands up and reaching.

She tore the Glock free from the bottom of the coffin. She worked the slide to chamber a round and saw the vampire's red eyes go wide. His brain understood what was happening, but his hands kept going for the skull. He caught it and crushed it unthinkingly between his pale fingers. Fragments of yellow bone and clods of dirt swarming with worms trickled down the front of his shirt. The shrieking stopped.

Caxton pressed the barrel of the pistol against his chest and fired. He fell backwards, his head smashing on the concrete floor. His eyes swiveled around to fix on her. "Pretty good," he said, and tried to get a knee under himself so he could rise and kill her. His limbs didn't seem to want to cooperate. "Shit," he said, and fell back.

"Go! Get help!" Hazlitt shouted at the half-deads. One of them rushed for the far exit, for the darkness there. Caxton pivoted on her heel and snapped off a shot and the half-dead's back erupted in a cloud of rotten flesh and torn clothing. She turned to shoot the next one but it was gone, already having fled the room. The third half-dead crouched down on the floor and hugged his knees.

She turned to Hazlitt next. She didn't point her weapon at him—you never pointed a weapon at a human being until you were prepared to shoot him. He stepped behind a cart of medical instruments and raised his hands. He was too smart, she decided, to actually try something.

Scapegrace had rolled over onto his side and was pushing himself up into a sitting posture when she looked again. His eyes wouldn't meet hers. "You nicked it," he said.

"What?"

"You nicked my heart," he finished. He pushed upward with one knee, but his arms were trembling. "That was pretty tricky." He got up on both knees. "You waited until I'd given all my blood to Her. You waited for the moment when I would be at my weakest. Pretty tricky. Listen," he said, rising to his feet. He lifted his hands into plain sight. "I'll go quietly, okay? Don't kill me." He wheezed as he spoke—had she punctured one of his lungs? She would have given anything for a chest x-ray just then. "Please," he continued. "You can lock me away forever, whatever you want. But please don't kill me. I'm not even eighteen years old."

"Don't," Arkeley breathed behind her. *Don't listen,* he was trying to say. Arkeley. Was he still alive? He wouldn't be for long unless she got him down and bandaged his wounds. She turned halfway around to look at him.

It was the opening Scapegrace had been waiting for. He flew across the room, a pale streak of lightning. Red blood erupted from Hazlitt's throat and chin as the vampire tore off half of the doctor's neck. Hazlitt gurgled out a scream. Caxton fired a round into the back of Scapegrace's head, just by instinct. It didn't even slow him down. She fired again into his back, but he just redoubled his efforts, pressing his face and his rows of triangular teeth deep into the hole he'd made in Hazlitt's neck.

Every drop of blood he drank would make Scapegrace stronger. He would be bulletproof in seconds. She needed to kill him instantly. Carefully, holding her breath, she lined up another shot and fired through the back of his T-shirt. The bullet tore through the vampire's body and made him double over in howling pain. He staggered away from Hazlitt and fell across a rack of IV stands. They clattered to the floor as his hands clutched and clutched at nothing, at air. His legs shook like rubber bands and he collapsed to the floor and finally, convulsively, died.

Hazlitt took one last look around the room, his face and chest and the whole front of his body one continuous sheet of flowing blood. Then he slumped to the floor as well, as dead as the vampire.

The half-dead in the corner jumped up and started running for the door. Caxton fired reflexively and missed him. She fired again and pulverized his left arm. The half-dead whined in pain but didn't stop. She fired a third time and his whole body blew to pieces.

There's a stake in your
fat black heart
And the villagers never
liked you.
They are dancing and
stamping on you.
They always knew it was
you.

— Sylvia Plath, Daddy

MALVERN

54.

"Five," Arkeley moaned.

She shoved the handgun into the empty holster at her belt. It almost fit. Climbing the stepladder, with shaking hands she managed to lower Arkeley to the floor. She found rolls of gauze and surgical tape in a rolling cart.

"Five," he said again, as if he'd just remembered something.

His injuries were terrible. The half-deads had really worked him over—his skin was a maze of cuts, most of them inflamed, and the skin that wasn't sliced or torn was bruised and even chewed in places. His eyes were swollen shut and his mouth was black and swollen with bruising. Then, of course, there were the fingers that Scapegrace had torn off. Caxton wrapped his left hand in gauze that instantly turned red with bright arterial blood. She wound more and more bandaging around the wound, tight but not too tight. At least it was his left hand. He would still have the use of his right hand. He could still shoot.

Except—he wasn't doing any shooting anymore. Not that night, probably not for months. He couldn't even sit up.

A cold flash went through her when she realized she had been expecting him to get up this whole time and reclaim his gun. She had really thought that her part was done and she could let him mop up.

"Five," he mumbled.

"Shh," she said.

It wasn't going to happen. He wasn't going to fight the half-deads. He wasn't going to walk out of Arabella Furnace. It was up to her to get out, to run and get help. Maybe—maybe—she could save his life, but it was all up to her.

"Five."

"Okay already," she said. "Five what? Five half-deads? I think there were more than that when I came in. If you tell me there are five active vampires here I'm going to soil my uniform." She smiled and patted his good hand.

He sucked in a painful breath and spoke in a rush. "There's only one more active vampire," he said. He waited a moment, then finished. "There are five bullets remaining in your clip."

Slowly she removed the Glock from her belt. She ejected the clip and counted the remaining rounds. There were only five left, just as he had said. That was impossible—she couldn't possibly have already fired eight bullets, could she? She went over the recent combat in her head and realized she had.

She slipped the clip back into the handgun and holstered it again.

"Be more careful," he said, his head rolling back and forth. "From now on."

She nodded in agreement. He probably didn't see it, though, because just then the lights went out.

It happened so quickly that Caxton thought it had to be in her head. She blinked, but the blue light didn't come back. Featureless darkness filled all the available space around her, so thick she felt as if it were rubbing on her dry eyeballs.

"Oh God," she said. "They know. They know something's up. What do we do now?"

Arkeley didn't answer. She reached over and grabbed his bloody wrist. He had a pulse, still, but he must have fallen unconscious.

Caxton searched her pockets, hoping she had some kind of light source on her. Something—anything. Scapegrace had taken most of her gadgets away from her: cell phone, PDA, handcuffs. "Oh, thank you," Caxton whispered, not knowing whom she was talking to. The vampire had ignored her mini-Maglite. He'd probably figured she couldn't hurt anyone with it. She took it out and pointed it at Arkeley. The miniature flashlight spat out a foggy cone of pale blue illumination that dazzled her eyes for a second. It gave off just enough light for her to see that he was still breathing.

A telephone was mounted on one wall. She grabbed the handset and pressed it to her ear. No dial tone rewarded her. She flicked the hook a couple of dozen times, trying to make it work, but no dice. Whoever had cut the power must have cut the sanatorium's phone lines, too.

Which meant they had to know everything. They knew where she was and what her first move would be.

If the half-deads—and the remaining vampire—knew she was in Malvern's ward then her first goal had to be to get away. She couldn't move Arkeley—he outweighed her considerably and she couldn't drag him—so she would have to leave him there on the floor. If the bad guys killed him out of spite, she would hate herself forever. She hoped they would be too preoccupied trying to kill her.

Waving her light around, she found the exit from the ward and slipped along the wall of the corridor beyond. The Glock stayed in her holster to prevent her from wasting a bullet if she jumped at her own shadow. That was an Arkeley kind of thing to do, and she was proud that she had thought of it. Of course, Arkelely would already have a plan by this point. He would already be putting it into effect.

"Think," she said, trying to break the layer of fear that covered her brain like frost. "Think." What could she realistically hope to achieve? She wasn't tough enough to take on another vampire and an unknown number of half-deads on her own. She'd only beaten Reyes because of Vesta Polder's amulet, and Scapegrace had died of surprise, not any special quality she possessed. So if she couldn't fight, what could she do?

She could run. She could get out of the hospital and call for backup. It was the only realistic plan. The half-deads would try to stop her, she knew. She tried to think like a faceless freak.

They hadn't attacked her directly yet—no, they wouldn't. They were cowards. Arkeley had told her as much. They would fall back, take away her ability to see and her ability to communicate. They would try to flush her out, to make her walk right into their traps. The half-deads would have secured the main entrance. Going out the way she came in would be suicide. She ducked down the first side corridor she saw.

She remembered her first visit to the sanatorium. She'd thought it was a big spooky maze then. With the lights out it was a lot more unnerving and a whole lot harder to find her way around. She knew generally what direction she was headed in: southeast, toward the greenhouse wing. Yes, that would be good. If she could just get outside, she would feel much safer. The moonlight might actually reveal something useful.

Her flashlight speared out before her, illuminating less than she would have liked. The corridor it lit up was a gallery of dim reflections and long shadows. Anything could be ahead of her, waiting for her. Anything at all. She kept her back to the wall and edged forward, a step at a time. There was nothing else for it.

She was halfway down the corridor, her eyes watching every doorway, when she began to hear a noise like something moving around inside the wall at her back. She shied away from it and heard it dash away from her, as if they'd scared each other off. It was a rhythmic skittering sound, or rather a whole group of sounds, the patter of tiny claws on wood, the thumping of a soft body dragging across broken plaster. Ahead of her, down the hallway, something oozed out of the wall and dropped to the floor.

She swung her light around and speared a rat with her flashlight beam. Its tiny eyes blazed as it looked back at her. Its nose twitched and then it bolted away.

"Nothing," she said, trying to reassure herself. It came out a little louder than she'd meant it to.

Ahead of her, at the end of the corridor, a half-dead hissed, "What was that?"

She stopped in her tracks. She stopped breathing. She switched off her flashlight. There was a tiny bit of light coming in through square inset windows in the double doors at the end of the hallway. A shadow moved across that light, a shadow like a human head.

"Did you see that?" someone else asked, with the same kind of squeaky, ratlike voice. Another half-dead. "Somebody had a light on and they switched it off."

"Get the others," the first voice said.

The double doors slammed open then, and what looked like a never-ending stream of human silhouettes flooded into the hall.

55.

Caxton reached for her weapon but stopped. She could hear dozens of feet pounding down the corridor toward her. She had only five bullets left. There was no way she could take on all the half-deads using the gun.

She switched on her light and pointed it at them. Their torn faces and their glassy eyes reflected the light perfectly. They were dressed in filthy clothes. One wore eyeglasses. A couple were missing hands or arms. There had to be at least twelve of them, and they were all armed: with kitchen knives, with sharpened screwdrivers, with hatchets or cleavers. One had a pitchfork. When the light hit them, their mouths went wide and they ran at her even faster.

If she stayed where she was they would simply cut her down. She flicked off the light and dashed sideways toward an empty doorway. The door itself lay flat on the floor of the room beyond, as if its hinges had rotted away.

There was a window at the far end of the room, but she

could see that it was barred. The room looked like a jail cell. Had it been the psychiatric ward?

She could hear them coming. She'd run into the room on pure instinct, just trying to get away. Had they seen her? She didn't know if half-deads saw any better in the dark than human beings. Had they seen her? She threw herself against the wall to one side of the door and breathed through her mouth. She heard them outside in the hallway, their feet pounding on the linoleum tiles, their hands thumping against the plaster walls. Had they seen where she'd gone? They had to be close. They had to be getting closer.

She thought she heard them walk right past the door. She had to be sure. She leaned out through the doorway to get a look and found one of them staring right back. His face was striped and raw where he'd torn away his own skin. His eyes were less hateful than pathetic, full of a weary sadness more profound than anything she could imagine.

Without even thinking about it, she reached up with both hands, grabbed his head, twisted, yanked, and pulled. He screamed but his flesh tore. It felt less like grappling with a human body than like pulling a branch off a tree. Bones crackled inside his neck as his vertebrae gave way, and suddenly she was holding a human head. The eyes looked right into her, sadness transformed entirely into fear. The mouth kept moving, but it no longer had the breath or the larynx to scream with.

"Ugh," she said, and threw the head into a shadowy corner of the room. Out in the hall, the half-dead's body kept walking but had lost all its coordination. It was just muscles twitching with no purpose. Guilt and disgust erupted inside of her and she thought she would throw up. She glanced into the dark corner, wondering if the head was still moving. Wondering how much that hurt, to be beheaded but not killed outright.

Then she remembered the half-deads who had taunted her

on the roof of Farrel Morton's camp. She thought about the one who had attacked her with a shovel—and the one who had stood outside her window and tricked Deanna into cutting herself to ribbons. The guilt flew away on moth wings.

The headless body kept walking, and soon enough it came up against a wall and started beating itself to pieces, its shoulder digging into the wall as if it wanted to push its way through.

The rest of the half-deads turned to look. They stood in the hallway in loose formation, their weapons out and ready but not pointed at her. They had walked past without knowing she was in the room—if she hadn't looked, they might have gone right past her. It was hard to tell in the dark hallway, but she thought they looked surprised.

The pitchfork the headless body had been holding on to bounced with a jangling sound on the floor. She scooped it up in both hands and felt its weight. It was heavy and overbalanced, the metal tines drooping low to the floor when she tried to lift it. It was a ludicrous weapon and one she'd never been trained to use.

She dropped it. It clanged on the linoleum. Then she drew her Glock.

The crowd of half-deads moved backwards. Away from her. That was good. Some of them raised their hands, though they didn't drop their weapons.

She pointed the handgun at one of them, then another. She made them wince. They couldn't know how many bullets she had left. She stepped out into the hallway, keeping them covered. She would shoot the first one that moved. Maybe that would scare them enough that they would scatter like frightened rats. She really hoped so.

One of them had a pair of kitchen shears. He worked them nervously, the blades glinting in the few stray beams of moonlight. Another one wore a dark blue Penn State sweatshirt with the hood up around his ruined face. He was carrying a ball-peen hammer. He could break her arm in a second if he got too close.

She took a step backwards. The half-deads took a step forward. It wasn't going to work. They would stop being scared in a moment and would rush her. There was no way she could survive if they all attacked her at once. If she didn't shoot one of them soon, they would call her bluff and it would be over.

She picked one. The one with the hammer. He didn't look as scared as the others. Taking her time, lining up her shot, she aimed right at his heart and fired, thinking even as she squeezed the trigger, *Four*.

The half-dead's chest burst open and a stench of rotten meat rolled across her. The others drew back.

Then they started moving toward her again. Their weapons brandished in their pale hands, they advanced on her as if they knew exactly what she was thinking. As if they'd been counting her shots, too, and knew she didn't have a chance.

She fired again, wildly, cursing herself even as she snapped off an unaimed shot. If it hit anything, she didn't stick around to see. She ran back along the corridor, back the way she'd come. She could feel them behind her, chasing her. She could hear their feet slapping on the linoleum in the dark. Could they see better in the gloom than she could? She didn't know. She didn't know at all. She flicked on her light, more interested in seeing where she was going than in hiding her position.

She pushed open a door and skidded around a corner, nearly colliding with a filing cabinet somebody had left in the middle of the hall. She pushed it over, adrenaline giving her the strength, and its clattering fall echoed all around her. Maybe one or two of the half-deads would trip over it.

Her breath froze her throat as it rushed in and out of her, and she ran, the light of her flashlight jumping up and down on the walls and floors ahead of her.

56.

Caxton rushed around a corner into a narrow hallway with no windows. She crouched down in the dark and tried to control her heartbeat and her breathing. Her blood was beating so loudly in her ears that she thought anyone nearby must be able to hear it.

Blood. That was the problem, wasn't it? She was full of blood. The half-deads wanted to spill it, maybe in revenge for what she'd done to them and their masters. Maybe because when you were undead all you had in your heart was jealousy directed at the living. They wanted her blood. Then there was the vampire, the unknown vampire haunting the sanatorium, also searching for her, also wanting her blood. But for a different reason.

She heard a half-dead moving nearby. Its feet made less sound on the linoleum than a cat might make padding through a garden, but she heard it. Nothing like fear to concentrate the senses.

She had three bullets left. She knew better than to think they would be any use to her. She could put one of them in her own heart—that way she would at least not come back as a vampire.

Alternatively, she could put one in her head. Then she would come back.

Would that be so very terrible? It would be a betrayal of Arkeley, true. But he had never liked her. If she made herself a vampire at least her life wouldn't end. It would change in many ways. But it wouldn't end.

"*Yes,*" Reyes said, inside of her head. He'd been quiet all night. Either he was losing his grip on her, fading away, or he was just biding his time.

"*Yes,*" someone else agreed. "*In the head.*" Someone else.

A full-body shiver made her twitch in the shadows. She heard the prowling half-dead stop, not ten feet away. She held her breath until he walked past her hiding place. When he was gone from earshot she let herself exhale a little.

Somebody else had spoken to her from inside her head. It hadn't sounded like Reyes at all. Somebody else was in there.

"All of you can just shut the hell up," she told them. A splintered chuckling sounded in the back of her throat as if she'd been laughing to herself. Not nice, she thought, but she didn't want to give them the satisfaction of a response.

She got up and made her way to the end of the dark hallway, using little bursts of light from her mini-Maglite to find her way. The corridor opened out at its end to a wider hallway full of flats of building supplies—stacks of shingles and neat bundles of replacement floor tiles, pallets of lumber, row after row of sealed white plastic buckets full of plastering compound. Moonlight streamed in through a hole in the ceiling and painted everything a ghostly silver, but even in that eerie light Caxton could see the supplies must have been left there untouched for years, bought for some project that had never really gotten started. Maybe they'd planned to fix the hole in the roof. The wood was worm-eaten and slimy to the touch, while some of the buckets had corroded away and spilled white powder in long sinuous drifts across the floor. She approached carefully, knowing that anything could be hiding in the shadows just outside the patch of moonlight. She glanced down at the powder spread across the floor. The wind coming down from the ceiling listlessly stirred the plaster. Slowly it worked at filling in a line of footprints. Laura was no tracker, but she could see the feet were no bigger than her own. The tracks were fresh, too, sharply defined. A barefoot woman had come that way recently.

"*Laura,*" someone said in a room nearby. Or had they? Caxton's mind wasn't just playing tricks on her, she had a whole

Vegas-quality magic show going on in there. She couldn't be sure of anything. What she had heard had sounded like a cough more than a word. And it sounded more like the building settling than like a cough. If she hadn't known better, she could have convinced herself it was just her imagination.

The footprints led her eye to a wide set of double doors across the hallway. Black paint on the doors said INVALID WARD. Someone was sending her a message—she was supposed to go through those doors. It was a trap. Arkeley had taught her about traps. Shaking more than she would have liked, Caxton stepped up to the doors and pushed one of them open. It slid away from her easily, its hinges creaking softly.

The room beyond was cavernous and extremely dark. Her light showed her that it had been stripped bare of anything that could be moved. All that remained in the room were cast iron bedframes painted with flaking white enamel. There were dozens of them, maybe a hundred. Some had been pushed into a corner and some effort had been made to stack them on top of one another. The majority remained exactly where they'd been when the sanatorium was abandoned, standing in neat rows that ran away from her into impenetrable darkness.

How many people, how many generations of people, had died in that room? How many men had lain in those beds, coughing away their lives until someone came to cart their lifeless bodies away? How many ghosts did they leave behind? Caxton's father had died like that, one little hitching cough at a time. He had died in a bed like—

Feather-light and soft, something tapped her shoulder.

A fear leaped on her then, not an emotion but a living, breathing thing that crawled around her shoulders and neck as if looking for someplace to hide. Caxton wanted to run. She wanted to scream. She tried to turn around and found that her body was completely paralyzed by fear.

Caxton stopped in her tracks and flicked off the light. Concentrating, she slowly began to breathe again.

"Laura." Wind in some trees, maybe, making branches rub together. Yeah, sure. Trees. She might have believed that the first time. Through sheer dint of repetition she knew what it had to be. It was a vampire, and the vampire was playing with her like a cat playing with a wounded starling. The skin on her arms erupted in goose pimples.

It might be Malvern. The bath of blood might have given the moribund vampire enough strength to call out like that from the other side of the sanatorium. Or it could be the other vampire, the unknown.

A cold breeze brushed across Caxton's face, ruffling her hair. There had been no wind in the passage before. Either someone had opened a door somewhere or—or—

She couldn't help it. She had to know. She flicked on the flashlight just in time to see a pale hand flash away from her, dripping red. She gasped in horror and spun around, trying to find where the owner of the hand had gone. She couldn't see anything. She flicked the light off again and brought her weapon down to low ready. *Three.*

A second passed, then another, and nothing happened.

Caxton wanted to turn the light back on. She told herself she was only handicapping herself by not having it on. Vampires could see living people in the dark. They could see their blood. She imagined the vampire looking at her at that very moment. Would the vampire see her frightened face or just the blood surging inside her veins? She imagined what that must look like: the branching network of her blood vessels, as if they'd been carefully surgically removed and hung from the ceiling by wires. A human-enough shape, but empty, a throbbing tracery, bright red jagged lines pulsing tremulously in the cold air.

The vampire had to be within striking distance. At any

moment he or she could pounce and tear Caxton apart. What was the holdup? Standing there waiting for her own destruction, imagining the pain to come, was almost worse than actually dying.

She flicked on the light and held it straight out, daring the vampire to show itself. The vampire obliged, stepping right into the path of the beam.

Thirty feet away, or maybe farther, the light revealed little more than a pale human outline. The vampire wore a white lacy dress that looked oddly familiar to Caxton, as if she'd seen it in a magazine. The colorless hands were full of blood.

Caxton had seen this apparition before. In the car, when she had passed out because she was so frightened. She had seen this vampire with bloody hands, beckoning, calling to her. Now the hands lifted, palms held out as if to catch Caxton's light. The red fell away through the fingers. It wasn't blood at all, Caxton saw. It was hair, clumps of short, red hair.

"It all came out at once, Pumpkin," the vampire said, moving closer. She moved so easily, she might have been skating across the floor. "I thought you might like to see it one last time before it's gone."

Caxton's bones hardened in place. She felt as if she were being fossilized. The sound that creaked up out of her wasn't a name, it was the noise rocks make when they freeze in the winter and crack and split. By the time it reached Caxton's lips, though, that noise sounded an awful lot like Deanna's name.

57.

Deanna touched Caxton's mouth, her chin. Her fingers trailed down across Caxton's throat and wove themselves around her belt. In the blue, uncertain light of the tiny flashlight Deanna didn't look half bad. Even if she was undead.

"It's good to see you," she said, very softly.

"Dee," Caxton sighed. "Dee. You can't be. You didn't—you didn't."

"I didn't kill myself?" Deanna asked. Her voice had that growling quality they got. Her skin was the color of skim milk. She could probably tie a steel bar in knots with her bare hands.

But she was Deanna, alive again. Or almost.

"I broke that window with my own hands. I cut myself up." Deanna's eyes wandered upward to Caxton's. "I guess that counts," Deanna said. Under the growl was a breathy quality to the voice. A sexy kind of flutter. It made Caxton's skin itch.

It would be technically incorrect to say that Caxton thought Deanna was actually alive. She knew better than that. Or rather, her brain knew better. Her body had its own ideas and its own memories. It remembered the shape of Deanna, the shape of Deanna when she was alive. It remembered her smell.

"How could you do this to us? You know what I am. What I've been working on," Caxton said. She stepped closer and touched Deanna's strangely lumpy jaw. "You're so cold," she said. She leaned forward and touched her forehead to the vampire's forehead. They used to do that, when they were alone and things were quiet. They used to press up against each other. It felt pretty much the same this time.

"I didn't have a choice. I mean—except I did. Congreve." The vampire closed her eyes and pressed her hands against her toothy mouth. She shook with weeping.

Caxton couldn't stand to see it. "Shh," she said. "Shh." She put her arms around Deanna's slender form. She wanted to press her tight until she warmed up again. Until she was a real girl again. A sob died in the middle of Caxton's throat. It didn't make it up to the surface. "How do you know about Congreve?"

Deanna pushed Caxton away. She used just enough of her strength to get out of the embrace, but underneath Caxton could feel just how much more power Deanna had, if she chose to use it. It was like being shoved gently away by a pickup truck.

Deanna wouldn't hurt Caxton, though. She would never harm her lover. Caxton could feel it in the way Deanna touched her, in the way they moved around each other.

"They're going to let us be together forever. That wouldn't have been possible otherwise."

Caxton shook her head. "Forever. Sure. Forever like one of them. Have you seen Malvern?"

Deanna laughed and it almost sounded like her old laugh. "Of course I have. She called me here." She was gone then, away from Caxton's body, and that felt wrong. Deanna sat down on one of the bedframes and hugged herself. Caxton kneeled down to bring their faces closer together. "Justinia is the one who made this possible. I was going to die, Pumpkin. I was going to die and I didn't know how else to save myself."

"Shh," Caxton said, and she reached with her thumbs to dry Deanna's tears. What leaked from the corners of the vampire's eyes wasn't water, though, but dark blood. Caxton wiped her fingers on her pants.

"Maybe you'd better tell me how this happened," Caxton said. Yes. That was good. She had to start thinking like a cop again. But it was so hard with Deanna right there, a Deanna who still moved and spoke and wept.

"Congreve was going to kill me. It wasn't anything personal. He was just in the neighborhood, hunting, and he found me. He came to the house one night when you were out at work. The dogs started singing and the light in the shed went on. I went to see what was happening. I grabbed the long screwdriver from the toolkit and I went back there and said, 'Whoever's in there, you'd better fuck off out of here. My girlfriend's a cop.' But nothing happened. So I went to the door of the shed, and that's when he grabbed me."

"Congreve?" Caxton asked. But how was that possible? She and Arkeley had killed Congreve long before Deanna's accident.

"Yes. His hands were really rough with calluses, and they held me so tight. He told me I was going to die, and I started screaming and begging. He told me to shut up and I tried. I really tried. He asked me if I was the artist, if the blankets in the shed were mine, and I said no, because I thought maybe he was some crazy religious guy or something and he wanted to kill me for my art. He made me look into his eyes then, and I saw he wasn't human at all. I couldn't lie to him then, not even if I'd wanted to. I said yes."

"Oh, God," Caxton moaned. "He hypnotized you. He transmitted the curse to you and you couldn't even know what was happening."

Deanna shrugged. "I don't like to think of it that way. He was an artist too, he said. A musician. He really got my work, Laura. That has to count for something, right? He said talent like mine shouldn't be wasted. He asked me if I wanted to live or die. Just like that. You know, I actually had to think about it." Deanna looked down at her hands. She picked at the front of the dress. Caxton realized, suddenly, where she'd seen it before. It was the Best Person dress that Deanna had worn to her brother's wedding. Had the Purfleets buried her in it?

"He made you like him. You must have said you wanted to live," Caxton said, trying to get back on track.

Deanna nodded. "Then he went away. And I started having those dreams. The dreams about you bleeding to death."

Caxton crab-walked backwards and sat down on a bedframe so she could face Deanna. They were two women, two living women sitting on beds, their knees almost touching. Two women just having a conversation. That was all, she told herself.

Deanna lowered her face until her voice was muffled by her

folded arms. "I fought the curse, as much as I could. I tried not to sleep. It's in your dreams that they make you hurt yourself. But that's the merciful part, isn't it? You don't feel a thing as long as you're dreaming. I wish I'd known what it was going to be like so I wouldn't have been so afraid. I'm really sorry, Laura. I'm sorry I got so scared. Otherwise I wouldn't have told them about you."

"What are you talking about?" Caxton asked, trying to keep her voice gentle.

"I told them I couldn't do it alone. I couldn't be one of them if it would mean leaving you behind. Mr. Reyes said he had the answer for that, though. He said they could take both of us. He really seemed to like the idea."

No, it hadn't happened like that. It couldn't have. Caxton felt like she'd gotten to the end of a jigsaw puzzle and found the picture didn't match the cover of the box. She shook her head. "That doesn't make sense, Deanna. Your story is all mixed up."

"What do you mean?" the vampire asked.

"This—this case—was all about me, at least, it was about me first. Because I stopped the half-dead at my sobriety checkpoint. That was how Reyes found out about me." That was the one thing she actually knew for sure, the one clue she'd really had firm and solid in her mind the whole time. It was why Arkeley had drafted her into his crusade in the first place. It was why the half-dead had followed her home. Because the vampires wanted her as one of their own.

"Pumpkin," Deanna said. "Does it really matter who did what first?"

"Of course it does." It meant everything. The vampires had come after her. They'd been obsessed with her. "This all began on the night of my sobriety check. When the half-dead followed me home."

Deanna shook her bald head, just a little. "No, Laura, no. It started weeks before that."

"Bullshit," Caxton huffed. She wrapped her arms around herself. "Anyway, how could you know that?"

"Jesus, stop already. You're not this stupid!" Deanna stood up and Caxton followed, but it felt as if she got to her feet first. Deanna was still rising. Eventually she raised herself up to a considerable height. Had she grown after being dead? Or maybe her posture was just better. "That half-dead didn't just accidentally run across your sobriety check. He was coming to get you."

"No." *No, no, no,* she thought. "No."

"Yes." Deanna reached out and grabbed Caxton's shoulders. Hard enough to pinch. Maybe even to hurt a little. She really wanted to convince Caxton that she was telling the truth. "Congreve sent him to find you, and bring you to him, so you and I could do this together."

"No," Caxton said again.

"Yes. Because I was scared to do it alone. And because Reyes wanted a matching pair of us. I was so confused when you woke me up that night as if nothing had happened. Then you scared away the half-dead. The one assigned to you."

No, Caxton thought, but she couldn't say it. If she said it, she thought, it might come out as a yes. Because she saw it could be exactly as Deanna said. It could be. But it wasn't. Because if it was, if Deanna had been cursed that whole time and Caxton hadn't even noticed, if she'd failed Deanna that badly—

"This whole thing, all the pain and suffering, was about me. And if you had just tried to talk to me, if you had just stayed with me that night I hurt myself—we could have been—we could have done it together—"

"No!" Caxton shrieked. She just wanted it to stop. She wanted it all to stop. She pulled out the Glock 23 and fired her last three rounds into Deanna's chest, one two three.

The noise obliterated all words. If only for an instant.

Then Caxton looked down at what she'd done. The white silk dress was scorched and torn but the skin underneath wasn't even singed. Deanna was completely unhurt.

"Oh God—you've fed tonight," Caxton wailed.

"You're my girlfriend. You're supposed to want to be with me forever, no matter what! We're supposed to want the same things. Why is this so hard for you?"

The fingers on Caxton's shoulder compressed like an industrial vise. Caxton could hear the bones in her shoulder creak and start to pop.

"Don't you love me anymore?" Deanna demanded.

58.

Deanna's fingers dug into Caxton's flesh like iron knives. Deanna's fingernails were just as short as they'd been in life, but still they tore through Caxton's jacket and shirt as if they were razor blades. In a moment they would break the skin.

And what would happen then? Deanna was already enraged. If she saw fresh human blood would she even stop to consider what she and Caxton had once meant to each other? Caxton was pretty sure she wouldn't.

She struggled to pull away, twisting her shoulders to the left and then the right. Deanna's face was a mask of anguish, her eyes wide, her jaw hanging open. All those teeth gleamed even in the minimal light of the invalid ward. Deanna's head was moving backwards, rearing to strike at Caxton's neck. The motion was painfully slow, perhaps unconscious. When it was complete Caxton would be dead. She'd watched Hazlitt die like that. She'd seen plenty of vampire victims.

Her arms and hands began to tremble. The death grip on

her shoulders was cutting off her circulation. The empty Glock fell from her hand and banged noisily on an iron bedframe.

Caxton gritted her teeth and focused every ounce of strength she had into pulling away, tearing herself out of the grip. Her jacket came off in long flopping pieces and she tumbled backwards, tripping on the bedframe, her arms flying wide to try to catch herself. Deanna seemed to loom up over her, as if she were growing even taller or as if she could fly up over Caxton's head. She was going to strike from above. Caxton rolled to the side.

The vampire's weight came down on the bedframe with a grinding, screaming noise of metal being twisted out of shape. Caxton was already rolling to a crouch and then up to her feet. Adrenaline made her feel like she weighed nothing at all, as if she'd been hollowed out and filled with air.

She didn't turn to look at Deanna. She just ran.

She ran without even bothering to turn on her flashlight. Her foot grazed a bedframe and she might have fallen down, but fear lifted her back up. She slammed painfully into the double doors at the far side of the invalid ward, her hip connecting with the push bar. The doors grated open and she rushed through.

Deanna was behind her, one hand reaching to grab the door almost before Caxton reached the hallway beyond. Caxton swiveled around sideways and ran down the hall with her mouth open, her breath bursting in and out of her body. Before she could find another doorway, Deanna smashed into her back, spilling her across the floor. Caxton got back up by sheer willpower and kept running.

Another door. The room beyond was lined with moldy tiles. She couldn't see more than three feet in front of her face. She sensed something wrong with the room, as if it didn't have enough walls or as if the floor was sloping downwards—

something—yes, it was the floor. There was something about the floor. She stopped short and fell back to hug the wall.

Deanna came bursting through the door like a pale comet blazing through limitless space. Her face was wide open, her mouth craned back to swallow Caxton whole. She looked in the gloom as if she were flying, truly flying—and then abruptly she disappeared from view.

Caxton tried to get some breath back into her body, but there didn't seem to be enough air in the world to fill the demand. The beginning of a splitting headache lit up the back of her skull as her brain shouted for more oxygen, more adrenaline, more endorphins, more anything. She pushed herself harder and harder against the wall as if it could absorb her, as if the tiles could part and let her inside, into a hiding place.

Deanna screamed in thwarted rage. The noise rolled around the room, reverberating strangely.

Caxton lifted her Maglite and switched it on. She played it across the grimy tiles, trying to understand what was happening. Five feet ahead of her, the floor stopped short. Had she kept running forward when she entered the room, she would have fallen into that pit. She looked at the door she'd come through and her light picked out faded black letters painted there: POOL ROOM.

The pool room—she'd heard Tucker mention it, once. She carefully folded up the twinge of guilt she felt for Tucker's death and scanned the room, looking to see where Deanna might have gone. She sniffed the air. Any scent of chlorine was long gone, and she was pretty sure the pool had dried up. She did smell something nasty and unnatural, though, something that made her nose wrinkle. It was the smell of a vampire. Wherever Deanna had gone, she was still nearby. Close enough to strike at any second. Was she playing some kind of game? Caxton didn't think so.

She had to know more. But she didn't want to move away from the wall. It felt as if her body had adhered to the tiles. She took one cautious step closer to the edge of the pool and pointed her light down over the concrete lip.

There was a sheer ten-foot drop to the bottom of the pool. Down there she saw tiles, more tiles, endless rows of them. They had been white and smooth once, but the black mold that had devoured the grout between them had spread across the crazed surface. Time and water had shattered some of the tiles and left the floor of the pool littered with tiny sharp fragments. A standing puddle of dark scum filled one corner of the pool. A little to the left she saw a massive bronze drain, completely black with tarnish. Caxton moved her light slowly across the bottom of the pool. She had to know, she couldn't just—

Deanna leaped up and nearly snatched the light out of her hand. Her jaws snapped at empty air and she fell back to land on her feet like a predatory cat. She stared up at Caxton with a look of pure and utterly simplistic hatred. There was a smudge of dark muck down the front of her white dress. She had run right through the door, ready to grab Caxton and kill her and feed on her blood. She hadn't looked where she was going and she'd fallen into the pool.

Caxton stepped back, away from the edge.

Time to run again.

She pushed through the door and back out into the hall. She estimated she had ten or maybe fifteen seconds before Deanna found a ladder or climbed up out of the shallow end of the pool. She couldn't count on any more time than that. With her light on this time, she retraced her steps. She had no intention of going back to the invalid ward, though.

It took her three or four seconds to find the door she wanted, the one marked CONSERVATORY. She pushed it open and emerged into moonlight so bright it dazzled her eyes.

Behind her she heard Deanna screaming in frustrated rage once more. It wouldn't be long, now, she told herself. She had better be ready.

59.

The first thing she had to do was make a choice. It wasn't an easy one. She had to decide she was going to kill Deanna. It didn't matter what they'd been. It didn't matter who had failed whom. She asked herself what Arkeley would say and knew he would say that Deanna was unnatural. A monster.

That didn't help nearly as much as she wanted it to. She could still love a monster, she knew, if she let herself. She could learn to love Deanna again, she could forgive her for what she'd done, and it wouldn't even be that hard. But it looked like she wasn't going to get the chance. Deanna would kill her unless she killed Deanna first. Her decision was made. She would kill Deanna if she could.

The second thing she had to do was figure out how.

The conservatory she'd finally found had once been a long, two-story space where brick walkways wound between tables and espaliers and giant flowerpots. The walls and the sloped roof had been constructed of wide panels of plate glass, held in place by a framework of steel girders. It must have been a lovely place once, she thought, a refuge for the dying patients. A place for them to get out of their beds and get some sun. Time and weather had changed the greenhouse, however. The plants had either died or flourished far beyond what the inmates might have ever hoped for. Vines crawled up the glass walls, choking off the grimy panes, littering the brick floor with curled brown debris. The far end of the conservatory had been smashed in altogether, perhaps by one of the violent storms that swept through the ridges of Pennsylvania from time to time. Yellow caution tape had been strung back there, tied from one girder to another to keep the staff out. She could see why—long spears of broken glass were there, lined up and stood on end, maybe by the same workers who had abandoned all that plaster compound and lumber outside the invalid ward.

Caxton needed a weapon. She waved her light around and found a piece of a steel stanchion that had once secured a trellis. It looked half rusted and like it might come loose with a couple of kicks. With a rage born of fear and desperation, she knocked it loose with her boot. She grabbed it up and immediately felt better, even though she knew her sense of security was an illusion. She had a steel bar the length of a riot-control baton with one jagged, wicked-looking end.

Next she needed to secure the door. She saw a terra-cotta pot the size of a refrigerator that she thought she might be able to use as a barricade. She went to grab it, knowing it would take every ounce of her strength to move it, when the door slapped open and Deanna came roaring through.

She was twenty feet away—and then she was right next to Caxton. Her pale arm lashed out like a camera flashbulb going off. Caxton's face went hot with pain, and her ears rang as if her head were a bell that had just been struck. She felt herself falling, tumbling backwards. Her nose ached almost immediately and she wondered if it was broken. She struggled not to fall over and then, when that appeared hopeless, she struggled to catch herself on her hands.

Deanna reached down, and even before she'd struck the ground Caxton was jerked back up into the air. Deanna punched her in the stomach and her breath flew out of her. Nausea wracked her body and she felt like she was going to throw up. Deanna's hand came down on her forearm. She felt the bones there creak and rub together unnaturally. She lost control of her hand and her pathetic metal bar went flying, skittering across the rough brick floor.

Caxton couldn't have kept standing if she'd been propped up. She dropped to her knees, knocking them badly, and grabbed at her stomach, feeling as if she'd been disemboweled. Deanna hadn't cut her at all, though. There wasn't a drop of blood on her, not even from her nose, which was hotly numb and sprained at the very least. She was in horrible pain and felt like she would never stand up again. But she wasn't bleeding.

Deanna had thought through her attack. She'd been careful to keep Caxton in one piece. "What do you want from me?" Caxton sputtered.

"You know what we want. You know what She wants." Deanna squatted down in front of Caxton and folded her arms across her out-jutting knees. "We want you to kill yourself and get this over with."

"That's what she wants," Caxton replied. "I asked what you want, Dee."

Deanna laid her head on her arms and looked away. She had to think about it. "This is just a little spat, what you and I are having right now. We can get over it and make up. I still love you. I still want to be with you. But there's no way that can happen as long as you're still human. So I want you to kill yourself, too."

Considering the way she felt right then, it didn't sound so bad. It would be an end to all the pain and all the fear. "I would resent you forever," she said. "I would hate you for what you'd turned me into."

Deanna smiled sadly. "No, I'm sorry, but that's not true. Maybe at first you would be upset. But then you would get hungry. You would want the blood more than you hated me. Once you tasted it—well, once I tasted it I knew that this isn't a curse. I don't care, Pumpkin, if I'm going to get old and withered.

I don't care about how bad the blood tastes. When I felt how strong it made me I didn't care about anything else. It'll be the same for you. I promise."

Caxton was pretty sure Deanna was telling the truth.

"But I'm so scared, Dee," she admitted. "You know about my mom." A tear gathered in the corner of her eye, but she squeezed it back. Too much.

Deanna reached forward and stroked Caxton's hair. "I know. I know you're scared. But it only takes a second." She grabbed Caxton's arms and lifted her up to her feet. "Come on. I'll help you."

"No," Caxton said. "Let me do it myself." She was still shaky, but she'd recovered enough to walk. She stepped over to where her iron bar lay on the bricks. "Let's go over here in the moonlight," she said. "I can't do it in a dark place."

Deanna's smile was perfectly pure and innocent.

Caxton walked up to the caution tape and lifted her bar. Deanna had hurt her pretty badly but had been careful not to spill a drop of blood. Caxton wasn't sure why, but she knew that had to be important. "Maybe I should do it like this," she said, and dragged the sharp end of the bar across her left wrist.

"Pumpkin, no," Deanna breathed, raising one hand to stop Caxton. Then she dropped the hand and just stared.

A line of ragged pain ran across her arm. A razor blade would have made a neater incision, but the wound wouldn't have bled so much. Caxton watched dark blood surge up inside the wound, filling the narrow channel in her flesh. It welled up and over the edges of the cut and spilled down her wrist. A drop splashed on the bricks, black in the moonlight.

"Oh, Pumpkin," Deanna said. She stared at the blood on Caxton's arm.

"What? Am I doing it wrong?" Caxton asked. Congreve, she remembered, had been unconscious, hurt, down on the ground and passed out, and a single drop of her blood had revived him. It had been like a shot of adrenaline pumped right into his heart. Reyes had tortured and damaged her, but he had never broken her skin.

Maybe they were afraid of the blood, as much as they wanted it. Maybe the blood made them crazy. Maybe it made them lose control.

Deanna's mouth was wide open. Her feet kicked at the bricks. A moment later she was running, her arms outstretched, her eyes closed as her jaws worried thin air. She almost seemed to be airborne. Her feet barely touched the ground and she moved as fast as a galloping horse, homing in on the blood.

Caxton timed it perfectly. She dropped to the ground and rolled to the left, and Deanna went right past her, moving too fast to stop easily.

With a crunching noise the vampire collided with the upright spears of glass, her arms flailing, trying to find something to hold onto, to stop her impact. Shattered glass filled the air like spinning, falling snow.

The sound . . . the sound was unearthly. A scream broken into pieces. A million tiny bells ringing.

A living human being would have been shredded. Deanna stood up slowly, her dress hanging in tatters from her limbs. Her skin was a maze of blood, dark, dead blood dripping away, rolling down her arms and legs. She tried to grab at it with her hands. She licked herself like a cat, trying to reabsorb all that lost blood.

It wouldn't work. "It has to be fresh." Caxton said. "It has to be warm."

Deanna looked up with red, confused eyes. She didn't understand what had just happened to her. Then she saw Caxton's dripping wrist and her mouth opened involuntarily. She took a step forward—and a jagged tongue of glass neatly impaled her foot. She let out a yowl.

Caxton stripped off her uniform tie and wrapped it around

her wrist, tugging at it until it hurt and then knotting it off as a tourniquet. No point in bleeding to death now, she decided.

She let Deanna take a few more painful, injurious steps toward her. She waited until all the blood had dripped away from Deanna's flawless body, already healed but paler now, very much paler. Deanna looked like she'd been carved from marble. The pink had left her cheeks altogether. The blood wouldn't protect her any longer. It would have been nice to have a Glock full of ammunition, but the jagged iron bar would serve just as well. Caxton brought it around in a long arc and plunged the sharp end right into Deanna's rib cage. A little to the left of her sternum.

Deanna screeched and howled and tried to form words, to beg, to plead. Maybe to say good-bye. Caxton pulled the bar out and struck again, and again. Three times had to be enough, she thought. It needed to be. She didn't have the strength to stab her partner a fourth time. Her arms felt like cut rubber bands.

Eventually Deanna stopped moving. Her red eyes stared up at the moon, her white face perfect still, untouched by horror or pain or death.

60.

It wasn't easy crawling out of the ruined conservatory, even with no more vampires on her trail. She got free at last, though, and headed for the front of the building, moving quietly, slowly, to avoid half-deads. She was going to go get help for Arkeley. That was the end of it. Once he was safely on his way to a hospital (assuming he wasn't already dead), the case would officially be closed.

Out on the lawn she got a weird surprise—colored light that bounced off the trees and flashed on the wet grass.

Light washed over her, lighting up her hands, her damaged

forearm. It shone in her eyes, red and blue, yellow, or white. No fewer than twelve patrol cars stood at odd angles on the sanatorium's front lawn. Two ambulances and the Granola Roller joined them. Captain Suzie stood up through the armored vehicle's sunroof, an MP5 at her shoulder. Her free hand waved Caxton on.

Anger lit up Caxton's face and made it hot. Where had all these people been? Why couldn't someone else have killed Deanna for her? While they waited out on the lawn she'd been inside fighting for her life.

Then the Granola Roller's rear door popped open and Clara jumped out, knee- and elbow-pads strapped over her sheriff's department uniform. Somebody shouted for her to stop, but she kept running until her arms were around Caxton's chest.

"You didn't get killed," Clara said. "When I got your text message I went right to your house."

"Text message?" Caxton asked. But yes—she'd sent one, right before she and Arkeley exited the shed. Hours ago.

"You said you needed my help but you didn't say what for. I went to your house and it looked like a war zone. The place was trashed and there were bodies everywhere. The dogs were whining like crazy."

"The dogs?"

Clara nodded. "They're okay. They aren't hurt anyway, just scared. I figured you would want to know."

The dogs were okay. That was something, some piece of good news to clutch onto. Caxton needed more. She needed more good, more life. More something to keep her from breaking down in hysterics.

"When I realized you weren't there I called my department and your troop and the Bureau of Prisons and everybody I could think of." Clara's face changed, then, from freeform worry to specific concern. "Hey," she said. "Are you okay?"

How could she possibly answer? After all that had happened.

After what she'd done. Was she even still real, still human? She wasn't sure. "I'm—no. I'm not okay."

Clara nodded. "You will be," she said. She leaned in and pressed her lips against Caxton's. After a moment of surprise Caxton yielded to the embrace. It felt as if she were melting in the other woman's arms. Half a dozen catcalls and cheers rose from the parked police cars, but Caxton didn't care. It had been a very long night.

"Thanks. Thanks for coming to my rescue," she said.

Clara's eyes were knowing, so knowing. Maybe she understood, just a little. It helped in ways Caxton couldn't even understand herself. The rolling, changing lights painted Clara's face now red, now green, now blue.

Caxton strode up to the Granola Roller and nodded at Captain Suzie. She looked around and found Clara's sheriff as well. He was out of his jurisdiction, but maybe the state police had temporarily deputized him. She would worry about the paperwork later. "Somebody give me a shotgun," she said. One was fished out of a patrol car's trunk and carried up to her. "There are an unknown number of half-deads inside that building," she said. "We need to find them all. But first we have to get Special Deputy Arkeley out of there. He's not in great shape." She realized too late that she had no authority over anyone there—she was just highway patrol, after all. "Does that sound good?" she asked.

Captain Suzie grinned down at her. "Lead the way, Trooper," she said.

Caxton took six heavily armed troopers with her, all of them carrying powerful flashlights. She remembered the way to Malvern's ward perfectly, but still she hated going back into the darkness of Arabella Furnace. She felt as if those shadows could hide anything. When they finally reached the plastic curtain outside the ward, she breathed a real sigh of relief. Nothing had jumped out at them. No pale shapes had darted from the shadows to tear them to pieces. "Okay, get that stretcher ready," she said, and pushed through the curtain.

She was surprised to find Arkeley sitting up inside. She was a lot more surprised to find Malvern walking under her own power.

The old, old vampire didn't look fully healed, not by a long shot. Her muscles were as thin and dry as vines in wintertime, and they wrapped around bones easily visible beneath her papery skin. Her tattered nightgown hung on her like a tent. Her face was drawn and spotted and her one good eye looked only half-inflated. But the blood Scapegrace and Deanna had brought to her must have been enough, just enough, to get her out of her coffin for the first time in over a century. She was standing up, walking even, advancing on Arkeley with her mouth open. Her teeth looked fully recovered—sharp, deadly, and numerous.

"That's right. Come here," Arkeley said. He was propped up on one arm. The other waved Malvern closer. "Come on, you old hag. You want it. You can have it."

He had cut his hand somehow. There was fresh blood on his palm. Maybe he had never stopped bleeding—that was the hand with no fingers, the hand Scapegrace had bitten in half. When flashlight beams converged on the hand it gleamed wetly.

Caxton could feel the need, the desire, radiating from Malvern's body. Every fiber of her newly reconstituted self wanted that blood. It would be all she could see, all she could think about.

Caxton knew exactly what Arkeley was doing. A judge had determined a long time ago that Malvern was a human being, that she enjoyed protection under the law against physical attacks by the police. If Malvern made the slightest move to harm or injure a human being, that changed. No court in the state would convict the state trooper who shot a vampire while she was attacking Arkeley. As soon as she touched him she was fair game.

She wanted to yell at Arkeley, to order her escort to drag him out of there. She wanted to save his life. She knew what he would say about that, however. His whole life, twenty years of it anyway, had been devoted to getting this one chance. He didn't want anyone to blow it for him now.

Caxton stood her ground. She could feel the troopers behind her bristling. They wanted to attack. She held up her hands to stop them.

"Come on. Come on and take it," Arkeley rasped.

Malvern glided toward him across the floor. Her hands, which hung at her sides, clenched into tight fists and then released again. She had to know. She had had plenty of time to lie back in her coffin and imagine what it would be like to take a bite out of the Fed who had imprisoned her—what dreams of vengeance would she have had? Yet she also had to know what would happen to her. What that mouthful of blood would cost her.

"You can't resist," Arkeley taunted. "If you were human, maybe, you could handle this. But you're a vampire, and you can't resist the smell of blood, can you?"

He scuttled toward her, his hand always outstretched, wagging in her face. He was verging on committing entrapment, but Caxton decided that if they asked her in a court of law she would lie for him. Anything to give him this win.

A thin, translucent eyelid came down over Malvern's eye. It shuddered gently, as if she were about to faint.

"Come on!" Arkeley shouted. His body was shaking too. He had to be running on fumes. "Come on!"

Her mouth closed slowly. Painfully. Then it opened and a creaking sound like a paper bag being folded up leaked out of her. "Damn ye," she said.

Then she turned around, slinked back to her coffin, and crawled over the lip. She lay back and let her wrinkled head rest on the silk lining.

"No!" Arkeley yelled, and slapped his injured hand against the floor. "I've spent too long on this. I've lost everything."

With hesitant, weak little motions Malvern reached up and grasped the lid of her coffin. Then she pulled it shut with her skeletal hands.

Acknowledgments

A lot of people assisted me with the writing and preparation of this book. I'd like to thank all my online readers. Every time I try to list them I end up forgetting people who deserved better, so this time I won't even try. You know who you are by now. Your comments and your support made this book possible.

I would certainly like to thank Alex Lencicki, who has been a great friend and a great business partner. Alex gave this book its first home and believed in it from the very start.

Jason Pinter, my editor, certainly deserves my thanks for his help in refining the manuscript and making this book stronger. Carrie Thornton has been encouraging my writing since before I had anything real to show and has never faltered in her support, for which I thank her.

Finally, I'd like to thank my wife, Elisabeth. When I was struggling with how to finish the story, she suggested one possible ending: "And then the goblin ate the vampire. The End."

About the Author

DAVID WELLINGTON grew up outside of Pittsburgh, Pennsylvania. He has since lived in Syracuse, Denver, and New York City, where he currently resides with his wife, Elisabeth.

In 2004 he wrote a novel about zombies called *Monster Island* and published it online on a friend's blog, posting short chapters three times a week. The serial drew enough readers that in 2006, Thunder's Mouth Press published it as a book. Two sequels followed.

Information about his books and other projects is available at www.davidwellington.net.

99 COFFINS
A HISTORICAL VAMPIRE TALE
$13.95 PAPER
(CANADA: $16.95)
978-0-307-38171-2

FROSTBITE
A WEREWOLF TALE
$14.00 PAPER
(CANADA: $17.99)
978-0-307-46083-7